It was a raw, blustery day, but the wind just gave them a handy excuse for having red faces. Catherine tried to hold back the tears as Adam hugged her. The platform was full of young men and women embracing each other; the train that was pulled up on the tracks was bound for Charleston, South Carolina. From there, the hundreds of Marine recruits it carried would board buses for the rest of the trip to Parris Island.

Ruth, Adam's mother, kissed him on the cheek, looked into his eyes for a long moment, then stepped back beside Catherine as the conductor came along the platform shouting, "Booaarrdd! All aboard!"

Catherine felt Ruth's hand close over hers and squeeze tightly. She returned the pressure. "He'll be all right," she heard herself saying.

With the other women and children being left behind, they stood there on the platform and watched until all the men were on the train and it had pulled out of the station and vanished in the distance.

★　★　★

"Reasoner has written a sure winner with *Battle Lines*. This World War II tale of ordinary people who find themselves thrown into the most extraordinary period in the twentieth or any other century, is real. I was right there with the Parker brothers and their friends Adam and Catherine. I really cared . . . in fact I still care. I want this story to go on."

—David Hagberg

"A shrewdly written and absolutely authentic look at what it must have been like for the generation before ours to find itself sliding inexorably toward war. The period detail has been applied with a light hand but a sure one, and even a casual reader would be hard put to set it aside and step out into the twenty-first century without blinking."

—Loren D. Estleman

BOOKS BY JAMES REASONER

BATTLE LINES

★ THE LAST GOOD WAR ★

JAMES REASONER

A TOM DOHERTY ASSOCIATES BOOK
NEW YORK

This is a work of fiction. All the characters and events portrayed in this book are either products of the author's imagination or are used fictitiously.

BATTLE LINES

Edited by James Frenkel

A Forge Book
Published by Tom Doherty Associates, LLC
175 Fifth Avenue
New York, NY 10010

www.tor.com

Forge® is a registered trademark of Tom Doherty Associates, LLC.

ISBN: 0-812-57917-8
Library of Congress Catalog Card Number: 2001017143

First edition: June 2001
First mass market edition: April 2002

Printed in the United States of America

0 9 8 7 6 5 4 3 2 1

This book is dedicated to my father,
Marion Reasoner,
and my father-in-law,
Paul Washburn

ACKNOWLEDGMENTS

Special thanks to Ed Gorman and Martin Greenberg for their faith in me, James Frenkel for the editorial guidance that made this a better book, Larry Segriff and John Helfers for smoothing the way, my friends in the Robert E. Howard United Press Association for their research assistance, especially Larry Richter and Morgan Holmes, and to Livia, Shayna, and Joanna for everything else.

PROLOGUE

The wind blowing off Lake Michigan was cold and raw. *Well, what do you expect?* Joe Parker asked himself as he turned up the collar of his coat and tried to huddle deeper inside it. *This is Chicago, after all. The Windy City. Of course it's cold.*

His brother Dale shook out a Lucky Strike and lit it, turning his back to the wind as he struggled to keep a match flaring long enough to fire up the smoke. He dropped the burned match on the marble steps of the Federal Building and ground his toe on it.

"You shouldn't do that," Joe said.

"Why not?"

"It's disrespectful. And look, it left a mark on the step."

Dale took a drag on the Lucky, blew out smoke that was immediately caught and shredded into nothingness by the wind. He shrugged and wiped the sole of his shoe over the charcoal smudge on the smooth marble, smearing it but not obliterating it. "Better?"

"I suppose."

Joe saw Dale roll his eyes as he turned away. "Where the hell are they?" Dale asked.

"They'll be here, don't worry."

"I'm not worried, I'm just ready to get this over with."

"So am I," Joe said. He took his hands out of his coat pockets and rubbed them together for a moment before putting them back in his pockets. He wished he had a good pair of gloves.

Uncle Sam will give you some soon enough, he told himself.

Three years in age and six inches in height separated the brothers. At twenty-two Joe was the older, but Dale was taller. He had caught up to Joe by the time they were both teenagers. Slender, with curly blond hair, he was also the more handsome of the two. Joe was shorter and stockier and had dark brown hair that he kept cut close to his head. Most people would not have picked them out as being brothers or even close relatives.

Dale flicked the half-smoked cigarette away. "The hell with this. I'm going in."

"We said we would go in together, all three of us."

"Yeah, well, that's when we thought Adam would be on time."

Joe looked at his watch. "Let's give them five more minutes." He glanced east along Jackson Boulevard toward the lake. "It won't even take that long. Here they are now."

Two more young people approached the Federal Building and started up the steps, arm in arm. The man was Joe's age and almost as tall as Dale, with an impressive width of shoulders in his black suit and overcoat. He had a cap pulled down tight on his black hair. The woman on his arm was a year or two younger. The fur collar of her coat framed pale, lovely features. Dark blond hair that swept in wings around her face was covered by a fur hat.

Joe smiled at her and said, "You look like a Russian cossack."

"I do?" Catherine Tancred said.

"I never saw a Russian cossack," her companion said, "but my Ukrainian grandfather did. From the way he described them, they weren't anywhere near as pretty as you, Catherine."

Catherine smiled at Adam Bergman. "Thank you. Compliments are always welcome."

Dale used his thumb to point at the main entrance of the domed, three-story Federal Building that had been

Chicago's main post office until a few years earlier. "Let's get in out of this wind."

"Aren't you the grumpy one," Catherine said as the four friends started into the building.

"It's my fault we're here."

Joe felt a flash of anger as he heard his brother's harsh tone of voice. Dale was upset, but he didn't have to take it out on the rest of them. "We all agreed this was best," Joe said.

"Yeah, I know, but we wouldn't have to be doing this if I'd just—"

"Kept your pecker in your pants?" Adam said.

Catherine tightened her grip on Adam's arm and shushed him. Quite a few people were walking in and out of the building. Dale stopped short and turned to glare at Adam. "Listen, I don't need this crap. Nobody's got a gun to your head."

Joe moved between his brother and his best friend. "We've already hashed all this out," he said. "Let's just go on and do what we have to do."

Dale and Adam stared at each other for a moment, then Dale nodded. "Yeah, let's do that." He turned and started walking across the tile-floored rotunda under the building's dome, and the other three went with him, Joe being careful to stay between Dale and Adam.

Adam's right. It never had to come to this. Or maybe it did.

They went down a corridor on the far side of the rotunda and through a door with a glass panel in its upper half. The symbol of the United States Army was emblazoned in gilt paint on the glass, with the words *U.S. Army Recruiting Station* below it. A thick-bodied man in a khaki uniform with the three stripes and a rocker of a staff sergeant on its arm patches stood behind a waist-high counter. He looked at Joe, Dale, and Adam and asked, "What can I do for you?"

The three young men exchanged a glance, then Joe

stepped forward and said, "We'd like to enlist in the Army."

"Now that's something I don't hear that often these days," the sergeant said. "Not since last October, anyway."

They all knew what he meant. October 16, 1940, had been "R Day"—Registration Day—when the newly established Selective Service System had required all men between the ages of eighteen and thirty-five to register for a potential military draft. Joe, Dale, and Adam had all gone to the Chicago office of the Selective Service and stood in line to fill out a registration questionnaire, DDS Form 40, and then had received DDS Form 2, their individual registration card, which they were told had to be carried on their persons at all times. People had already started referring to the cards as draft cards, and Joe, Dale, and Adam each had theirs tucked neatly into their wallets.

The drafting of young men into the military had begun shortly after that. Consequently, voluntary enlistment into the armed services had dropped off considerably. Why volunteer, the thinking went, when you were just going to be called up anyway? Why not enjoy however much time was left to you as a civilian?

Joe wished they could, but that option had been taken away from him and Dale.

"You mean we can't sign up?" Dale asked the sergeant.

He held up his hands. "Now, I didn't say that. I'll be glad to take care of you boys. I just want to make sure you know what you're getting into."

"We know," Joe assured him. "What do we do now?"

"Well, there's forms to be filled out." The sergeant chuckled. "Always forms to be filled out." He glanced at Catherine as he moved toward a gate in the counter. "You boys come on in. The, ah, young lady can wait there on the bench—"

Adam took a step backward. "You go ahead," he said to Joe and Dale. "I've changed my mind."

Dale frowned, but Joe felt a surge of relief. Adam

wasn't in the same sort of trouble he and Dale were. Adam had come along because he and the Parker brothers had done almost everything together for years, and because his grandparents were sitting in the Ukraine with the barrels of the Nazis' guns pointing right at them.

"If you wait for the draft to take you," the sergeant said, "you can't be sure of getting the sort of assignment you want, son."

Dale said, "I should have known you'd back out."

Joe got ready to get between them again. Adam was touchy sometimes; he might just take a swing at Dale for saying something like that. But after a tense few seconds, Adam shook his head and said, "I'm not backing out. I just decided I don't want to join the Army. I'm going over to the Naval Service office and enlist in the Marines."

"The Marines!" the sergeant exclaimed. "You don't want to join the Marines, son. You're too smart to be a leatherneck."

Adam smiled thinly. "You don't know me, Sergeant. Maybe I'm as dumb as they come."

Catherine looked up at him and said, "I thought you wanted to stay with Joe and Dale, Adam."

"Even if I join the Army, there's no guarantee the three of us will be sent to the same place," Adam said. "I want to fight—and what else do the Marines do?"

The sergeant put a sorrowful look on his face as he shook his head. "You'll be sorry."

"I'll take my chances."

Joe reached out and put a hand on Adam's arm. "You're sure?"

Adam nodded. "I'm sure."

Joe saw that his friend was telling the truth. "All right, then. I won't try to talk you out of it."

"You wouldn't have succeeded anyway."

Joe knew that. Adam had always been as stubborn as a mule, he thought.

Catherine's voice shook a little as she said, "I'm still not sure why any of you have to enlist."

"We all talked about it," Joe said.

"I know, but . . . surely there's some other way."

As if sensing a couple of potential recruits about to slip away from him, the sergeant said quickly, "Miss, why don't you have a seat?"

Catherine ignored him and looked instead at Joe and Dale and Adam. She nodded slowly and then, without saying anything else, went over to the bench against the wall and sat down. On the opposite wall, brightly colored posters proclaimed that being in the Army was both a duty and an adventure for every patriotic young man. Catherine was looking at them, but she didn't seem to see them.

Adam put his hand out to Joe and said, "Good luck." Without hesitation, Joe shook his hand and nodded his thanks. Adam turned to Dale and extended his hand, repeating, "Good luck."

Dale didn't move as quickly as his brother had to take Adam's hand. A couple of seconds went past before he clasped Adam's hand and murmured, "Thanks."

Adam stepped back, and Joe and Dale went through the gate in the counter that the sergeant held open. For the next twenty minutes they sat at desks and filled out forms; then, suddenly, they were standing up again and had their right arms raised. They repeated the oath of enlistment, and then the sergeant said, "Welcome to the United States Army. You're to report to the induction center at Fort Sheridan in thirty days—"

"Can we go now, sir?" Dale asked.

The sergeant's formerly affable personality seemed to fall away from him. He glowered at Dale and said sharply, "Don't call me sir. That's what you call a commissioned officer. And don't interrupt." He clasped his hands together behind his back. "Now, what's this about not waiting the usual thirty days to report?"

"We'd like to go now," Joe said, stopping himself before he added *sir*.

"You're in that much of a hurry to be in the Army?"

Not exactly, Joe thought. They were in a hurry to be

out of Chicago. He realized abruptly how hot it was here in the recruiting office. His coat was unbuttoned, but he wished he could take off his tie and unfasten the top button of his shirt, too. His heart was racing, and his pulse sounded like thunder in his head.

He was willing to bet that Captain Combat never felt like this . . .

ONE

"Listen to this," Joe said. He read from the magazine with the garish cover that he held. " 'We give you Bill Combat, a fighting man in the bloody skies of today! Death flies the Swastika across the ceiling, but Captain Combat knows the Nazis must be stopped. Here in living pages we tell his thrilling story, which you will long remember when the battle smoke has cleared!' "

From the other bed in the rear bedroom of the Greenwood Avenue house, where he lay in undershirt and shorts, Dale said, "The guy's *name* is Combat?"

"Yeah. Bill Combat."

"Who the hell is named Combat?"

"The guy in this story, for one."

Dale shook his head. "You can do better than that."

"Why do you think I became a pulp writer?"

Dale grinned and rubbed his thumb and fingers together and said, "Moolah, my friend, moolah."

"Oh, yeah, like I'm getting rich. *Thrilling Adventures* hasn't paid me yet for that last yarn of mine they published, and it came out two months ago."

"That headhunters of Borneo thing?"

"And it even got the cover!" Joe tossed the magazine aside and swung his legs out of bed. In his pajamas, he walked across the room to the small table where his typewriter was set up.

As Joe pulled back the chair, Dale said, "You start pecking on that thing, Pop's gonna bitch about the noise." He lowered his voice and went on in a growling tone,

"Why do you have to do that this late at night? Don't you know that decent people with decent jobs are asleep by this hour? Oh, yeah, you don't have a decent job, do ya, ya bum?"

"Pop's never called me a bum," Joe said as he sat down in front of the typewriter and picked up the top sheet from the stack of paper beside it on the right. "And you're so funny you ought to be on the radio with Jack Benny and Fred Allen. Now go twiddle your thumbs or something, I'm busy."

He read over what was written on the page, then set it back on the stack. From the pile of blank pages on the left, he picked up a sheet and rolled it into the typewriter, adjusting it carefully. He frowned in thought, then began hitting the keys.

"What're you working on?" Dale asked after a moment.

" 'Gun-Slammers of Cougar Basin.' I think I can peddle it to *Ten Story Western*."

"What's your hero's name, Bill Gunfighter?"

"Shut up." Joe continued typing. It wasn't easy to work with Dale in the room, but he knew that if he kept plugging away, eventually he would get caught up in the flow of the words and his shabby surroundings would fall away from him and he'd feel as if he was actually in the story, riding the dusty trails of Cougar Basin with Rance Jarrett, the drifting gunman who was going to wind up saving Peggy Dane's ranch from the villainous Arch Sundeen . . .

A fist pounded on the door of the bedroom, and Sam Parker said loudly, "Hey! Don't you know what time it is?"

Joe stopped typing and looked around. Dale smirked at him. "Sorry, Pop," Joe called through the door. "Just a little more, and then I'll stop."

"It better not be long." Sam Parker's dragging footsteps receded down the hall.

Told you so, Dale mouthed.

Joe lifted the middle finger of his left hand at him and turned back to the typewriter. *Where the hell was I?*

Somebody rapped lightly on the window.

Joe's breath hissed between his teeth in frustration. He could reach the window from where he was sitting, so he pushed the curtains aside. The window was raised several inches already since it was a warm night. Joe grasped the bottom and pushed it up even more. Adam Bergman stuck his head in through the opening.

"Hi, fellas. What're you doing?"

"I was trying to work," Joe told him.

From the bed, Dale added, "And I was trying not to die of boredom."

"It's too nice a night to work," Adam said, "and I got a cure for your boredom, Dale. Catherine and I are going to Caskey's Pier. Why don't you come with us?"

"It's late, in case you didn't know," Joe began, but Dale was already getting out of bed.

"Sounds good to me. There a hot band there tonight?"

"Jasper Thorn's Melody Makers."

Dale let out a low whistle. He reached for his pants.

"Wait a minute," Joe said. "It's late. Do Catherine's parents know where she is?"

"What they don't know won't hurt 'em," Adam said. "C'mon, Joe, it'll be fun."

Joe shook his head. "I appreciate you thinking of us, but Dale and I both have to work in the morning."

"Speak for yourself," Dale said. "I hate that damn job. I'm gonna be quitting in a couple of weeks anyway when school starts. What's it matter if they fire me now?"

"Two weeks' wages, that's what it matters," Joe said. He stopped himself from adding, *Two weeks' wages that I won't have to earn.* He had been the family's chief breadwinner for two years now, ever since that damned bull had crushed Sam Parker's leg and ended his job at the stockyards. And he had never begrudged all the hard work he did to support himself and his brother and their parents. But Dale's cavalier attitude about money bothered him, always had. Things weren't as tight as they had been a few years earlier, in the depths of the Depression, but a fella was still lucky to have a job.

"And don't talk like that in the house," Joe added. "Ma might hear."

"Wouldn't want her to die of a damn heart attack because of her baby boy's damn language, would we?" Dale finished buttoning his shirt and tucked it in. "Where's Catherine?"

"Waiting in the car." Adam jerked a thumb toward Greenwood Avenue. He was still leaning in the window with his elbows hooked over the sill. Even though the bedroom was on the first floor, it was built up several feet from the ground to allow more room for the basement. Joe knew that Adam was standing on a box to reach the window. He and Dale kept an old orange crate behind the shrubs to make it easier for them to come and go through the window. Not that they snuck out a lot at night, Joe thought. Well, he didn't, anyway. Dale was a different story.

Dale finished tying his shoes. "Let's go." He looked at Joe, who was still in his pajamas. "You're not coming?"

"I want to write a little more, like I told Pop, and then I'm going to sleep."

Dale shrugged. "Your loss. See ya."

Adam hopped down from the window. Dale swung a leg over the sill and bent as low as he could. Because of his height, he had more trouble going in and out this way than Joe did. But a moment later he was gone, and Joe was left facing the typewriter.

The page had only eight lines on it. What with all the interruptions, he had barely gotten started. It wasn't like he was rolling or anything, so if he quit for the night, it wouldn't be any great loss. . . .

He heard the roar of an engine from the street as a car powered away from the curb. That would be Catherine's Plymouth, Joe told himself. There was no longer any point in trying to talk himself out of working. He might as well get back to it, he thought with a sigh.

Rance saw the gunman reach for—No, not "reach for," "grab for." *Rance saw the gunman grab for his pistol, and he flung himself to the side as he slapped leather. The Colt bucked in his hand and sent lead fanging at the killer. Lefty staggered back, crimson blooming on his shirt front as his revolver slipped from nerveless fingers. "Yuh . . . yuh polecat!" he gasped.* Should that be "damned polecat?" Joe asked himself, then shook his head. No, he'd leave it like it was. Now he needed to have Peggy witness the shooting, so she could see for herself for the first time just what a gunslick Rance really was, and she'd be drawn to him but sort of afraid of him at the same time. . . .

The typewriter keys continued clicking into the night.

TWO

Dale felt himself pushed back against the plush upholstery in the backseat of the Plymouth convertible as Catherine pressed down hard on the gas pedal. He grinned. The girl liked to drive fast.

He ought to ask Adam if she was fast in any other ways, he thought.

Nah, that was none of his business, Dale decided. Besides, if Adam was getting any, sooner or later he'd break down and tell Joe all about it. Joe and Adam had been best friends for a hell of a long time, ever since that business with the Harrigan boys. And Joe was his brother, Dale thought, so it was only reasonable to assume that they wouldn't have any secrets from each other. So eventually Adam would tell Joe if he was screwing Catherine, and then Joe would tell Dale all about it.

Dale wondered if Adam knew that Joe was still a little sweet on her himself.

On the Plymouth's radio, Glenn Miller and the boys were blasting out "Tuxedo Junction." Dale lit a Lucky and asked around it, "Where'd you say we were going? Caskey's Pier?"

Adam turned around in the front seat and nodded. "That's right."

"I feel like dancing," Catherine added.

"Sounds good to me." Dale leaned back and looked out the window as the Chicago landscape rolled past. In the distance he could see the lights of the Loop.

Riding in a car was a lot better than riding the Illinois Central or the El. Dale hated the crowded railroad cars and the stale air inside them. He liked to be out in the open where he could feel the wind in his face. That was why he always enjoyed riding in Catherine's car. But it was even more fun to drive, so that he could feel the engine responding to *him*.

Too bad she wouldn't let him crawl under the hood and modify it. A race was coming up down at Green Valley, and he bet that if he had a couple of weeks to work on the Plymouth he could get it to where it was fast enough to kick the tails of those bozos who raced down there. Man, wouldn't he grin when they were eating his dust!

But the convertible didn't really belong to Catherine, of course. It was one of her father's cars, and Dr. Tancred would know if somebody had been monkeying with it. That was a shame. He would just have to wait until he could afford to fix up the Ford he had bought earlier in the summer. He'd gotten it cheap because it was just a junker, but he'd done the deal on the q.t. anyway so that Joe wouldn't pitch a fit about the money. Since then, Dale had kept the car out back of a garage that belonged to a buddy of his, and he swung by there whenever he had a chance to work on it. Joe didn't know a thing about it, and Dale wanted to keep it that way.

Maybe Joe was right about not quitting his job just yet, Dale thought. He was supposed to be saving his wages for college, but the Ford really needed a new carburetor. The old one was shot.

Dale leaned forward and said, "Uh, I can't stay out too late. . . ."

"That's all right," Adam said. "You can always catch a train back to Kenwood if you need to."

"Yeah, I suppose so." Dale took a deep drag on the cigarette and then snapped the butt out of the car. He didn't want to be a wet blanket. He would dance and drink as long as Adam and Catherine wanted to, and in the morning he'd just go to work sleepy and hungover if he had to. It wasn't as if it would be the first time.

★   ★   ★

God, she's beautiful! Adam thought as he watched the
lights of the ballroom on Caskey's Pier sparkle on Catherine's golden hair. He lived in mortal fear that sooner or
later she would realize what a big ugly brute he was and
ask herself what she was doing wasting her time on him.

She turned her head, looked up at him, and smiled as
she caught him watching her.

"Better look where you're going," she warned him teas-
ingly. "You might run into something."

"It'd be worth it."

He meant it, too. Ever since he'd first seen her three
years earlier, when he was a freshman at the University
of Chicago, he had known that she was the girl for him.
She'd been a junior in high school at the time, and the
only reason she'd been at the university was because her
father was giving a lecture about the political situation in
Europe and she had come along with him. That was the
luckiest night of his life, Adam had thought many times
since then, not because he'd gotten to listen to Dr. Gerald
Tancred talk about the Dangers of Foreign Entanglements
for All Americans, but because he had seen the beautiful
blond-haired girl who had left with the doctor afterward,
and fallen in love at first sight.

Dr. Tancred was a popular speaker and had many
friends on the faculty of the university, so he lectured
there often. Adam made sure he attended each and every
one of the talks, even after his mother asked him pointedly
why he was going to see "that isolationist fascist." Adam
couldn't very well explain that he didn't care about Dr.
Tancred's political views; he just wanted to see Catherine.
When she actually enrolled at the university as a premed
student after graduating from an exclusive private high
school on the North Side, that was the second-happiest
day of Adam's life.

"What are you thinking about?" Catherine asked him.

"Oh, just remembering things."

"Good things?"

"Very good things."

"You." She squeezed his arm and started to blush, and he couldn't tell her he wasn't thinking about *that*. There were too many people around.

Not that those weren't very good memories, too. . . .

Music swelled up from the bandstand, and Dale moved up alongside them, cigarette canted jauntily between his lips. "Listen to those hot notes," he said. "Think I'll go ask one of those cuties to cut a rug with me." He nodded toward a line of young women on the opposite wall of the dance hall that extended out over the waters of Lake Michigan on Caskey's Pier.

"Go ahead," Adam told him. "I've got the best dance partner in town right here." He held out his arms to Catherine, and she came into them.

The number was a fast one. Catherine kicked up her heels and shook a leg with the best of them, just as Adam had said. He was glad, though, when the music slowed down and she moved closer to him, sliding her arms around his neck as he wound his around her waist. Her breasts brushed lightly against his chest. "Baby . . ." he murmured. He was getting sentimental over her, all right, just like the song said.

She leaned her head forward so that the fragrance of her hair sent his senses swirling. His arms tightened around her even more so that her belly bumped against his groin.

He was getting hard. Had she felt it? Even after the things they'd done together, he experienced a surge of embarrassment. Carefully, so as not to draw attention to what he was doing, he put a little more space between them.

Catherine closed the gap almost immediately, and Adam felt the warm pressure of her body against him once more.

He wanted to close his eyes and moan. Didn't she know what she was doing to him? She had to know. But she wasn't a tease. Adam was certain of that. Whatever she was doing, she wasn't doing it just to torment him.

That meant she wanted him, too, just like he wanted

her. He knew logically that was true. She wouldn't have done some of the things she'd done in the past if she didn't. But he still had trouble making himself believe it in his heart.

The slow dance number came to a close, and Catherine tipped her head back and looked up at him with a softness around her mouth and blue fire in her eyes. She came up on her toes and brushed her lips across his. "Thanks for the dance, mister," she whispered.

Adam swallowed, wondering what the hell had happened to his ability to talk.

Catherine smiled. "I could use a beer."

He finally found his tongue again. "Yeah, so could I."

He slipped his arm through hers and led her toward the bar. It was crowded. Caskey's was one of the most popular spots in town on a warm summer night like this. A cool breeze was usually blowing in from the lake, the music was good, and the bartenders didn't check too closely to make sure all the customers were of age.

After a while, Adam was able to work his way through the press of people in front of the bar and snag a couple of bottles of beer. He shouldered a path back to Catherine and handed one of them to her. "Let's go outside," he suggested.

"Okay."

Sliding glass doors at one end of the dance floor led out onto a long terrace at the end of the pier. Lights winked far out on the lake, and they were pretty if you didn't stop to think that they were probably on garbage scows and coal barges. That was the way a lot of things in life were, Adam told himself: it was smarter just to accept the beauty and not think too much about what was underneath it.

They went to the wooden railing along the edge of the pier and leaned against it as they sipped their beers. Quite a few couples were strolling on this part of the pier, enjoying the night air and the view down the Gold Coast.

Light spilled out from the ballroom, but it was still dim enough out here that a guy could safely do a little necking with his girl, too. Adam was doing some serious thinking along those lines.

"I tell you, as far as I can see, Hitler's not that bad a fellow."

"What? What are you talking about?"

The voices came from two young men who were walking past, about twenty feet from Adam and Catherine.

"What I mean is, he's not doing anything to bother *us*, is he?"

"Yeah, well, what about the people in France?"

"What do I care about a bunch of Frenchies?"

"But he's bombing the hell out of England, and the British are our allies. I think Roosevelt—"

"Screw Roosevelt. Don't you know he's one of those damned Jews, too? That's the only reason he doesn't like Hitler, because he's worried about all his little hymie cousins over there in Europe . . ."

The words faded out as the two young men walked on down the pier. Adam didn't realize until after they were out of earshot that he was clutching the beer bottle in his hand so tightly that it was in danger of shattering. He was holding his breath, too, and his pulse was going a mile a minute. He jumped as Catherine put her hand on his arm and quietly said his name.

"Don't pay any attention," she said. "He's just a stupid . . . he doesn't . . . just don't pay attention to people like that."

Adam drew a deep breath. "Ignore them and they'll go away." He shook his head. "I don't think so. They never have so far."

He bent over and carefully placed his beer bottle on the pier.

Catherine's grip on his arm got tighter. "No, Adam," she said. "Please don't. We came here to have a good time."

He couldn't get free from her without jerking loose,

and he didn't want to do that. But rage was boiling up inside him and it had to get out some way. It got even worse when one of the young men let out a bray of laughter down the pier.

"Probably made another joke about the damned Jews and how Hitler ought to kill all of them—"

Catherine moved closer to him, put a hand on the back of his neck, and drew his head down to hers. In the shadows of the pier, her lips found his and kissed him hungrily, urgently.

She was only doing this to distract him, a voice in the back of Adam's mind told him. She just didn't want him getting into a fight and making a scene.

It was working, he realized. His anger was slipping away like the tide going out. He could argue with bigots anytime; there was always one around handy.

But it wasn't every night that a fella got to stand on a pier with water lapping gently below it and a warm breeze blowing and stars shining brilliantly in the sky while he kissed the prettiest girl on the whole blasted planet.

Adam Bergman did the intelligent thing. He forgot all about those ignorant bastards and kissed the girl.

THREE

Dale leaned in under the raised hood of the Ford and fitted the head of a wrench around a bolt. He strained against it for a moment until the wrench slipped and his knuckles banged against a sharp corner of the engine block. He said, "Shit!" and jerked his hand up. Ignoring the grease on his hand, he lifted the bleeding knuckle to his mouth and sucked on it for a second.

"Your own fault for buying a Ford," Harry Skinner said. He had just come out of the back door of the garage carrying a tire. He tossed it on a pile of tires and came over to the car where Dale was working. He was a tall, slender man in his thirties with a seemingly permanent mocking grin on his face. "You buy a pile of crap like that, you bleed."

"Shut up," Dale muttered. "I gotta break that bolt loose so I can get that old gasket off. It's gotta be replaced."

"Move over, Junior," Harry said. "Let the expert show you how."

Dale hesitated, then shrugged and handed over the wrench. Harry bent over the exposed engine.

Dale started to reach toward his pocket and then remembered that he didn't have any cigarettes. He'd smoked his last one earlier in the day and didn't have enough change to buy another pack. He didn't have any money at all, period. He would have bummed a smoke off Harry, but Harry, the son of a bitch, didn't smoke.

Harry straightened up and dropped a rusted bolt in Dale's hand. "There you go. Now you can get that gasket off. I told you you needed to let the expert do it."

"Yeah, yeah. Thanks, I guess."

Harry stepped back and wiped his hands on his coveralls. "Say, I guess I won't be seein' as much of you after this week."

"What do you mean by that?"

"Well, college starts next week, don't it?"

"Yeah." Dale spat into the weeds that grew up between old engines and stacks of tires in the lot behind Harry's garage. "But I'm not sure I'm going."

"Ho, ho. You don't go, your brother'll kick your ass."

Anger flared inside Dale. "My brother hasn't been able to kick my ass since I was twelve."

"Well, then, your old man will."

"He's a cripple," Dale said.

"I don't care. He'll take his cane to you."

"Yeah. You're probably right. But I still don't know if I'm going or not."

"Listen," Harry said. "I joke around a lot, but I mean this, kid. You're already enrolled, your brother wants you to go, your folks want you to go. So go already! You're a smart kid. You might make something of yourself, you never know."

"Well . . . I guess it's better than working in the hardware store and listening to old man Grissom bitching at me all day."

"Damn right."

Dale nodded toward the concrete-block building. "But you own your own business, Harry, and you're doing fine. And you never went to college."

"Yeah, well, lemme tell you, it took a hell of a lot of hard work and even more luck to make it through the hard times these last seven or eight years. Plenty of folks didn't."

"You don't need a college degree to stand in a breadline."

Harry shook his head. "All right. Don't listen to me. Don't listen to your brother. But if you don't go to school, what're you gonna do?"

Dale put a hand on the fender of the Ford and said, "Race this baby."

Harry stared at him for a long moment, then said, "Good Lord, you really mean it."

"Damn right I do." Dale felt his enthusiasm growing. "There's a track down at Green Valley where all you have to do is come up with the entry fee. Once I fine-tune the old girl a little more, I can take those jokers who run down there. I know I can. I've been hitching down on the weekends some and watching the races. I can beat 'em, Harry."

"You think so?"

"I know it."

Harry pushed his lips in and out a couple of times, then nodded slowly. "You're gonna need a better carburetor on this heap of junk, then. I think I can come up with one."

"Really? You want to help me?"

"Hey, you're a pal," Harry said. "And you've helped me out plenty of times here at the garage and never took no money for it. Least I can do is find a good used carb for you. I still think you ought to go to college, though. It's too good an opportunity to just throw away."

"Yeah, yeah, you're starting to sound like my sainted brother." Dale punched him lightly on the shoulder, then turned toward the Ford's engine. "Say, you think we could come up with some way to increase the compression a little on these cylinders?"

"I don't see why not. Lemme take a look."

★   ★   ★

Catherine hesitated in the hallway, then moved quickly forward, trying not to make too much noise. That was easy on the thick carpet. She went past the open doorway and thought she had made it. Like they sometimes said in the movies and in those stories Joe wrote, the coast was clear.

"Catherine?" Dr. Gerald Tancred's voice came through

the open door from his study. "You're not going out this late, are you?"

Catherine stopped in her tracks and closed her eyes for a second. She thought about making a dash for the front door. But she couldn't do that, and she knew it. With a sigh, she turned back toward the study. By the time she stuck her head into the room, she had managed to put a smile on her face.

"It's really not that late, Dad—" she began.

"I've asked you to call me Father. And dinner was an hour ago."

Catherine didn't lose her smile. "I just need to run out for a few minutes. I thought I'd take the convertible—"

Her father carefully placed his fountain pen on the sheet of paper in front of him where he had been making notes on the day's patients. He always did that after dinner, retreating into his study to get his thoughts down on paper while they were fresh in his mind.

Not that it really mattered, Catherine thought. Most of the patients who came to see him weren't really sick at all. They were just rich, bored, middle-aged women who enjoyed the attention—even if it was just medical attention—from a handsome, suave, European doctor.

Her father *was* handsome, Catherine had to give him that, with his tall, regal bearing and aristocratic features and thick dark hair just starting to turn a distinguished gray in places. And he was a good doctor when he had the chance to do some real healing. He'd been first in his class at the University of Heidelberg, back in '19. He had practiced in Berlin for six years, acquiring a number of loyal patients, a wife, and in due course a daughter. Then, in 1925, he had immigrated to America, bringing the wife and the daughter—Catherine—with him.

The first few years had been lean ones, working in first one clinic and then another, and supporting a wife and two children now—Catherine's brother Spencer had come along by then—but by the early thirties Dr. Gerald Tancred had been established here in Chicago. He had bought this mansion on the North Shore in '35, when the real estate market, like everything else, was depressed. Every day he made the short drive to his office in the Loop in a Packard sedan. His clients included the wealthy and the famous, and he and his wife Elenore were invited to all the best dinners and parties. He despised Franklin Roosevelt with a passion and secretly wished his wife and Roosevelt's wife hadn't been given such similar names. And, Catherine thought, he really had no idea how to go about loving his children.

Spencer was at a boarding school back east, and Dr. Tancred would have much preferred that Catherine attend Sarah Lawrence or Radcliffe rather than the University of Chicago. That would have gotten her out of the way, too. But as long as she was living at home, Dr. Tancred felt that he had to keep a tight rein on her behavior. It was somehow expected of him.

After placing the pen on the desk, he steepled his hands in front of his face and gravely regarded her over them. "Your sophomore year begins next week," he said.

Catherine nodded. "That's right." She didn't see what that had to do with anything.

"So I understand why you feel that you have to . . . have some fun before buckling down to another year of serious work. You want to . . . sow some wild oats, as they say. I was young once, too, you know."

Maybe so, but even then he wouldn't have known a wild oat if he tripped over one, Catherine thought.

"I just need to run down to the drugstore," she said. She hoped he would jump to the conclusion that she needed some sort of female product. Then he would leave her alone. Even though he was a doctor, he was incredibly reticent about that sort of thing where his own family was concerned.

"And who do you plan to meet there? Your friend Adam?"

"No," she said. It wasn't really a lie. She wasn't going to meet Adam at the drugstore. She wasn't *going* to the drugstore. They had made plans to meet at Madison Park.

Her father looked down at his paperwork, obviously torn between the desire to get back to it and the urge to continue interrogating his daughter. He cleared his throat and said, "You won't be out late?"

"Of course not."

"All right, then."

She came over to the desk, leaned over it, and planted a quick kiss on his cheek. "Good night, Dad. I mean, Father."

"Good night." He reached for his pen.

Catherine hurried out of the study. As she passed the parlor, her mother called to her, "Good night, dear," but didn't look up from the copy of *Collier's* she was reading. Music played softly from the cathedral radio in the corner.

" 'Night, Mother," Catherine replied, and then she went out the front door and got into the Plymouth convertible she had left parked on the circular drive in front of the house earlier in the day. She started the car and drove away at a sedate pace, waiting until she was three blocks away from the house before she pressed harder on the accelerator and sent the vehicle leaping down the street.

At moments such as this, she could understand why Dale Parker liked to drive fast. She knew Dale wanted to race cars; she had heard him talking about it with Joe and Adam. If she hadn't been a woman, Catherine thought with a smile, she might have liked to be a race car driver herself. But women didn't do such things. It was daring enough that she was enrolled in the premed program at school and planned to someday become a doctor. There had been women doctors before, although not all that many. But Catherine couldn't ever remember hearing anything about a female race car driver.

She wheeled through a tight turn and headed for Madison Park. She couldn't wait to see Adam again. She wanted to kiss him and feel his arms go around her and hold her. That was all she thought about these days. That, and the times they had gone a little farther than simple necking. . . .

A wicked little thrill went through her. They hadn't gone all the way yet, of course, but they had touched each other intimately enough so that she knew the power of the feelings they aroused in each other. Sooner or later, they would get carried away and wouldn't stop, she thought.

And when that time came, she wouldn't really care, because she knew that despite all the obstacles, she loved Adam Bergman with all her heart. Thinking about that, she drove on into the Chicago night.

FOUR

From its founding in 1890, the University of Chicago was intended to be more than just another college.

Its first benefactor was John D. Rockefeller, who made a personal donation of $600,000 to the university and arranged for the prominent educator William Rainey Harper to serve as its first president. The first classes were held in 1892 with the campus still largely unfinished, but its faculty was complete, with distinguished, award-winning professors recruited from all over the country. Most were specialists in academic research in fields such as physics, medicine, and sociology. The University of Chicago would not concern itself only with the dry dispensing of the facts of the past. Its faculty and students would spend more time looking forward than backward.

In the nearly fifty years since then, the school had lived up to its promise. And it was as impressive physically as it was academically, with its campus sprawled along the northern edge of the Midway, the mile-long stretch of grassy parkland that connected Washington Park on the west with Jackson Park—the site of the Great Columbian Exposition of 1892—on the east. The university was a haven of beauty and learning here on the south side of Chicago.

And today it was a busy place as well, as its more than fourteen thousand students streamed into its buildings for the first classes of the Fall 1940 semester.

Joe walked past Mitchell Tower, modeled after Magdalen Tower at England's Oxford University, and across Hutchinson Commons. He was starting his junior year. When he had first enrolled at the university, he had hoped that he would have his undergraduate degree by now and be starting his graduate work. The necessity of working one and sometimes two full-time jobs had made that impossible.

Things had gotten a little easier once he'd started writing and had cracked the pulp markets a couple of years earlier, but the payments for his stories were usually pretty small and frequently slow in coming. Still, they had enabled him to stick with just one job most of the time and increase his course load at school by a few hours each semester.

Dale walked alongside, head down. "I don't get it," he said. "You saw how I struggled all the way through high school. Hell, I was lucky to graduate. Why'd you strong-arm me into going to college?"

"I didn't strong-arm you."

"Huh. Next thing to it."

"You saw how proud Mom and Pop were when I started college. Think how they must feel now that both of their sons are getting a college education."

"So I'm here to make Mom and Pop feel good."

"I didn't say that." Joe pointed to one of the massive buildings. "That's the library. I expect you'll be spending a lot of time there studying."

When Dale didn't answer, Joe glanced over to see that his brother had stopped and was now turned around on the sidewalk, peering back in the direction they had come from. Joe saw several young women walking along the sidewalk in that direction, their lightweight summer skirts swirling around their legs, and Dale was grinning broadly as he watched them.

"Say, maybe this college stuff won't be so bad after all."

Joe tugged on his sleeve. "Come on, Romeo."

"Don't start spouting Shakespeare at me," Dale said as he fell in step beside Joe again. "You're the literature major, not me. Captain Marvel's more my speed when it comes to reading. Shazam!"

"What *are* you going to major in?"

Dale shrugged. "Hell if I know. You signed me up for the basics and said I didn't have to decide yet."

"You'll have to decide sometime."

"Yeah, but not yet." Dale turned his head to watch another coed walk past, pert-breasted in a white blouse. "I think I'll major in *that*."

Joe tried not to roll his eyes. A moment later, he was distracted from Dale's grumbling by someone calling his name behind them.

Joe stopped and turned around to see a young man hurrying along the commons to catch up to them. He smiled and said, "Hi, Ken. How was your summer?"

Kenneth Walker joined Joe and Dale and said, "Quite exciting. I was here almost every day working as Dr. Foster's laboratory assistant."

"You mean you went to school all summer, and you call that exciting?" Dale said.

Ken looked at him and said to Joe, "This must be your brother."

"I'm afraid so."

"He doesn't *look* like a Neanderthal."

Dale frowned. "Hey. Was that a crack?"

"Forget about it," Joe said. He went on to Ken, "So you're starting graduate school?"

"Yes. I'll be a teaching assistant in the science department, too."

"You look more like a halfback," Dale said.

That was true, Joe supposed. Ken Walker had the sort of blond, athletic good looks that made people think of heroics on the football field. He also had absolutely no interest in sports, but possessed a keen mind when it came to physics, chemistry, and biology. Joe knew that as well as anybody, because Ken had helped him make it through a biology course when they were both freshmen at the university. Joe had returned the favor by tutoring Ken in literature and grammar so that he could pass the introductory English course. They didn't have a thing in common but had been friends ever since anyway, even though Ken had been able to progress through school at a much faster pace.

"Dale's taking Introductory Biology," Joe said. "Maybe he'll be in one of the classes you're teaching."

"It's possible," Ken agreed.

Dale made a face. "It's not bad enough that I've got my big brother riding herd on me, but now I'm going to have a pal of his for a teacher?"

"Don't worry," Ken said seriously. "Just because you're Joe's brother doesn't mean that you'd get any special treatment in one of my classes."

"Then why—Ah, never mind," Dale said with a wave of his hand.

"Don't pay any attention to him," Joe said to Ken. "He doesn't want to be here."

"Where else would anyone want to be on a gorgeous autumn day such as this other than school?" Ken asked and, again, he was completely serious.

Well, I suppose it's good that there's somebody *in the world more straitlaced than I am*, Joe thought.

★   ★   ★

Despite the fact that he had looked forward to this day, Joe was tired when he finished his last class and walked down the steps of Cobb Hall. His spirits lifted a little when he saw Adam and Catherine standing arm in arm at the bottom of the steps, obviously waiting for him.

"How did it go?" Adam asked.

"Hard, just like always. How was law school?"

Adam closed his eyes for a second and groaned. "Don't ask. All of my professors seem to be planning on chewing us up and spitting us out all semester."

"It can't be that bad," Catherine said.

No, Joe thought. *Nothing could be bad with a girl like Catherine on your arm.*

Most of the time, he wasn't jealous. After all, he had

gone out with Catherine exactly twice before she met Adam. That had been during her freshman year here at the university. On the first date, he had taken her to the Orpheum to see *The Big Broadcast of 1938*. She had seemed to have fun, but there hadn't been any good-night kiss. For their second date, he had taken her to dinner at the downstairs grill of the Blackstone Hotel. He was sure the main dining room upstairs would have been more to the taste of a girl such as Catherine, but just taking her to the grill had strained his finances enough. When he had taken her home—with him feeling damned uncomfortable just being in the exclusive North Side neighborhood, let alone dating somebody from there—she had given him a quick peck on the lips, just warm enough and friendly enough to make him think that there really might be something there between them.

But then the next week Adam had come along and Catherine had fallen head over heels for him, and to tell the truth, Joe was a little glad. He couldn't afford her. Neither could Adam, of course, but he didn't seem to care about that.

They had all become good friends, and Joe figured that having Catherine for a pal was probably better in the long run than if she had been his girlfriend. Still, he couldn't help but wonder every now and then what it would have been like. . . .

"We're going to get burgers and beers over at Pascoe's," Adam said. "Why don't you find Dale and come with us?"

Reluctantly, Joe shook his head. "I can't. I'm working the evening shift at the hardware store now. I told Mr. Grissom I'd be there by five."

"You're sure?"

Joe shrugged. "Afraid so."

"Well, we'll miss you. What about Dale?"

"He's supposed to go straight home after his classes so he can get to work studying for them."

"Do you really think he'll do that?"

"He'd better," Joe said grimly. Dale had quit his job at Grissom's Hardware, just as Joe had planned, so that he would have plenty of time for schoolwork.

"Okay. See you later."

" 'Bye, Joe," Catherine said.

" 'Bye, Catherine," he called after her as she and Adam turned away.

Yeah, she was beautiful, all right, he thought. Just the sort of cool, elegant dame who'd waltz into a gumshoe's office and hire him to retrieve a piece of ice from her blackmailing boyfriend before her rich, older husband found out about it. Joe nodded slowly. That might do it, all right. He had been trying to figure out what to write next ever since he had finished "Gun-Slammers of Cougar Basin" and sent it off to *Ten Story Western*. A detective yarn might be just the thing. He knew Rogers Terrill at *Dime Detective* was looking for stuff, but if the story turned out good enough, he might even try it at *Black Mask*. If it didn't go, there was always *Thrilling Detective*. And he could always sex it up a little if need be and send it to *Spicy Detective*.

" 'Homicide Hangover,' " he muttered to himself as he started across the commons, surrounded by students coming and going. " 'Corpse Parade.' Or maybe 'The Dame Cried Danger.' "

One of these days, he told himself. One of these days people were going to walk into their local bookstore and plop down good money for the latest bestseller by Joseph Parker. Yeah. Had to happen.

One of these days.

FIVE

Dale pressed down on the gas pedal and ran the engine up. "Man, listen to that baby purr!" he said to Harry Skinner as he let up on the accelerator and the roar died down.

Harry leaned his arms on the open window of the Ford. "I never thought the heap would sound that good, to tell you the truth," he said.

"It wouldn't have without your help, Harry." Dale grinned up at his friend.

Harry brushed a loosely balled fist against Dale's chin. "Ah, don't go gettin' all sappy on me," he said. "All I did was scrounge up some parts and give you a hand now and then."

Dale couldn't resist. He pumped the gas again. "C'mon, Harry. Let's see what she'll do on the road."

Harry straightened and waved a hand at the garage. "No can do, kid. I got a business to run. Why don't you go hunt up your brother and see if he'll take a spin with you?"

The mention of Joe made Dale frown. "He's at work, and he doesn't know I've even got a car. Besides, he thinks I'm at the library studying."

"Yeah, how are them courses of yours going?"

Dale closed his eyes for a moment and bit back a groan before saying, "You never heard such a crock of shit in your life, Harry. Those professors are all a bunch of musty old bastards who look like they crawled up out of a grave. And they just stand up in front of the class and ramble on and on about nothing. Blah, blah, blah. It's enough to drive a guy nuts."

"Yeah, well, I bet you'd learn something if you'd just pay attention."

"Don't you start in on me, too. I thought you were a pal."

"Just tryin' to look out for your best interests."

Dale changed the subject by saying, "Next Saturday, I'm going down to Green Valley and run this baby in one of the races."

"You got the entry fee?"

"Well . . . not yet," Dale had to admit. "It's twenty-five bucks, and I can't ask Joe for it. I thought I might put the touch on Catherine—"

"That North Side girlfriend of that Jewish buddy of yours?" Harry reached for the back pocket of his coveralls and brought out a thin, battered, black leather wallet. "Never borrow money from a dame, kid, even a rich one," he said as he slid a couple of bills from the wallet. "Take anything else they wanna give you, but never money."

Dale held up both hands, palms out, as Harry thrust the bills at him. "Put that back," he said. "You've done way too much for me already, Harry—"

"Hell, I'm thinkin' of it as an investment. How much is the prize in that race?"

"Three hundred for the winner, a hundred for second place, and fifty bucks for third."

"See? All you got to do is come in third and I get my twenty-five back and you get twenty-five out of the deal."

"How's that an investment?" Dale asked. "Don't you have to make a profit for it to be an investment?"

"Nah. There's profit enough in havin' you tell people that you rebuilt this heap at Harry Skinner's garage. Free advertising's the best kind, I always say."

Harry might have a point about that, Dale thought. If he could make a splash on the racing circuit and let people know that Harry had helped him, it would be good for the garage's business. Dale nodded and reached for the grease-stained bills that Harry was still holding out to him.

"One more thing," Harry said. "You got to tell Joe and

your folks about the car. It ain't right to sneak around behind your family's back."

Dale hesitated for a moment, then nodded and took the money. "All right. Thanks, Harry. But I'm not going to come in third."

"Now, don't start thinkin' them pessimistic thoughts before you even enter the race."

Dale laughed. "Third, hell. I'm going to win the damned thing."

★   ★   ★

Joe heard somebody tap a car horn and looked up to make sure he wasn't too close to the curb. He had just left the hardware store on Forty-third Street and was about to walk the four blocks back to the Parker house. He was surprised to see a Ford that was nine or ten years old come to a stop in front of him.

Dale grinned at him from behind the wheel of the car. "Hey, big brother, want a ride home?" he asked.

Joe stared at him for a long moment before he was able to say, "Where in the world did you get this car?"

"Bought it," Dale said matter-of-factly. "Back in June, in fact. I've been keeping it at Harry Skinner's garage ever since then and working on it whenever I could." Dale paused, then went on, "Harry made me sort of promise to tell you about it."

"You bought it in June," Joe repeated. "Where did you get the money?"

"Well, I had my first week's wages from old man Grissom there—" Dale nodded toward the hardware store. "And there was that money I got from Aunt Edith for my birthday."

"You were supposed to put that away for school expenses this fall!"

Dale cut off the engine of the car, swung open the door, and stepped out on the sidewalk. "Look, Joe," he said sharply. "I came up with the dough, all right? The car was cheap because it wasn't running—"

"Because it was junk, you mean."

"Not anymore! Didn't you hear that engine purring like a kitten when I pulled up? Harry helped me out, found some parts for me and helped me fix it up."

"You're supposed to be studying in your spare time, not monkeying with some car."

Dale sighed in exasperation. "Don't you get it?" he asked as he slapped a hand on the fender of the Ford. "I'm going to race this car. I'll make more money that way than I ever will from anything I learn at that damn college!"

Joe struggled to control his anger. "You don't understand—" he began.

"*You're* the one who doesn't understand! You think your way is the only way to do anything. You think you've got all the answers!"

Joe stared at his brother for a moment, then couldn't stop himself from laughing bitterly. "All the answers?" he repeated. "If I had all the answers, you think I'd be running myself ragged trying to keep up with school and a job and riding herd on you at the same time? You think I like sorting nuts and bolts for hours and then going home to work on my assignments and my writing until after midnight?"

"I'm not asking you for any help," Dale said.

"No, but you're squandering the help I'm trying to give you!" Joe realized he was almost shouting. He glanced around at the people going past on the sidewalk. Nobody was staring directly at him and Dale, but Joe knew they all had to be aware of the argument. He took a deep breath and went on, "Look, we can talk about this at home—"

"That's where I was going. Remember, I offered to give you a lift?"

"Yeah. Well, I suppose that would be all right." Joe went around the front of the car to the other side and opened the door. He looked across the roof of the vehicle at Dale and said, "You know Pop's going to blow his top when he finds out about this."

Dale shrugged. "Pop blows his top so much I don't even pay attention to it anymore."

Joe understood the feeling. He got into the car and pulled the door shut. Dale got in, turned the key, and stepped on the starter. It ground noisily for a second, then caught. The engine roared smoothly.

"It does sound pretty good," Joe admitted.

A cocky grin tugged at Dale's mouth. "You bet it does. It'll sound even better crossing the finish line first at Green Valley next week."

"You're talking about that racetrack?"

"Damn right. Next Saturday." Dale pulled away from the curb and then glanced over at Joe. "You coming?"

"To the race, you mean?"

"Slow on the uptake today, aren't you? Of course to the race."

"I don't know. I'm supposed to work. . . ."

"You've got a whole week to work things out with Mr. Grissom. Maybe you can just work Saturday morning."

"Yeah, maybe, if I work some extra evenings." Abruptly, Joe nodded. "I'll figure out something. But yeah, I'll be there."

"Good. I want to see the look on your face when I win that race."

★　★　★

Dale hurried into the house and found his mother in the kitchen. The smell of baking bread came from the oven. Any other time Dale would have stopped to enjoy the aroma, but today he was more interested in showing off his car. "C'mon, Ma," he said as he caught hold of Helen Parker's hand. "I got something to show you." He started tugging her toward the front of the house.

"Dale, what in the world—?" she said.

"You'll see," he promised.

They were passing the parlor when the tip of Sam Parker's cane thumped hard on the floor and he asked, "What's going on here?"

Dale hadn't seen his father when he went by the parlor earlier. That was probably because all the drapes were pulled and the lamps weren't on. Sam Parker spent a lot of his time sitting in darkened rooms. That was enough to make anybody go nuts, Dale had often thought, even somebody who hadn't had his leg crushed by a bull so that he could never work again.

Dale wanted to ignore his father's question and keep going, but his mother hung back. "Just a minute, dear," she said. "Wait for your father."

Reluctantly, Dale nodded. "Okay."

Sam Parker came out of the parlor, dragging his bad leg behind him as he balanced on his cane. He was shorter than his wife; Dale had gotten his height from Helen. Once broad-shouldered and immensely strong, Sam was now just big and sloppy, with his muscles gone to rolls of fat around his middle. He was mostly bald, with gray hair around his ears and the back of his head, and two days' worth of beard stubble covered his jowls. He was pretty damned pathetic as far as Dale was concerned, and he couldn't see how the old man had let himself go like that. His mom was still sort of pretty in a middle-aged, graying-blond sort of way. He thought she could have done better than a self-pitying old fart like his pop.

But she wouldn't, of course. She'd stick by him through thick and thin. For better or worse. That was what she'd said when she married him. At least, Dale figured that was the case. He hadn't been around then, of course.

"C'mon out on the porch, Pop," Dale forced himself to say pleasantly. "I've got something to show you."

"Can't you bring it in here? My leg's starting to hurt."

Yeah, like the leg ever stopped hurting. He never stopped bitching about it, anyway, Dale thought. But he said, "No, I can't bring it in. You've got to go out on the porch."

"Come on, Sam," Helen said. "I'll give you a hand." She moved around so she could take hold of his left arm, the one he didn't use for the cane.

Slowly, they went along the hallway to the front door. Joe was waiting on the porch, and he opened the door for them. They stepped outside. A September twilight was falling, filling the Kenwood neighborhood with soft shadows and the yellow glow of lamplight in windows, but there was still enough leftover sun in the sky to show the car parked at the curb.

"Ain't she a beaut?" Dale asked proudly.

"Whose car is that?" Sam said.

"Mine. That's what I wanted to show you."

Slowly, Sam turned his head toward Dale. "Where'd you get the money to buy a car?"

"Don't worry, it didn't cost much—"

"You steal that car, boy?"

Dale took an involuntary step back, his eyes widening. "Of course not! I wouldn't steal a car."

"You must've stole the money, then. What'd you do, hold up a store?"

"He worked for it, Pop," Joe said quickly. Dale was glad Joe didn't say anything about him using the birthday money he'd gotten from Aunt Edith.

"This boy never earned enough to buy a fancy car like that."

"Fancy?" Dale said. "You call that fancy? There's nothing fancy about it, Pa, except that the engine runs like a top."

"Dale's a lot of things, Pop, but he's not a thief," Joe added.

Dale looked narrowly at him. "Thanks a lot."

"I'm just trying to help out here—"

"Well, don't." Dale turned back to his father. "I didn't steal the car, and I didn't steal the money. But that car's mine, and if you don't like it, you can just go take a flying—"

"Dale!" Helen Parker said. "Don't talk to your father in that tone of voice."

Dale threw his hands in the air. "I give up. I just thought you might like to see the car because you're my folks. I thought you might be happy for me."

"It looks like a very nice car, dear."

"It's ready for the scrap heap," Sam said.

Dale stared at him. "A minute ago you were saying how fancy it was!"

"What, the El's not good enough for you? You're too good to ride the train or take a streetcar?"

"Why don't we all go inside?" Helen suggested. "I don't want my bread to burn."

"That sounds like a good idea, Ma," Joe said.

Dale and his father were still glaring at each other. Neither appeared ready to budge. But then Dale said, "I'm going out. Why don't you come with me, Joe?"

"Going where? It's almost dark."

"I just want to take a drive."

Joe shook his head. "Sorry, I'm too tired, Dale. And I can smell that bread cooking."

"Go on," Sam said to Dale. "Speed around like a maniac. You'll wreck that jalopy is what you'll do."

Dale's jaw was taut with anger, but he didn't say anything else. Instead, he turned and stalked down the walk to the curb. He got into the Ford and slammed the door behind him. The engine came to life as he stepped on the starter.

He should have known better, he told himself as he drove away from the house. Joe had been mad at first, but he would come around. He had already started to. And his mom didn't seem too worried about it, either. But the old man . . .

The old man would never be anything but a major pain in the ass, Dale thought. Sooner or later he was going to stop trying to impress his father.

And that day was coming, sooner rather than later.

SIX

Adam couldn't help it. A thrill of excitement, mingled with a touch of bittersweet regret, went through him at every crack of the bat against the ball, every "ooh" and "ahh" from the Wrigley Field crowd as an outfielder made a nice running catch.

That could have been him down there, he thought. Maybe even should have been.

"What good can a ballplayer do for people? Entertain them, that's all. My boy will make a difference. A real difference."

Ruth Bergman's voice was echoing in her son's head as Catherine leaned over to Adam and said, "This is fun. I'm glad we came."

Adam nodded. "Yeah, so am I."

Afternoon sunlight was splashed over the stadium with its ivy-covered, red-brick walls. The Cubs were playing the Brooklyn Dodgers, trailing three to one in the seventh inning. Since it was late in the season, the Cubbies were already well out of the pennant race, but the fans didn't seem to care. They had come here today to soak up some sun and some beer and to begin to mark the passing of yet another baseball season.

Back in the spring, the Cubs had offered Adam a contract after one of their scouts had seen him playing for the university team and invited him to a tryout. He would have had to start out in the minors, of course, but the scout had assured him that the club would call him up later in the season if he could just hit his weight in the minors. They needed his speed in the outfield, the scout had said.

Adam was confident he would have been able to do better than that. He'd always had a good eye for a pitch, developed in countless stickball games. He hadn't been able to hit for power, though, until he'd been in high school.

And then only because of what had happened with the Harrigan boys . . .

"Jewboy! Hey, Jewboy! Who've you been about cruci-fyin' today?"

"Lookit him run! Lookit the little kike bastard run!"

"We'll teach 'im a lesson, sure an' we will!"

Adam knew he shouldn't have ventured this far west on Forty-second Street. Even at twelve years old, he knew that much. But his mother had sent him for bread, and the market close to their house had been out so he had kept going toward another market he had seen before from the streetcars. He hadn't even thought about the fact that most of the kids over here were Irish. They all went to the same school, Shakespeare Elementary on Forty-sixth Street, and there was an uneasy truce between them and the Jewish children on the playground. Now, though, Adam had fool-ishly ventured right into their territory.

So of course he ran. He recognized the three rangy, redheaded Harrigan brothers from school. Only one of them was older than him, and the other two were younger, but they were all bigger than he was. If he didn't get away from them, they'd give him a beating. He was sure of it. If he could get to the streetcar stop at the end of the block, the conductor wouldn't let the Harrigans hurt him. The conductors didn't allow any tomfoolery on the streetcars.

The car at the stop pulled away just before Adam got there. At the same moment, a hand fastened itself on his collar and jerked him back roughly. "Gotcha, Jewboy!"

Adam felt himself turned around. He barely had time to open his mouth before a fist sank into his belly. He

wanted to yell in anger and pain, but all that came out
was an embarrassing little squeak.

"Christ-killer!" The boy hit him again, then moved
around behind him and grabbed his arms. "I'll hold him
while you guys work him over."

Through a blur of tears, Adam saw the other two Harrigans closing in on him, their fists doubled. One was nine
years old, the other ten, but the hatred in their eyes was
ancient. The closest one swung, hitting Adam for the third
time in the belly. Adam thought he was going to throw
up and hoped he wouldn't, because that would probably
just make them madder at him. The one holding him
twisted his arms painfully.

"Let him go."

The words were shouted from somewhere off to the
side. The boy holding Adam jerked his right arm so hard
Adam thought it was going to be torn off his shoulder.
"Stay outta this, Parker," the boy said. "This ain't none
o' your business."

"There's three of you, and you're all bigger than him.
It ain't fair."

"What ain't fair is that the damn Jews are a bunch o'
Christ-killers. My pa said so."

"Yeah, well, your pa's an ignorant bastard."

With a howl of rage, the boy let go of Adam and threw
himself at the newcomer. Adam's vision was still blurred
by tears, but he recognized the smaller boy as Joe Parker.
He knew Joe a little from school, but they'd never been
friends. A younger blond boy was hanging back behind
Joe, probably his brother.

All three of the Harrigans jumped Joe, and he met the
first one with a straight right-hand punch in the face.
Blood spurted from a mashed nose, and the owner of the
nose yelped in pain and surprise. But then the other two
Harrigans crashed into Joe, and they all went down on
the sidewalk.

Why doesn't somebody stop them? Adam asked himself. All the adults walking past seemed to think it was

funny that the boys were fighting. They probably thought it was just a friendly scuffle.

But it wasn't friendly at all, Adam knew. It was deadly serious.

And he couldn't stand by and let Joe Parker get beat up just because he'd tried to come to his rescue.

Adam wiped the back of his hand across his runny nose, then yelled incoherently and jumped on the back of the closest Harrigan.

The next few minutes were full of gouging and flailing and kicking. Adam got in some good licks, probably because the Harrigans weren't really expecting him to do anything except run. Eventually, he and Joe found themselves back on their feet, facing the Harrigans. All five of them were scraped and bloody and had rips in their clothes. The oldest Harrigan pointed at Joe and said, "Parker, you son of a bitch, you'll be sorry you crossed us. Sure and we'll settle the score."

"Anytime," Joe said, panting slightly from the exertion of the battle.

"And you, Jewboy. You're dead." The threat was made with bared teeth, and Adam had no doubt that Harrigan meant it.

But for now, the fight was over. Both groups backed away from each other until finally the Harrigans turned and sauntered off down the street. Adam waited until they were gone before he bent over and picked up the cap that had been knocked off his head earlier.

"Thanks, Joe," he said. "You didn't have to do that."

"If I hadn't, they'd've killed you."

"I don't get it. You're Irish, too, aren't you? Why'd you stick up for a Jew?"

Joe grinned. "You're Jewish?"

"My name *is* Bergman."

"Well, I'll be damned," Joe said with an adolescent's pride in cursing. "All I saw was the Harrigans beating up some skinny little stick of a kid. I didn't even know it was you at first. You better get to where you can run faster before you come back to this neighborhood. Either that, or don't come back."

"Or get big enough and strong enough to beat up the Harrigans."

"Oh, yeah. Sure, Bergman." Joe didn't sound as if he believed for a second that might happen.

"I'll do it," Adam promised. "You'll see."

"Yeah. Come on, Dale. We gotta get home."

Dale Parker said, "Your coat's torn, Joey. Mama's gonna be mad."

"I ain't worried. So long, Bergman."

Adam watched them go and thought, *I'll do it. I'll get so big and strong the Harrigans and people like them won't ever bother me again.*

The trick was figuring out how to do that. He had seen an advertisement for a strength-developing course on the back of an issue of *Argosy* that a kid had smuggled into school one day, but you had to send off for that and it cost money. Adam had heard that lifting weights would make you strong, but he couldn't afford to buy weights, either.

Maybe lifting other things that were heavy would work, he thought. There were plenty of things in the world that were heavy.

He started exercising every day, and he ran, too, because he'd heard that professional boxers did that to improve their wind, whatever that meant. The Harrigans were too busy bullying other people to get around to wreaking vengeance on him, and after a few years had gone by, they wouldn't have wanted to. By the time he was a freshman in high school, he was five-feet-five-inches tall, weighed a solid one-fifty, could outrun anybody else in the school, and hit a baseball like nobody's business. He and Joe Parker had been friends ever since that day Joe had rescued him from the Harrigans, and most of the time Adam didn't even mind putting up with Joe's little brother Dale.

Joe was on the baseball team, too, and the team won

the city championship two years running. Adam led the team in batting average and runs batted in and played a smooth center field. He was a good enough athlete that the University of Chicago wanted him to play football for them and offered to help him out with his books and tuition if he did. Money had always been tight in the Bergman household, since Adam's father had died when Adam was seven, but he knew his mother's dream had always been for him to go to college. This was the only way he'd ever be able to do that, he decided.

Football wasn't nearly as much fun as baseball, but he was able to play both sports, one in the fall and the other in the spring, and that was all right. He entered the pre-law program and did well enough with his grades. The idea of being a lawyer wasn't something he had dreamed of ever since he was a kid, but it was okay. Playing for the Cubs would have been better, but his mother had finally put her foot down about the sports. He was going to law school, and that was it.

Adam had been able to accept that decision, but he had to admit that having Catherine around made it a little easier. They had been going together for over a year. If he had signed with the Cubs and they had sent him to one of their farm teams, there was no telling where that would have been. And even if he had made the major league team, there were still long road trips that would have taken him away from Catherine.

The university was almost like a second home to him by now. He didn't mind staying on there and continuing his studies.

Except at moments like these, on a sun-splashed afternoon with the deep green of the playing field under the blue, cloud-dotted sky and the air filled with the roar of the crowd and the crack of the bat and the smell of hot dogs and peanuts and beer. . . .

"Adam?" Catherine said. "Are you all right?"

He smiled. "I'm fine."

"Well, you looked like you were a million miles away for a minute."

No, not a million miles, he thought. Just the distance from where he was sitting here in the grandstand to the playing field below.

SEVEN

Green Valley Raceway was forty miles south of Chicago near Kankakee, one of dozens of dirt-track ovals scattered across the Midwest that catered to a loosely organized racing circuit. Surrounded by farmland, unpainted wooden grandstands rose around the track. It was a far cry from the Brickyard at Indianapolis, but the races were well-attended. Most of the spectators were from the Chicago area, since it was so close. Many of the drivers, as well, came from Chicago.

Dale wanted as many people in the stands cheering him on as possible, so he'd made an outing of it, inviting Adam and Catherine as well as Joe and Harry. Harry had ridden down with him in the Ford, while Joe rode in the back seat of Catherine's Plymouth roadster.

Dale had asked his parents if they wanted to come, too, but Sam had muttered something about damned foolishness, and Helen had said, "Oh, I don't think so, dear. All that dust and sun. But good luck to you. Just be careful. And don't drive too fast."

There wasn't a thing in the world Dale could say to that.

A good crowd was on hand for the race. The parking lot was full of cars, everything from battered old Model As and the Ts and pickups to sporty new roadsters and solid-looking coupes. People streamed from the parking lot into the grandstands, most of them dressed informally for a Saturday afternoon's entertainment.

Some of the spectators sported more expensive clothing, however, such as the young woman Dale noticed as he pulled into the parking lot and headed for the gate where the entrants were lined up to enter the pits. The woman wore a red dress that clung to the smoothly curving lines of her body, and a matching red hat with a little feather in it was perched on her black hair. Dale slowed to admire the shapely calves below the hem of her skirt. The seams of her silk stockings ran perfectly straight.

She must have felt his eyes on her, because she turned and looked over her shoulder at him. Her dark eyes met his. A woman as good-looking and sexy as her must be used to guys staring at her, Dale thought. She didn't seem to be offended by the boldness of his stare. She gave him a smile and then walked on, but there seemed to be a little extra sway and bounce to her rump.

"Look at that," Dale said to Harry. "That butt moves like perfectly oiled ball bearings."

"I didn't know you had so much poetry in your soul, kid."

"What? Was that some sort of crack?"

Harry pointed. "Just drive over there and get yourself registered for this race. You still got that dough I loaned you?"

"Of course I do. What'd you think, that I went out and blew it somewhere?"

Harry didn't answer that question, Dale noticed.

He parked the car at the end of the line and got out. Harry did likewise. As Dale leaned against the Ford's fender and looked over the other cars lined up for the race, he felt a twinge of worry. They looked a lot sportier— and faster—than this clunker he was driving.

But it was what was under the Ford's hood that counted, he told himself, not what the car looked like. A fancy paint job wouldn't have made it a bit faster. Nor would a few rust spots here and there slow it down.

When he'd won a few races, he could get the car painted and the interior fixed. Maybe if he won enough, instead of getting the rips and tears in the upholstery patched, he'd just have new seat covers put in. Really gussy it up. Then nobody would turn up their nose at his car.

While Dale was tending to the details of entering the race, Adam, behind the wheel of Catherine's car, parked the Plymouth on the gravel lot and got out. He hurried around to open the passenger door for Catherine, but Joe had beaten him to it. On a nice day like this, the top was down and Joe had simply hopped out, bracing one hand on the car's body as he did so.

"Hey, are you trying to move in on my girl?" Adam asked. His tone made it clear he was joking.

"Just trying to be a gentleman. Will milady alight from her carriage?" Joe bowed and held the door as Catherine got out of the car.

Catherine was wearing a blue dress and a blue hat with a broad, floppy brim. She fluttered her fingers and said in a thick Southern accent, "Why, thank you evuh so much, kind suh."

"If you two are going to clown around, you need to decide if you're in medieval England or Mississippi," Adam told them. "Let's find a beer stand."

They joined the crowd streaming into the track, standing in line to buy tickets and then finding seats after buying beers and some bags of peanuts. Catherine sat between Adam and Joe, popped some peanuts into her mouth, then pointed and said, "Look, there's Dale!"

Sure enough, Dale was pulling the Ford slowly into one of the pit areas. He stopped the car and got out. Harry Skinner got out, too, and began examining the tires.

"That's Dale's friend Harry?" Catherine asked. She had never met the garage owner.

"That's right," Joe said. "He loaned Dale the entry fee."

"That was nice of him," Adam said.

"Yeah." A part of Joe wished that Dale had come to *him* for the money. After all, they were brothers. He might have been able to give Dale the entry fee.

And he probably would have given him a lecture along with the money, Joe realized. Maybe he had been too hard on Dale. True, Dale wasn't applying himself at college as much as Joe had hoped, but there was still time for that.

"I heard on the radio this morning that the Germans are bombing London again," Adam said suddenly. "Edward R. Murrow was broadcasting from the top of a hotel. You could hear the bombs going off." Adam's eyes were narrowed, as if he were looking at something off in the distance.

"What?" Catherine said. "Oh. The Germans. Yes, my father mentioned something about it this morning, too. He said they've started calling it the Blitz."

"The RAF has their hands full. I'm not sure the British government ever really believed the Nazis would attack London itself until the bombs started falling."

Joe felt a little left out as he listened to the conversation. He had a pretty good idea what was going on with the war in Europe, of course. You couldn't read a newspaper or listen to the radio without getting the war news. But when the German air force—the Luftwaffe, that was what it was called, he remembered—had started pounding the British capital a month earlier, in mid-August, Joe had been busy getting ready for school to start and finishing up that Western story. It wasn't that he didn't *care* about the war. He just had so much to do.

"When France fell, I knew Hitler would come after England next," Adam went on. "He's never going to be satisfied until he's got all of Europe under his thumb."

"We don't know that," Catherine said. "They could still negotiate some sort of peace treaty or something."

Adam looked over at her. "After he's bombed the hell out of London? I don't think the British are in much of a mood to negotiate with Hitler right now."

"Well, it's a long way over there. I just hope President Roosevelt doesn't drag us into all that."

"That's your father talking," Adam said angrily. "He's an isolationist."

"That's not true! He just doesn't think we should be fighting England's war for them."

Adam leaned forward so he could look past Catherine at Joe. "Is Arthur Yates still at school? I haven't seen him this year."

"Yeah, I ran into him the other day," Joe said. "He's going for his master's in sociology."

"He's from London, isn't he?"

"That's right. He said he'd heard from his family and they were all all right. Some of the bombs had fallen close to their neighborhood, but so far their house hadn't been hit."

"But that was a few days ago, you said."

"Yeah."

"Who knows what's happened over there since then?" Adam looked at Catherine again. "I'll bet it doesn't seem so far off to Arthur, or to my grandparents in Kiev. Hitler's looking that direction, too, you know."

"I don't want to have this argument with you, Adam," she said.

He shrugged. "I'm not arguing, just pointing out a few things."

Joe tried to lighten the mood by saying, "You're in law school. You get extra credit for arguing." When they both just looked at him, he shifted his attention to the track and went on, "Look, they're bringing the cars to the starting line."

One by one, the cars rolled up to the line and stopped. The drivers killed their engines. The noise of the crowd became louder with anticipation. After a few minutes, the track announcer said over the loudspeakers, "Gentlemen, start your engines!" just like at Indy.

The engines roared back to life, then the sound subsided to a throbbing rumble. On the elevated stand next to the track, the starter lifted his flag, paused dramatically, then let it fall. The cars leaped away from the starting line.

Joe watched his brother's Ford and saw to his dismay that Dale hadn't gotten off to as good a start as the other drivers. He wasn't that far back, though, and he didn't seem to be losing any more ground.

Inside the Ford, Dale clutched the steering wheel tightly and clenched his teeth together. "Shit!" he hissed. The engine had hesitated when he tromped on the gas, just a little but enough to throw him behind the other cars. That hesitation had been a problem right from the start with the Ford, but he'd thought that he and Harry had worked out the kinks in the engine so it wouldn't happen again. Now he was starting out in a hole.

Since he was past the start, though, he didn't have to worry about the hesitation anymore. He pushed down hard on the accelerator and felt the engine respond. The Ford's speed began to creep up. On the first turn, Dale had the Ford up to sixty. As he entered the long straightaway, the needle on the speedometer climbed to seventy and then eighty. He took the next turn without slowing.

He had never driven on a racetrack like this with banked turns, but he found that he took to it naturally. The first few laps were pretty much a blur to him. He drove on instinct more than anything else.

But then the pieces began to fall into place for him. He knew what he was doing and why. He knew when he had to use the brakes and when it would do to just ease off on the gas a little. And as he drove a new excitement began to well up inside him, a sensation he had never known before. He suddenly knew without question that he was doing what he had been born to do.

He had started out last. This was a hundred-mile race, so that gave him some time to work his way through the pack. First one car and then another and another fell behind him. He looked at the gauges on the dashboard even though he already knew he had enough gas in the tank. The oil pressure and the temperature were holding up well, too. Now if his tires would just last . . .

He swooped past another two cars and couldn't help but let out an exultant laugh. Fancy as they were, those jalopies couldn't beat him.

In the stands, Catherine asked, "Is this all there is to it? We watch him drive around and around?"

Joe and Adam were both leaning forward slightly, their attention focused on the track. Joe could tell that Dale had passed quite a few of the other cars already. He didn't say anything. Adam just nodded distractedly and said, "Yeah."

"All right. But it doesn't seem like much of a sport to me."

Joe had never really thought about it but, before today, he would have said that auto racing didn't seem like much of a sport to him, either. But now he was caught up not only because he was watching his brother race but because of the excitement of the crowd. At a moment such as this, everything—not just the war in Europe—seemed far away.

Adam cupped his hands around his mouth and shouted, "Pull a Barney Oldfield, Dale!" even though he knew Dale couldn't possibly hear him.

Catherine leaned over to Joe and asked, "Who's Barney Oldfield?"

"A famous race car driver."

"Oh. Well, I suppose I might as well get in the spirit of the thing." She leaped to her feet, put two fingers in her mouth, and let out a piercing whistle, then shouted, "Come on, Dale!"

Joe and Adam both looked up at her in amazement.

Dale wasn't aware of anything except what was directly in front of him and beside him on the track. He wasn't worried about anyone catching him from behind. He swept around the turns, roared down the straightaways, and slowly moved closer and closer to the front of the pack. More than fifty laps had fallen behind him, he realized. The race was more than half over.

Suddenly, from the corner of his left eye, he saw a car spinning wildly out of control. It careened off the track and crashed through the bales of hay that separated the track from the infield. Dale saw the car roll over a couple of times and come to a stop upside down. Flames licked out from its engine. A man climbed quickly onto the tower beside the track and began waving the yellow caution flag.

Dale bit back a groan as he slowed the Ford. It took a while for the engine to build up to its top speed. Having to slow down now would put him at a disadvantage again. He couldn't disregard the caution flag, though, or he would be disqualified.

The slower pace gave him a chance to take stock of the situation. He counted eight cars ahead of him now, and none of them would have been out of his reach if he'd been able to continue running at top speed. He didn't know what effect this delay would have.

It took several laps before the fire was put out and the injured driver pulled from the wreck of his car. Dale saw the man being carried off on a stretcher and wondered if he was going to be all right. He hoped so. Nobody had ever said racing didn't have its risks, but if his mother found out that a guy had been killed in the same race in which Dale had driven, he would never hear the end of it.

When the signal came to bring the race back up to full speed, Dale was ready. The Ford didn't hesitate this time because he didn't have to push down on the accelerator so hard. The speedometer needle began creeping up again. As he passed the pits, he saw Harry holding up a scrawled sign with the number 78 on it. Only twenty-two miles to go.

Dale didn't know if that would be enough time or not.

The track had been watered down before the race to settle the dust, but by now clouds of the stuff were beginning to billow up behind the cars. Dale had the windows in the Ford closed, but he could still taste the grit in his mouth and throat, and feel it on his lips. The dust made steering trickier, too, because it interfered with the drivers' vision. Dale blinked his eyes as he passed another car and continued to close in on the leaders.

The Ford hadn't let him down. It was still running perfectly. Even if he didn't win, he was proud of what he and Harry had accomplished with their work on the engine.

Another car fell behind him and then another. The leaders were bunched up, hogging the track. Dale eased forward, looking for an opening. When one came, he tromped on the gas pedal again and sent the Ford squirting between two of the cars. Now there were just three in front of him.

But the man on the tower was waving the flag that signified the final lap.

Dale zoomed through the next-to-the-last turn. He edged the Ford up beside the third-place driver. The man glanced over at him, face intent behind a pair of goggles. Dale wished he had thought of getting some goggles for himself. Next time, he thought.

Then he was past the car and in third place. If he could just hold on, he was assured of fifty bucks prize money he could split with Harry.

But the second-place car was within reach, he thought. He might not be able to come in first, but he could still grab second and double the prize money. He would just have to take the final turn faster than any of them before . . .

With the Ford's engine howling, Dale started into the turn. He didn't slow down; in fact, he pressed harder on the accelerator. For a dizzying second, he felt as if he was weightless, like a spaceman in one of those yarns Joe sometimes wrote for *Thrilling Wonder Stories.*

Then he was out of the turn and into the straightaway and the Ford leaped forward like it was alive. Dale whipped past the second-place car and roared on past the tower as the man standing on top of it waved the checkered flag. The race was over.

Dale took his foot off the gas, and as the car slowed he began to tremble. Every muscle in his body seemed to be jumping around like Carmen Miranda. He had to hold tightly to the steering wheel to keep the car under control as he slowed to a stop.

Harry was there before he could even open the door. Harry jerked it open himself and reached in to grab Dale. Whooping with excitement, he pulled Dale out and bear-hugged him. Even though Dale was bigger, Harry was bouncing him up and down on the track beside the Ford.

"You did it, kid! You did it!"

"It . . . it was just second place," Dale managed to say.

"Second place against some of the top cars and drivers in the Midwest! Hell, kid, you were great!"

Dale grinned. The trembling was going away now. "Yeah, I guess I was, wasn't I?"

Joe came running up to him, followed by Adam and Catherine. They all gathered around him and pounded him on the back in congratulations, and Catherine gave him a big hug and kissed him on the cheek. "I never dreamed a car race could be so exciting," she said. "But Dale, I was scared when that car wrecked. You could get hurt doing things like this!"

"Yeah," he admitted, "but I could win a hundred bucks, too!"

Dale glanced over at the grandstand. A flash of red caught his eye. That good-looking woman he had seen earlier when they got here was sitting in the front row at the finish line. She was smiling, and she was close enough so that Dale could tell she was looking straight at him. He lifted a hand, about to wave at her.

She stood up abruptly and turned to walk toward the ramp that led down out of the grandstand.

Well, Dale thought, *I guess she put me in my place. Fancy dame like that likes to watch the races but doesn't want to get caught smiling at a guy with dust on his face, even when he almost wins.*

Next time he *would* win, he promised himself. He had learned a lot out here today, and he would put that knowledge to good use the next time he entered a race. He hoped that was soon.

"Come on, let's find a roadhouse and celebrate," Harry said. "I'm buyin'!"

EIGHT

The papers the next morning, September 16, were full of stories about the German air raids on London. Joe read them with a little more interest than usual after listening to the argument between Catherine and Adam the day before. According to the reports filed from London, the outnumbered pilots of the Royal Air Force, flying Spitfires and Hurricanes, had valiantly turned back the Nazi attack, downing a large number of Messerschmitt fighters and Heinkel bombers while losing a comparatively small number of their own planes.

Joe couldn't find anything in the newspaper about the race at Green Valley. Dale would be disappointed that he didn't make the paper, he thought.

Dale was still so excited when he came into the kitchen for breakfast that he didn't seem to care, though. He sat down at the table and snatched up the comics section to read *Terry and the Pirates*. He picked up a slice of toast from the plate in the center of the table and began taking bites from it.

Helen Parker came into the room straightening her hat. "I'm off to church, boys," she said. "I don't suppose either of you want to come with me?"

"Not today, Ma," Joe said.

"Me, neither, Ma," Dale added, his nose still buried in the comics.

Helen's sigh spoke volumes about the way she felt about her sons' churchgoing habits. "Your father is resting in the parlor," she told them. "Try not to disturb him." She went out the back door and left Joe and Dale sitting at the kitchen table.

"Think the old man's drunk again?" Dale asked.

"This early in the day?"

"Never stopped him before."

Joe shrugged. He folded the front page of the newspaper so that the headline about the Nazi Blitz was prominent, then held it out toward Dale. "What do you think about this?"

Dale frowned, clearly not happy about being taken away from the comics. "What? You mean the war?" He shrugged. "Pretty bad. I'm glad I'm not a Limey. They're sitting ducks for old Adolf."

"Adam and Catherine were talking about it yesterday. Adam seems to think that we're going to wind up getting in the war."

"Well, he's Jewish, and he's still got relatives over there somewhere, doesn't he? Hitler's been pretty hard on the Jews, what with all those programs and all."

"Pogroms."

"That's what I said. I bet Catherine didn't think the U.S. should get involved, did she?"

Joe shook his head. "Not really."

"That's because she's been listening to her old man. He's rich, and all the rich guys hate Roosevelt."

Joe frowned at his brother. He wasn't used to Dale making political observations. "How do you know that?"

"Because Roosevelt's a Communist."

"No, he's not! Where did you hear that?"

Dale shrugged. "I dunno. Around."

"Well, the president's not a Communist."

"Why are you sticking up for him? You weren't even old enough to vote in the last election."

"I'm old enough now," Joe said. "Maybe I'm just trying to figure things out."

Dale flicked a fingernail against the comics section of the newspaper. "I'll tell you what I'm trying to figure out. Who's a better lay, Blondie or Winnie Winkle?"

Joe didn't have an answer for that.

★ ★ ★

Over the next month, Dale drove the Ford in three more races, spending nearly every weekend driving to one race-track or another in Illinois, Indiana, or Wisconsin. He collected a third-place finish in the first race, then won the next two. In one of them, the top prize was a thousand dollars. Suddenly, he was rolling in dough, as he gleefully put it.

Joe deposited a check for sixteen dollars from *Weird Tales*—six months after it should have been paid to start with—and tried not to feel jealous.

Earlier in the month, the United States had traded fifty outdated destroyers to Great Britain in exchange for ninety-nine-year leases on air and naval bases in Newfoundland and the West Indies. Now the president was talking about sending supplies, including guns, tanks, and ammunition, to England, even though the United States was still officially neutral. He called it the Lend-Lease program, because the British were supposed to send all the stuff back eventually. In the radio address he made to announce the program, Roosevelt talked about how when your neighbor needs your garden hose to help fight a fire, you don't offer to sell it to him. You let him borrow it with the understanding that he'll give it back when the fire is out.

Joe listened to that speech on the big cathedral radio in the parlor and thought that it would take more than a garden hose to put out the fire of Nazism.

A lot of the talk now was about the war and when—not if—the United States was going to get into it. There was still plenty of fierce opposition to the idea of the war, but the president was able to get Congress to go along with registering young men for a military draft. When he heard about the passage of the Selective Service Act, Dale said to Joe, "See, I told you Roosevelt was a Communist."

"I still say you're crazy."

"Maybe." Dale lit a cigarette, then said around it, "She was there again on Saturday."

"Who?"

"The girl at the race. I told you about her."

"Oh, yeah," Joe said. "The mystery girl."

"She's been at every one of my races. I don't think that's a coincidence, do you?"

"To tell you the truth, I haven't given it much thought."

"Well, I have," Dale said. "I think she's coming to see me."

"They'll never take you in the Army."

"Why not?"

"They don't have a helmet big enough to fit that swelled head of yours."

"No, I mean it," Dale insisted. "Why else would she show up every time I drive in a race?"

"Maybe she just likes the races," Joe said.

Dale took a drag on the Lucky and shook his head. "No, it's gotta be me. You can make all the cracks you want, but I'm convinced of it."

"Well, then, I won't waste my breath."

"I'd appreciate it."

Maybe Dale was on to something, Joe thought, although he wouldn't admit that to his brother. Maybe the girl *was* coming to the races just to watch Dale.

"She's sure a looker," Dale said. "Got plenty of money, too, judging from the clothes she wears."

"I hope the two of you will be very happy."

"You'll see," Dale said. "Me and her, we'll wind up together." He grinned. "That is, if I don't get drafted and get my ass shot off."

★ ★ ★

Joe, Adam, and Catherine were all on their feet cheering and applauding as Dale's car zoomed past the tower and the checkered flag waved in the autumn air. Dale had just won another race, this time at a small track in Rockford.

The prize was small, too, but Dale considered this race to be nothing more than practice. A big one was coming up at the Milwaukee Mile. If he could win that race, it would mean some nationwide recognition.

Harry was waiting for him in the pits, as usual, and Joe, Adam, and Catherine joined them a few minutes later, having made their way down from the bleachers. Dale's muscles still trembled after each race, but the trembling wasn't as bad now. He shook hands with Harry, Adam, and his brother, and got a hug from Catherine. He didn't really pay much attention to their congratulations, though, because his eyes were scanning the bleachers in search of the young woman he had seen at every one of his races.

She was here today, too, he saw with a thrill of excitement. She was wearing a dark gray tweed suit and a matching hat. It was amazing how on her even a conservative outfit like that could look sexy. Dale watched her leaving the track and wondered if he ought to run after her.

What would he say to her, though, if he caught up to her? *Hello, I was wondering if you have the hots for me?* But why else would she be at all of his races?

"Come on, let's get a drink," Harry said. That had become their routine after every race. They would find the nearest roadhouse and have a few beers, sometimes with a burger or a steak. "Dale, you hear me?"

"What? Oh, yeah." The girl was gone now, having disappeared in the crowd. "Yeah, that sounds good, Harry."

Dale had started wearing coveralls when he raced, as well as a pair of goggles and a cap. It helped with the dust. While the others waited, he went into the restroom next to the concession stand and washed his face, then changed into his regular clothes. When he came out, he had almost forgotten about the mystery girl.

Almost—but not quite.

A mile down the road was a tavern called the Shamrock. They had seen it on their way to the track, and they went there now, taking both cars. It was dusk when they

parked the Ford and the Plymouth on the gravel lot outside the long, low building and got out. Joe opened the
door, and loud music, cigarette smoke, and the smell of
stale beer rolled out.

The five of them went in, pausing for a moment to let
their eyes adjust to the smoky dimness of the tavern's
interior. Harry pointed to an empty corner booth and said,
"Over there." He led the way.

The booth had a single bench that curved around a large
table. The seat was upholstered in red leather and had
plenty of padding. Joe slid in first, followed by Catherine
and Adam to his left and Harry and Dale to his right. A
waiter came up to the table and asked what they would
have.

"Beers all around," Dale said, "and keep 'em coming.
What's good to eat?"

"In this place? I'll bring you a bowl of peanuts."

Dale chuckled and nodded. The waiter left, and Dale
leaned back against the seat. The trembling had completely stopped.

Dale had just lit a cigarette when the waiter came back.
The neck of a large bottle stuck out of the bucket of ice
he was carrying.

"Wait a minute," Joe said. "That's champagne. We
didn't order that."

"The lady did," the waiter said. "She said a champion
shouldn't have to drink beer." He set the bucket on the
table and began to work on the cork in the bottle.

"What lady?" Dale asked.

"At the bar."

They all looked and saw the attractive young woman
sitting there in her gray tweed suit and hat.

"Uh-oh," Joe said. "The mystery woman."

"It's about time." Dale stood up.

Joe leaned forward. "Where are you going?"

"The lady bought us champagne. The least I can do is
thank her and ask her to join us."

The cork came out of the neck of the champagne bottle with a loud pop.

"Dale, wait a minute," Joe said, but Dale ignored him. He made his way across the crowded room toward the bar, the Lucky Strike dangling from the corner of his mouth. On the bandstand at the far end of the room, a sweating drummer worked out a long, pounding solo.

Dale took the cigarette out when he reached the bar. The stools on both sides of the young woman were occupied, and the men siting on them were vying for her attention. Dale touched her shoulder with his left hand.

She turned around on the bar stool and said, "Well, hello."

"Hey, buddy," the man on her left said. "I was talking to this dame."

She looked at him, smiled sweetly, and said, "And I was doing my best to ignore you. Why don't you run along?"

"Hey!"

Dale jerked a thumb over his shoulder. "Thanks for the champagne. Would you like to join us?"

"I certainly would. Thank you." She slid off the stool and linked her arm with Dale's.

"Hey!" the man said again. He sounded more than half drunk.

Dale leaned close to him and said in a voice that could barely be heard over the music and the buzz of conversation in the tavern, "Shut up and leave the lady alone or I'll stomp your head in, you stupid jerk."

"You . . . you punk kid!" the man sputtered, but he didn't make move to budge off his stool.

Dale led the woman toward the booth. "Sorry about that."

"I just appreciate you rescuing me from an evening of boredom. I'm Elaine." She didn't offer a last name.

"Dale Parker."

"I know. I've watched you race. You're very good."

"Thanks." Dale grinned. "You ain't half-bad yourself, Elaine."

"Such flattery," Elaine said mockingly. "Keep it up—and it's liable to get you everything you want."

Now she didn't sound like she was kidding at all, Dale thought, and he couldn't help but notice that his lips, mouth, and throat had suddenly gone dry.

NINE

This was trouble with a capital *T*, Joe thought as he watched his brother laughing and guzzling champagne.

Dale had his left arm around the shoulders of the young woman he had introduced only as Elaine. She was sitting between him and Harry Skinner, and she seemed to find everything Dale said as funny as Dale himself did.

Joe glanced at Harry, Catherine, and Adam. Harry wore a cautious look on his face, as if he wasn't sure what to make of Elaine. Adam was being friendly enough to her, but he was so in love with Catherine that he didn't really pay much attention to any other woman, not even one as beautiful as Elaine.

And she *was* beautiful. Joe couldn't deny that. With that fair skin and those sparkling dark eyes and hair as black as midnight, she had an exotic loveliness to her. And she was older than Dale, probably in her mid-twenties, which gave her an air of intrigue. Joe couldn't really blame his brother for losing his head over her.

Catherine wasn't taken in by her, though. Catherine watched her warily. Some people might think she was just being jealous and protective of her own man, but Joe knew her better than that. Or he thought he did, anyway. The only thing he was sure of was that Catherine didn't particularly like Elaine. She was being polite about her dislike, however.

"It must be frightening, driving that fast," Elaine said.

Dale shook his head. "Nah, there's not really time to be scared. You just have to keep your eyes open."

"I've seen some bad crashes at the races."

"I take my chances fair and square, just like the other

guy. If my number comes up . . ." Dale shrugged. "Well, at least I've had some laughs and made some dough."

"You must have won quite a bit by now."

Uh-oh, Joe thought. *She's angling to find out how much money he has.*

The thing was, she didn't really look like a gold digger. That outfit of hers would have cost more than the top prize in some of the races Dale had won. And there was a fancy gold wristwatch on her slender wrist that was even more expensive. Earrings with what looked like real diamonds in their settings dangled from her ears. Any woman who could afford baubles like that couldn't be after the sort of money that a small-time race car driver collected.

But the prize was a lot bigger for the upcoming race at the Milwaukee Mile. And if Dale won that, he would probably be invited to other races all over the country. Like it or not, Joe realized that his brother was on the verge of being a big shot.

"I'm going to win a lot more," Dale said confidently. "Harry and I are going to fix up the Ford until it's the fastest car in the whole damned country. Aren't we, Harry?" Dale's speech was getting thicker now. He had downed several glasses of champagne. The stuff tasted like soda pop, but it had a lot more kick than Nehi.

"You betcha, kid," Harry said. "Say, maybe you better slow down on that hooch."

Dale drained the last of the champagne that was in his glass. "I'm fine," he said. "In fact, I think I'll have another." He reached for the bottle. The ice in the bucket was mostly melted by now.

"Adam, we really ought to go," Catherine said. She glanced at the clock over the bar. "It's after eleven, and it'll be midnight by the time we get home."

"Sure, baby." Adam started to slide out of the booth so that Catherine could get out.

"Wait a minute," Dale said. "You're not leavin' already? Hell, it's the shank of the evening."

"Why does an evening have a shank?" Joe heard himself asking. He'd only had a few glasses of the champagne, but he supposed he wasn't used to it. Nobody answered his question, which he thought wasn't surprising.

Adam helped Catherine out of the booth, then stuck out his hand to Dale. "Congratulations again," he said.

"Thanks," Dale said. He shook Adam's hand, then went on, "You don't have to leave."

"Yes, we really do," Catherine said. She put a smile on her face. "It was nice to meet you, Elaine."

"Likewise."

Neither of them sounded like they meant it for a second, Joe thought. At least they'd kept their claws in during the evening.

He stood up and said, "Good night, Catherine. See you, Adam."

"Do you want a ride back to town with us, Joe?" Adam asked.

Joe looked at Dale, who was blinking his eyes rather fuzzily. "No, that's all right. I'll catch a ride with Dale and Harry," he said. He trusted Harry to keep an eye on Dale, but Joe wanted to be around after they had dropped Harry off at the garage.

With waves of farewell, Adam and Catherine left the tavern. Joe sat down again and said, "We ought to start thinking about heading home, too, Dale."

"It's too early yet. I was thinking about ordering another bottle of champagne instead."

Elaine said, "Oh, I couldn't possibly have any more."

"What would you like to do, then?" Dale asked her.

"What did you have in mind?"

Harry elbowed Joe in the side. "Scoot out. I gotta hit the can."

Joe was suddenly aware of a pressing need in his own bladder. "All right," he said as he slid over the smooth leather of the seat. He stood up and started across the bar toward the men's room. Harry fell in alongside him.

"We're like a couple of dames going to the ladies' room

together," Harry said with a laugh. "You're a college boy. You got any idea why they do that?"

Joe shook his head. "Not a clue." That answer would apply equally well to just about anything he was asked about female behavior, he thought.

The men's room was busy. Joe had to wait in line a few minutes in front of one of the urinals. Harry was in an even longer line in front of the other one. When Joe finished and went back out, he stopped short as he looked toward the corner booth where they had left Dale and Elaine. Feeling extremely stupid, he said, "Shit!"

They were both gone.

★   ★   ★

"I can't believe this is happening," Dale gasped as Elaine's lips rose from his for a second.

"Believe it, honey." She kissed him again, hungrily.

They were in the front seat of the fanciest car he had ever seen, a sleek Cadillac roadster that was parked in a dark corner of the Shamrock's parking lot. The whole parking lot, in fact, was dark, since the Shamrock's owner didn't believe in wasting a lot of money on electricity. The closest light was a streetlamp at an intersection nearly a block away.

Dale sat on the passenger side of the front seat. Elaine had hiked up her dress so she could straddle him. Her thighs, clad in sheer silk stockings, were pressed against his hips. She ground her belly against his as she kissed him.

Dale's pulse was playing a drum solo in his head just like the one he'd heard in the club earlier. For all his talk about women, he was, technically, a virgin. The closest he had come to being otherwise was a little messing around with Sally Ann Jessup, who lived a few blocks away from him on Drexel Avenue. They had gone up under the old abandoned toboggan ramp at Forty-second Street a few times and kissed while he felt her breasts through her clothes, and once the back of her hand had accidentally bumped his erection through his pants. That was it.

But his luck was about to change, Dale thought as he tightened his arms around Elaine. She was far and away the hottest girl he had ever met.

She had both hands on the back of his neck, holding him tightly. There was no need for that; he wasn't going to try to get away. Not in a million years. Her tongue slid boldly between his lips and into his mouth. He had never tasted anything hotter or sweeter or more exciting.

At first when she'd said she wanted to show him her car, he had hoped that something like this would happen, but he hadn't really believed that it would. She probably really wanted to show him the Cadillac, he warned himself. But then, after leading him out to the parking lot and listening to him go on for a few minutes about how great a car it was, she'd told him to get in and see for himself how soft the upholstery was. He did that, opening the passenger door and sitting down, then saying, "Yeah, this is really nice—"

That was when he'd looked over and seen her lifting her skirt, and then she was in the car with him, on top of him. She pulled the door shut so that the dome light went out.

When she finally broke the kiss again, Dale couldn't seem to get his breath for a few seconds. Finally, he was able to say, "Elaine, you're . . . you're the nicest girl I've ever met."

"I told you what that flattery would get you," she teased. Her hands went to the buttons of her suit jacket. She unfastened them quickly and deftly and stripped the jacket off. She wore a white silk blouse under it. Dale's eyes had adjusted to the darkness well enough so that he could see her cupping her breasts through the blouse. Then she reached out, took his hands, and brought them to her breasts.

"Oh, my God," Dale breathed. His fingers tightened, sinking into her flesh through the clothes.

"I want you to touch me," Elaine whispered. "Open my blouse, Dale."

He reached for the buttons, but his fingers were trembling as badly now as they had after that first race. He felt his face burn with shame. She was going to know how inexperienced he was. She was going to laugh at him.

Instead she smiled and waited patiently while he fumbled the buttons open. When he had the top four buttons undone, she spread the blouse apart and shrugged it off her shoulders. The black bra she wore stood out in sharp contrast to the white blouse and her pale skin.

"This, too," she said. "Take it off."

Still shaking, Dale reached behind her and found the clasp. Wonder of wonders, it came open almost immediately, and he felt a flood of relief. Then he started worrying about a flood of another kind. He was as hard as an iron bar, and he didn't want to ruin everything by losing control of himself too soon. He had heard guys talk about mentally reciting baseball statistics at times like this, but he was damned if he cared about bases on balls and strikeouts right now.

Elaine peeled the bra off and draped it over the steering wheel. Her nipples were dark in the faint light. She lifted herself a little and cupped her right breast to offer it to Dale. His lips fastened over the little bud of hard, pebbled flesh.

He wasn't sure how long they sat there like that while he sucked first one nipple and then the other, but at last Elaine whispered, "I have one final surprise for you, honey." She took his hand and guided it under her hiked-up skirt.

Ohmigod! She's not wearing any panties!

It was official now, Dale thought. He had died and gone to heaven.

TEN

Joe heard a car door shut somewhere on the other side of the parking lot, then its engine came to life and the car pulled away. Headlights flicked on, sweeping over him as the car drove past and turned onto the road with a slight screech of its tires. The driver was going a little too fast but seemed to have the vehicle under control. Joe thought it was a Cadillac.

He smelled cigarette smoke and walked toward the spot the car had just left. He didn't think anybody had come out of the tavern after him, which meant whoever had been in the car and whoever was out here smoking had to have been in the parking lot before him. "Dale?" he called.

No one answered, but a moment later Joe spotted the tiny orange glow of the coal at the end of a cigarette. The smoke smelled like one of Dale's Luckies, too. As Joe came closer he saw a man sitting on the gravel of the lot with his back propped against the fender of a car. "Dale?" Joe said again.

The coal glowed brighter as the man inhaled on the cigarette. He blew out a cloud of smoke and said, "Perfect timing, big brother." Dale's voice was still thick. He lifted something to his mouth, upended it. Joe heard a faint gurgle.

"Where have you been?" he asked.

"You wouldn't believe me if I told you, big brother."

"What's that you've got there?" Joe knelt and sniffed the air. "Smells like whiskey."

Dale held a flask out toward him. "Want some?"

The flask looked expensive, as though it was made out of silver. "Where did you get that?"

"It was . . . a present. Maybe . . . a good-bye present." Dale took another long swallow from the flask, and then his shoulders started to shake with sobs.

"What the hell? What's wrong with you, Dale?" Joe answered his own question by saying, "You're drunk as a skunk, aren't you? Give me that."

Dale jerked the flask out of Joe's reach. "Already offered," he said. "You didn't want any." He lifted it and downed another slug.

"Damn it, Dale, don't make me fight you for it!"

"Like you could take it!" Dale tossed his cigarette away and then used that hand to brace himself as he stood up. He kept his hand splayed on the fender of the car for balance as he tipped his head back and emptied the flask down his throat. He tossed it aside. It clattered away on the gravel.

Joe heard footsteps. "There you guys are," Harry said. "I came outta the can and you were both gone. I thought you'd run off and left me out here."

"Dale's drunk, Harry," Joe said.

"Well, he won a race today. I reckon he's got a right to celebrate."

"I'm not drunk," Dale said, but he swayed and would have fallen if he wasn't leaning against the car.

Harry's foot hit the flask. "What's this?"

"A gift from a lady," Dale said. "A token from a lady fair."

"Man, he really is sauced, ain't he? Where'd he learn to talk like that?"

"Prince Valiant," Joe said.

Harry picked up the flask and tucked it behind his belt. "I guess we'd better get him home."

He moved up on one side of Dale. Joe took the other side. They got their arms around him and steered him away from the car where he was leaning. Joe looked around for the Ford, and after a moment he located it. "Over there. Careful with him."

Harry grunted. "What'd he do, come outside with the ball-bearing girl?"

"What?"

"Elaine. First time he ever saw her, down at Green Valley, he said her butt moved like a couple of well-oiled ball bearings."

"I don't really know what happened," Joe said. "When I came out of the men's room, they were gone. I came out here to look for them, and I found him smoking a cigarette and guzzling down whiskey from that flask."

"It was good stuff, too, from what I can smell on him. That's why he got drunk so fast, putting a few slugs of whiskey on top of all that champagne. You think they had a fight or something?"

"I don't know. She's the one gave him the flask, I think."

Dale said, "N-never . . . never see her again . . ."

"Might be the best thing for you, buddy," Harry told him. "A dame like that . . ."

They reached the Ford, and Joe and Harry bundled Dale into the backseat. Dale tried to sit up, then slumped over sideways. A second later, he started to snore.

"You want to drive?" Harry asked.

Joe shook his head. "You helped him rebuild this car. You know it better than I do."

"It's just a car." Harry opened the door and climbed behind the wheel. Joe got into the front seat on the passenger side. "Dale don't really understand that yet," Harry went on. "He thinks there's something special about this jalopy. He don't know there's hundreds of cars out there we could fix up to be just as fast or faster than this one. What's special is the way he drives it." He turned the key and ground the starter.

As the engine caught, Joe said, "Racing is the first thing he's ever been really good at. I guess that's why he thinks this car is special."

"Well, he'll learn." Harry drove out of the parking lot and turned toward Chicago. "He's just a kid. He'll learn a lot of things before it's all over."

★ ★ ★

Harry drove back into Chicago and headed for Greenwood Avenue. "I can catch a streetcar back to the garage, or even hoof it if I have to," he said. "It ain't that far."

"You live at the garage?" Joe asked. He didn't really know Harry all that well, he thought, despite having been around him quite a bit over the past few weeks.

"Yeah, I got a cot in the back room, a little icebox, and a hot plate. All the comforts of home."

"Where is home?"

Harry glanced over at him, his eyes narrowing in the light of the streetlamps they were passing. "You really want to hear about this?"

"Sure." A snore drifted up from the backseat, and Joe went on, "I don't think we're going to be getting much conversation out of Dale."

Harry chuckled. "Nope. He won't say much until tomorrow morning. And then he's going to be cussin' because his head feels like it's going to explode."

"He's been hungover before and lived through it. So, where are you from?"

"Minnesota, originally. My family had a big farm up there. Lost it in the Depression. Things weren't as bad as in that Dust Bowl, down in Okie country, but they was bad enough. My pa passed away, and us kids sort of scattered out all over, tryin' to find someplace to make a living. My ma went to live with my sister in Cedar Rapids. I wound up in Chicago."

"How'd you get the garage?"

"Well, I'd always been the one to work on the tractors back home, so I knew engines. Went to work for the fella who owned the garage before me. I sent a little money to my ma and saved the rest of my wages. I knew the old man wanted to retire and sell the place, so when he got ready to do that, I scraped up part of the down payment and borrowed the rest from the bank. Didn't see any reason to keep payin' rent on a room when I could live at the garage."

Joe looked a little more closely at Harry. He realized that Harry probably wasn't even thirty years old yet, though he looked older. Hard times did that to a man, Joe supposed. But Harry had come through those times all right and made something of himself.

They were on Greenwood Avenue now. Joe pointed out his parents' house and said. "You're sure you can get back to your place all right? You can take the car and Dale could come get it tomorrow."

"Nah. If he woke up in the morning and this crate was gone, he'd be scared something had happened to it. I'll be fine." Harry brought the Ford to a smooth stop at the curb in front of the house. All the windows inside were dark, and Joe knew his parents had gone to bed. He hoped he and Dale could get inside without waking them.

He turned and reached over the seat to grasp Dale's shoulder and give it a hard shake. "Come on, Sleeping Beauty," he said. "Time to wake up."

Dale snored again, then shifted around on the seat and began to cough.

"We better drag him out," Harry said. "He's liable to puke."

They got out and closed their doors quietly, then Harry opened the back door and reached in to grasp Dale's coat. He hauled Dale part of the way out, then Joe was able to lean in and get a grip on his brother's coat, too. Together, they spilled Dale out of the seat and onto the sidewalk, and true to Harry's prediction, Dale rolled over and began to vomit. Joe wrinkled his nose at the stench.

"You'd a never got that smell outta the car," Harry said.

"You're right. Thanks."

"When he's done, we'll get him on his feet. He'll feel better for a few minutes."

When Dale finally reached the dry heaves, Joe and Harry took hold under his arms and hoisted him upright. Dale groaned. "I hope she was worth it," Joe said. Dale didn't make any response.

They marched Dale around the side of the house to the window of the back bedroom the brothers shared. Joe slid the window up noiselessly, glad that he kept it oiled. "Let me climb in first," he said to Harry. "Then I'll help you with him."

Harry kept Dale balanced while Joe stepped up on the crate and climbed in the window. He turned on a lamp, then reached out and hooked his arms under Dale's arms. He leaned back, pulling as hard as he could. Dale had gotten some of the vomit on his clothes, and Joe realized to his disgust that it was now on him, too. But there was nothing he could do about it. Dale came up and through the open window. Joe almost lost his balance, which would have sent both of them sprawling on the floor with a thump, but he was able to catch himself and Dale without falling.

He lowered Dale onto one of the twin beds. Dale was muttering something. Joe couldn't understand all of it, but he caught enough to know that Dale was apologizing to Elaine. Apologizing for what? Joe wasn't sure he wanted to know the answer to that question.

He stepped back to the window and bent down to whisper, "Thanks, Harry. We'll be seeing you."

Harry sketched a salute in the air and said, "Don't worry about the kid. He'll be all right."

Joe wished he could be sure about that.

Harry turned and walked away into the night. Joe swung around toward the beds and thought that he ought to get Dale's clothes off, as well as his own. He'd have to hide them somewhere until he had a chance to wash them. If he put them in the laundry, his mother would wash them and would no doubt smell the boozy vomit on them. That would lead to all sorts of trouble.

The door of the bedroom swung open, and Sam Parker

stood there. "So," he said. "Sneaking in at all hours of the night, eh?"

"Pop," Joe said, startled. "We didn't want to wake you and Mom."

Sam sniffed. "I can smell why. It smells like a brewery in here. Either that, or a whorehouse. You boys been out whoring, Joe?"

"Of course not! Dale won the race in Rockford this afternoon, and we just had a few drinks to celebrate. Please, Pop, don't tell Mom."

Sam came into the room, his cane thumping on the floor. "I was sitting up in the parlor when I heard you drive up. It's hard to sleep with this leg hurting so bad. When you didn't come in the front door or the back door, I asked myself, now why would my boys be sneaking into the house after midnight? Because they don't want their old pa to know what they've been doing, that's why!" His voice rose on the last sentence.

"Please, you're going to wake up Mom—"

"Shut up!" Sam roared. Balancing himself carefully, he swung the cane at Joe, slashing it through the air. Even though the blow missed by a good six feet, the violence of the gesture made Joe take an involuntary step backward. "You drink until you throw up on yourselves, you consort with whores, of course you don't want your mother to know about it! You're no-good bums, the both of you! I ought to throw you out of my house!"

The words were out of Joe's mouth before he could stop them. "Then who'd support you?"

Sam's face paled with fury. "I put a roof over your head and food on the table for years, you ungrateful little bastard!"

"Well, you're not doing it now. If not for what I earn, we probably would have lost the house. And Dale's making more money racing than you ever did at the slaughterhouse."

The cane thumped on the floor again as Sam shuffled forward, then he lifted it over his head. This time, he was within striking distance, Joe knew. What was he going to do if the blow fell? Would he take the cane away from his father? Had it come to that?

"Sam!" Helen Parker said sharply from the doorway. "Stop that! Put that cane down."

He turned his head and looked back over his shoulder at her, but he didn't lower the cane. "He's got it coming!" he said hotly. "He's been mouthing off at me, the drunken little whoremonger!"

"Please, Sam." Helen came closer to him, and her tone was more conciliatory now. "You're just angry because you're tired and you don't feel good. Why don't you come along to bed? We'll talk about it in the morning."

Sam finally brought the cane down, but he jabbed it toward where Dale lay on the bed. "Look at your youngest son! He'll be too hungover in the morning to talk about anything."

"Then we'll wait until he feels better," Helen said firmly. "Please, Sam, I don't want you and the boys fighting."

"But you didn't hear what he said to me." Sam's voice was thick now, as if he could barely get the words out. "You didn't hear what he said."

Joe felt a wave of guilt wash over him. "Pop, I'm sorry. I didn't mean—"

"Yes, you did. You meant every word of it." Sam's shoulders slumped, and he turned toward the door. His bad leg dragged behind him as he limped out of the room. Helen tried to put a hand out to help him, but he shied away. She looked at Joe, and he saw the anger and sorrow on his mother's face.

"I really didn't mean it," he said. "It's just that he came in here and started yelling at me . . ."

"I know." Helen looked at Dale. "Is your brother all right?"

"He's just drunk. Pop was right about that." Sam had probably been right about the whoremongering, too, Joe thought, but he didn't want to get into that, especially with his mother.

"Put those dirty clothes in the hamper. There's no point in trying to hide them from me now."

He should have known better in the first place, Joe told himself. No matter how old he was, his mother still had that uncanny ability to seemingly read his mind.

"I *am* sorry about all this."

"So am I." She shook her head as she looked at the still-snoring form of her youngest son. "He's really going to be miserable in the morning. But maybe he's the lucky one."

"I don't understand," Joe said.

Her expression was bleak as she looked at him. "He got to sleep through tonight."

ELEVEN

"So you're saying that time travel is impossible?"

"I suppose theoretically, anything is possible, but traveling in time would create so many paradoxes that I just don't think it would ever be practical." Ken Walker took a bite of his egg salad sandwich. "But does it have to be practical? We're talking about, what do you call it, scientifiction? Bug-eyed monsters and all that?"

Joe said, "Well, yeah, but I want the story to be as plausible as possible. I'm thinking about sending it to John Campbell at *Astounding*, and I hear he's a real stickler for scientific accuracy."

"Better not put in too many cosmic ray blasters, then."

Joe winced. Ken's sarcasm was probably well deserved, but it didn't help at the moment. The detective yarn Joe had started had hit a snag in the plot, so he thought that switching to something else for a while might help. But Ken seemed to think that the idea he had for a time travel story was ridiculous.

They were sitting on the grass under a tree on the commons at the university, eating lunch. Students moved around them, on their way to and from classes. Joe wondered if Dale had actually gone to class today, or if he'd slipped away from the campus again.

Ken finished his sandwich and began folding up the brown paper in which it had been wrapped. He would use the paper again to wrap tomorrow's sandwich, Joe knew. Ken was thrifty, if not downright frugal. He came from a family that had never been rich, just like the Parker brothers.

"What you might want to do," Ken said slowly, "is

have your hero get caught in a time loop, so that things keep repeating themselves."

Joe frowned. "I never heard of that."

"There's a theory that time is actually an endlessly repeating cycle, and perhaps in a small segment of time, that cycle could be speeded up. That's pure speculation, of course, and borderline gibberish." Ken grinned. "But it sounds good."

"Yeah, it does," Joe had to admit. "Thanks for the advice."

"Any time. No pun intended. Say, there's Arthur." Ken got to his feet and waved over one of the students walking along the commons. Joe got up to greet him as well.

The newcomer was slender, with dark curly hair and glasses. He looked worried, but he managed to put a smile on his face as he said hello. He shook hands with both Joe and Ken.

"How are you, Arthur?" Joe asked. "Things have been so busy this semester I haven't had a chance to look you up."

Arthur Yates nodded distractedly. "I'm fine, I suppose. It's a shame we don't run into each other more often these days."

Ken shrugged. "It's been a long time since we were freshmen. Different paths, and all that."

True enough, Joe thought. As a graduate student in sociology, Arthur didn't take any of the same classes as Ken. And, of course, both of them were far ahead of him. He was still just a lowly junior, and an English major at that.

"What do you hear from London?" Joe asked, and then immediately regretted the question as Arthur winced. It was easy to see the pain in the young Englishman's eyes.

"A friend of mine was killed in one of the bombing raids last week," he said. "A very good friend. She . . . she lived in the next block."

Ken put a hand on Arthur's arm. "I'm sorry, Arthur."

"I am, too," Joe said. "I should have kept my big mouth shut."

Arthur shook his head. "Actually, no. I'm glad you asked. And I'm glad I ran into you two chaps today. I wouldn't have wanted to leave without saying good-bye."

"Leave?" Ken repeated. "Where are you going?"

"Back home."

"To London?" Joe exclaimed.

A thin smile that was totally devoid of humor touched Arthur's lips. "That *is* my home, yes."

"But . . . but the bombing!"

"My friends and family are all undergoing the ordeal," Arthur said. "I've decided that I can do no less. I can't continue hiding out over here like a coward."

Ken said, "You're not a coward. It was your family who wanted you to come here and go to college."

Joe remembered the story. Arthur's mother was an American. She had lived in Washington, D.C., and had married a British Foreign Service officer who had been serving at the embassy there. When he went home, she went with him. But by the time their only child had grown up and was ready to go to college, war clouds had already begun to gather over Europe with Adolf Hitler's rise to power in Germany. Arthur's parents had decided that it would be better for him to attend school in the States. As far as Joe knew, that decision had been all right with Arthur.

But now things were different. Arthur's homeland was under attack. Now that he thought about it, Joe could understand why Arthur would want to go back there. If he had been in England and the Nazis had started bombing Chicago, he would have wanted to go home as quickly as possible.

"I'm afraid my mind is made up," Arthur was saying. "I've already begun the process of withdrawing from the university. By the end of the week, I hope to be on a ship bound for Liverpool."

Joe put out his hand. "Good luck, Arthur."

Ken frowned as his friends shook hands. "You're not going to try to talk him out of this, Joe?" he said. "It's insane, and you know it."

Arthur looked at him coldly. "Applying the scientific method to human emotions rarely works, Kenneth."

"But . . . you're safe here. The Germans aren't going to attack the United States."

"No," Arthur said. "And the United States is going to stay out of the war as long as possible, too." A faint hint of accusation could be heard in his voice.

"President Roosevelt wants to send supplies—"

"Yes, and we'll be grateful for them, I'm certain. But you're still standing on the sidelines. I can't say as I blame you. After all, it's not really your fight, is it?" Arthur managed to smile again. "Good-bye, lads. I have your addresses. I'll write, if there's a chance."

"Good-bye, Arthur," Joe said.

"Good-bye," Ken echoed. He sighed as he watched Arthur walk away across the commons. "Do you think he's right? *Should* we be in the war?"

"I don't know. I haven't got my own life figured out, let alone what the whole country should do."

"But if it comes down to that . . ."

"Maybe it won't," Joe said.

He wished he could believe that.

★ ★ ★

Dale ducked into the telephone booth in the back corner of the drugstore next to the soda fountain and pulled the door shut. The light went on over his head. He reached in his pocket and dug out a scrap of paper. A telephone number was written on it. He hesitated, then took a deep breath and thumbed a nickel into the slot on the phone. He dialed the number before he could change his mind and back out. While he waited for the ringing to start, he peered through the glass of the door at a display of Bromo-Seltzer without really seeing it.

The number rang four times before a voice he instantly recognized said, "Hello?"

"Elaine?"

"Dale? Is that you?" She sounded surprised and not particularly happy.

He shouldn't have called her, he told himself. But why would she have given him her number if she didn't want him to call? When he'd found the piece of paper in his shirt pocket after that night at the Shamrock, he knew that the number scrawled on it in feminine handwriting had to belong to her. He shuddered when he thought about how close he'd come to not finding it. His mother hadn't done the laundry yet, and when the memory of Elaine slipping something into his pocket had cropped up in his hungover brain the next day, he had practically raced for the hamper. Luckily, the paper was still there in his shirt.

It had taken him several days to work up the courage to call. Today he had come into this drugstore near the University of Chicago campus and told himself that the time was now or never.

Now he had her on the other end of the line, and he said, "I've been thinking about you ever since last Saturday. I . . . I . . . That was such a special night, Elaine—"

"You're sweet, Dale. But I really can't talk now."

"I want to see you again." He rushed the words out so she couldn't interrupt.

"I don't know . . ."

He felt his heart start to crack.

"When are you racing again?"

His spirits took a leap. "At Kokomo in a couple of weeks."

"Look for me. Maybe I'll be there."

"I will," he promised.

"But between now and then . . . don't call me, all right?"

Dale swallowed hard. "Sure." Whatever she wanted, he had to go along with it. As long as there was a chance he would see her again, he would do anything. "You . . . you're not upset?"

"About you calling me? I'm the one who gave you my number, honey. I've got nobody but myself to blame."

He really didn't want to broach the subject, but something compelled him to. "No, I meant about . . . about what happened Saturday night. In your car."

Elaine laughed. "I told you, you're sweet. And I take it as a compliment that you couldn't hold back. Don't worry about it, honey." Her voice became lower, more throaty. "You'll do better next time."

Next time! There was going to be a next time. Dale could hardly believe it.

"All right," he said. "I'll see you at Kokomo."

"Look for me," she said, and then the phone clicked in his ear as she hung up.

Dale put the phone receiver back on the hook, then leaned against the wall of the booth and closed his eyes for a moment as relief washed over him. Saturday night they had barely gotten started before it was all over, and from the way she had almost booted him out of the Cadillac after that, he was sure she hated him. But she had slipped her number in his pocket and she had given him the silver flask full of whiskey, and now she had said she would see him again the next time he raced.

More than that, she had come right out and said that they would do it again. He had to be the luckiest guy on the face of the earth.

He reached for the door of the phone booth and started to open it, then looked down at himself and realized that he couldn't walk out into the drugstore in the condition he was in now. He'd have to wait a few minutes for certain things to subside and hope that nobody wanted to use the phone until then. To make sure that they didn't, he picked up the receiver and held it to his ear again, unobtrusively holding down the hook with the thumb of his other hand. Now it looked like he was making another call.

Somebody had left a folded newspaper on the little shelf next to the phone. Dale's eyes strayed down to it, and he started reading the headlines. The Nazis were making noises about occupying Romania in order to "protect" its oil fields, and Mussolini's Italian forces had taken over some little country in Africa that Dale had never heard of. The Germans were bombing London again, too, but the RAF was still making them pay heavily for every bomb they dropped. Dale wondered briefly what it would be like to fly a plane. It might be something like being behind the wheel of a race car, he thought, only high in the sky.

Wouldn't Elaine think he was really something if he became a pilot?

He glanced down at his crotch again, saw that he was respectable, and hung up the phone. Being careful not to think too much about Elaine, he left the booth and hurried out through the drugstore. He had already forgotten all about becoming a pilot, and about the war as well.

TWELVE

Catherine leaned back against the wall of the alcove that enclosed the side door of her parents' house. Adam's arms were around her, and she was holding him just as tightly. His tongue slipped into her mouth as he kissed her. She darted her own tongue against his in welcome.

It was dark here, which was why Catherine preferred to come in this way. She and Adam could stand here in the alcove and neck for a while before she went in. It had been a nice evening—they had gone to the movies and seen the new Errol Flynn picture, *The Sea Hawk*, then had coffee at a diner and finally come back here—and kissing Adam was the perfect way for it to end.

Almost perfect, she corrected herself. Perfection would have been if Adam didn't have to say good night. Perfection would have been if he could have stayed with her and they both could have taken off all their clothes and spent hours in bed making mad, passionate love to each other.

Catherine's arms were twined around his neck. As their tongues continued their caresses, she took her right arm down and moved her hand between them. She had felt him growing hard against her belly, and now she pressed her palm against his erection through his trousers. Adam broke the kiss and gasped as she closed her hand and squeezed lightly.

"I wish you could be inside me," Catherine whispered. "I'm so wet for you."

"Oh, dear God . . ."

She moved her fingers to the buttons of his fly. "Do you want me to take it out and hold it?"

His voice was choked. He could barely say, "Yes."

They had done this before. Not often, but several times. Catherine knew it was shameless of her, but she didn't care. They had never actually made love and they had decided—well, she had decided, she supposed—that they wouldn't do that until they were married. But the passion they felt for each other was too strong to be completely denied. As long as they could give each other some satisfaction with their hands and their mouths, it would be easier for them to resist the temptation to go all the way.

That was what she wanted to believe. She finished opening his fly and reached inside to fill her hand with him.

The heat of his flesh was incredible. It almost seared her palm. She buried her face against his broad, muscular chest and breathed in the scent of him. He slid his hands down her back to her hips and then cupped her buttocks. She tightened her grip and then began to slowly stroke up and down, the movements small but maddeningly sensuous.

It didn't take long, of course. Catherine had the handkerchief from her purse ready. Later, she would wash it out herself in her bathroom, so that Mrs. Loftus, the housekeeper, would never see any evidence of what had happened.

Adam leaned over and rested his head on her shoulder for a moment, nuzzling against the side of her neck. "I love you," he said, his voice husky and a little breathless.

"I love you, too," Catherine said. "When we're married, we'll do so many things together. I won't let you out of bed for weeks at a time."

Adam laughed. "I'll be your prisoner?"

"My love slave." Catherine would have thought the line was corny if she'd heard it in a movie, but right here and right now, it sounded perfect.

Adam pulled away from her slightly and buttoned his trousers. "Can I . . . do anything for you?" he asked. Catherine was used to the slight awkwardness in his voice at moments such as this. He was a little embarrassed, and she thought that was awfully sweet.

"I'm fine," she said quietly. "I had a wonderful time tonight, Adam."

"Yeah. Me, too. That guy Flynn . . . he makes good movies. That sword fight with that Lord Wolfingham guy was a doozy."

He didn't want to talk about what had just happened. Catherine understood that, too. She came up on her toes and brushed her lips across his in a quick kiss. "I'll see you at school tomorrow."

"Sure. You bet."

"Good night, Adam."

"Good night." He put his hands on her shoulders and leaned closer to give her a proper good night kiss. Then he turned and made his way along the flagstone walk to the gate in the fence around the side yard. Even though it was dark, he had no trouble finding his way. He was used to leaving by this path.

Catherine had already unlocked the side door with her key. All she had to do was turn the knob and open it quietly, then slip inside. Her mother would be asleep by now, and her father would be in his study reading medical journals or whatever he did in there at night. Catherine smiled. Maybe he was in there reading lurid novels and just didn't want anyone to know.

Dr. Gerald Tancred wasn't in his study at all, she realized a moment later. He was standing in the side hallway, waiting for her. He wore a robe over his pajamas, and his arms were crossed over his chest. The light from the main hall was behind him, making him seem even larger and more impressive.

"Father!" Catherine said. "What are you doing here?"

"What am I doing here? This is still my house, isn't it?"

"Of course. I just meant . . . Well, I didn't expect to see you standing there. Have you been . . . waiting for me?"

Oh, God! she thought. *He was standing here just a few*

feet away while Adam and I ... while I had hold of ...
She couldn't force her mind to go any farther. Her face
was already burning with shame.

But he couldn't know exactly what they had been doing, she told herself. The side door, like the other doors
in the house, was thick and heavy, and they hadn't made
much noise. Their words had been spoken mostly in whis-
pers, and in the dark.

"It's late," Tancred said, not really answering her question about whether or not he had been waiting up for her.

"Not really that late," Catherine said. "It's only eleven."

"You have classes tomorrow."

"None of them are early."

"Still, you need your sleep." His arms uncrossed, and
he made a curt, slashing gesture with his right hand. "You
should not be out at all hours. You are still a girl."

"I'm a young woman." *Old enough to be in love. Old
enough to be talking about getting married.*

"And you were with that Jewish boy again, no doubt."
He came a step closer. "What were you doing out there
in the dark with that Jew, Catherine?"

Well, that was putting it bluntly enough, she thought.
She lied and said, "Nothing. We were just saying good
night."

Tancred's voice rose. "Did he put his hands on you?"

Catherine backed up a step. "Father, why are you doing
this?" she asked. "I thought you liked Adam. He ... he's
a good student, and an athlete, and he ... he's just a fine
young man ..."

"*Juden.* That is what he is."

Catherine stiffened. Her father had said that one too
many times. "You're starting to sound like a Nazi."

Tancred's hand came up quickly, and for a second
Catherine thought he was going to slap her. He had never
laid a hand on her in anger, and she was so shocked that
she didn't move. If he wanted to strike her, there was
nothing stopping him.

He caught himself and lowered his arm. "I do not want you to see Adam Bergman again," he said.

"You can't mean that."

"I do mean it. I forbid you to see him."

"I have to see him," Catherine said. "We go to the same university."

"You know what I mean. He will no longer court you."

The old-fashioned term made Catherine laugh, even though she knew it was not a good time to do so. Her father's back was already as straight as a ramrod.

"He's not courting me. We're dating. That's what Americans do. And that's what we are, Father. Americans. We're not in Germany anymore. We haven't been for a long time."

"If we were in Germany, you would respect me. Children there respect their parents."

"Children there go into the Hitler Youth."

"Stop it!" His hands clenched into fists. "Why must you bring that man into everything? First you call me a Nazi, then you say I want you to join the Hitler Youth! All I want is for you to stop seeing someone who is totally unsuitable for you."

"That's my decision to make," Catherine said.

Tancred shook his head. "No. Not as long as you live here. I say what you will do and what you will not do. And I say you will not see Adam Bergman again."

Catherine felt tears begin to slide down her cheeks. "You can't mean that."

"I do."

"I won't do it."

"You will!"

The argument had finally woken Catherine's mother. Elenore Tancred moved into the side hallway, knotting a robe around her waist. Her short dark hair was tousled from sleep. "Gerald," she said. "What are you doing? Why are you shouting?"

"He's trying to ruin my life, that's what he's doing,"

Catherine said. She knew she sounded melodramatic, but at the moment she didn't care.

Tancred looked over his shoulder at his wife and leveled a finger at his daughter. "I have told her that she can no longer see that Jew."

"You mean Adam?" Elenore said. "But he's such a nice boy."

"Does no one listen to me?" Tancred's voice shook with anger and frustration. "He is Jewish. He is not a suitable young man for our daughter!"

Elenore moved up beside him and put a hand on his arm. "Why don't we talk about this in the morning? You know you're too upset tonight because of that telegram."

"Telegram?" Catherine said, frowning. "What telegram?"

Her mother looked at her. "Your brother—"

"Brother!" Tancred said. "She has no brother, just as I have no son!"

Catherine moved forward, the argument with her father suddenly all but forgotten. "What's wrong with Spencer?" she asked. "Is he hurt?" Her brother Spencer, two years younger than she, was in his final year at a boarding school in Connecticut.

"He's fine," her mother assured her. "He sent us a telegram asking us to meet him at the train station tomorrow."

"The train station? But it's the middle of the semester."

"He has been . . . asked to leave the school."

"Kicked out!" Tancred said. "He has been thrown out of school like the common hoodlum he is!"

Catherine's head was spinning. This was the first she had heard of Spencer being in some sort of trouble. He had never been an exceptional student, getting by with mediocre grades, and there had been a few typical schoolboy pranks in which he had been involved . . . But to be expelled from school? Catherine could hardly believe it.

"What did he *do*?" she asked.

"He didn't really go into the details—"

Again Dr. Tancred interrupted his wife. "He said he

was thrown out for running a gambling ring!"

Catherine was shocked, but at the same time she almost wanted to laugh. That was just like Spencer, to be so blunt about things. She wasn't sure what the truth of the situation might be, but one thing was certain, Spencer wouldn't sugar-coat it.

"He'll be back tomorrow, you said?"

Elenore nodded. "That's right."

"It'll be good to see him again."

"Good!" Tancred said. "How can it be good when he has been thrown out of school?"

Elenore tugged on his arm. "We'll talk about it tomorrow, Gerald. Once Spencer is home, we'll find out everything about it."

"I suppose." Grudgingly, he allowed his wife to lead him down the side hallway. Before they turned into the main hall, though, he looked back toward Catherine and shook a finger at her. "But do not think I have forgotten what was said tonight! You will *not* see that boy again. I forbid it!"

Catherine's mother pulled him on around the corner. For a long moment, Catherine stood there in the side hall, then she said aloud, "Forbid all you want. You won't keep me from seeing Adam."

She was as sure of that as she had ever been of anything in her life.

THIRTEEN

Kenneth Walker was on his way up the ramp that led from the physics laboratories underneath Amos Alonzo Stagg Field. The stadium was named after the famous football coach, and the university's team played its home games there. Ken had never seen one of those games, but the labs in the stadium's bowels had been like a second home to him for the past few years.

He was carrying a folder with the results of his latest experiment in it, and as he walked he couldn't resist opening the folder for a peek at the charts and reports it contained. He knew he had done a good job, and he thought his faculty advisor, Dr. Allen Chamberlain, would be pleased.

"Ken? What are you doing down here at this hour?"

Speak of the devil, Ken thought as he glanced up from the folder in his hand. Dr. Chamberlain was coming down the ramp with several other men, all of them in white lab coats. Except for one man, Ken recognized them as professors from the physics and chemistry departments. The stranger wore a lab coat, too, and looked very much at home in it. He was about forty years old and balding, with a smile on his pleasantly homely face.

Ken came to a stop as the group approached him. "Hello, Dr. Chamberlain," he said. "I was just checking on some results from the experiment I've been running."

"At one o'clock in the morning?"

Ken looked surprised. "It's not that late, is it?"

Chamberlain fished out a pocket watch. "It's 1:16, to be precise."

"Oh. It was a little after seven when I got here. I

thought I'd be through by eight, and I knew it had taken a little longer than that . . ."

"The young man must have gotten lost in his work," the stranger said. "I've done that myself many times, Allen."

Ken sensed that the man was defending him. Chamberlain nodded and said, "Yes, but I'll have to have a talk with the guards. No one was supposed to be down here tonight."

"No one came by the lab and checked to see if it was empty," Ken said. He didn't want to get any of the security guards in trouble with the university, but he didn't want to be blamed for something that wasn't his fault, either.

Chamberlain seemed to accept that. "No harm done," he said. "In fact, this may be a bit of good fortune. Ken is one of the best graduate students in the department. Maybe *the* best." He glanced at Ken. "Don't let that go to your head, Walker."

"No, sir."

The stranger was taking an even greater interest in him now. "You were thinking about bringing this young man in on the project with us?"

"You won't find a better assistant, Enrico."

Ken's heart began to pound faster and harder when he heard Chamberlain say the stranger's name.

"Well, then, perhaps you should go ahead and introduce us."

"Of course. This young fellow is Kenneth Walker. Ken, say hello to Dr. Enrico Fermi of Columbia University."

Union Station, fronting on the Chicago River on Canal Street, was actually a set of two impressive buildings. The one in front, with its peaked roof and double columns flanking the main entrance, was the smaller of the two. Behind it was a larger, blockier, four-story structure with columns all along the front and illuminated letters along the top that spelled out UNION STATION. The rail yards were across Adams Street and Jackson Boulevard to the east and west. Dozens of sets of tracks passed underneath the streets and converged on the dual buildings of the station.

There was something unavoidably exciting about being in a train station, Catherine thought as she stood with her father and mother and waited for her brother. The faraway places seemed so much closer when you looked at all the trains and listened to the announcements over the loud-speaker and watched the hordes of people coming and going, bustling through the station on their way to or from who knew where.

Almost anything seemed more possible in a train station.

Except, she thought, getting her father to unbend from his rigid stance. He was still angry this morning, both at her and at Spencer. A part of her mind was glad that Spencer had been thrown out of school; his transgressions might help distract Dr. Tancred from his battle with her over Adam Bergman. No sooner had that ungenerous thought passed fleetingly through Catherine's mind, however, than she felt guilty for thinking it. She loved her brother and didn't want to see Spencer in trouble.

It was too late for that, of course. He was already in trouble. But no one would have known it from the cocky grin plastered on his face as he made his way through the crowd toward his parents and sister.

He hadn't changed much, she thought as she spotted him. It had only been a few months since she had seen him last, she reminded herself. He was three years younger and a couple of inches shorter, a little stocky, a grinning fireplug with crewcut blond hair. As he came up to them, dragging a pair of suitcases that seemed almost as big as he was, he called out, "Hi, Mom and Pop! Hi, Sis!"

Elenore stepped forward and hugged him. "Hello, Spencer." Catherine embraced him as well.

Spencer turned to Dr. Tancred and held out his hand. "What do you say, Pop?"

"I say you are an embarrassment and a disgrace to this family," Dr. Tancred responded coldly. He didn't take Spencer's hand, and after a moment the young man lowered it.

"Well, that's about what I expected." The grin didn't leave Spencer's face, but Catherine saw the brief flare of pain in his eyes at his father's harsh words. "At least *you* never disappoint *me*, Pop. You're as predictable as the sunrise."

"Stop your blathering. I canceled appointments with several patients to come down here this morning, only because your mother insisted that I do so. Come along. Let's get home, so I can get back to the office."

Catherine reached out to grasp the handle of one of the trunks. "Let me help you with this," she said.

"No, that's all right, I'll get a porter." Spencer snapped his fingers, caught the attention of one of the red-jacketed porters waiting in the terminal, and pointed to the bags. The man moved forward to take them.

Dr. Tancred's Packard was parked in front of the station. The porter placed the trunks in the back end of the car. They barely fit, and the lid wouldn't close. He tied it down with a piece of twine, then said, "Thank you, suh," as Spencer handed him a dollar. Dr. Tancred frowned at the extravagant tip.

Spencer saw his father's reaction and said, "Money's no object, Pop. I told you about the gambling ring. What I didn't tell you was that it made me a pile of dough."

"Why must you talk like someone from a . . . a gangster movie?" Dr. Tancred said.

"Everybody at school talks this way."

"You are no longer *at* school, are you?" his father pointed out.

Spencer shrugged, held the front door open for his

mother, and then piled into the backseat with Catherine. As Dr. Tancred drove through downtown toward their home, Catherine thought that this was almost the way things had been when she and Spencer were children: the two of them sitting in the backseat, their parents up front. They could have almost been on a family outing.

Only there had never been very many outings like that. Her father had kept long office hours and seen as many patients as possible. That was how they had been able to afford all the luxuries they had. Plenty of people had lost everything during the Depression, but not the Tancreds. Due to her father's hard work, they had flourished.

"Well, I suppose you want to hear all about it," Spencer began.

"When we get home," Dr. Tancred said. "That will be soon enough."

At least he hadn't refused to come down to the station at all, Catherine told herself. He might be cold and angry, but he had come. That was one small point in his favor.

Spencer unloaded the trunks when they got home, refusing Catherine's offer of help. "Come to my study when you are done," Tancred said.

Both of their parents were waiting when Spencer and Catherine came into the study a few minutes later. Tancred looked at Catherine and said, "This does not concern you, Catherine."

"I think it does," she said, her chin coming up defiantly. "Spencer is my brother, and I love him."

"You don't have to worry, Cathy, he's not going to horsewhip me or anything," Spencer said.

"I wouldn't be so sure of that," she warned him.

"I have never laid a hand on my children in anger," Tancred said stiffly. "I do not intend to start now. But I will have an explanation of your behavior, young man." He glanced at Catherine. "Stay if you wish, but do not interrupt." He looked at Spencer again, waiting. Elenore sat on a sofa in front of the dark, glass-fronted bookshelves that ran from floor to ceiling along one wall of the study. Her hands were clasped together in her lap.

Spencer opened his mouth to speak, closed it without saying anything, spread his hands, and finally blurted, "Those guys at school were such pigeons, Pop! They were just begging to be taken to the cleaners. But I didn't cheat any of 'em. The game was on the up-and-up, I swear it."

"You have been educated at some of the finest schools in the country, Spencer. Kindly speak as you would to an intelligent person, not to another hoodlum."

"All I did was set up a floating crap game in the dorm," Spencer said. "Nobody had to play if they didn't want to. And nobody played who couldn't afford to lose. Their dads have to have plenty of money, or they wouldn't be going to school there in the first place."

That made sense to Catherine. Her father looked far from convinced, however.

"Nothing would have happened if one of the losers hadn't gotten sore and figured that the dice must be loaded. But they weren't, I tell you. This guy was just a bad loser." Spencer sighed. "But he went to the headmaster anyway and told him about the game."

"Didn't he get in trouble himself for gambling?" Catherine asked, defying her father's edict that she stay silent.

Spencer shook his head. "The headmaster wanted the guy who was running the game—me. He promised that nobody else would get in trouble if they spilled the beans."

"But that's not fair!" Catherine burst out.

"I'll say."

Dr. Tancred said slowly, "Spilled the beans. Hundreds of dollars for tuition, and he uses expressions such as spilled the beans."

"I'm sorry," Spencer said. "The headmaster promised the other students immunity if they would testify against me. Is that better?"

"It's still unfair, as Catherine said," Elenore said. "But you did wrong, Spencer. We did not raise you to be a gambler."

He shrugged. "I'm sorry, Mom. I knew it was against the rules, but I didn't think I was really hurting anybody. It was just . . . fun."

"Fun." Dr. Tancred practically spat the word. "We did not send you to school to have fun. You were sent there to learn. But it appears all you learned was how to be a criminal." He toyed with a pen on his desk for a moment, then stood up. "I shall write a letter to your headmaster apologizing for your abominable behavior and offering to make restitution to all the boys from whom you stole. Then I will ask for your reinstatement to the school."

"No! I'm not going back there."

"Probably not, as my request will almost certainly be denied. But I will make the attempt, anyway. Until we hear the school's final decision, you will stay here in this house and study independently."

"You mean I can't go out of the house?"

"Only to church with your mother and sister and myself."

"You can't mean that! That's like . . . like putting me in prison or something."

Dr. Tancred smiled thinly. "What your gangster friends would call the Big House. Yes, that is an apt analogy."

"I won't do it. You can't keep me locked up here like that."

"Your only other choice is to be disowned and leave this house forever."

"Gerald!" Elenore exclaimed. "You can't mean that."

"I most certainly do. That was almost my decision to begin with, but I decided that I would make one more effort on behalf of our son." Tancred looked hard at Spencer. "If you fail one more time . . ."

"I know," Spencer said, his voice shaking slightly with emotion, "I'm out on my keister."

Dr. Tancred reached into the bookshelves behind him and pulled out a volume on biology. "Go to your room and begin your studies," he said as he held the book out to Spencer. "That, or leave."

And she had believed that he was awfully high-handed with her about Adam, Catherine thought. She couldn't believe he was being so hard on Spencer. She watched tensely as Spencer glared across the desk at their father for a moment, then grudgingly reached out and took the book from him.

"I won't go back to that school," he said again.

"We will see." Now that he had laid down the law as he saw it, Dr. Tancred was calmer, almost serene. He folded his arms across his chest and watched as Spencer turned and stalked out of the study.

Catherine saw her mother chewing lightly on her bottom lip. Elenore didn't necessarily agree with what her husband had done, but she wouldn't go against him. Catherine knew that from experience. Ultimately, Gerald Tancred made the decisions in this household.

Sooner or later, Catherine thought, her father would be the one to get the education, and it would be a bitter lesson indeed when his wife and children finally defied him.

For the moment, though, there was nothing any of them could do, so she turned and quickly followed her brother out of the room. Her father didn't stop her, didn't bring up the matter of Adam again, and she was grateful for that.

She had already missed one class today. She wanted to get to the university before she missed any more.

FOURTEEN

Dale was so distracted by searching the stands for Elaine that he almost didn't win the race at Kokomo. Going into the final turn, he found himself running in second place. He cut the curve as sharply as he could, gunned the Ford's engine even as he was straightening the wheel, and felt the car leap forward. He edged in front of the first-place car with a good ten feet to spare before they reached the finish line.

Elaine came up to him afterward in the pits as he stood with Joe and Harry. She looked beautiful in a dark blue dress and a matching hat with a floppy brim. She put her arms around his neck and kissed him hard on the mouth.

"Congratulations," she said.

"Almost better than a first-place check, ain't it, kid?" Harry asked with a grin.

"No almost about it, Harry," Dale said. "This is the prize I want."

Joe looked away and rolled his eyes.

Adam came down from the stands to join them, too. Catherine wasn't with him today. Now that Joe thought about it, he couldn't recall seeing the two of them together at school all week. He hoped that they hadn't had a fight.

After Adam had shaken hands with Dale and congratulated him—with Elaine still hanging on to Dale—he turned to Joe and said, "Can I talk to you a minute, Joe?"

"Sure. What's up?"

They walked a few yards away from the Ford. With all the engine noise going on, no one could hear what Adam was saying except Joe.

"Has Catherine said anything to you about being mad at me?" Adam asked.

Joe frowned and shook his head. "She hasn't said anything like that. Of course, I haven't seen her much this week. In fact, I've barely spoken to her, just said hello whenever we passed each other on campus." He hesitated, then went on, "I noticed that you two weren't together. What happened?"

"That's what I want to know!"

"You didn't have a fight or anything?"

"Not that I know of. Everything was fine the last time we went out. We went to the movies and then I took her home and . . . Well, everything was all right. But she's been avoiding me ever since!"

Joe couldn't help but wonder why Adam had stopped short of telling him what had happened when he took Catherine home after the movie. *You're better off not knowing*, he told himself firmly.

"I'm sorry I can't help you, Adam. I just don't know why she would be avoiding you. But next time I see her, I can ask if you'd like."

Adam shook his head gloomily. "No, that might just make things worse if she thinks I've been complaining about her to you. Maybe she'll come around."

"Sure. You know how girls are. A guy can never figure 'em out."

Adam nodded toward the car. "Looks like Dale's got that one figured out."

Joe looked and saw that Elaine was still draped all over Dale. Harry came over to join him and Adam and said, "Those two don't need me in the way. I think Dale said they were going out for dinner and dancing as soon as he changes his clothes."

"Do you fellas want to ride back to Chicago with me?" Adam asked. "I've got my mom's car."

"I guess," Joe said. "Thanks."

"Glad to do it. Anyway, Dale's definitely going to be busy."

★ ★ ★

Elaine had been right. The second time was definitely better than the first time had been. So much better, in fact, that the difference was like night and day. Breathless, Dale rolled over in the bed and reached for his pack of cigarettes on the nightstand. Beside him, Elaine lay on her back, her bare breasts rising and falling quickly. Her dark hair was splayed out on the pillow around her head and looked beautiful, like a cloud of sable, Dale thought.

And Harry thought he didn't have any poetry in his soul.

"That was . . . very nice," Elaine said.

Dale fired up a Lucky, snapped his Ronson closed, and said, "Yeah." He blew smoke toward the ceiling of the little room. The garish colors of the neon sign outside the motor court cabin splashed over the closed curtains of the single window. A burst of dance music came through the opened door of another cabin, then was abruptly cut off.

They had stopped in here after dinner, drinks, and dancing at the best roadhouse in Kokomo. It had been Elaine's suggestion. *Doesn't that place look so cute and cozy? Wouldn't it be fun to stop?* Dale hadn't been about to say no to that suggestion and everything it implied.

He had been a little nervous, of course, after what had happened last time, but he had forgotten all about that once he and Elaine had gotten into the room. Then he'd been awash in the sea of sensation that caught up both of them as they kissed and began tugging at each other's clothes. They had gotten undressed in a hurry, and then Elaine had fallen back on the bed, urging Dale to come with her.

He had gone to her willingly.

Now he felt good, so good that he thought he might swell up and burst from the sheer joy of what had happened.

Elaine sat up in bed and said, "We've got to get you back to the racetrack."

Dale looked over at her. The only light in the room was what came through the thin curtains from outside, but it was enough to show him the smooth, sleek lines of her bare back. He couldn't resist trailing his fingers along her spine. Elaine shivered.

"That feels nice, but we can't do anything else."

"Why not?" He reached the very base of her backbone and slid his fingertip into the top of the cleft between her buttocks.

"Because there's not time."

"I've got all night."

"I don't."

He stiffened, and his eyes narrowed. "Why not? There some place you have to be?"

"As a matter of fact, yes." She swung her legs off the bed and stood up gracefully.

Dale sat up and watched her. Even though he was a little angry, he couldn't help but admire the play of muscles under her skin as she began to get dressed in the clothes she had so hastily discarded a short time earlier.

"You left in a hurry last time," he said after a moment. "I thought you were mad at me because of . . . well, you know what I thought. But maybe you had to be somewhere that night, too."

She fastened her bra and then lifted her slip over her head and began to wiggle into it. "Look, Dale, you're a nice guy, and I love what we did here tonight, but we all have responsibilities—"

He stood up, nude, and stepped over to her. He put his arms around her waist and pulled her against him. The slip was down only to her waist, and his arms kept it from falling any farther. He kissed her. His erection pressed hard against the cotton panties she wore.

Elaine tore her lips away from his and whispered, "Again?"

"I want you, baby."

"You son of a bitch." Her open mouth found his.

This time he lay on his back and she straddled him. It was even better, Dale thought.

★　　★　　★

He didn't argue with her when she got up to get dressed the second time. He was tired, and he supposed she was right about it being time to go back by the racetrack so that he could pick up his car. They had left it there after he changed from the coveralls he wore while racing, taking her Cadillac to the roadhouse and then here to the motor court instead. She could drop him off at the track, and they would go their separate ways once more.

"Is it all right if I call you again?" he asked as he pulled on his shirt.

"I'd rather you didn't. I'll call you if you'll give me your number."

"We don't have a phone."

"Oh."

"You can leave messages for me at Harry's garage, though." He recited the number there.

Elaine nodded. "I'll remember it."

"Why don't you want me to call, Elaine? Afraid your husband will answer?" He had checked her ring finger and hadn't seen a ring, not even a telltale band of paler skin where she usually wore one. But why else would she have to leave, and why else would she be so leery about him calling her?

She gave a low, throaty laugh. "My husband? That's a good one. I'm afraid you'll disturb my mother."

"Your mother?" Dale wasn't sure whether to believe that one or not.

"That's right." She turned toward him and tugged her hat down on her dark hair. "And the reason I have to get back is because the nurse will only stay until midnight, and I don't want Mother left alone any longer than necessary. She's not well, you know."

"No, I don't know. I don't much of anything about you,

except for your first name and the fact that you're a hell of a lay." Dale didn't know why he said it, unless it was because she thought he was stupid. Beautiful or not, she wasn't going to take him for a sap.

"You're a bastard, you know that," she said coldly.

"But you can't deny it's the truth."

"No. *I am* a hell of a lay. And that's all you need to know." She took a deep breath and controlled her temper with a visible effort. "But just in case you're curious, I'm telling you the truth. I live with my mother, and she's ill. About the only times I get out are when I go to the races. I like the races."

"You like race car drivers."

"Yeah, I do. Don't kid yourself, Dale. You're not the first driver I've known. Just the best."

"What?" He was surprised.

"The best driver . . . and the best at other things, too." Her voice softened. "You could go a long way, Dale. You could be famous. And when you are, you'll forget all about me."

He shook his head. "No, I won't. I couldn't ever forget you, Elaine."

"We'll see." She turned toward the door, then stopped and looked over her shoulder at him. "When's your next race?"

"I don't know. I haven't heard about the Milwaukee Mile yet."

"Harry will know as soon as you do, won't he?"

"Yeah, sure."

"I'll be in touch. And I'll see you then."

"Elaine . . ." He reached out to her as she started toward the door.

"You've already made me a little late," she warned him. "And I'm dressed now. Don't get me all mussed up again, Dale."

He grimaced. "I'm sorry I made that crack. I guess I should have believed you."

After a moment, Elaine said, "It's all right. I don't want

to make this into any more than it is. I like watching you race, and I like going to bed with you. That's enough, isn't it?"

"Sure. Nothing serious, right? Just fun."

"Yeah." She leaned up and kissed him again. "Now come on. I'll take you back to the track."

"Lemme get my shoes on."

Dale finished dressing quickly, then picked up his almost forgotten cigarette from the ashtray on the nightstand. He took another drag on the Lucky, then crushed out the butt. He glanced around the room, knowing that he would probably never be here again. Elaine stood in the open doorway, silhouetted by the light from the neon sign.

He would go along with what she wanted for now, he told himself. If she wanted to think of their affair as just for laughs, then fine. Let her think that.

But Dale knew differently. He knew, with the supreme confidence of youth, that he was going to marry this woman, and that they would spend the rest of their lives merrily screwing their brains out.

FIFTEEN

Adam's spoon clattered against the bottom of the bowl as he scraped up the last of the soup. It was funny how the colder the weather was, the better soup tasted, he thought. But that was definitely true. A chilly wind was blowing outside, and the soup had been delicious.

His mother smiled from across the kitchen table in their apartment on Fifty-second Street. She liked to see him eat, and he'd always had a hearty appetite.

Ruth Bergman worked as a secretary and bookkeeper in the Loop, in one of the tall office buildings on Michigan Avenue. She rode the El every day, and Adam knew she came home tired, but that never stopped her from having a hot meal ready for him at dinnertime. That was just one of the reasons he appreciated her and tried to do whatever he could to make her life easier. When he had his law degree and a successful practice, he would see to it that she never had to work again. That was a promise he had made to himself when he was in high school, and he intended to keep it.

"How did the draft registration go?" she asked as he set his spoon beside the empty bowl.

Adam shrugged. "There wasn't much to it. We just filled out some forms, and they gave us our draft cards."

"You have it?"

"Sure. The guy in charge said we had to keep them with us at all times."

"Can I see it?"

The request surprised and puzzled Adam, but he reached for his wallet to comply. He slipped the card out of the wallet and handed it across the table.

Ruth looked at the draft card for a moment, then sighed. "And this gives the government the right to come and take you and make you fight in a war."

"Not yet," Adam said. "They haven't said when conscription will start. Maybe they won't even have a draft."

"They will," Ruth said with surety. "There's no way the United States can stay out of the war. We're already helping England as much as we can without violating our neutrality."

Actually, once the Lend-Lease program was passed in Congress and went into effect, it would be neutrality be damned, Adam thought. The officially neutral stance of the U.S. government would be at direct odds with what they were actually doing. And that was all right with Adam, because Lord knew England needed the help and Hitler needed to be stopped. Hitler had taken the Sudetenland, Poland, and France without much trouble, but if the British could deal him a defeat, maybe he would slink back into his hole in Berlin and stop giving the rest of Europe such fits.

It was a hope, anyway. Maybe a futile one, but still a hope. Unfortunately, Europe wasn't the only continent being threatened by the little madman.

"I thought you wanted us to get involved," Adam said to his mother. "You've been talking for years about what a threat Hitler is, not just to people like Grandpapa and Grandmama but to everybody else, too."

"Yes, but . . ." Ruth looked down at the draft card in her hand, clearly torn between her worries about her parents in Kiev and her concern for her son. "I suppose I wasn't really thinking about what it might mean."

Adam didn't know what to say to that, so he didn't say anything. But he was grateful a moment later when a knock sounded on the front door of the apartment.

"I'll get it," he said as he stood up. He went through the living room and opened the door to the hallway.

Catherine stood there. She wore a camel hair coat and

high brown boots and a lighter brown beret. Adam thought she looked achingly beautiful.

"Hi," he said, startled. She had barely spoken to him for weeks now, and they hadn't been out on a date in that time. Now she'd showed up on his doorstep, unannounced, and he didn't know whether to be thankful or angry.

Still, the sight of her was breathtaking. He felt the need for her springing up instantly inside him. Frustrated and peeved at her behavior he might be, but he still wanted her more than anything else on earth.

"Hello, Adam," Catherine said. "I need to talk to you."

"Sure. Come on in." He stepped back a little so she could come into the apartment.

Catherine hesitated, and Ruth called from the kitchen, "Who is it, dear?"

Catherine lifted a hand and Adam thought for a second she didn't want him to tell his mother she was there, but he wasn't going to lie about it. "It's Catherine, Ma," he said.

Ruth came out of the kitchen. She smiled at Catherine and said, "Hello."

Catherine nodded. "Mrs. Bergman, how are you?"

"I'm just fine, dear. And you?"

"I'm all right, thank you."

Adam listened to the exchange and wondered if the slight edginess between his mother and Catherine would ever go away. That tension was only natural, he supposed. A mother would have to feel a little threatened by the woman who might well take her only child away from her.

"Well, don't just stand there, Adam," Ruth said. "Ask your friend in."

"I already did," Adam said. He looked at Catherine, who hadn't made any move to come into the room but was still standing on the threshold.

"Could we go down to the coffee shop?" Catherine asked, and Adam thought he heard a note of desperation in her voice. Something was wrong. He knew it; she hadn't been angry with him for some unknown reason. Something else was bothering her. And although he was a little ashamed of feeling that way, he was glad he wasn't to blame for whatever it was.

He reached for his overcoat, which was hanging on a coat tree near the door. "Sure."

"You're going out?" Ruth asked.

"Just for a little bit." Adam slipped into the coat and looked at Catherine. "Right?"

Catherine managed to smile. "I won't keep him out late, I promise."

"Adam's a grown man. He can do whatever he likes."

His mother might say that, Adam thought, but she didn't really mean it. In her mind, he would never really be a grown man.

He took his cap off its hook. "I'll be back," he promised.

He and Catherine walked side by side but didn't touch each other as they left the apartment house and walked down the block to a nearby coffee shop. The lake was six blocks away, and the wind off it was more than chilly, it was frigid, Adam thought as he pushed his hands deeper in his overcoat pockets. Not even Halloween yet, and already winter was knocking on the door.

Catherine didn't say anything until they were sitting opposite each other in a booth with cups of coffee in front of them. Then she said, "My brother Spencer is home."

"I thought he was at some ritzy prep school Back East."

"He was. They expelled him for gambling. My father tried to get him reinstated, but the headmaster refused."

Adam took a sip of his coffee and then shook his head sympathetically. "That's a tough break."

"He and my father are at each other's throats constantly. They argue all the time. Father says that Spencer will have to finish his senior year of high school in public school here in Chicago."

"Well, I don't suppose that'll hurt him." Adam paused,

then asked, "Is that why you haven't had any time for me lately? Because of your brother?"

"Maybe. A little. But mainly my father has forbidden me to see you again, and he's been watching me like a hawk, even while he's arguing with Spencer. I was only able to get out tonight because he was called to the hospital for an emergency."

Adam's fingers tightened on his cup. "He's forbidden you to see me? Why?" He was afraid he knew the answer to that question already.

"Because . . . well, you know . . ."

"Because I'm Jewish," Adam said bitterly, "and not good enough for his beautiful Aryan daughter."

Catherine leaned forward. "It's not like that! You make him sound like a Nazi."

"Oh, yeah, I forgot. I'm not just a Jew, I'm poor, too. That's the other reason he doesn't want the two of us going together, isn't it?"

Her silence was all the answer he needed.

"Damn!" He pushed his cup aside so abruptly that a little of the coffee slopped over the side. "That damned bigot!"

"Adam, please. I don't agree with him, but he *is* my father."

"That doesn't make him any less of a bigot. And I'm not too sure about that Nazi business, either." Adam saw the pain in her eyes and immediately regretted the harsh words, but then he decided he wasn't sorry about them after all. All he was doing was speaking the truth. He asked, "What are we going to do about this?"

Catherine looked at him squarely across the table and said, "Get married."

The answer took him by such surprise that all he could do for a moment was stare at her. Finally he was able to repeat, "Married?"

"That's right. I've been thinking about it for weeks. Father will feel differently about you when you're my husband. He'll have to."

Slowly, Adam shook his head. "I don't know . . ."

"I do. Once we're married, he'll see that there's nothing he can do to keep us apart, so he won't even try. We may not agree with him, but he's not stupid, Adam. He'll know when he's beaten."

Adam thought Catherine was underestimating her father. But she was starting to seem so excited, with enthusiasm shining in her eyes, that he couldn't bring himself to argue with her.

Besides, getting married to Catherine was what he had wanted almost from the moment he met her. Why was he being difficult about it?

"You're sure?" he said. "I mean, this isn't very romantic. I'm supposed to propose to you on bended knee, aren't I?"

She glanced around the busy, noisy coffee shop. "Well, I must admit some flowers and moonlight would have helped the ambience, but . . . Yes, Adam, this is what I want. I want to be your wife. We've talked about it before, and we both know that marriage is what we want."

"Yeah, in theory." He saw her eyes widen slightly, so he hurried on, "I mean, sure, we've talked about it, but it was always about how we'd get married someday. Not now. Someday. After I'm through with law school and you're through with medical school."

"Do you really want to wait that long?"

"To get married?"

She leaned forward and whispered, "To consummate our love."

He forced himself to chuckle. "If you're going to put it that way . . ." He gave a little shake of his head and reached across the table to take her right hand gently in both of his hands. "I love you, Catherine. I've loved you for a long time. And I want you for my wife more than anything else in the world." He paused, then added, "It won't be easy, though."

"I know that. We'll have to arrange everything secretly."

"You were going to convert, so that we could be married in the temple."

"I will," she promised, "only it'll have to wait for a while. We'll be married in a civil ceremony first, and then we can get married in the temple later. That'll be all right, won't it?"

Adam wasn't sure. He knew it definitely would *not* be all right with his mother. Nor was Dr. Tancred likely to be pleased when he discovered that his daughter was going to convert to Judaism.

But maybe Catherine was right. Maybe the civil ceremony would be enough for right now, and they could work out everything else later. One thing was certain: once they were married in the eyes of the law, Dr. Tancred would not be able to keep them apart.

His fingers tightened on her hand. "It looks like we're engaged."

"Oh, Adam, I love you."

"Since you're being the practical one tonight and I'm being the romantic one, don't you think you should kiss me?"

"Right here in the middle of the coffee shop?"

"What's the matter, don't you *want* to kiss me?"

"You are terrible. Come on." She slid out of the booth and tugged him with her. Adam disengaged one hand long enough to drop a couple of quarters on the table, then allowed her to lead him out of the building.

"Where are we going? It's cold out here," he said as they walked along the sidewalk.

"Don't worry. I'll keep you warm, baby."

They had reached a tiny island of grass next to Grove Avenue, on the edge of Washington Park. The grass was green during the spring and summer but already brown and dead now. Still, it was a little haven from the busy city around them. Adam stopped and said, "This turnabout business is cute as hell, but that's enough." He turned to her and put his arms around her. "There's something I have to say. Catherine Anne Tancred, will you marry me?"

She tipped her head back slightly to look up at him and said in a husky voice, "Yes. Yes, I'll marry you."

Adam's mouth came down on hers and their arms tightened around each other in an embrace that did, indeed, keep out most of the cold.

There, Adam thought fleetingly before giving himself over to the sensations of holding and kissing the woman he loved, the woman who was going to be his bride. That was more like it.

SIXTEEN

Halloween came and went, and a few days later Franklin Delano Roosevelt was elected to an unprecedented third term as president of the United States. To a large part of the country, Roosevelt's reelection was not a treat at all but rather a belated trick. With that mandate from the voters, the opposition in Congress to the Lend-Lease program was bound to steadily erode. It was only a matter of time until FDR got what he wanted.

Dale didn't give politics much thought. He was too busy racing, and Elaine was waiting for him after each of the races. That was more than enough to keep him occupied. He was bitterly disappointed that he hadn't been invited to race at the Milwaukee Mile, but on the surface at least he was upbeat, telling anyone who would listen how those bozos in Milwaukee would regret passing him up. He was going to be the top driver in the country, and then they'd be begging him to race on their track.

Joe thought about the war in Europe every time he walked past International House, the huge, castlelike structure at the eastern end of the Midway where the University of Chicago's foreign students lived. Arthur Yates had lived there, until he withdrew from the university and went back home to London. Joe couldn't help but wonder if he was all right. None of Joe's letters to him had been answered, despite Arthur's promise to write. The German Blitz had eased somewhat, but London was still being bombed from time to time.

Adam and Catherine were together again, though not as often as before. Still, whatever had been causing trouble between them seemed to have been resolved, and Joe was glad of that. He wanted to see his friends happy. Adam and Catherine certainly appeared to be happy, judging by the way they held hands all the time and kissed whenever they thought no one was looking, and sometimes when they obviously didn't care if anyone was looking. From time to time, though, Adam admitted how worried he was about his grandparents in the Ukraine. Hungary and Romania appeared to be on the verge of joining the Axis powers, and once they had capitulated to Germany, the path through them to the Ukraine would be wide open for the Nazi hordes.

"Gun-Slammers of Cougar Basin" brought Joe a $75.00 check from Popular Publications, and it was slated for the February issue of *Ten Story Western*. The editor told him that it might even get top billing on the cover and asked for more stories. Joe had finished the time travel story and sent it off to John Campbell at *Astounding*, so instead of trying to pick up the mystery again, he started another Western. Only a fool ignored a sympathetic editor and a ready market.

The week of Thanksgiving—the same week that, on the other side of the world, Hungary and Romania did as expected and "allied" themselves with Germany—the time travel yarn came back in the mail with a two-page, single-spaced letter from Campbell pointing out everything that was wrong with it—and that was a lot, Joe thought as he read the letter and tried not to wince at the blunt rejection. Campbell thought the story's basic premise made it too weak to fix up and resubmit, but he asked, at the end of the letter, to see any other science fiction stories Joe might have. That made him feel a little better. It was on to *Amazing* or *Thrilling Wonder Stories* with the time travel yarn, he thought.

Christmas was approaching rapidly, and so was the end of the semester. Joe was doing all right in his classes, carrying A and B averages in all of them. Dale, on the other hand, was struggling and in danger of failing more than one course. That came as no surprise to Joe, consid-

ering how much time and energy his brother spent on
racing—and Elaine. Joe had offered to help tutor him, but
Dale wasn't interested.

Now that winter had arrived, there were fewer races.
The final one of the year, in fact the final one for several
months, was held in Chicago itself, at a dirt track on the
far west side. As if the weather wanted to cooperate and
allow the racing season to end in style, the clouds and
snow of the past few weeks blew away in midweek, so
that by the Saturday of the race, the sky was clear and an
unseasonably warm breeze was blowing.

Christmas carols played over the racetrack's loudspeakers as the crowd made its way into the stands. Dale stood
in the pits and watched the spectators, and Joe knew who
he was looking for.

"Don't worry, she'll be here," he heard himself saying
to Dale. "She hasn't missed a race yet, has she?"

"No, but you never can tell when something might have
happened."

"You know, if you were half as worried about your
grades as you are about that girl—" Joe stopped short and
held up his hands, palms out. "No, I promised myself I
wasn't going to lecture you today. Besides, you still have
finals next week. You can still pull out passing grades in
all your courses."

"Yeah, sure," Dale said, but he didn't sound convinced
of that. He didn't even sound like he was paying that
much attention to his brother.

Harry had the hood of the Ford raised and was making
a few last-minute adjustments to the engine. He straightened, closed the hood, and wiped his hands on a rag.
"Well, she ought to be about as fast as she can be," he
said. He was talking about the car, but he might as well
have been talking about Elaine, Joe thought.

That wasn't really fair, he told himself. He shouldn't
be upset just because Dale had some beautiful, hot-
blooded girlfriend who wanted to jump into the sack after

every race, while he, Joe, had nothing but work waiting for him each and every day . . .

"Mr. Parker?"

Joe and Dale both turned, even though to them, "Mr. Parker" was their father. They saw a stranger walking toward them, a man in his forties wearing an expensive suit and a homburg hat. He had on fine kid gloves, too. He tugged the gloves off, slapped them together in his left hand, and held out his right hand to Dale.

"You're Dale Parker, aren't you?"

Dale shook the stranger's hand. A slightly puzzled frown was on his face. "That's right."

"I recognize you from pictures in the newspapers. I'm quite a race fan, but I'm not able to get out to see them as often as I'd like." The man laughed. "My name is Victor Mason."

"Dale Parker. But you know that. This is my brother Joe, and my buddy Harry Skinner."

Victor Mason nodded to them. "Gentlemen. I'm pleased to meet you."

"Likewise," Harry said.

Mason turned back to Dale. "I've been following your progress ever since you drove in your first race at Green Valley, Dale. You don't mind if I call you Dale, do you?"

"No, that's all right."

"Anyway, I've taken quite an interest in your exploits on the track. You seem to be a very talented driver. You've won a great deal more than you've lost."

"Thanks." Dale shrugged modestly, but Joe knew that he enjoyed the attention from racing fans such as Victor Mason. "I just try to do the best I can."

"I'd like to see you do the best you can, too. That's why I have a business proposition for you."

Joe stepped forward. Typical fans didn't talk business. Dale didn't have much experience in the world—if you didn't count Elaine, that is—and Joe wanted to look out for his brother's best interests.

"What sort of business proposition?" he said.

Mason nodded toward the Ford. "Next racing season, how would you like to be driving a better car, an actual race car, Dale?"

Dale slapped the Ford's fender. "This baby's been pretty good to me."

"Of course, but I sponsor a racing team, or rather my bank does, and I'd like for you to be a part of it."

"Your bank?" Joe said. Mason was trying to ignore him now, but Joe wasn't going to allow that.

Mason barely glanced at him. "I'm the president of Fidelity Bank and Trust, on LaSalle Street."

"Hey, I do business with you guys," Harry said.

"What do you say, Dale?" Mason went on. "I'm willing to back you so that you can either make more improvements to this car or build yourself a new one from the tires up."

Dale rubbed his chin. "I don't know, Mr. Mason. I mean, it's tempting and all, but it sort of sounds like . . . well, work. I got into racing because it's fun. It's the most fun I've ever had."

"I understand. But you'll think over my offer, won't you?"

"Sure, I guess I can do that," Dale said, ignoring the way Joe was shaking his head.

Mason reached inside his coat and brought out a small leather case. He opened it and took out an embossed card on heavy paper. He went back to his pocket for a fountain pen that probably cost more than Joe made in a month. "Here's my business card," Mason said as he uncapped the pen and began to write on the back of the card. "I'm putting my home address on the back. I'd like for you and your brother and your friend to join me for dinner at my house next Saturday. What do you say?" He held out the card.

"Gee, I don't know . . ." Dale looked at Joe and Harry. "What do you think, guys?"

I think going to dinner with a rich banker is about the

dumbest thing we could do, Joe thought. He didn't trust Mason.

But maybe he was being unfair to the man, he told himself. The Parkers had always been a middle-class family, with the typical ingrained distrust of the wealthy and powerful. Maybe Victor Mason really was just a racing fan who wanted to lend Dale a helping hand. What harm would it do to have dinner with him? At least they would get a good meal out of the deal.

"I suppose we could do that," Joe said warily.

"Yeah, I'm always up for a good feed," Harry added.

Dale nodded. "Okay, then," he said to Mason.

The banker grinned and nodded. "Excellent." He shook Dale's hand again, then pumped the hands of Joe and Harry. "I know I come across as a bit of a stuffed shirt, boys, but you'll see. I'm just a regular guy."

They waited until Mason had started toward the stands and was out of earshot before Harry said, "Yeah, a regular guy in a fancy suit and a homburg hat. He's about as much a regular guy as Daddy Warbucks. But what the hell, maybe he can give you a hand, Dale."

"With somebody like that backing me, I could be racing at Indianapolis someday," Dale said with a dreamy quality in his voice.

"Don't set your sights so high," Joe warned. "We'll go see what he has to say, but don't count on anything coming of it."

Dale laughed. "You're a fine one to talk, Mr. I'm Going to Be a Rich and Famous Author Someday."

Joe flushed. "I never said that—"

"Yeah, but you thought it enough times, I'll bet. What if some rich guy like Mr. Mason offered to help you out so you wouldn't have to work while you wrote some fancy-shmancy novel? Wouldn't you jump at the chance?"

"I don't know . . ."

Dale punched him on the shoulder. "Of course you would. You'd be a damn fool not to. Well, I'm not a damned fool, Joe." He turned and studied the crowd in the stands again. "Now, where the hell's Elaine?"

★   ★   ★

She wasn't there, and Dale was so upset by her absence that he ran third in the race, his worst finish in quite some time. He slumped in the backseat of the Ford, fuming, as Harry drove back toward Chicago. Joe turned around in the front passenger seat and said, "You can't expect her to have every Saturday free. Didn't you say her mother was sick?"

"Yeah, but it's not every Saturday," Dale said. "Just the ones when I'm racing."

Joe shook his head. "Things come up unexpectedly, things that people can't get out of. Look at it this way. Now you can go home tonight and study instead of—"

Instead of going out dining and dancing with a beautiful woman and then getting laid. Joe was glad he had stopped short before saying something that stupid.

Harry chuckled, and Joe knew he must have completed the thought for himself. "Yeah, kid," Harry said. "Go home and study—for a change. It'll be good for you."

Dale slumped down lower in the backseat. "Yeah, maybe. But just wait'll next season. I'll win every race, and all of our pockets'll be stuffed full of dough. Then I'll show Elaine the best time of her life. Just wait and see."

SEVENTEEN

Harry tugged at his collar and the knot of his tie. "How do I look?" he asked. "I ain't used to gettin' dressed up like this."

"You look fine," Joe assured him. Harry was in the backseat of the Ford, Joe and Dale in the front with Dale at the wheel. Both of the Parker brothers were in their Sunday best.

That had brought some caustic comments from their father as they were leaving the house. "Going off to see your fancy friends," Sam Parker had said with a sneer. "Next thing you know you'll be too good for your own family."

Helen had fussed over them, brushing imaginary lint from their coats and straightening their ties. "Don't let your father bother you, boys," she said. "He's just being an old grump, as usual."

That was putting it mildly, Joe thought. His father had long since passed the stage of being a grump.

Now they were on their way to the exclusive North Shore neighborhood where Victor Mason lived. Harry asked from the backseat, "You think there'll be caviar? I never had that stuff, but I seen Ronald Colman eat some in a movie once. What is it, anyway?"

Joe looked back at him. "Fish eggs."

"No, really, what do they make it from?"

Dale said, "I think it's really fish eggs, Harry."

"No shit." Harry shook his head. "And rich people really eat that? I think I changed my mind. I hope they don't have no caviar."

"I'd settle for a nice, thick, juicy steak," Dale said. "With a good wine."

"Like you'd know a good wine from a bad one," Joe said.

"I might. Hey, I got a little culture." Dale checked the street signs and turned onto a narrow blacktop road. A tall brick wall fronted by shrubbery ran along the left side of the road. Up ahead was a wrought-iron gate flanked by stone pillars. "Is that it? It looks like the entrance to a museum or something."

Joe saw a brass plaque on one of the pillars with a number on it. "That's it," he said. "We're here."

Dale swallowed hard, suddenly nervous. "Yeah. This must be the place."

"I can't believe we're really here," Catherine said.

"Neither can I." Adam brought the car to a stop in front of the cottage. A small sign hanging from a post in the front yard read JUSTICE OF THE PEACE. Adam had no trouble reading the words, even though twilight was settling down over the area.

They were in a small town on the shore of Lake Michigan, about halfway between Chicago and Milwaukee. A lot of planning had gone into what was going to happen this evening. One of Catherine's friends from the university lived here, and with the semester over and the Christmas holidays begun, the girl had gone home until after the New Year. Adam had been a bit leery of bringing her in on the plan, but Catherine had insisted that she could be trusted.

"Gloria's such a romantic she'll do anything to help us," Catherine had explained. "You don't have to worry about her, Adam."

He'd gone along with the idea. For one thing, he hadn't been able to come up with anything better himself. Gloria had asked Catherine to spend the weekend before Christmas with her, and Catherine had driven up on Friday evening. As far as Gloria's parents knew, the invitation was only for one night, but Catherine's parents weren't expecting her back until Sunday afternoon. Catherine had met Adam at a restaurant in town, and now they had the whole night in front of them.

A night that she would spend as Mrs. Adam Bergman, Catherine thought with a shiver as Adam got out of the car and came around to open her door for her.

She was surprised that her father hadn't been more suspicious. If Dr. Tancred had not been so distracted by his continuing troubles with his son, he might have questioned why Catherine wanted to go spend a holiday weekend with a girl with whom she had never seemed that close in the past. Catherine was thankful for Spencer's stubbornness; he was insisting that he wasn't going to finish high school, that he was going to get a job instead. Dr. Tancred wouldn't hear of such a thing.

Adam took Catherine's arm and led her up the walk to the cottage. There was a nice little inn just down the road, facing the water, and Catherine thought the justice of the peace probably did a booming business in marrying eloping couples.

That was what she and Adam were doing, she told herself: eloping. Running off to get married in secret. And they had agreed—after quite a bit of long and sometimes heated discussion—to keep the marriage a secret. Catherine would continue to live at home, and Adam would live with his mother at their apartment. But they would see each other whenever they could, and they would continue making their plans to have a real wedding later on.

In the meantime, though, they would be together as often as possible, beginning with tonight.

They went up onto the porch and Adam knocked on the door. Inside, music was playing softly on a radio. The Pied Pipers, with that skinny Italian kid taking the lead, were crooning "I'll Never Smile Again," backed by Tommy Dorsey's orchestra. Adam hoped that wasn't an omen. He knocked again, and the music cut off. A moment later, footsteps sounded on the other side of the door, and it swung open. A short, mostly bald man in suspenders and a loosened tie stood there, holding a pipe. "Yes?" he said.

"Are you the justice of the peace?" Adam asked.

The man had looked a bit annoyed at first, but now he smiled. "Indeed I am, my boy. And you don't have to say anything else. I know why you're here. Come in." He stepped back to usher them inside and turned his head to call over his shoulder, "We have a nice young couple here looking to get married, Mother."

A woman's voice came from somewhere else in the house. "Oh, that's wonderful, Carl. I'll be right there."

"My wife," the JP said as Adam and Catherine stepped into a warm parlor with lace doilies on all the furniture and a piano sitting against one wall. An embroidered sampler that read *Bless This House* hung over the piano. "She'll play for the ceremony." The JP looked over the top of his glasses at Adam. "You *do* have the proper license, young man?"

"Yes, sir, of course." Adam reached into his coat to get the marriage license.

"And twenty dollars, hmmm?"

"I've got that," Catherine said. She opened her purse. She noticed that the justice of the peace looked faintly disapproving, as if he didn't like the idea of a bride paying the fee for her own wedding. He was probably old-fashioned enough to think that the man had to pay for everything.

Catherine didn't mind. She wanted this marriage as much as Adam did. It was only fair that she help pay for it.

"Very well," the JP said as he took the folded bill she handed him and put it in his pocket with the marriage license. "Just let me get my coat . . ."

He left them alone in the parlor. Adam and Catherine looked at each other for a long moment, then Adam said,

"I can't believe we're really going to do this."

"I know what you mean." Suddenly, Catherine was assailed by doubt. "Are you sure we're doing the right thing?"

"Do you love me?"

"Of course!"

"And I love you." He put his hands on her shoulders. "We were meant to be together, Catherine."

"Yes," she whispered. "We were."

He slipped his arms around her and kissed her.

From the doorway, with his wife beaming behind him, the justice of the peace said with a chuckle, "Well, I always give couples a few minutes alone so they'll have a chance to bolt if they decide they're doing the wrong thing. I don't reckon that's going to happen here. Come along, Mother, let's get these fine young people married."

Victor Mason's house looked like a museum, too, Joe thought as Dale brought the Ford to a stop in front of the columned entrance. The driveway had curved up through a huge expanse of lawn. The grass was dead now, but in the summer the place would look like a park. It was almost big enough to be a park.

The house was three stories tall and made of red brick. Marble columns flanked the entrance. A portico extended out over the driveway in front of the double doors. As they got out of the car and gazed around in awe, Harry said, "How many people live here, anyway?"

"Probably just Mr. Mason and his family," Joe said, rubbing his hands together to keep warm.

"I seen smaller hotels. You could put an army in this joint."

"Don't mention the Army," Dale said.

Joe knew what he meant. That was a worry that lurked in the minds of most young men these days. They could make all the plans they wanted, but there was always the possibility that their lives would be totally disrupted if they were drafted.

At the end of October, conscription had begun with President Roosevelt symbolically reading the first draft numbers to be drawn. So far, Joe and Dale had not been called, but each day's mail might bring a draft notice for one or both of them. The chances of them being called increased every day. For a country that was officially neutral, it sure looked as if the United States was getting ready to go to war.

Still, neither of them wanted to just sit and wait for the worst. It was better to go ahead and live their lives. The first semester of the school year was over, and Dale, to Joe's surprise, had managed to squeak by with passing grades in all his courses. Christmas was coming, and there were plenty of things in the world to look forward to and be happy about.

So they were here tonight in front of this mansion, ready to perhaps make a deal with Victor Mason for financial backing of Dale's racing career.

Dale squared his shoulders and said, "Let's go." He stepped up to the double doors and pressed a gilt button set into the wall beside them.

An elderly, white-haired man in servant's livery opened the doors a moment later and greeted them with a solemn, "Good evening, gentlemen."

Dale swallowed. "I'm Dale Parker," he said. "This is my brother Joe and our friend Harry Skinner."

The butler didn't smile. "Yes, sir, Mr. Mason is expecting you. If you'll come in, please . . ."

They stepped into a high-ceilinged foyer, and the servant swung the doors closed behind them.

"Mr. Mason is waiting for you in the library. You're to have drinks there before dinner."

"Oh. All right. Thanks."

"Right this way, gentlemen."

As they followed the servant down a hallway lined with paintings, Harry leaned over and whispered to Joe, "I thought all butlers had to have English accents, like it was a law or something."

Joe just shrugged.

The butler showed them into a large room. Most of the walls were covered with floor-to-ceiling bookshelves, and the areas that weren't had dark wood paneling on them. A massive desk dominated one side of the room. A bar was on the other side, and that was where Victor Mason stood, a glass in his hand.

"Dale!" he said, coming forward with his hand outstretched. "Good to see you again. And Joe and Harry, too, of course." He shook hands with each of them, then waved toward the bar. "I thought we'd have a drink before dinner. Scotch all right with you boys?"

Mason was dressed more casually tonight, in slacks and a double-breasted tweed jacket, but his clothes were still elegant and expensive. Joe felt more than a little shabby in his plain black suit.

"Sure, Scotch is fine," Dale said, and Joe didn't point out that legally Dale was too young to be drinking liquor.

The butler had left the room unobtrusively. Mason poured the drinks himself, splashing dark brown liquid into heavy glasses of cut crystal and adding an inch to what was left in his own glass. He passed the others around, then lifted his glass and said, "Gentlemen, start your engines."

Dale and Harry chuckled at the bad joke, and Joe managed a smile. They all clinked their glasses together, then drank. Dale threw back all of his, Joe noticed. Joe sipped on the Scotch, not really caring much for it.

"My wife is waiting for us in the dining room," Mason said. "I hope you don't mind if she joins us. She does so like to entertain. But don't worry, we'll come back in here after dinner for brandy and cigars, and we can discuss our business then."

"Sounds good to me," Dale said as he put his empty glass on the bar.

"Well, then, shall we go?" Mason put his hand on

Dale's arm and started toward the door of the library. Harry finished off his drink and set his glass next to Dale's. Joe left his on the bar, too, with the whiskey nearly untouched.

Mason led the three of them down a long hallway toward another pair of double doors. He opened them to reveal a beautifully furnished dining room with French doors at the far end that overlooked a garden. In summer, the view would be a lovely one, Joe thought.

Then Dale stopped short in front of him, and as Joe moved to the side and stepped farther into the dining room, he saw the woman standing at the far end of the long mahogany table. She wore a black gown that clung to the lines of her body and a diamond necklace that glittered in the light of the chandelier that hung over the table. Joe thought she was beautiful.

He had thought the same thing the first time he saw her, several months earlier at Green Valley Raceway.

"Gentlemen, this is my wife, Elaine," Victor Mason said.

EIGHTEEN

Dale felt like somebody had just swung a sledgehammer into his gut. *She'd lied to him! Sick mother, my ass!* His eyes met Elaine's, and he saw fear there for a second.

Then it was gone, replaced by a look of cool, almost disinterested politeness. Dale took his cue from that. What was important now was that nobody panic. They might get through the evening yet. Mason was on his way along the length of the table, and he hadn't been looking at either Dale or his wife during that moment of shocked recognition.

Dale's head swiveled sharply on his neck as he glanced back at Joe and Harry. Both of them looked surprised, too, but thankfully they were trying to bring their reactions under control. Joe managed to do so before Harry did. He dug an elbow sharply into Harry's side. Harry jerked his head and then deliberately stared down at the table until he had brought his expression back to normal.

Dale hoped the smile on his face didn't look too sick. *The bitch.* He would never forgive her for this.

"Hello, gentlemen," Elaine said. Unbelievably, only a couple of heartbeats had passed.

"This is Dale Parker, his brother Joe Parker, and their friend Harry Skinner," Mason said.

Joe stepped forward. "Pleased to meet you, Mrs. Mason," he said. His voice sounded a little odd to Dale, but Mason probably wouldn't notice that.

"Yeah, likewise," Harry said. "This is some joint you got here."

Dale knew he ought to say something. He said, "Thanks for having me—I mean, us. Over for dinner."

Elaine smiled at her husband as he came up beside her. "Darling, when you said you had invited some business associates for dinner, I thought you meant someone from the bank."

Mason took her arm and kissed her on the cheek. "No, these gentlemen are involved in something a lot more enjoyable and a lot less stuffy than banking. Dale is a race car driver."

Elaine's look of polite interest never faltered as she said, "Really? I'm afraid I don't follow car racing, Mr. Parker, but I'm sure you're an excellent driver."

"One of the best," Mason said. "Well, shall we sit down?" He snapped his fingers, and a servant that none of the guests had noticed until now opened a door so that several women in maid's uniforms could begin serving dinner.

Just let me get through this without giving anything away, Dale thought, *and I swear, I'll never have anything to do with a married woman again!*

★　★　★

"A married woman," Catherine said sleepily. "That's what I am."

"My wife," Adam murmured into her ear. "Mrs. Adam Bergman." He tightened his arms around her. He couldn't believe how wonderful the long, sleek, naked length of her felt pressed against him as they snuggled under the covers of the bed.

The little lakeside inn wasn't busy at this time of year, so they'd had no trouble getting a room. The clerk had surely known from their anxious, eager laughter as they checked in that they were newlyweds. He had smiled tolerantly and handed over a key, saying, "Room Seven. It's around the back, so you folks won't be disturbed."

Nothing could disturb them now, Adam thought. They were married.

Making love to Catherine had been every bit as exciting

as he had thought it would be. They had taken it slowly, undressing each other, stroking and kissing each new area of flesh that was uncovered, until they couldn't withstand the sweet torment any longer and had slipped under the covers to consummate their marriage. As difficult and frustrating as it had been at times, Adam was glad now that they had waited.

The only light in the room came from the embers in the small fireplace. Adam slid his hand lightly along Catherine's side and over the swell of her hip. "Honey? You dozing off?"

"Oh, no. Just resting for a minute." Catherine turned over in his arms so that she was facing him. She lifted a leg and slipped it over his thigh. Her erect nipples brushed against his chest. "I don't intend to waste any of tonight sleeping. Do you?"

"Not a minute," Adam said. He lowered his head and took one of her nipples into his mouth, sucking gently on it. She ran her fingers through his hair, then they tightened on his head as he darted his tongue against the bud of pebbled flesh and sent new sensations coursing through her.

There would be plenty of time for sleep on other nights. Tonight was the only honeymoon they would have.

Somehow—and Joe was never sure exactly how—they all got through dinner. He supposed the food was good, and Mason said the wine was excellent. Joe didn't know, because he didn't really taste anything. He was too worried that someone would make a slip and inadvertently reveal that his brother had been having a red-hot affair with their host's wife for the past few months.

Mason carried most of the conversation over dinner, talking animatedly about the British diplomat Lord Lothian's recent trip to the United States to drum up support for U.S. aid to Britain. The Lend-Lease bill proposed by

President Roosevelt would be coming up for a vote soon after the first of the year, and Mason was in favor of it. If Joe had not been so distracted by the situation with Dale and Elaine, he might have been surprised by Mason's stance on the issue. Most Republicans were adamantly opposed to the United States getting involved any further in the European strife. How much of that opposition was sincere and how much was simply because Roosevelt was a Democrat, Joe didn't know.

Finally the meal was finished, and Elaine stood up. The four men rose quickly to their feet. "I'm sure my husband plans to take you back to the library for brandy and cigars, gentlemen, so I'll say good night now."

"Good night, Mrs. Mason," Joe said. "And thank you. It was a lovely meal." He was a damned liar, he thought, but he was far from the only one in the room.

"Yeah, quite a spread," Harry said. "Much obliged."

Dale nodded and said stiffly, "Good night, Mrs. Mason. Thank you for dinner."

Mason took Elaine's hand and bent to kiss her briefly on the lips. "I'll be up later, sweetheart."

"Take your time. I know how you like to talk business."

Mason smiled. "Yes, and if all goes well, you may be seeing a lot of Dale around here."

Elaine's smile didn't waver. She left the room.

Mason waved expansively toward the door. "Shall we repair to the library, boys?"

The ordeal wasn't over yet, Joe thought, but at least things might get a little easier now since they wouldn't be in the same room as Elaine.

In the library, Mason filled brandy snifters and handed them to his guests. "Martell," he said. "Enjoy it. There may not be any more until we kick those Nazis out of France. Damned rude of them interfering with the grape harvest over there."

Joe wasn't sure if Mason was making a joke or if he was serious.

Mason turned to Dale. "What about it, Dale? You've

given plenty of thought to my proposition, I hope."

Say no! Joe mentally shouted at his brother. *Damn it, say no so we can get out of here!*

"I've thought about it," Dale said slowly, "but I haven't made up my mind yet."

Mason took a sip of his brandy and asked, "What's the problem? Maybe I can sweeten the pot a little."

By throwing your wife in on the deal?

"Harry backed me starting out," Dale said. "I'm not sure I'm ready for a full-fledged partner, though. And that's what you're talking about, isn't it, Mr. Mason?"

"Please, call me Victor. And I just want to give you a helping hand, Dale." Mason shrugged. "Of course, if I sponsored you, I'd expect some sort of return on my investment. . . ."

"I thought you said the bank would sponsor me."

"Well, the bank can't actually do that, of course. Banks are such stuffy institutions, and there are federal regulations about which endeavors are proper for banks to be involved with . . . But don't worry, Dale. I have plenty of money."

Dale glanced around the library, and by extension the rest of the luxurious mansion. "Yeah, anybody can see that."

"So how about it? What do you say?"

Dale took a deep breath. "Let me think about it some more."

No! Joe almost yelped. *You can't get mixed up with this guy. If you do, he's bound to find out sooner or later about you and his wife.*

"You're sure?"

"Yeah," Dale said with a nod. "I'm sure."

Mason clapped him on the shoulder. "Well, then, if that's the best I can do right now, I suppose I'll have to be satisfied with your answer." He wagged the index finger of his other hand at Dale. "But don't you go setting up a deal with anybody else, all right?"

"I promise," Dale said. "If I go partners with anybody, Mr. Mason—Victor—it'll be you."

"See that you remember that." Mason stepped back and rubbed his hands together lightly. "Now, about those cigars I promised you . . ." He turned toward the desk, where a large humidor sat. "Thank goodness those U-boats haven't completely stopped the shipping in the Caribbean yet. I can still get my Havanas."

★ ★ ★

"What the hell were you thinking about?" Joe tried not to yell at his brother as Dale drove back toward their home an hour later, but it was difficult. "Why didn't you just tell him no?"

"I didn't want to be rude to him after that nice dinner," Dale said defensively.

Harry said dryly from the back seat, "Uh, kid, speakin' of bein' rude, about what you been doin' with the guy's wife . . ."

"I know, I know." Dale clenched a fist and thumped it against the Ford's dashboard. "Damn her! She lied to me."

"You thought she was married, remember?" Joe said.

"Yeah, but then she told me that cock-and-bull story about her poor old sick mother . . . Damn! I'm an idiot for believing her, aren't I?"

Harry said, "Most guys think with their pecker most of the time. You ain't no different than anybody else. Well, maybe a little more so, since you're only nineteen and that's a prime pecker-thinkin' age—"

"The important thing," Joe said, "is that you stay away from Elaine. You can never see her again."

"I don't want to, after the way she lied to me," Dale said, but Joe didn't think his brother sounded completely sincere.

"And if Mason gets in touch with you again, tell him you thought over his offer some more and you're just not interested."

Dale nodded. "Not interested. Right."

"You have to steer clear of him."

"I know. Geez, I'm not a complete fool, Joe."

"I'm just saying—"

"I know what you're saying. We got lucky tonight because Mason didn't tumble to the truth, but we can't push our luck."

"That's right."

"Don't worry," Dale said. "After tonight, I never want to see Elaine again, that damned slut."

Joe sighed and wished that he could believe that.

NINETEEN

Christmas of 1940 was probably the most solemn holiday Joe could remember. People had their trees and their decorations up, of course, and lights were lit on the buildings, but corps of Air Raid Wardens had been formed and blackout drills were carried out several times in December. When the sirens blew, the entire city of Chicago was plunged into darkness, all the festive glitter extinguished in a matter of seconds. It was unthinkable that any enemy bombers could penetrate all the way to the heart of the nation . . . but if the unthinkable happened, Chicago would be ready.

And it was difficult for many families to celebrate as they normally would because sons and brothers were gone, drafted into the Army or the Navy and sent hundreds of miles away from home for training. Those absences made the holidays even more poignant for those left behind. For the boys themselves, Joe thought more than once, spending Christmas so far from home and under such circumstances must have been really miserable.

He had gotten a twenty-dollar check from Culture Publications for a weird-menace story he'd sold to *Spicy Mystery*. The story had appeared ten months earlier without the promised payment on publication, but that wasn't unusual. Culture was always a slow pay. This time it had worked out well for Joe. He had taken the money and bought a pair of gloves for Dale, a fancy scarf for his mother, and a cap for his father. They had all seemed pleased, even Sam, when the family opened their presents around the tree on Christmas morning.

That afternoon Adam came by, and he, Joe, and Dale

went down to the drugstore, which didn't close even on Christmas, for a soda. Adam didn't celebrate Christmas, of course, but that didn't stop him from wanting to be with his friends on their holiday.

"How's Catherine?" Joe asked as they sat at the soda fountain counter.

"She's fine," Adam said, making rings on the polished wooden surface of the counter with the condensation on his glass.

"I don't see the two of you together as much as I used to."

Dale said, "Maybe she finally wised up and told this big lug to take a hike."

Adam shook his head. "You can crack wise all you want. Catherine and I are fine. Better than fine."

Joe leaned forward a little, hearing something strange in Adam's voice. "What do you mean by that?"

"Nothing," Adam said quickly.

"No, there was something there," Joe persisted. "Trouble with her parents?"

"Look, I'm just trying to make it easier for her right now. Her family's in enough of an uproar, what with her little brother getting kicked out of school and fighting with her father all the time."

"Yeah, that's a shame about Spencer," Dale said. He sucked the last of his soda through the straw.

"But you don't have to worry about Catherine and me," Adam went on. "There's nothing to worry about at all."

Joe nodded. "Okay, if you say so."

"I say so." Adam stood up. "I've gotta get going. I'll see you guys later."

"So long," Joe said. He turned on the stool to watch Adam shrug into his overcoat, put on his cap, and head out into the street. A few flakes of late-afternoon snow were falling.

"They're doin' it," Dale said.

Joe frowned. "What?"

"Catherine finally went all the way with him. That's

why he's acting that way. He's getting laid regularly."

"You're crazy."

Dale shook his head and smiled smugly. "Nope. Don't forget, big brother, I've got more experience in this area than you do."

"Yeah—with a married woman."

"Keep your voice down," Dale said, glancing at the soda jerk at the other end of the counter. "I don't want Mom and Pop to find out about that."

"I don't blame you," Joe said. "I'm just glad you haven't heard anything else from Mason. Maybe he got the idea that you don't want him to sponsor you and has forgotten all about it."

"Yeah," Dale said. "That'd be nice, wouldn't it?"

On December 29, President Roosevelt was scheduled to make an important address to the nation on the radio. During his first two terms in office, the country had gotten used to his fireside chats, and nearly everyone who had access to a radio was planning to listen in on this one. The Parkers gathered in their parlor after supper. Sam was in a bad mood and made a few grumbling comments as Dale tried to tune in the station on the big cathedral radio. Dale leaned close to the speakers and listened closely to the bursts of static as he gingerly turned the tuning knob.

Suddenly, a deep, resonant voice filled the room as an announcer said, "Ladies and gentlemen of America, the president."

Roosevelt's familiar aristocratic tones came from the speakers. "This is not a fireside chat on war. It is a talk on national security, a security that hinges on the survival of our friends and allies in Great Britain."

The president did a good job of presenting his case, Joe thought as he continued to listen to the speech. There was no possibility of compromising with Hitler, as England's previous policy of appeasement had proven to be disastrously mistaken. Peace in our time, as the former British prime minister, Neville Chamberlain, had put it, was now nothing more than a dashed hope, buried in the rubble of London neighborhoods that had been bombed by the Germans. The threat of military aggression would not end in England, Roosevelt went on, but would ultimately threaten the United States itself unless Hitler was stopped.

Someone knocked on the front door of the Parker house.

"Who the hell?" Sam said.

Joe was the closest to the door. He stood up and said, "I'll get it." He went into the foyer while President Roosevelt continued speaking on the radio.

Joe swung the front door open and saw Elaine Mason standing there wearing an overcoat with a fur-lined collar and a fur hat on her black hair. The snow flurries had continued, and a few flakes were caught in the fur of the hat. They were slowly melting. Joe's hand clenched on the door in surprise as he recognized Elaine.

"What are you doing here?" he said, keeping his voice low so that his parents wouldn't hear him over the president.

Elaine's eyes were wide with fear or excitement or both. "I have to see Dale," she said. Joe was thankful she followed his lead and kept her voice pitched quietly.

Joe started to shake his head. "I don't think that's a good idea—"

She reached out and put a gloved hand on his arm. "Please. I have to."

From the parlor, Helen Parker called, "Joe? Who is it, dear?"

"A, uh, a friend from school, Ma," Joe lied. With his free hand, he made a shooing motion at Elaine. He kept his other hand solidly on the door, using his arm to block her from coming in.

She didn't budge. Her eyes glittered dangerously as she said, "I'll start yelling for him in a minute."

Joe held up his hand, knowing when he was beaten.

Besides, this wasn't his fight. "Stay there," he said, then he turned his head and called, "Hey, Dale, come here a minute, will you?"

Dale's lanky form emerged from the parlor a moment later. He looked irritated. "Ma says you should bring him in, whoever he—" He stopped short at the sight of Elaine, and after he had stared at her for a second, he whispered, "Good Lord!"

Joe jerked a thumb toward the front porch. "Go talk to her, then get her the hell out of here." He knew he was being rude but didn't particularly care. Elaine had lied to Dale and nearly gotten them all in a lot of trouble.

Dale looked as if he would have rather turned and run, but he forced himself to move past Joe into the doorway. "Elaine," he said quietly. "What do you want?"

"I have to talk to you."

Dale shook his head. "I don't have anything to say."

Joe put a hand in his brother's back and shoved a little. "Then don't say it outside." He closed the door behind them.

President Roosevelt was still making his speech when Joe came back into the parlor. Helen looked up from the divan and asked, "Where are Dale and your guest?"

"They went outside to talk for a minute," Joe said. Not wanting to get into it any more than that, he went on, "What's the president saying now?"

From the radio speakers, Roosevelt's words came. "We must be the great arsenal of democracy. There will be no bottlenecks in our determination to aid Great Britain. No dictator, no combination of dictators, will weaken that determination."

"The arsenal of democracy," Joe repeated. "Good line. We're going to war, aren't we?"

"Roosevelt says he's not sending any armies to Europe," Sam Parker said. "But you mark my words, we'll wind up there sooner or later."

Helen shook her head sadly. "I can't imagine my boys fighting in a war. I just can't imagine it."

Her husband snorted contemptuously and said, "You think they'd take these two? What kind of soldiers would they make? A mama's boy who spends his time making up stories and a dunce who's not good for anything except getting into trouble." Sam shook his head. "Don't worry, Helen. Our boys are safe."

The harsh, sarcastic words made Joe's face burn with anger and resentment, but he bottled up the reaction. He didn't want to go to war. He wasn't convinced he would ever make much of a soldier. But he didn't want to hear his father talking about him like that, either.

From the radio, President Roosevelt said, "Thank you, good night, and God bless."

★   ★   ★

Elaine came into Dale's arms as soon as the door closed behind him. She lifted herself on her toes and her mouth found his. He stood stiffly, not returning the embrace or the kiss. But his lips parted instinctively as her tongue prodded hotly and wetly against them, and he felt his resolve start to weaken.

What would it hurt to kiss her? he asked himself. His arms went around her.

He had missed her so much. He couldn't deny that. For months, the thought of being with Elaine had kept him going through all the boring classes at the university and the usual harassment from his father at home. Elaine and the racing were the only two things that really mattered to him. The times when he was with her or behind the wheel of the car were the only ones when he felt truly alive.

But she was married, he reminded himself. And her husband was a rich, powerful man. If he found out . . .

Dale broke the kiss and stepped back. "This is no good, Elaine," he said, his voice hoarse with emotion. "You've got to get out of here. We can't see each other anymore."

"That's what I thought at first, too. My God, I . . . I was

so scared when Victor brought the three of you into the dining room! I swore then and there that if I could just get through the evening, I'd never see you again."

"I felt pretty much the same way."

"But then . . ." Her voice faltered, and it was a moment before she could go on. "But then I started to miss you, Dale. The longer it went on, the more I wanted you. I won't lie to you. I thought we were just having a few laughs together and that I could give you up just like snapping my fingers." She shook her head, making the dark wings of hair sweep around her face. "But I can't. I just can't! Damn it, Dale, I think I—"

He grabbed her by the upper arms. "Stop it! Don't you say it! Don't you dare say it! It doesn't matter what either one of us feel. We have to do what's right."

She looked up at him for a long moment, trying to read his face in the light that filtered onto the porch through the windows. Then she laughed, a brittle sound. "Who am I talking to? I thought Dale Parker didn't give a damn about anything except winning races and getting laid."

"Yeah," Dale said. "That's what I thought, too. Funny, ain't it?"

She jerked away from him. "Bastard. You won't even let me say it, will you?"

"I can't," he whispered. "I can't risk it."

"This isn't over."

"It has to be."

"*We're* not over." She turned and went down the porch steps.

Dale stood there and stared down at the planks of the porch, afraid to look up while he could still hear the clicking of her high heels on the sidewalk. He didn't know where she had left her car. Probably not too close, in case anybody was following her. He hoped she had that much sense, anyway. Finally, the sound of her footsteps faded off into the night.

A few weeks earlier, he would have found the idea of having a beautiful girl crazy in love with him tremendously appealing and exciting. Now he just wished he had never seen Elaine Mason.

But at the same time, he wanted her. He wanted to feel her in his arms again, to taste her mouth again, to hold her close with nothing between them but air . . .

The door opened, and Joe stepped out onto the porch. He pulled the door closed behind him. "Is she gone?"

"Yeah," Dale said. "Gone."

"You did the right thing. *If* you sent her away."

"I did. I sent her away." Dale gave a little shake of his head, took a deep breath, and turned to his brother. "I missed most of the president's speech. What'd he say?"

"We're going to send as much help as we can to England."

Dale reached for his cigarettes. "Good. Hitler's got to be stopped."

"This may mean we'll get into the war. It sounds pretty certain, in fact."

Dale lit the Lucky Strike and blew out smoke. "Right now I think I'd rather face the Nazis than . . ."

He looked off into the darkness where Elaine had disappeared and didn't have to finish the sentence.

TWENTY

The second semester wouldn't start until after the middle of January, so Dale planned to use the first two weeks of the new year to work on the Ford. As the worst winter weather set in, he didn't want to be driving it around Chicago and risking a wreck on slippery roads. He was going to store it at Harry's instead; Harry had already made a space for the car in a corner of the garage.

That was where Dale and Joe were on January 10, 1941. Outside the sky was overcast and a cold wind blew. The garage was a little chilly, too, since the radiator in Harry's office wasn't nearly enough to heat the whole place. Dale had the Ford's hood up and was tinkering with the spark plug wires. Joe sat on a nearby work bench, his feet dangling. He didn't have to work at Grissom's Hardware this afternoon, and he was hoping that he and Dale might take in a movie later. *The Great Dictator*, with Charlie Chaplin, was playing at the Orpheum.

Harry came out of the office. He had been going through the mail that the postman had dropped off earlier, and now Harry had one of the letters in his hand. His hand was shaking a little, Joe noticed, and that was surprising. Hardly anything ever rattled Harry.

"Say, Joe, would you take a look at this?" Harry asked. "I think I know what it means, but I want to be sure."

"Okay." Joe took the paper, which was thick and had embossed lettering at the top. It was from the Fidelity Bank and Trust, he saw, on LaSalle Street. Something about that was familiar to him, but he couldn't recall just what it was.

As he read the letter, he began to frown. "What the hell

is this?" he said after a moment. "They can't do this, can they?"

"They're callin' in my loan," Harry said. "That's it, ain't it? I thought that's what it said, but I wasn't sure."

"But why would they do that? You've made all your payments, haven't you?"

Harry nodded. "Every one. Right on time, too."

Joe jabbed a finger against the letter from the bank. "This says they've determined that you're a bad credit risk. I just don't understand."

Harry wiped the back of his hand across his mouth and said, "They're a bank. They can say any damn thing they want and they don't even have to back it up. They say I got thirty days to pay 'em the rest of the dough I owe 'em. I can't do that, Joe."

Dale lifted his head from under the hood of the Ford. "What are you two yapping about? A guy can't concentrate on his work around here for all the noise."

Joe pushed himself down from the work bench and waved the bank letter at Dale. "The bank's going to foreclose on Harry!"

"What! They can't do that."

Harry said, "They've done it."

"Well . . . well, you'll just have to fight them!"

"I ain't got the money to pay 'em, kid, which means I sure ain't got the money to hire some shyster to take them to court. And don't think they don't know it, too."

"Let me see that." Dale snatched the sheet of paper out of Joe's hand, not worrying about the grease he got on it from his fingers. "This is crazy. I still say they can't just—"

"What?" Joe asked, a moment after Dale had fallen silent abruptly.

"Fidelity Bank and Trust," Dale said. He turned the letter so that Joe and Harry could see the printing on it. "It says so, right there."

"So?" Harry said.

"That's Victor Mason's bank."

"Oh . . . my . . . God," Joe said. "That's why the name sounded familiar to me." He looked at the signature on the letter. "This is from some vice president named Reese. But I'll bet he works for Mason."

"Of course he does." Dale turned sharply and leaned on the Ford's fender, the letter still clutched in one hand. "That bastard! He found out somehow about me and Elaine, and he's trying to get back at me through Harry!"

"Or he knew all along," Joe heard himself saying.

Dale glanced at him. "What?"

The more Joe thought about it, the more plausible it sounded to him. "He knew about the two of you before he ever came to the track and invited you to dinner. He was just playing with us. Like a cat that catches a mouse and pretends to let it go before he swats it again."

"I dunno," Harry said. "It'd take one sick son of a bitch to do something like that."

"He's a banker," Dale said disgustedly. "What else do you need to know about him?"

"Wait a minute, wait a minute," Joe said. "If this is just Mason's way of getting revenge on you, Dale, then the bank can't legally get away with it."

"Why not? Whether something's legal doesn't matter anymore. All that counts is whether or not you're rich enough to fight back."

"The kid's right, Joe," Harry said. "I might beat 'em if I had the money to put up a fight, but I'd still lose the garage. The big boys win either way."

Dale dropped the letter and smacked his right fist into his left palm. "Damn it! This is my fault, all my fault."

"Probably," Joe said. He knew that wouldn't help matters, but he couldn't stop himself.

"Maybe we can come up with the money. How much was it again?"

Harry picked up the letter. "Thirty-five hundred bucks. There's no way, Dale."

"You let me and Joe worry about that. We'll come up with something." Dale took hold of Harry's shoulders.

"You're not going to lose this place, Harry. I swear it."

"I sure hope you're right, kid. The garage is all I got in the world."

Dale turned and reached for his coat. "Come on, Joe. We got to think about this."

They could think all they wanted, Joe told himself, but it wasn't going to do any good unless they could come up with three thousand five hundred dollars.

And that seemed about as unlikely as him winning the Pulitzer Prize.

★ ★ ★

Helen Parker was crying when Joe and Dale got home. They heard the quiet sobbing coming from the kitchen and went straight there. As they came into the room, they found their mother sitting at the table, dabbing at her eyes with her apron.

"What's wrong, Ma?" Dale asked. "The old man giving you trouble again?" The mood Dale was in, he was ready to tear into his father.

Helen shook her head. "No. No, your father's upstairs resting. He doesn't know anything about this."

Joe pulled out a chair and sat down next to her. "What is it, then? What's wrong?"

"I was at the market and . . . and Mr. Hennessey said he couldn't give us credit anymore."

"Why would he do that? We've always paid our bills on time."

"I don't know. All I know is that he said I couldn't have any more groceries until I paid this month's tab in full. And then he said I couldn't charge anything else, even if I paid him what we owe."

"I don't understand . . ." Joe began, then he broke off and looked up at Dale. *Mason*? he mouthed.

Dale shrugged and shook his head. He didn't know, either, but it seemed likely that Victor Mason's hand was somewhere in this.

"Ma, does Mr. Hennessey have a mortgage on his store?" Dale asked.

Helen looked up at him in confusion. "Why, I don't know. I . . . I suppose he must. Nobody can buy anything without a mortgage."

Thank God the house was paid off and the family didn't have any direct dealings with Fidelity Bank and Trust, Dale thought. Mason couldn't get at them that way.

But that just meant that Mason would have to strike at him through Harry, and by forcing the grocer to close their account, and who knew what else?

"It'll be all right, Ma," Joe told her. "There are other markets. Nothing says we have to buy from Mr. Hennessey."

"No, but he was always so good to us. When money was so tight, right after your father's accident, he let the bill ride for months at a time . . . I just can't imagine shopping anywhere else." Helen sighed. "But you're right. I suppose we'll have to."

"I ought to go down to Hennessey's and bust him one in the chops," Dale said.

His mother stood up quickly. "Oh, no! That wouldn't do any good, and I don't want you fighting, Dale. I forbid you to go down there and cause a scene."

Dale wiped his mouth and grimaced. His insides were jumping around like crazy. His pulse throbbed in his head like Gene Krupa pounding the skins. He was mad and scared at the same time. He forced himself to say, "All right, Ma. No trouble. I promise."

But he was going to get to the bottom of this. That was a promise he was making to himself, and he intended to keep it.

Hennessey's Market was on the bottom floor of a three-story building on Fifty-first Street. Joe and Dale came into the market that evening not long before it closed for the day. Hennessey was standing behind the meat counter with a butcher's apron on, and when he saw them come in he reached over and wrapped his fingers around the wooden handle of a cleaver with its blade stuck in the chopping block. "Help you boys?" he asked.

Dale started to say something, but Joe moved forward, cutting him off. "Our mother told us what happened, Mr. Hennessey," Joe said.

Hennessey eyed Dale nervously. Dale was the one most likely to take a swing at him, he knew. "I don't want any trouble, Joe," he said. "I been friends with your family for a long time. No hard feelin's, it's just . . . business."

Joe stuck his hands in the pockets of his jacket. "Just answer a couple of questions for me, Mr. Hennessey," he said.

"Sure, if I can."

"Do you have a mortgage on this place?"

"Well, yeah, I—" The man from the bank had told him to keep his mouth shut if anybody asked him that question, and he had forgotten.

"With Fidelity Bank and Trust?"

"That ain't none of your business," Hennessey answered in a surly voice. "I told you, Joe, I'm sorry—"

"You told us, all right," Joe said quietly. "You told us all we needed to know. Come on, Dale."

Dale eyed the grocer intently for a moment, then turned and followed his brother out of the market. Hennessey heaved a sigh of relief. At the same time, he felt sick to his stomach. The Parkers were good folks, and he didn't like making trouble for them, even if it was none of his own doing, not really. *Damn a world where a little guy's got to let the banks push him around!* he thought.

But what was he going to do? What could anybody do?

Nothing happened for a few days, and Joe came to fully understand the meaning of the old saying about waiting for the other shoe to drop. Mason had thrown a couple of punches. Joe didn't think he would stop with that.

Dale was all for going down to LaSalle Street and confronting the banker. Joe had his hands full talking him out of that idea. If Mason was really after revenge, that might just make things worse. There was still the slimmest chance what had happened were coincidences.

Joe didn't believe that for a second, but he was going to hang on to the hope anyway.

On another snowy afternoon, he and Dale went to the university to register for classes. They stood in line to pick up their registration forms. The young woman who was working behind the table handed Joe his packet of paperwork, then said to Dale, "What was your name again?"

"Dale Parker. I'm his brother."

She looked down the list of names in front of her and then flipped through the stack of registration packets. "I'm sorry. You're not on the list, and I don't have a packet for you."

"What do you mean? I went to school here last semester, and I signed up to attend again this semester." Dale glanced at Joe. "Somebody saw to that."

The young woman shook her head. "I'm sorry, sir. Why don't you go over to the registrar's office and ask there? It's in the administration build—"

"I know where it is," Dale said. "Come on, Joe."

Joe had a bad feeling about this already, and when they reached the registrar's office and asked why Dale hadn't been allowed to register for classes, Joe's suspicion was confirmed. The middle-aged woman behind the counter said, "Our records show that Dale Parker has been placed on academic suspension for a semester."

"What? But I passed all my courses!"

"Not exactly." She pointed to the papers she had taken from a file cabinet. "You can see for yourself. You failed three courses."

"That's a damned lie!" Dale shouted.

Joe grabbed his arm and pulled him back from the

counter. Hurriedly, he said to the woman, "I saw my brother's grades, ma'am. He passed everything. Just barely, but he passed."

The woman turned around the paperwork. "See for yourself. He had failing grades in English, history, and biology."

Joe looked down at the records. "Those grades have been changed."

"That is impossible. We don't make that sort of mistake."

"Yeah, well, somebody sure made a mistake, lady—" Dale began again.

Joe stopped him by saying quietly, "I wonder just how much money Fidelity Bank and Trust donates to the university each year."

The woman frowned. "I don't know what you mean, young man."

Joe believed her. Whoever had been responsible for this was a lot higher in the university administration than a clerk in the registrar's office. And he was willing to bet that there wouldn't be any way to prove a bit of it. Men like Victor Mason were probably damned good at covering their tracks when they wanted to be.

"Come on, Dale."

"But I want to go to school!" Dale laughed humorlessly. "I never thought I'd hear myself saying *that*!"

"Come on," Joe said again. "We've got to figure this out."

He was beginning to get the sickening feeling, though, that they already had all the answers they needed.

There just wasn't a damned thing they could do about it.

TWENTY-ONE

The secretary said into the phone, "Mr. Mason, I have two young men out here who don't have an appointment, but they seem to think you'll see them anyway . . . Their names?"

"Parker," Joe said tightly. He had made Dale promise to let him do all the talking before he would agree to come down here to LaSalle Street with him.

The secretary repeated the name, then glanced up at Joe and Dale in surprise. "Yes, sir," she said, then hung up the phone. "Go right in."

"Thank you," Joe managed to say. The words tasted bad in his mouth.

Mason's office was on the twenty-fifth floor of the towering skyscraper that housed Fidelity Bank and Trust. Joe had never been that high in a building before. Doc Savage's office was on the eighty-sixth floor of the Empire State Building, he recalled, although the writers who wrote the novels never actually called the building by its real name.

About now, he and Dale could have used the help of a big bronze adventurer whose profession was righting wrongs.

Joe put those thoughts out of his head as he and Dale marched into Victor Mason's office. This was deadly serious business.

The office was all glass and chrome and dark wood, with a high enough ceiling so that their steps echoed hollowly. A big window overlooked the Loop, providing a spectacular view. Mason stood up from a leather chair behind a huge desk and said cheerfully, "Hello, boys.

What can I do for you? Have you finally made up your mind to accept my proposition, Dale?"

Dale clenched his fists and started forward. "I'm not going to accept anything but beating the shit out of you, you—"

Joe grabbed him and pushed him back. Mason hadn't moved and didn't seem the least bit frightened. In fact, judging from the faint smile that curved his lips, he was amused.

Joe said, "We're here about what's been happening to our family and our friends."

"Oh? And what would that be?"

"You know," Joe said. "You foreclosed on Harry's garage, you made Mr. Hennessey cut off our credit, and you ruined Dale's grades at the university. What were you planning to do next? Have some goons jump us and beat us up?"

Mason reached down and picked up a gold cigarette case from the desk. He opened it, took out a cigarette, and lit it with a matching gold lighter. As he blew out the smoke, he said, "Really, do I seem like the sort of man who would resort to such crude methods to get what I want?"

"What *do* you want?"

"To tell you the truth, I don't actually know yet. I thought I'd spend a few weeks making your lives miserable first. I'm enjoying that a great deal."

"So you admit it," Joe said.

Mason's narrow shoulders rose and fell in a shrug. "Why not? What can you do?"

He was right. Their sheer helplessness was almost overwhelming, Joe thought.

Dale was breathing hard, barely able to keep his emotions in check. In a thick voice, he said, "You're just doing this because of Elaine."

"Of course. I'll admit that. My pride was wounded when I found out she was having an affair with you, Parker." Mason started out from behind the desk. "But I was hardly surprised. You're not the first."

Dale drew in a breath. "I'm not?"

Mason laughed. "Good Lord, did you really think so? I knew when I married a woman nearly twenty years younger than me that I would have to keep an eye on her, and she hasn't disappointed me. Well, of course, she *has*, in a way, but at least she proved my suspicions correct. More than once."

"Look," Joe said, "Dale didn't know she was your wife. He didn't even know she was married. She told him she lived with her sick old mother."

Mason looked at Dale scornfully. "And you believed her?"

"We're sorry," Joe hurried on. "Dale is sorry. As soon as he knew, he put a stop to it."

"Oh? Was that before or after . . . let me see . . . December twenty-ninth?" Mason reached down and picked up a manila folder from his desk. "You see, I have a detailed report from the private detective agency I employed. Complete with dates, places . . . and photographs."

A growl rumbled in Dale's throat. "You sonofa—"

Mason slapped the folder down on the desk. "She went to your house on the twenty-ninth," he said. "To your *house*! In a neighborhood she shouldn't have even been seen in."

With an effort, Joe controlled his own temper. "We just want to make this right—"

"You can't," Mason said. "I'm the only one who can make it right, and that's what I'm doing. And I've just started."

"What do you mean by that?"

"You have a friend named Adam Bergman. A Jewish boy."

Dale pointed a quivering finger at Mason. "Adam doesn't have anything to do with this!"

"He was there several times when you were out carousing with my wife, as was another friend of yours, a Miss Catherine Tancred. I'm acquainted with her father. A very respectable man."

Joe shook his head. "Just leave Adam and Catherine out of it."

"I haven't done a thing concerning them . . . yet. In the future . . ." Mason shrugged again. "Who knows? Right now, I don't believe you've thought about what else I can do to *you*."

"You'd better just leave us alone—" Dale began.

Mason went on as if he hadn't even heard the interruption. "There's the electric service to your house, not to mention the coal deliveries. Both can be cut off due to nonpayment of your bills."

"We pay our bills," Joe said.

"Mistakes happen. Just look at your brother's school records." Mason held up a hand to forestall any more arguments. "Then there's your job at Grissom's Hardware. It's amazing how many businesses in the greater Chicago area owe money to this bank, Mr. Parker. And it's equally amazing what people will do to stay on the good side of their bankers.

"Imagine yourselves sitting in a dark, cold house, unable to find work, unable to buy food, not even able to get the medicine your father takes for the pain in his crippled leg. Imagine that, both of you." Mason suddenly began to shake, and his voice rose as he continued, "Imagine it getting worse and worse and worse, because I'm just getting started with you, you contemptible little worms!"

Dale started forward again, and this time Joe didn't stop him.

Mason was caught up in the grip of his fury, but he had the presence of mind to move his foot and step on a button underneath his desk. A second later, before Dale could reach him, a door on the other side of the office opened and two large men stepped into the room. They wore the uniforms of bank guards, and each man had a pistol holstered on his hip.

"Mr. Parker and Mr. Parker were just leaving, boys," Mason said, his voice still trembling with rage. "See them out, will you?"

"Sure, Mr. Mason," one of the guards said. Both of them started toward Joe and Dale.

Joe caught hold of Dale's sleeve. If they put up a fight, they would be beaten badly. They might even wind up in jail. That wouldn't help anything.

"Come on, Dale. Let's get out of here. Let's go."

The urgent words must have penetrated Dale's brain, because he gave a little shake all over, like a dog, then said, "Yeah. It stinks in here."

They left the office, and the guards marched behind them all the way to the elevator. "You fellas don't have any more business here, do you?" asked the one who had spoken before.

"No," Joe said. "We don't have any more business here."

Because Victor Mason had won, and they all knew it.

★　★　★

Adam leaned back against the upholstered seat of the restaurant booth and said, "You mean he threatened Catherine and me, too?"

"I'm sorry, Adam," Dale said. He dragged his fingers through his hair in frustration. "I never meant for this to happen."

Catherine reached over and patted his arm. "We know you didn't, Dale."

"Don't be so easy on him," Adam said. "He's brought trouble down on all of us."

"I didn't mean to," Dale said.

"Doesn't matter if you meant to or not." Adam sighed. "Well, at least you came clean with us. We can be grateful for that, anyway."

Joe said, "You're in law school, Adam. Can Mason get away with this?"

"You're talking about an official with one of the largest banks in the country. Legal or not, he can get away with just about anything he wants badly enough. And he's per-

;onally wealthy on top of it, which just makes things
worse."

Dale said, "So he can make our lives a living hell, and
here's not a damned thing we can do about it?"

"Not as long as you're here in Chicago. And even if
you left town, Mason's influence might be able to follow
you."

Dale put his elbows on the table and dropped his face
into his hands in despair. "It's not fair, it's just not fair,"
he said in a muffled voice.

"You're telling a Jew about life not being fair?"

"Adam," Catherine said. "You could be a little more
sympathetic. Dale is our friend."

"And if he wasn't, you and I wouldn't be in for some
trouble from this guy Mason." Adam reached over and
clapped a hand on Dale's shoulder. "But I suppose Catherine's right. I'm sorry, Dale. We know you didn't mean
to cause trouble. If there was anything I could do to
help . . ."

Joe was frowning. "You said Mason could do anything
he wanted as long as we stayed here in Chicago."

"Yeah, but—"

"I know. He could have us followed and keep causing
problems for us no matter where we went. But maybe not.
Maybe there's something bigger and more powerful than
the Fidelity Bank and Trust."

"Oh?" Adam said skeptically. "And what would that
be?"

Joe looked around the table and said, "The United
States Army."

TWENTY-TWO

"You're insane," Adam said a few minutes later when Joe had explained his plan. "You'd actually join the Army just to get away from Mason?"

Dale had listened intently as Joe spoke, and his mood of despair had gradually lifted. "Why not?" he asked now. "Joe's right—Mason can't do anything to us once we're in the Army. And besides, we're liable to be drafted anyway. Might as well go now as later."

Catherine said, "What about your parents, though? Even if you enlist, Mason might keep on trying to make things hard for them."

Dale frowned. His hope was that once he and Joe were out of Chicago, Mason would lose interest in them, and in their folks as well. But there was no way of knowing for sure that he would.

"Maybe if we went to him and told him we were leaving, he'd be reasonable."

"How reasonable has he been so far?" Adam asked.

Dale shook his head. "I don't care. Joe's idea is the best one anybody's come up with. No plan is perfect."

Joe stared down at the table. A few moments earlier, he had been convinced that he had hit upon the perfect solution. Now he was rapidly losing faith in it, despite Dale's show of confidence. There was Harry Skinner to consider, too. He would still lose his garage.

"Well, you can enlist if you want," Adam said, "but don't expect me to go along with this cockeyed scheme."

"Nobody asked you to," Dale said.

Adam glanced at Catherine. "I've got a good reason to

stay right where I am." She reached over and took his hand.

"Of course you do," Joe said. "You don't need to enlist, Adam. I know we've been friends for a long time, but I was just talking about what Dale and I should do."

"As long as we're clear on that. And there are no hard feelings."

"No hard feelings," Joe said, and meant it. He slid out of the booth. "Can you guys take Dale home?"

"Sure," Adam said.

Dale asked, "Where are you going?"

"I need to look up something—some research for a story—at the public library. I'll take the El home later."

Adam said, "So you've given up on that crazy scheme of joining the Army?"

"I don't know what we'll do," Joe said honestly. "Nothing right now, I guess."

He left the restaurant and began walking the downtown streets of Chicago. He buried his hands in the pockets of his overcoat and hunched his shoulders against the cold wind. Although he wasn't really thinking about it consciously, his steps inevitably took him back toward the LaSalle Street skyscraper that housed the Fidelity Bank and Trust.

It was late afternoon, and many of the bank's employees were leaving for the day. Joe found himself standing across from the bank's entrance, watching the steady stream of people coming out of the building. He wasn't surprised when he saw Victor Mason push through the revolving door and start toward a Packard sedan that had pulled up at the curb in a No Parking zone. A uniformed driver was behind the wheel of the sedan.

Joe crossed the street quickly before Mason could reach the car. "Mr. Mason!" Joe called. "Can I talk to you for a minute?"

Mason stopped short, the grains of dry snow on the sidewalk making a gritty sound under the soles of his Italian shoes. "Parker," he said. "We've nothing to say to each other. And I warn you, my driver is right there in the car if you intend to cause trouble."

"No trouble," Joe said with a shake of his head. "You like to make business propositions. I've got one for you."

Mason seemed intrigued in spite of himself. "What could you possibly offer me that would be of any interest?"

"Dale and me out of Chicago for good." The situation was desperate enough, Joe thought, that he had to take the chance.

"You mean you'd leave town, run away?"

"I mean we'd enlist in the Army." Joe spoke quickly, trying to overcome the dubious expression on Mason's face. "Look, Mr. Mason, we're probably going to be drafted anyway. But we can enlist now and be out of your hair for good. All we ask is that you lay off our friends and family."

"I don't have to do anything I don't want to do," Mason said.

"I know that. But it's a fair trade, don't you think? You get rid of us, Harry gets his garage back, and our folks get to go on living a normal life."

Mason shook his head. "That's not enough. How can I be sure you'd never come back?"

"There's a war going on in Europe, a big war," Joe said grimly. "Chances are, the United States is going to be in the middle of it sooner or later, probably sooner. Guys like me and Dale, you know they're going to put us in the front lines." There was a hollow feeling in Joe's stomach as he spoke the words. He was trying to convince Mason to accept the deal, but at the same time, he knew he was speaking the truth. If the United States entered the war, as seemed inevitable, there was a very good chance that he and Dale would not survive.

Mason frowned in thought. "I suppose that's true," he said after a moment. "You haven't really offered me a business proposition at all, Parker, but more of a sporting one. I'd be wagering my revenge on your brother against the chances of him never coming back from the war."

Joe's mouth and throat were dry. He swallowed, nodded, and said, "That's right."

"Interesting. But as you say, you'll probably be drafted anyway, especially if we do get into the war."

Joe had to risk making Mason even angrier. "Your wife already came to see my brother once. You can't be sure she won't do it again—unless Dale's nowhere near Chicago."

Mason's face, already ruddy from the cold, flushed even more. But he said, "You're right." He nodded abruptly. "I'll give you a week, no more. If you're not in the Army and out of Chicago by then, I'll go ahead with my plans."

"But if we enlist, you see that nothing else happens to my folks?"

"I'm a banker, not God," Mason said. "I can't give you a guarantee like that. But I will say that I won't do anything else to make their lives harder."

That would have to be good enough, Joe thought. He said, "What about Harry's garage?"

Mason shrugged and waved a gloved hand negligently. "A mistake in the paperwork in his loan file. Easily corrected."

Joe tried not to heave too obvious a sigh of relief. "All right, then," he said. "We have a deal."

Mason sneered. "A deal presumes an arrangement between equals. I'm granting you a favor, Parker. Don't forget it." He started toward the Packard again. The driver hopped out and came around to open the rear door for him. Mason said over his shoulder, "And don't forget, you have one week. And if I ever find out that you've returned to Chicago after that, you can forget about everything that's been said here today."

Joe nodded. "I understand." Groveling to Mason like this made him feel about two inches tall, but the humiliation was worth it if he managed to deflect the banker's quest for revenge on Dale and everyone connected with him.

The driver closed the door behind Mason and got behind the wheel again. The Packard rolled away down LaSalle Street. Joe stood there and watched it go as the snow began to swirl down more heavily in the canyon between the lofty skyscrapers rising all around him like cathedrals.

It was hard to believe that less than a month had passed since they were married, Adam thought as he sat with Catherine in the backseat of the Cadillac. They were snuggled together with her head resting on his shoulder. The car was parked on one of the blacktop lanes that circled through Grant Park. They had already dropped Dale off at his home on Greenwood Avenue and then had come here. An early twilight was settling down over the park. A thin layer of snow lay on the dead grass, and the bare branches of the trees were outlined with white, too. It was beautiful here, Adam thought.

Catherine sighed. "I wish we didn't have to go."

"I know." Adam's arm tightened around her shoulders. "Someday soon, we can be together all the time."

Like a respectable married couple, instead of a pair of lovesick teenagers necking in the backseat of a car. Adam was beginning to wonder if they had done the right thing by going ahead and getting married secretly. Having to leave Catherine was killing him. On the other hand, he wouldn't trade the moments they had been able to share together for anything.

"The family's expecting me for dinner," Catherine said with another sigh.

"I know." Adam bent his head and kissed her, his mouth lingering on hers for a long, sweet moment. When he finally broke the kiss, he reached for the door handle.

Catherine caught his arm. "Just a minute more," she said.

Adam smiled. He was glad to oblige.

★ ★ ★

She dropped him off at an El station near downtown, and he rode back to the Madison Park Station in a car crowded with workers going home for the day. The holidays were over, and everyone's mind was back on the day-to-day activities of their lives.

And the war. Adam heard plenty of talk about the war from his fellow passengers.

Nearly everyone seemed to be in favor of the Lend-Lease program now, even though the Germans were rattling their sabers and warning that American aid to England would make the United States a willing participant in the war, with all the consequences that implied. Adam heard the sentiment expressed more than once that the U.S. ought to quit dragging its feet and declare war on Germany.

Adam couldn't help but agree. The Nazis tried to keep a lid clamped tightly on their activities, but word had filtered out of Germany that their hostile actions toward the Jews and members of what they considered the other "undesirable" groups were continuing. All Jews over a certain age were required to wear a yellow Star of David and a sign on their clothing proclaiming *Juden*. The Nazis claimed that was for the Jews' own protection, but Adam knew differently. Hitler's storm troopers just wanted to know who to round up when the time came.

Adam had heard the stories of how the Czar's cossacks had committed atrocities against the Jews in the Ukraine, back in the days before the Russian revolution. He was glad that his grandparents had sent his mother and the other children to live with relatives in America, even though it had meant separating the family. What was going on now in Europe promised to put the atrocities of the cossacks to shame before the Nazis were through.

And a part of him, he had to admit, wanted to march right over there and help put a stop to it before it could spread far enough to threaten his grandparents. He had told Joe and Dale that they were insane to consider joining the Army, but at the same time, deep down, he felt the urge to do so himself.

You're a married man. There's nothing you can do about the draft; you just have to take your chances there. But don't go running off to join up like a damned fool . . .

The train stopped at the Madison Park Station. He got off and walked the six blocks to the apartment building where he and his mother lived. A glance at his watch as he climbed the stairs told him it was late enough that his mother would be home already. She would probably have supper started.

Adam didn't smell any food cooking as he unlocked the door and stepped into the apartment. "Mama?" he called. She might have been delayed downtown.

Ruth Bergman's voice came from the kitchen. "In here."

Adam stiffened. Something was wrong. He had heard it in the tone of her voice. He took off his overcoat and cap and quickly hung them up, then walked into the kitchen. He found his mother sitting at the table, the day's mail in front of her. She was staring at the envelopes as if they were some sort of ugly insects that had invaded her kitchen.

No, not all the envelopes, Adam realized a moment later. Just one. A long one with official-looking printing in the corner.

"This came for you today," Ruth said. "I found it when I got home a little while ago."

"Mama . . ." Adam put his hand on her shoulder and felt the tenseness there.

"You had better read it. It's from the government. It must be important."

Adam's chest was tight and his throat seemed to have

closed up. He reached onto the table for the envelope and picked it up. The paper of which it was made was thick and substantial, just what you'd expect from the government.

He slid his finger under the flap and tore it open roughly. The folded paper inside was heavy, too. He took it out and opened it and read the words printed on it.

"You've been drafted, haven't you?" Ruth asked, a tiny quaver in her voice.

"Yes," Adam said. "I have." He felt dizzy and disoriented. He dropped the letter and the envelope on the table and leaned forward on his hands, breathing deeply for a moment as he collected his thoughts. There was only one thing to do now. "I'm not going to let them draft me," he said.

Ruth's head jerked up. "What?" she said. "But . . . but you have to. God knows I don't want you to, but the law says . . ."

Adam felt calmer now. He tapped the letter. "This says I have to report in two weeks. By then I'll have enlisted with Joe and Dale Parker."

TWENTY-THREE

Catherine heard the shouting even before she came into the house. It was her father, of course. Spencer usually didn't yell. He just grinned that cocky grin of his and drove their father almost insane with rage.

"A stock boy at a grocery store!" Dr. Tancred bellowed from his library as Catherine entered the house through the side door. "What sort of job is that for a son of mine?"

"The only kind I can get right now, Pop," Spencer replied. "Don't worry, though. So many guys are getting drafted that I'll probably be promoted pretty quickly. I might even make produce manager."

His mocking tone produced the expected result. Tancred's fist slammed down against the desk, rattling his paperweights. Catherine heard the impact as she paused in the hall just outside the open library door.

"If you had gone back to school as I demanded, we would not be having this conversation," Tancred said.

"I'm seventeen, almost eighteen," Spencer replied coolly. "The truancy laws don't apply to me anymore. I'm too old."

"You are not too old to be whipped like the troublesome pup you are!"

"Don't try it, Pop," Spencer warned, and now the usual good-natured tone of his voice had disappeared.

The clash between them had never come to actual physical violence, and Catherine didn't know what would happen if it ever did. She didn't want to think about such things. Instead, she stepped quickly into the doorway and said lightly, "You two are back at it again, I see."

They both turned to look at her. "Hi, sis," Spencer said. "Where've you been?"

"Out with that Jew, more than likely," Tancred said as he glared at Catherine. "Oh, I know you are still seeing him, regardless of your poor father's wishes."

"Poor father," Spencer said. "That's a hoot."

Tancred's angry expression swung back to him for a second. "Stay out of this." He jerked toward Catherine again. "And you, young lady, have no business interfering between your brother and myself. I know you wish to protect him, but he must stand up for himself and take the blame for his foolishness."

"Do you see me trying to duck out on anything?" Spencer asked. "I'll take my medicine, whatever it is."

Tancred snorted in disgust. "Medicine is what you should be studying, so that someday you can be a doctor. But you go to school and learn how to run a—what did you call it?—floating crap game! And if you go to work at the market, I'm certain you'll be in the back alley pitching pennies with the other lowlifes who work there in no time!"

"You shouldn't talk about people like that, Father," Catherine said. "You don't know that the people who work at the market are lowlifes. From what I've seen, they're just good, common people."

Tancred glowered at her again and said, "You sound like a Communist! If you want to preach the glory of the masses, go to Russia! I'll not have that sort of talk in my house."

Catherine took a deep breath. Getting drawn into an argument with him wouldn't accomplish anything. She would never change his views. She said, "All I wanted was for you and Spencer to stop fighting. Dinner should be ready soon, shouldn't it?"

Her father took out his pocket watch and flipped it open. "It *is* time for dinner," he said grudgingly. He looked at Spencer. "But we will discuss your future plans after we have eaten."

"Fine by me," Spencer said.

Catherine sighed. A temporary truce was the best she could hope for, she supposed. She took off her coat and draped it over her arm. "Come on, you two. Let's find Mother. I'll bet she's waiting in the dining room."

That was indeed where they found Elenore Tancred. The maid was just putting dinner on the table. Elenore stood with a glass of wine in her hand. She was smiling, and Catherine found herself wondering just how many glasses of wine she had had during the afternoon. Being trapped between two family members as strong-willed as her father and Spencer would be enough to drive anybody to an extra glass or two of wine, Catherine thought.

"Hello, dear," her mother greeted her. "How was your day?"

At least my husband—my husband you don't know anything about—didn't decide to join the Army with Joe and Dale. I've got that much to be thankful for, anyway.

"It was fine, Mother. Just fine."

★   ★   ★

Ken Walker's footsteps echoed hollowly in the tunnel that led to the labs under Stagg Field. He walked quickly, but he wasn't really paying much attention to where he was going. His mind was on the letter he had gotten earlier in the day.

He reached a heavy door and opened it, stepping into a large, low-ceilinged room filled with worktables and scientific apparatus. On one side of the room, a gray, lead-lined partition closed off a small area. A six-inch-square window of extremely thick glass was set into the lead wall, and several men in lab coats were gathered around it, peering through.

Just inside the lab door, a man in a nondescript brown suit sat on a stool. He was in his twenties, and despite the fact that he wore civilian clothes, something about him always reminded Ken of a soldier. Ken didn't know his name; there were several other men who looked and dressed much like this one, and one of them was nearly always in the lab. Ken had a pretty good idea why they were there, but since their presence didn't seem to bother Dr. Fermi or Dr. Chamberlain or any of the other scientists, Ken didn't care, either.

He thought they should have tried a little harder to conceal the M1911A1 Colt .45 automatic pistols they carried in shoulder holsters under their coats, though.

The scientists clustered around the window that looked into the bombardment chamber turned around, talking animatedly among themselves. They wore goggles of thick, smoked glass which they pushed up on their foreheads. The rubber straps of the goggles left lines on their faces. Dr. Fermi glanced toward Ken, noticing him for the first time. The Italian physicist came over to him.

"You are late, Ken. You missed the experiment."

"I know, Dr. Fermi. I'm sorry. I had something on my mind."

"A problem?" Fermi was all business most of the time, but he was also friendly to his colleagues.

"I got this—" Ken dug an envelope out of one of the deep pockets of his lab coat. "—in the mail today."

Fermi smiled. "A letter from your girlfriend?"

Ken shook his head. "I don't have a girlfriend. No, sir, it's from the Selective Service. I've been drafted."

"Drafted?" Fermi's eyes widened in surprise. "You mean, into the Army?"

"Yes, sir. Or wherever they want to put me. I suppose I could end up in the Navy or the Marines."

Fermi's smile had disappeared. He turned his head and called, "Dr. Chamberlain? Could you come over here, please?"

Chamberlain hurried over to join Fermi and Ken. Although Fermi was a visiting professor from Columbia University and was still spending part of his time in New York, there was no doubt in anyone's mind about who was running the project here at the University of Chicago.

Fermi was a Nobel Prize winner and one of, if not *the*, leading authority in the world on the subject of atomic fission.

"What is it, Doctor?"

Fermi nodded toward Ken. "Our young friend here has a problem. Show him, Ken."

Ken held out the letter from the Selective Service System. "I've been drafted, sir."

"What?" Chamberlain took the letter and read it quickly. He looked as upset as Fermi did. "We can't have this. This is totally unacceptable."

"What can we do?" Ken said. "If the Army says I have to go, then I have to go."

"Not necessarily," Fermi said. "There are certain jobs that are considered essential to the government's needs, and men in those jobs can be exempted from the draft, I'm told."

Ken shook his head. "I'm just a laboratory assistant. I don't see how that can be considered essential. There are plenty of people who can do what I do."

Fermi and Chamberlain both glanced at the man in the business suit standing beside the door of the lab. Fermi said quietly, "But there are only a limited number of people who know what we are doing here. And the United States government would prefer that it stay that way."

He's telling me this is some sort of top-secret project, Ken thought. *I knew that. Dr. Chamberlain told me not to blab about it to anybody. And they've got a G-man standing guard over the lab.*

What in the world had he gotten himself into?

Whatever it was, it looked like he was in it to stay. He took the letter from the draft board back from Dr. Chamberlain and asked, "Do you think you can get me out of this, Doctor?"

Chamberlain glanced at Fermi and then nodded. "I think it can be arranged."

A contrary streak in his personality that Ken rarely indulged chose that moment to emerge. "What if I don't want to get out of it? If my country needs me, isn't it my patriotic duty to serve?"

"There is more than one way to serve your country, my young friend," Fermi said. "What we are doing here may make more difference for years to come than any contribution you could make in the armed forces."

"We're splitting atoms," Ken said. "I don't see how that—"

Fermi held up a hand to stop him. "You know the ultimate goal: a controlled chain reaction of nuclear fission. You know what such a thing could produce."

"In theory, yes, but—" Ken broke off and glanced again at the G-man. The man was taking more of an interest in the conversation now than he had at first. He wasn't looking too friendly, either. The carefully bland expression the agent usually wore had disappeared.

"I'm about to talk myself into a deep, dark hole, aren't I?" Ken asked.

"We want you to keep working here with us, Ken," Dr. Chamberlain said. "We'd like to take care of that draft notice for you. But we'll all understand if you feel that you have to honor it."

And if I try to I'll wind up disappearing somewhere for the duration of the war that's coming. I won't see the light of day again for a long time, if ever.

If Joe Parker had written this in one of his pulp stories, Ken wouldn't have believed it. G-men and super-science and secret weapons . . . it was all just too much.

But it was his reality now. The world had been changing ever since Hitler had risen to power in Germany, and it wasn't changing for the better. Whatever innocence had been left in the world after the last "war to end all wars" was being stripped away and could never be returned. Ken could either be part of the effort to save what decency remained, or he could turn his back on it, with possible highly unpleasant repercussions for himself. He told himself not to cast his decision in noble terms. It was a pragmatic world now and growing more so all the time.

He looked down at the draft notice in his hand and then looked up at the lab-coated men who were waiting for his answer.

"I want to be part of the team," he said, mindful of his choice of words since they were underneath a football stadium. "Count me in."

TWENTY-FOUR

The way Catherine's face lit up when she saw him standing on the sidewalk made Adam feel that much worse. He was glad to see her, of course, but he was about to hurt her, and he didn't like that idea at all.

She brought the Plymouth to a stop at the curb, and he got in. "Hello, husband," she said as she leaned over from behind the wheel to give him a kiss.

"Hello, wife," he said just before their lips came together. "Where are we going tonight?"

"I was thinking about the Palmer House."

"That's the most expensive hotel in Chicago!" The exclamation was out of his mouth before he could stop it.

Catherine's expression tightened a little as she eased the Cadillac back into the traffic. "So?" she said. "I can afford it."

"That's not what I meant," Adam began, but then he fell silent as he realized that was exactly what he meant. *She* could afford to pay for a room at the Palmer House, but he couldn't. It was bad enough that they had to sneak around and go to hotels and motor courts as if they were having some sort of tawdry affair, but if they walked into the Palmer House and Catherine paid for the room, he would feel like some sort of . . . gigolo.

He doubted if he could explain that without hurting her feelings even more, though, so he tried to steer the conversation in another direction by saying, "We'd be more likely to run into someone who would recognize you there."

"Maybe, but I don't care." Her hands tightened on the steering wheel. "I'm getting tired of hiding our marriage,

Adam. I'm proud to be your wife. I want to tell the world."

"So do I," he said. *And maybe that's exactly what we should do. What could her father really do about it, anyway?*

Disown her, to start with, he told himself grimly. Kick her out of the house. And with a husband about to go into the service—even if she didn't know that yet—she would need the help and support of her family in the months to come.

He had to tell her. He had put it off for days now, unwilling to shatter the fragile spell they created in the moments they snatched together. But it just wasn't fair to keep Catherine in the dark any longer.

"The Palmer House it is," he said. "Nothing's too good for Mr. and Mrs. Adam Bergman."

★　★　★

The Palmer House deserved its reputation for luxury. Adam had never felt a softer, more comfortable bed. He lay back with Catherine sprawled on top of him, both of them naked but warm under the covers. Catherine's head rested on his broad, hairy chest, which was rising and falling quickly as he tried to catch his breath from their recent exertions.

"How can it get *better* every time?" Catherine asked.

Adam stroked her hip. "You're complaining?"

They were still joined. Catherine shifted her hips back and forth and giggled. "Not at all!"

Adam put his arms around her and sat up, cuddling her in his lap. She wrapped her legs around his back and her arms around his neck and kissed him. Her mouth opened and their tongues came together and they sat there for several long moments, so closely entwined that it seemed to Adam they were no longer two separate beings but one instead. It was difficult to tell where each of them ended and the other began. That wonderful intimacy was going to make it that much harder to tell her what he had to tell her, but at the same time it demanded truthfulness.

He broke the kiss and whispered, "We have to talk."

Catherine stiffened in his embrace. "Uh-uh," she said as she slowly shook her head. "Talk bad. Love good. You Tarzan, me Jane." She giggled again.

He wasn't going to let her distract him. "No, I mean it," he said. "There's something you have to know, Catherine."

"I know you love me and I love you." This time there was a faintly pleading note of desperation in her voice. "That's all I want to know. That's all I need to know."

There was no way to soften the blow, Adam thought. He said, "I've been drafted."

Catherine spasmed in his arms and buried her face against his chest, and for a moment he thought she was crying. Then she started to hit him, thumping her fists against his body, and she said, "No! Don't tell me that! Damn you! Don't tell me that!"

He leaned back and caught hold of her wrists. "Catherine, stop it! I'm sorry, but you had to know—" He stopped when he saw her face, saw the way it was twisted by pain and sorrow and loss. And then the tears came, flowing down her cheeks. She sagged against him, crying so hard that she began to hiccup.

All he could do was sit and hold her, stroke her hair and tell her that everything was going to be all right, even though neither of them could know that.

Finally she said something, but Adam couldn't make out the words. He said, "What?"

"Why did you have to tell me *now*? Now, of all times!"

"I . . . I didn't think it was fair to keep lying to you and telling you that everything was fine. I thought you'd want to know."

"But not *now*! Not when I was so happy!"

That set off a fresh round of crying. Adam waited it out, rocking back and forth on the bed as he cradled her.

When she spoke again, her voice was calm and under control. "Let go of me."

"Are you upset?"

"Of course I'm upset. But if you mean, am I angry at you . . . only a little. Now let me go."

Reluctantly, Adam released her. She slid back on his thighs, still straddling him, then swung her legs off the bed. She stood up and reached for the robe she had dropped at the foot of the bed after she had taken it from her small overnight case earlier. They wouldn't be staying overnight, of course, but they didn't like to check in at a hotel without at least one piece of luggage. Catherine slipped into the robe and belted it around her waist.

"You did the right thing," she said as she turned back toward the bed. "When did you find out?"

"A few days ago, when the draft notice came in the mail. It was the day Joe and Dale decided to join the Army, in fact."

"The day you said you weren't going to enlist with them."

He shrugged. "That was before I knew about the draft notice."

"It must have come as a terrible shock to you." She was still calm, almost eerily so.

Adam shrugged. "We knew it was possible I'd be drafted, of course. But I guess I've been so happy being married to you that I just didn't want to let myself believe it could happen. I put it out of my mind as much as possible."

"When are you supposed to report?"

"The notice gave me a couple of weeks, but I'm not going to wait that long."

Catherine frowned. "What do you mean?"

"I've been thinking about it. With Joe and Dale enlisting, it seems to me the best thing to do would be to sign up like they are. At least that way I might have a little say in where I wind up. If I wait and go in as an inductee, I'll have to just go wherever they tell me."

"You mean you want to enlist with Joe and Dale?" Catherine laughed, but there wasn't much humor in the sound. "All for one and one for all, just like the Three Musketeers, is that it?"

"Well . . . we've been friends for a long time. But I'm considering some other options, too."

"Like what?"

"They're planning to enlist in the Army. I was thinking about the Marines."

"The Marines? Why?"

"Because of what Hitler's doing in Europe." Adam leaned forward, warming to his subject despite the fact that he was sitting there naked and Catherine was only a few feet away clad in a thin robe and nothing else. "The way I see it, if we get into the war the way everybody says we will, the Marines will probably be the first ones to go over there and try to knock the Nazis out. The leathernecks always throw the first punch."

"And that's what you *want*? To be the first to have a chance to die?"

"Hitler has to be stopped, and I'd like for it to be before Germany has a chance to invade Russia. My grandparents are still in Kiev, and if the stories about what the Nazis are doing to my people are true—"

"Your people?" Catherine broke in. "I'm your people, Adam. I'm your wife, your family."

"I'm still a Jew."

"That doesn't mean you're responsible for saving all the Jews in the world!" She looked a little shocked at her own outburst, but she continued, "You have responsibilities here, Adam."

"If I don't enlist, I'm going to be drafted, remember?" he pointed out. "One way or another, I'm going to have to leave you, Catherine."

Putting it in words that blunt made a sharp pain go through him. Now that he and Catherine were together, truly together, it was going to be even more difficult for them to be apart. Maybe it would have been better, a small part of his brain said, if they hadn't gotten married.

But then they wouldn't have had the times together that they'd had, and Adam knew he wouldn't have traded those moments for anything. He stood up and went to her, drawing her into his arms. She was tense and stiff at first, but then she slipped her arms around his waist and leaned against him.

"I don't want to lose you," she said huskily.

He tried to keep his tone light. "Hey, nothing's going to happen to me. I was an All-American outfielder, remember? I could've played for the Cubs. I know how to take care of myself."

"War's not like playing baseball."

"I know. But I'll be fine. I'll be the most careful soldier you ever saw."

Catherine sniffled a little. "You'd better be."

He put his hand under her chin and lifted her head so that he could kiss her. He kissed her cheeks, where the tears had run, and her eyes and her nose and her mouth. As their tongues met, her hands slid down over his hips and her fingers dug into his bare buttocks. He found the belt of her robe and pulled it loose, then spread the robe open and drew her more tightly to him. With their mouths still locked together, they turned back to the bed.

Their passion was even more intense this time, with an urgency born of the bittersweet knowledge that one way or another their time together was coming to an end.

TWENTY-FIVE

Everything had gone as planned. Joe and Dale had been surprised that Adam had decided to enlist, but they hadn't tried to talk him out of it. He didn't say anything to them about receiving his draft notice, nor did Catherine mention his indecision about joining the Army or the Marines, since he hadn't really made up his mind until the last moment. But by the time the day was over, Joe and Dale had been sworn into the United States Army, and Adam was a member of the United States Marine Corps.

The next day was the earliest that Joe and Dale could report to Fort Sheridan, north of Chicago, where they would undergo all the red tape of being processed into the Army. Adam would have to wait another week to catch a train to Parris Island, South Carolina, where the Marine Corps Recruit Training Depot was located.

"We've got tonight," Dale said as the four of them left the Federal Building. "We ought to go out and have one last blowout of a party."

"I think I'd rather stay at home with the folks tonight," Joe said. He was worried about what his mother would say when she found out he and Dale had enlisted. His father, he was sure, would have some sort of bitter, sarcastic comment to make, and Joe wasn't really worried about how he would take it. But Helen Parker was a different story.

"Why don't we have dinner together," Catherine suggested, "and then Joe and Dale can go home."

"I suppose that would be all right," Joe said.

"If it's the best we can do," Dale added with a frown at his brother.

"We'll meet at Ciro's," Catherine said. "Dinner is on me."

Joe started to protest, but Adam said with a grin, "There's no use arguing with her. I've learned that."

Joe nodded. "Okay. How about six o'clock? There's something I have to do first."

"I'll go with you," Dale said grimly.

"No, you won't. Do you want to just make things worse?"

"Damn it, I'm the one who caused all this—"

"Just go say so long to Harry," Joe said. "He's going to miss you. I'll take care of everything else."

"You're sure?"

"I'm certain."

"Well, all right." Dale summoned up a smile as he looked at Catherine and Adam. "Ciro's at six." They nodded.

With a wave, Joe started walking through the cold canyons of downtown toward LaSalle Street.

★   ★   ★

Mason's secretary knew now to admit Joe to his office with only a perfunctory check. Mason was sitting behind his desk as Joe walked into the large, luxuriously appointed room.

"I hope after this I'll never see you again, Parker," Mason said distractedly. He had several sets of documents spread out on the desk in front of him.

"I don't plan on ever seeing you again, either," Joe said. "I just want you to know that Dale and I are in the Army. We leave Chicago tomorrow."

"Excellent. Now get out."

Joe stayed where he was. "First I want your word that it's all over and you won't cause any more trouble for our family or our friends."

"That was the arrangement, wasn't it?" Mason asked impatiently.

"I want your word," Joe insisted.

Mason sighed and placed the fountain pen he was holding on the desk. "Very well, if that's what it will take to satisfy you. I give you my word that neither I nor anyone else connected with this bank will be responsible for any misfortunes that may befall your family, your friends, your acquaintances, or anybody you may have bumped into in the street. Satisfied?"

Oddly enough, Joe was. He nodded and said, "Thanks."

"Get the hell out."

"I'm going." Joe turned toward the door, then paused. "It's funny, you know."

"What?" Mason asked in exasperation. "What's funny?"

Joe waved a hand at his surroundings. "While you're sitting here in this fancy office, you'll know that maybe Dale and I are overseas somewhere, fighting to keep it safe for you."

Mason sat back in his plush leather chair, his mouth open. Joe left with the satisfaction of knowing that he had rendered the banker speechless.

★ ★ ★

"You mean it?" Harry said. "I ain't goin' to lose my garage?"

"That was the deal Joe worked out with Mason," Dale told him. "We join the Army and get out of Chicago, and Mason takes the screws off everybody we know."

"But geez, kid, the Army . . . I dunno if that's a good idea."

Dale shrugged. "They would have drafted us anyway. You know that."

"Yeah, more'n likely." Harry clapped a hand on Dale's upper arm. "Thanks, Dale. To you and Joe both. There ain't many guys who'd do something like this for a pal."

"Adam enlisted, too. In the Marines."

"That Jewish buddy of yours? The one with the snazzy girlfriend? Why'd he go and do that?"

Dale waved a hand. "Ah, he gave us some eyewash about wanting to go to Europe and kick Hitler's ass. He's still got some grandparents over there somewhere, and I suppose since he's a Jew he thinks he's got some sort of obligation to go."

"It's more'n just the Jews who wanta stop that crazy little paperhanger. If I was a few years younger, I might be itchin' to sign up myself."

"You stay right here in the garage, Harry. That's where you belong."

"Don't worry, kid," Harry assured him. "The closest I'll ever come to the Krauts is maybe workin' on an old Mercedes Benz. Say, you want to go out and have a drink or something?"

Dale shook his head regretfully. "I'd like to, but Joe's got this idea in his head that we ought to spend our last night in Chicago at home with the folks."

"And he's right," Harry said. "That's just what you should do." He put out his hand. "Good luck to you, Dale."

Dale took his hand. "Thanks, Harry. There's just one more thing. You'll look after the Ford for me, won't you?"

"Sure thing. I'll keep her in top-notch shape for when you get back." Harry was still pumping Dale's hand. He said, "Ah, hell," and threw his other arm around Dale's shoulders, hugging him. "Take care o' yourself, kid," he said in a voice choked with emotion.

"I will, Harry," Dale promised. He was starting to feel a little misty-eyed himself, so he got out of there quickly, before the feeling could get any worse.

They would board the El at the Kenwood Station, transfer to the Illinois Central at Union Station downtown, and take it north to Fort Sheridan. The platform at the Kenwood Station was crowded with commuters as Joe and Dale walked up the stairs toward it the next morning, the chilly wind whipping their overcoats around their legs. Each of them carried a small suitcase. The sergeant at the recruiting station had told them not to bring much with them, since all their personal belongings would just be boxed up and shipped back home once they arrived at their induction center, wherever that might be.

They joined the group of passengers waiting for the next train and stood quietly, each thinking their own thoughts. Joe didn't know what was going through Dale's head, but he couldn't stop seeing a mental image of his mother's sad, tear-streaked face. Just as he had expected, she had taken the news badly. Joe didn't blame her; he wouldn't have wanted to be left there alone with the old man, either. But the blow would have fallen sooner or later. At least money wouldn't be too tight, what with the race winnings Dale was leaving behind.

More than anything else, Joe thought, their mother had been disappointed because her boys—her two college boys, the first ones on either side of the family to go on past high school—had had to abandon their educational careers.

But everything would work out, Joe told himself grimly. It had to.

"Hey, you two! We were afraid we'd miss you."

They turned to see Adam and Catherine approaching along the platform. Catherine hugged both Joe and Dale, and Adam shook hands with them. There was a lot of hugging and hand-shaking going on these days, Joe thought. All across the country, in fact, as thousands of young men said good-bye to their friends and families and headed off to whatever fate awaited them.

Catherine kissed Joe on the cheek. "Take care of yourself," she said. Tears shone in her eyes.

"I plan to. Somebody has to look after this joker." Joe jerked a thumb toward Dale. He wanted to keep things as light as possible, otherwise he was liable to start bawling and he didn't want that.

"When you get where you're going, send Catherine your address," Adam said. "I'll get it from her, and I'll be sure to write."

"Yeah, me, too." Joe wished Adam hadn't changed his mind and enlisted in the Marines. They had been friends for so many years . . . But even if Adam had joined the Army, there was no guarantee they all would have been assigned to the same outfit. It was time to face facts, Joe told himself. From here on out, their fates were totally in the hands of other people.

A rumbling sound from the rails told them that the train was approaching. All four of them turned to look along the elevated tracks.

"Dale!" a woman's voice cried from behind them.

Dale turned and said, "Shit!" as he saw Elaine struggling to make her way through the crowd toward him. "What the hell's she doing here?"

The train was nearly at the station now. Joe looked at it and tried to judge how soon it would be there. He wished it would hurry so that he and Dale could get on it before Elaine could reach them.

She was too close, though, and as she elbowed her way past the last of the commuters in her path, she ran up to Dale and threw her arms around his neck. He stood there, stiff and straight and unsmiling, as she said, "Oh, my God, Dale, don't go!"

"I've got to," Dale said. "I'm in the Army now, and besides—" His tone became angry and scornful. "Joe made a deal with your husband."

Elaine flinched under the words. "I'll leave him, Dale," she said. "I swear I will. I don't want to be married to him anymore. I just want you."

"You say that now, but it wouldn't be long before you'd be missing his money." Dale grimaced. "Ah, the hell with it! Give it up, Elaine. It's not going to happen."

His voice softened slightly. "It doesn't really matter now what either one of us might want."

She was crying now and, to Joe's amazement, he thought they were genuine tears. She really didn't want Dale to leave. She started kissing him, pressing her lips to his mouth and saying between kisses, "I'll do anything . . . anything . . ."

The train shuddered to a stop and the doors of the cars opened. Dale took hold of Elaine's shoulders and gently but firmly moved her back away from him. "I have to go," he said.

"No!" she wailed.

Joe glanced at Adam and Catherine. They looked as uncomfortable as he felt. Leaving would have been bad enough without this embarrassing scene.

Besides, Mason might still have his private detectives watching Elaine. Joe didn't want them reporting back to Mason about how she had thrown herself at Dale one last time.

Joe put a hand on Dale's arm and said, "Let's go," but as Dale started to turn away, Elaine clutched at him desperately.

"Isn't there anything I can say or do to make you stay?" she pleaded.

Dale's jaw was taut. "I've already had your best, baby," he said coldly. "It wasn't good enough."

Elaine looked like he had slapped her. Her face went pale, and her hands fell away from him. "What?" she whispered.

"You heard me." Dale inclined his head toward the nearest car of the train and said to Joe, "Come on. Let's blow this joint."

Joe grabbed his suitcase and followed Dale toward the train. He waved at Adam and Catherine and called, "So long! I'll write!"

"You'd better," Adam called after him. He had an arm around Catherine's shoulders, and Catherine was crying again. A few feet away, Elaine stood stock-still on the platform, her face like stone.

Joe and Dale crowded through the door into the car and found seats. As they settled down into them, Joe said, "Tough guy. George Raft couldn't have done it any better. 'Let's blow this joint.' "

Dale laughed hollowly. "Hey, after some of the dialogue you've written in those pulp stories, you shouldn't be talking."

"I guess you're right." Joe was sitting by the window, and he scanned the platform, looking for Adam and Catherine. He couldn't see them any longer. There were too many people. . . .

The train began to move.

"Well," Joe said, "we're on our way."

Dale pressed the balls of his hands to his eyes. In a muffled voice, he said, "Do me a favor."

"What?"

"Get struck speechless for once, okay?"

Joe started to get mad, but then he realized that his brother was right. Sometimes it was better to just sit back and shut up.

TWENTY-SIX

The only forts Joe was familiar with were the ones he'd seen in the movies and read about in Western stories, and they were all old-fashioned stockades made out of upright logs with the top ends sharpened.

Fort Sheridan didn't look a thing like that.

Instead, the place where Joe and Dale got off the bus with all the other recruits and draftees who had come from the train station was simply a collection of fairly ugly wood and cinder-block buildings behind a tall wire fence. A pair of sergeants was waiting to usher the group through the gate in the fence. One of them barked, "Atten-*hut!*" and the men who had straggled off the bus and still, by and large, thought of themselves as civilians, tried to stand at attention and form into orderly ranks. It was a pretty awkward effort, and Joe didn't like the glares that the sergeants sent their way.

The two noncoms moved among the new arrivals, snapping, "Straighten that back!" and "Feet together!" and "Pull those shoulders back!" By the time they reached the rear of the group, the ranks looked a little better. One of the sergeants returned to the front of the assembled newcomers, while the other one stayed behind them. That made Joe a little nervous.

"I'm Staff Sergeant Markham," the noncom in front of them announced in a loud voice. "Staff Sergeant Robeson and I have the responsibility of getting you men properly inducted into the United States Army. You may believe that you are already members of the Army because you signed some papers and recited an oath. But I am telling you here and now that you are *not* members of the Army until *we* are through with you! Is that clear?"

A ragged chorus of "Yes, sir!" came from the recruits.

Staff Sergeant Markham leaned toward them. "What did you say?"

"Yes, sir!" The answer came more clearly and at a higher volume this time.

Staff Sergeant Markham still wasn't satisfied. "What!" he bellowed.

"*Yes, sir!*" Joe felt a little foolish shouting like that, but he did it anyway.

"Very good," Markham said. He turned on his heel, more sharply and precisely than it seemed a human being could turn. "Follow me!"

If they were supposed to stay in step, they did a poor job of it. Joe tried, but his feet just didn't seem to want to do what he told them to do. Awkwardly, with a definite hitch in his gait, he marched with the other recruits into a large building. They entered a room with open cubicles along the walls. Toward the rear of the room, several men in white coats were waiting, each of them holding a clipboard with papers on it.

From behind them, Staff Sergeant Robeson called, "Fall out and get undressed, then form a line in the center of the room!"

One of the recruits said anxiously, "Undressed? You mean like down to our shorts, Sarge?"

Robeson was in front of him almost immediately, shouting, "Don't call me Sarge! My rank is staff sergeant! And I mean get buck naked, mister!"

Joe and Dale looked at each other, and Dale rolled his eyes. Joe hoped neither of the noncoms saw that and, thankfully, they didn't seem to. Stripping down to the buff was probably only the first of the indignities they would be subjected to today, Joe told himself.

He went into one of the cubicles, took off his clothes, and left them neatly folded on the small bench provided for that purpose. Goosebumps popped up all over him, and he started to shiver. The room was heated by several large radiators, but it was still late January outside and a few chilly drafts made their way around the doors and windows. Feeling uncomfortable both mentally and physically, Joe went back to the center of the room and joined the line of naked men forming there. Dale was right behind him.

A soldier with the single stripe of a private first class on the sleeve of his khaki uniform came along the line and handed each man a piece of paper with a number on it. A loop of string was attached to each piece of paper. "Put this around your neck," the PFC said over and over as he passed out the numbers.

Joe was seventeen, which made Dale eighteen. Joe supposed they would be taken in numerical order, and he was right. There were four doctors, so the recruits were examined four at a time. When Joe's turn came, he was weighed and his height was measured, then the doctor used a stethoscope to listen to his heart and lungs. The man in the white coat peered into Joe's mouth to check his teeth. His eyesight was checked next, and he was beginning to wonder why this examination couldn't have been performed with him still dressed. He found out when the doctor leaned over to closely scrutinize his genitalia. Joe felt himself flushing with embarrassment, and he felt a sense of relief when the doctor muttered, "Short-arm inspection okay," and made a checkmark on the paperwork on his clipboard. The doctor said, "You're fit for general service, son."

"Thank you, sir."

The doctor smiled wearily and said, "Don't thank me. Now get dressed and report to Room Two for psychiatric screening."

There were four doors at the end of the room, each of them marked with a number. Joe went back to the cubicle where he had left his clothes, pulled them on hurriedly, and started toward Room Two. He wasn't sure what the psychiatric screening would involve, but he was confident it wouldn't be as bad as the physical exam. At the very least, it wouldn't be as cold.

Room Two was spartanly furnished with a desk and two chairs. The man sitting behind the desk was thin and had two small silver bars on the collar points of his uniform shirt. His eyebrows were bushy tufts that stuck out comically. Joe kept a carefully neutral expression on his face.

"I'm Captain Bessemer," the officer said. "Shut the door and sit down."

"Yes, sir." Joe wasn't sure if he was supposed to salute or not. He didn't, and Captain Bessemer didn't seem to mind.

The captain looked at the papers on his desk. "Name?" Joe told him, and Bessemer wrote it down. "Do you know the purpose of this screening, Parker?"

"To make sure that I'm mentally sound and fit to serve in the Army, sir?"

"Indeed. My job is to weed out any neuropsychiatric undesirables. Do you think you're an NP, Parker?"

"An NP, sir?"

"Neuropsychiatric," Bessemer said impatiently. "I just explained that."

"Sorry, sir. No, sir, I don't think I'm an NP."

"Have you ever been sick?"

"Physically, you mean?"

Bessemer nodded.

"Well," Joe said, "just the usual stuff. I had chicken pox and measles when I was a kid, and an occasional case of the grippe."

"But you wouldn't describe yourself as sickly?"

"No, sir."

"How do you feel now? Are you nervous about being here?"

Joe wondered if that was a trick question. Who wouldn't be nervous under these circumstances? He said, "I'm okay, sir. Maybe a little nervous."

"About what?"

"Everything is so different."

"Think you'll have trouble adjusting to Army life, do you?"

Joe sensed a trap. If Captain Bessemer decided he was an NP and disqualified him, he would have to go back to Chicago. As firmly as possible, he said, "No, sir, I don't. I believe I'll do just fine in the Army, sir."

Bessemer grunted, scribbled something on the form in front of him, and then looked up at Joe. "Have you ever had deviant sexual feelings for another man?"

"What?" Joe couldn't stop the exclamation. "No, of course not."

"Never?"

Joe shook his head. "No, sir. I'm not a pervert."

Bessemer wrote on the paper again, then put it inside a manila folder and pushed the folder across the desk toward Joe. "Take this down the hall to Room Nine."

Joe stood up and took the folder. "Yes, sir. Thank you." He supposed he had passed the screening.

Bessemer didn't say anything else, just waved him out of the room. As Joe emerged, Dale came out of the next room, also carrying a folder. His screening had gone a little more quickly than Joe's had.

"You pass?" Dale asked.

Joe nodded. "Yeah. I guess I'm not crazy."

"No, but that captain who talked to me was. He wanted to know if I was some sort of faggot." Dale shook his head. "As if he couldn't tell by looking that I'm a hundred percent, red-blooded male."

Joe jerked a thumb toward the hallway at the back of the room. "Come on. Let's find Room Nine."

That turned out to be a larger room with several desks behind a wooden railing. Joe and Dale waited in a short line to be admitted through the gate in the railing. Each of them went in turn to one of the desks. The officer at the desk where Joe sat down introduced himself as Lieutenant Gibson.

"I'll take your fingerprints," the lieutenant said as he nudged an ink pad toward Joe. Joe inked one finger at a time and pressed it on the card that Gibson placed in front of him. When he was done, Gibson handed him a rag to wipe his fingers. That got some of the ink off, but not all of it.

"This is your preassignment interview," Gibson went on, after blowing on the fingerprint card to dry the ink and then placing it in the folder with the rest of Joe's documents. "What do you think you might like to do in the Army, Parker?"

The question took Joe by surprise. "I haven't really thought about it, sir," he said honestly. "I didn't realize that I'd be given a choice."

"Well, we can't guarantee that you'll be given whatever assignment you request, but if you have any special talents, we'd be foolish to waste them, wouldn't we?"

I can write stories about cowboys and detectives and spacemen, Joe thought, but he didn't suppose the Army had a special pulp-writer brigade. However, he did possess one talent related to that.

"I can type," he said.

Gibson made a note. "How fast?"

"Sixty words a minute." When a story was really rolling along, that was true.

"Accurately?"

"Yes, sir." Paper cost money, which meant he was limited to how much he could rewrite. He had learned to get it right the first time as much as possible.

"How are you with arithmetic?"

"Pretty good, sir. I usually made A's in school in my math courses."

"College man, are you?"

"Yes, sir. I'm a junior—I was a junior—at the University of Chicago."

Gibson frowned slightly. "According to your records you're twenty-two years old. But you were only a junior?"

"Yes, sir." Joe told himself not to be ashamed of that fact. "I could only attend college part-time because I was working to support my family, too."

Gibson nodded. "I see. Well, it sounds to me like the

Quartermaster Corps would be the perfect place for you, Parker. How does that strike you?"

"Fine, sir." Joe wasn't exactly sure what the Quartermaster Corps did, but he knew it had something to do with supplies. That meant that when the United States got into the war—he was no longer thinking in terms of "if"—he would probably be stationed somewhere in the rear, rather than in the front lines. The less he was shot at, the better, as far as he was concerned.

Gibson made a final note on the paperwork, then added Joe's folder to a stack already on his desk. "Report to Sergeant Markham and Sergeant Robeson on the parade ground," he said. He pointed toward a door at the rear of the room.

Joe stood up. "Yes, sir." He thought he ought to at least attempt a salute, since he had evidently passed all the tests he would have to pass. He brought his arm up and touched his stiff fingers to his temple. Lieutenant Gibson looked surprised but returned the salute. Joe turned, trying to imitate the precision with which Sergeant Markham had performed the move earlier, and walked out of the room.

Dale was right behind him as they stepped outside and found themselves on a large stretch of open ground. A cold wind whipped across it, making Joe tug his jacket more tightly around him. Dale didn't seem bothered by the wind. He was grinning as he said, "That part of it went pretty good. I told the guy I wanted to be a mechanic. That's really all I'm good at."

"I told my guy I can type and do math, and he said they'd put me in the Quartermaster Corps."

"Sounds good to me," Dale said. "The Quartermaster Corps and the Motor Pool must work pretty closely together. Got to have trucks to carry all those supplies."

That made sense to Joe, too. He found himself wondering if it was possible that he and Dale might not even have to go overseas.

The newcomers were forming into ranks again. Sergeants Markham and Robeson stood in front of them, hands behind their backs, seeming to not feel the chilly wind at all. Joe kept getting colder and colder as he waited, and when the group was finally assembled again and Sergeant Markham told them to raise their hands for the oath, Joe's teeth were chattering so badly that he could hardly get the words out. Taking the oath again seemed redundant to him, but he was already starting to learn that the Army had its own way of doing things.

Markham shouted, "I will now read the Fifty-eighth Article of War, covering desertion, and the Sixty-first Article of War, covering absence without leave. Listen up!" He read the two sections from a small book he held up in front of him, and as Joe listened to the penalties for the infractions covered by those articles, he realized that he had placed himself in the hands of something entirely different from the society he had always known. The Army had its own rules, and it enforced them strictly. A mistake here had consequences far beyond what might occur in the civilian world.

When Sergeant Markham was finished reading the articles, Sergeant Robeson said, "Now you will report to the company clerk's office and be issued your life insurance policy in the amount of ten thousand dollars. Following that, you will be assigned to barracks for the night. Tomorrow you will depart by train for the reception centers to which you will be assigned." He paused, then asked, "Any questions?"

The recruits had better not get used to that, Joe thought. From here on out, they would be given orders, not asked if they had questions.

"When do we get our uniforms?"

"At the reception center."

"And our rifles?"

Robeson smiled thinly. "Soon enough," he said. "Move out!"

As they began marching, Dale said from the corner of his mouth, "Ten thousand bucks life insurance. We're worth a hell of a lot more dead than we ever were alive."

"Let's just hope Mom and Pop never collect," Joe said.

TWENTY-SEVEN

The barracks to which Joe and Dale and their fellow inductees were assigned at Fort Sheridan was yet another of the drafty cinder-block buildings. The long main room had upper and lower bunks along each wall. The men were not assigned to specific bunks, since they would only be here one night, but were allowed to claim whichever ones they wanted.

"I call the upper," Dale said as he came to one of the pairs of bunks.

"You can have it," Joe told him as he sat down on the edge of the lower bunk. It had a bare mattress and a bare, thin pillow, with a folded blanket and sheet at the foot of the bunk.

Dale pulled himself up to the upper bunk and stretched out on it. His feet hung a short distance over the end. "I wonder when chow is," he said as he took out a cigarette.

A young man sat down on the bottom bunk next to Joe's. He looked around the room, his eyes wide behind thick glasses. His gaze settled on Joe. He must have heard them talking, because he asked, "Are you guys buddies?"

"Brothers," Joe replied. He put out his hand. "I'm Joe Parker. That's my brother Dale up there."

"Reuben Gilworth." He shook hands with Joe. "From Milwaukee."

"We're both from Chicago."

"You're not far from home, then."

Joe looked around the barracks. "Might as well be a million miles," he said.

Reuben smiled faintly. "Yeah, I know what you mean. You get drafted?"

"No, we enlisted."

Reuben's wide eyes widened even more. "Enlisted? Why?"

From the top bunk, Dale said curtly, "Seemed like the thing to do at the time."

"Oh. I didn't mean any offense. It's just that I was drafted."

"What'd you do before that?" Joe asked.

"I worked in a pharmacy. You know, making deliveries, helping out, soda jerking. I thought I might go to school and be a pharmacist someday."

"With that experience, maybe they'll make you a medic," Joe said.

Reuben nodded. "Yeah, that'd be nice, I guess." He looked down at his pudgy body. "I don't suppose I'd ever make much of a fighter."

"You never know."

Sergeant Markham appeared in the door of the barracks. "Fall in for chow in twenty minutes! All bunks must be made up neatly before then."

Joe stood up and reached for his sheet and blanket. "I guess we'd better get started."

Dale let out a groan and said, "I was just getting comfortable."

"Don't get used to it," Joe advised him dryly.

★   ★   ★

Catherine felt Adam's eyes on her as she came along the sidewalk toward him. She had asked him to meet her downtown today, and they were supposed to rendezvous in front of Marshall Field's. Adam wasn't the only one watching her, of course. She knew she looked trim and attractive in her long, dark coat and the rakish hat perched on her blond hair. She was accustomed to admiring glances from the men she passed.

She wondered how she would look in navy whites.

As she came up to Adam, he put his hands on her upper

arms and leaned over to kiss her. "You look beautiful,"
he told her.

"Thank you."

"What's up? Why did you ask me to meet you here?"

"I thought we'd go shopping."

"Shopping for what?"

"You'll see." She linked her arm with his and turned
toward the busy entrance of the huge department store.
"Come on."

She led him inside. Even though the Christmas rush
had been over for several weeks, the store was still
crowded. They made their way to the furniture department, and Catherine paused in front of a set made up of
a comfortable-looking sofa and two armchairs.

"That's what I want in the living room," she said.

"You mean at your parents' house?" Adam asked.

"No, silly. In our house."

Adam frowned in confusion. "Our house? We don't
have a house."

"We will someday, after the war, and when we do,
we'll have to furnish it. These things take some planning,
you know. Furniture doesn't spring into existence by
magic."

"No," Adam said slowly, "I guess it doesn't."

"Come on." She tugged lightly on his arm. "I want to
go look at the beds."

They crossed the sales floor to a large display of beds,
and Catherine stopped in front of one with a white satin
cover on the mattress. The bed itself was pine, only lightly
stained, and had a sturdy look to its arched headboard and
the two posts that rose at the foot.

"That's it," Catherine declared. "Don't you think so,
Adam?"

"It's a fine bed," he said guardedly.

She knew he was watching her out of the corner of his
eye as if she had gone mad, and she felt the warmth of
tears in her own eyes. She blinked them back. She wasn't
done yet, and she wanted to finish.

"That dressing table would go with it, and that chest over there," she said, pointing. "Now, we have to think about the nursery, because I'm sure we're going to conceive a lot of children in that bed." She couldn't stop herself from giggling.

"For God's sake, Catherine," Adam said in a half-whisper. "Are you drunk?"

"Of course not. I'm your wife, Adam, and wives have to think about these things. . . ."

This time she couldn't stop the tears. They began to roll, scalding hot, down her cheeks.

Adam took her arm. "Let's get out of here." He started leading her toward the exit, his grip firm enough so that she couldn't pull away from him. Catherine couldn't stop crying now, and she was sorry that she was making a scene and embarrassing him. She hadn't meant for it to happen this way.

A few minutes later, he settled her in a booth in a coffee shop a couple of blocks from Marshall Field's and sat down opposite her. He pulled some paper napkins from the dispenser on the table and handed them to her. "Wipe your eyes," he said, not unkindly. Catherine could tell from the expression on his face that he was torn between anger at her behavior and concern for her. "What was that all about?"

"I'm sorry, Adam," she said as she wiped away some of the tears. She knew she was ruining her makeup, but at the moment she didn't really care. "I didn't mean for that to happen. I truly didn't."

"Why did we go in there?"

"I thought . . . I just thought it would be nice to . . . to dream for a few minutes about how things are going to be after the war. . . ."

A waitress came up to the table and asked, "What can I get you folks?"

Adam glanced up. "Coffee for both of us. That's all."

"Okeydokey. Be right back."

Adam turned his attention back to Catherine. "That was

a nice idea, I guess. I'm sorry it upset you so."

"Don't you ever think about how things would be if there wasn't a war?" she asked.

"Sure I do. I think about it a lot." Adam hesitated, then went on, "But even if there wasn't a war, there'd still be your father. He's the real reason we've kept our marriage a secret, isn't it?"

"I suppose so . . ."

The waitress came back with cups, saucers, and the coffee pot. She filled the cups, then said, "There you go."

"Thank you," Adam said.

"Anything else? We got some nice pies today."

"No, that's all."

"Suit yourself, honey. Just lemme know when you want that java warmed up."

When the waitress was gone again, Adam leaned closer to Catherine and said, "Look, we have to just take things as they come right now. Dreaming about the future is okay, but we don't have any way of knowing how it's all going to turn out."

She reached across the table and caught hold of his hand. "I know we'll be together," she said. "I know that with all my heart."

His fingers tightened on hers. "Yeah. You're right about that."

She took a deep breath, knowing that she couldn't hold the news inside her any longer. "I hope we'll be together during the war, too, at least part of the time."

Adam looked doubtful. "I don't think the Marines would let me come back here to Chicago—"

"You don't understand, Adam. I'm going where you're going. I've joined the Naval Nurse Corps."

His hand clenched painfully on hers. "What?"

"Wherever they send the Marines, they'll have nurses in the rear to take care of the men who are wounded. That's where I'll be. You won't be wounded, of course, but I'm sure you can get passes to visit me."

With his free hand, he pushed the untouched coffee

cups aside so that he could lean even closer to her. "Are you crazy?" he said. "You can't enlist!"

"Why not? I'm old enough, and the Nurse Corps needs women with medical training. I'm in premed at the university, and I grew up as a doctor's daughter, for goodness' sake. I've been around medicine my whole life, Adam."

He was still thunderstruck. "But you can't . . . you just can't . . ."

"It's already done, sweetheart. I enlisted this morning."

He slumped back against the padded seat of the booth. "I can't believe this. I never wanted you to do anything like this."

"I know you didn't. But I couldn't bear to be parted from you. Wherever the Marines send you, I won't be far behind. I swear it."

Adam shook his head. "Your father's going to have a stroke."

"He'll be upset," she said. "That's why I want you to come with me when I tell my parents about it."

Adam's head jerked up. "You want me to—I don't know, Catherine."

"You're my husband," she pointed out.

"Yeah, but having me there might just make your father even angrier. He's going to think this is all my fault, you know. He thinks I'm a bad influence on you."

She managed to smile. "Well, you are, you know. I can think of quite a few times when you've been a very, very bad influence on me, and I've loved every minute of it."

He put his hands flat on the table and blew out a breath. "All right," he said. "I *am* your husband, even though they don't know that, and I ought to be with you when you tell your folks."

"You're not going to try to talk me out of enlisting?"

"It's too late for that, isn't it? You said you'd already signed up."

"I might be able to get out of it."

He laughed humorlessly. "I don't know much about the

Marines yet, but I know that once you've signed your name and sworn the oath in any service, you don't get out until your time is up. No, I'm afraid you're a swabbie now, or whatever they call lady sailors."

"All right, then. Let's go tell my parents."

Adam dropped a quarter on the table to pay for the coffee they hadn't drunk, then muttered as he stood up, "I wish they'd already issued me a rifle."

TWENTY-EIGHT

They went into the Tancred house through the front door.
"I'm not going to sneak in," Catherine insisted. "This is
too important for that, and besides, I'm tired of it. We
haven't done anything wrong."

Adam wasn't so sure about that, but he didn't argue
with her. Now that Catherine had gotten over the crying
jag that had overtaken her in Marshall Field's, she was
cool and collected and very focused on what she wanted
to do. Adam didn't want to do anything to upset her again.

Inside, he was anything but calm. The news that Catherine had enlisted in the Naval Nurse Corps had staggered
him emotionally. The one anchor he'd been able to hold
onto in the storm that had swept over his life was the idea
that no matter what happened, Catherine would be safe
here in Chicago with her family. Now there was no way
of knowing where she would be sent, and although he
hoped the female reservists, especially the nurses, would
be kept far away from any combat zones, he still felt
uneasy. Catherine was gambling that they would be stationed somewhere close to each other, but there was no
way of knowing that, either. They might wind up on opposite sides of the world.

Of course, that had been true when it was only him
who was going off to serve . . .

In the foyer, he helped Catherine off with her coat, then
she took it and his overcoat and hung them up in a small
closet. She shut the door and then reached for his hand.
"Come on," she said. She led him toward the parlor.
Adam heard music playing, the low, melodious sound of
some classical composition.

As they walked into the parlor, Adam saw that the music was coming from a huge Philco radio placed against the wall opposite the fireplace. Dr. Gerald Tancred was sitting in an armchair, his legs crossed, a newspaper held up in front of him. Mrs. Tancred was on the divan, reading a book. Adam didn't see Spencer anywhere.

Dr. Tancred glanced over the top of his paper, then looked again as he realized that his daughter was not alone. Slowly, he lowered the newspaper. "Catherine," he said. "I heard you come in, but I didn't realize you had . . . company."

Tancred said the word as if it tasted bad in his mouth, and Adam felt a surge of dislike for the man. He knew the feeling was mutual, and although he wished it was otherwise, some things just couldn't be helped.

"Hello, darling," Mrs. Tancred said from the divan. She looked at Adam. "It's good to see you again, Adam."

"Thank you," he said. "It's nice to see you again, too, ma'am." He turned his attention back to Tancred. "Good evening, Doctor."

"Good evening," Tancred said coolly. His newspaper was now folded in his lap, but he hadn't set it aside.

This meeting wasn't going to go any better than the few occasions in the past when he had visited the Tancred house, Adam sensed. Catherine's mother was always polite to him, but while Dr. Tancred was unfailingly civil, his disdain and outright dislike for Adam were never far beneath the surface of his words and expressions.

Mrs. Tancred came to her feet. "Please, sit down. I'll get us some tea."

"No, Mother," Catherine said. "Thank you, but Adam and I have something to tell you."

When she didn't go on, an awkward silence settled over the room for a long moment, broken only by the music of the string quartet coming from the radio. Then, as Mrs. Tancred's hand lifted slowly to her mouth, she said, "Oh, my God. You're going to have a baby."

"No!" Catherine and Adam exclaimed at the same time.

"Of course not," Catherine hurried on. "It's not that at all, Mother. You . . . you shouldn't even think such a thing."

Mrs. Tancred closed her eyes and sighed in relief. "Thank God."

Adam knew she didn't mean that to be as insulting as it sounded. He also knew that a certain degree of luck was involved in the fact that Catherine *wasn't* pregnant. They had taken precautions, of course, but accidents happened.

Still, the plan was to keep the marriage a secret at least until they had gotten over the hurdle of Catherine's enlistment in the Naval Nurse Corps, so Adam was glad they had gotten the subject of babies out of the way.

From his chair, Dr. Tancred asked, "If it's not that, what is it?"

Catherine looked at Adam. They hadn't discussed who was going to go first, so he decided he might as well take the bull by the horns, thinking at the same time what an apt analogy that was where Dr. Tancred was concerned.

"As you may know, sir, I've joined the Marines," Adam said.

Tancred nodded. "Admirable of you," he said grudgingly. "When do you ship out, or whatever they call it?"

"In just a few days. I'll be taking the train to Parris Island, South Carolina, for my basic training."

"Good luck to you." Tancred was no doubt thinking that South Carolina was a long way from Chicago and was glad that so much distance would soon separate his daughter and Adam Bergman.

"Thank you, sir. I want to do my part to help put a stop to some of the things that are going on."

Tancred sniffed. "Then you believe, do you, that it is the responsibility of this country to take care of the rest of the world?"

Catherine shot him a warning glance, but Adam ignored it. The last thing Adam wanted this evening was to get into an argument with Tancred over isolation versus intervention. However, he couldn't let the doctor's question pass without a response.

"I think if we can help make things better, we should," he said. "As a physician, isn't that part of your creed, too?"

" 'First, do no harm'," Tancred quoted. "I believe it will do this nation great harm for it to become involved in unnecessary overseas adventures."

"Daddy," Catherine said, "I've enlisted, too. In the Navy."

That simple statement made everyone in the room stare at her, including Adam. He couldn't believe she had been so blunt about it. He had assumed they would ease into the subject and work their way up to the fact of her enlistment. But instead, with her customary directness, Catherine had laid the whole thing out in front of them.

While a shocked silence gripped the room, Spencer strolled into the parlor, whistling. He headed toward the Philco, saying, *Gangbusters* will be on in about five minutes—" Then he stopped, realizing that he had walked into a tense situation. He looked at the strained expressions on the faces of his parents, Catherine, and Adam, then said, "Hey, what's going on here? Sis, you're not knocked up, are you?"

"Spencer!" The exclamation came jointly from Catherine and both her mother and father.

He held up his hands, palms out. "Hey, I was just asking."

"Spencer, leave the room," Dr. Tancred said tightly.

Spencer gestured toward the Philco. "But *Gangbusters*—"

"Now!"

Elenore Tancred put a hand on her son's arm. "Perhaps it would be better if you went to your room. Please."

"Okay, okay." Spencer rolled his eyes. "Geez, you'd think you were all about to fight a war in here."

When Spencer had left the parlor, Dr. Tancred set his newspaper on the small table beside his chair and stood up. Facing Adam, he said, "I would ask you to leave my wife and daughter and me alone, Mr. Bergman."

"I'm not going anywhere," Adam said stubbornly. "Not as long as Catherine is here."

"This is a family matter."

And I'm family now, "Papa." I'm your son-in-law, whether you know it or not.

Catherine touched his shoulder. "Let me talk to them, Adam. It'll be all right."

He looked at her with a skeptical frown. "Are you sure?"

Catherine nodded and said, "Of course. I'll explain everything. Why don't you go down the hall to the billiard room?"

He asked himself what the hell he had been thinking when he got involved with a girl whose family even *had* a billiard room in their house. But he knew that Catherine was probably right. She knew better than he did how to handle her parents.

"Down the hall?" he asked.

"Yes. It's the second door on the right."

"Well . . . okay." He glanced at the angry features of Dr. Tancred and the pale, drawn face of Mrs. Tancred. "If you're sure."

"I'm sure." Catherine came up on her toes and brushed a kiss across his lips. Adam didn't know if it was a good idea or not to remind Tancred that Catherine was in love with him. But the kiss was warm and sweet anyway, and he enjoyed it.

"Billiard room," he said as he turned toward the parlor door.

He eased the door shut behind him, then took a deep breath and walked down the hall. He found the billiard room with no trouble and stepped inside. What he thought of as a pool table covered with green felt sat in the center of the room, beneath a hanging chandelier. A small bar sat to one side. He thought about fixing himself a drink, but mentally nixed the idea. That wouldn't help matters.

He'd left the door open part of the way, and from it came a whispered, "Pssst!" Adam looked in that direction and saw Spencer Tancred slipping quietly into the room.

"I thought you went upstairs," Adam said.

"Do I look like I'm nine years old?" Spencer asked. "I'm grown up now. They can't send me to my room anymore."

Adam shrugged. He really didn't mind the company. He didn't know Spencer all that well, but the boy had come with Catherine several times to baseball games in which Adam had played. Spencer tapped him lightly on the arm now and said, "How's the ol' slugger?"

"I've given it up," Adam said. "Unless the Marines have a team, I don't suppose I'll be playing ball for a while."

"Boy, that's something, enlisting like that. I wish I could."

"You want to be a Marine?" Somehow, that surprised Adam.

"Sure. Or the Army or the Navy would be okay, too. Anywhere I could join so I could go fight that crazy little Kraut, Hitler."

"You're too young to be fighting anybody," Adam told him.

"I'm just four or five years younger than you. I bet plenty of guys my age will wind up in the war."

"You sound pretty sure it's going to come to war."

"Don't you listen to Edward R. Murrow on the radio? The Nazis are bombing the hell out of London. They've gobbled up France and Poland and all the little countries in Europe, and that Mussolini guy in Italy is in his Uncle Adolf's pocket. Hell, yes, there's going to be a war, and we'd better fight it pretty soon, while we've still got a chance of winning. Otherwise it's going to be too late."

Adam chuckled. "FDR could use you writing his fire-side chats."

"You really think so?" Spencer asked with a broad grin. He changed the subject by continuing, "Say, I'm sorry for that crack about Catherine being knocked up. I didn't mean anything by it. I just figured the two of you must've been . . . you know . . ."

"Your sister's a lady," Adam said coldly.

"Sure, sure. And me being her brother, I'm supposed to be the one who defends her honor against cracks like that. I'm ashamed of myself, I really am. I didn't mean to be a wisenheimer."

"Just don't let it happen again."

Spencer shook his head. "It won't. But what *was* all the ruckus about in there?"

Adam didn't see that it would do any harm to tell him. "Catherine has joined the Naval Nurse Corps."

Spencer looked just as shocked as his parents had been at that news, but a pleased grin quickly replaced the expression of surprise. "Really?"

"Really."

"That's great! Does that mean Catherine gets to fight the Nazis, too?"

"She's going to be a nurse," Adam explained. "She won't be fighting anybody, just patching up the guys who get wounded."

"Maybe she'll be stationed close to where you are. Say, I'll bet that was the whole idea, wasn't it?"

Before Adam could answer, Catherine came into the billiard room. Her eyes were a little red and puffy from crying, but she was smiling. "Well, I wouldn't say that they *understand*," she said, "but they've accepted my decision to enlist."

"Pop didn't try to talk you out of it?" Spencer asked.

"Oh, he tried to talk me out of it, all right. But I convinced him that even if it hadn't already been too late to do anything about it, I wasn't going to change my mind." Catherine shook her head. "I just wish it hadn't hurt Mother so badly. She feels like I'm abandoning her."

"Hey, I'm still here," Spencer said.

Catherine ignored him and turned to Adam. "Let's go get something to eat. I want to get out of here."

"I don't know if that's a good idea," Adam said slowly.

"Since you've enlisted and all, you'll have to leave your parents soon enough. Maybe you should spend time with them as much as you can."

Catherine shook her head. "No, I want to be with you."

Spencer said, "If you're going out for a burger or something, I could use one. Meals here are too fancy, and a guy doesn't get enough to eat."

Catherine looked from her brother to Adam. "I don't know...."

Adam suddenly felt generous, and while Spencer could be annoying at times, he genuinely liked the kid. "Sure, come on," he said. Besides, if Catherine was determined not to use the time she had left before reporting to be with her parents, she could at least spend some of it with her brother. Adam was an only child, but he knew the importance of family. That was one reason he had enlisted.

"This is gonna be great," Spencer said. "Lemme get my coat." He hurried out of the room.

Catherine said, "Are you sure about this?"

"Sure. I like your brother."

"He's a hotheaded loudmouth."

"You can say that about him. He's *your* brother."

"And I'm going to miss him," Catherine said. "I'm going to miss all of them...."

Adam saw the wistful look in her eyes and drew her into an embrace. As he hugged her, he thought about how right she was. No matter how much she might fight with her parents—especially her father—Catherine still loved them. Being separated from them would be difficult, and it would be even more so under the uncertain conditions.

"It'll be all right," Adam promised as he stroked her thick blond hair.

"You promise?"

"I promise. By the way, I'm still a little peeved at you myself for going off and enlisting like that."

She lifted her head. "Is that so?"

"Yeah." He kissed her. "But I have to admit ... if I can see you sometimes, maybe it'll all be worth it."

"It will be," Catherine whispered. "Whatever it takes to keep us together is worth it."

He was kissing her again a few seconds later when Spencer came back into the room, laughed, and said, "Come on, you two, break it up. There, that sounded more brotherly, didn't it?"

TWENTY-NINE

The Army recruits were up early the next morning, early enough so that Dale grumbled considerably during the march over to the chow hall for breakfast. In their civilian clothes, they still didn't look much like soldiers, Joe thought. Maybe once they were issued uniforms, things would be different.

Breakfast was coffee, scrambled eggs, sausage, and pancakes. The food was bland but actually not too bad. After they had eaten, they marched back to the barracks, where they stripped the bunks and cleaned up the place for the next batch of brand-new soldiers who would be housed there overnight. Then they assembled once more on the parade ground as buses began to pull in through the main gate of the fort.

Sergeant Markham and Sergeant Robeson were still in charge of the group. Once they had everyone standing at attention, they went along the ranks handing each man a manila envelope with his name typed on it. "These are your orders," Robeson said. "You will board those buses and return to Union Station in Chicago, where you will board trains bound for the reception center at Camp Wolters, Texas."

Joe and Dale looked at each other, and Dale mouthed the word *Texas?* Joe knew that he had given considerable thought to where they might be sent, and he assumed that Dale had, as well. But for some reason the idea that they might be going to Texas had never crossed his mind.

"Hope the Injuns don't get us," Dale said from the corner of his mouth.

"Shh," Joe hissed back. Then he winced as he saw Sergeant Markham striding toward them. He had hoped that neither of the noncoms would notice them talking.

"Parker!" Markham said in a voice that was just under a shout. "You have a problem with going to Texas?"

"No, sir," Joe said. "Not at all, sir."

"I let you dumb-ass recruits get away with it yesterday, but don't call me sir, you idiot! Sirs are officers!" Markham jabbed himself in the chest with a blunt thumb. "Sergeants *work* for a living!"

"Yes, Sergeant Markham!"

"That's better. Now, I'll ask you again: you have a problem with going to Texas?"

"No, Sergeant Markham!"

The sergeant swung sharply toward Dale. "What about you, Parker?"

"No, Sergeant Markham! No problem at all, Sergeant Markham!"

"That's what I like to hear. Now get on those buses! Move out!"

The men broke ranks and headed for the buses. As they climbed aboard, Dale said, "That was a close one. If he'd had time, I'll bet Markham would have had us running laps or doing push-ups or something."

"You'd better learn to keep your mouth shut while you're in formation," Joe warned him.

"What, now you're bucking to be an officer?"

"Just sit down," Joe said. "We've got a long trip in front of us."

"Yeah, I guess so." Dale sat down in one of the seats, and Joe sat beside him. Dale reached for his cigarettes and went on, "Still, Texas? Couldn't they have found a civilized place to send us?"

"They don't have wild Indians down there anymore. That's just in the movies."

"What about cactus? Do they have cactus?"

Joe shrugged. "I don't know. But I guess we'll find out."

The bus was loaded now. It lurched into motion as a

buzz of conversation filled it. The recruits were excited to
be on the move. Some of them were pretty quiet, though.
Joe glanced across the aisle and saw Reuben Gilworth
sitting and staring pensively out the window. Reuben was
about as reluctant a soldier as anybody could ever want
to see, Joe reflected. If the Army could make a warrior
out of somebody like Reuben, then Joe might turn out to
be the next Sergeant York.

Joe gave a little shake of his head as he caught himself
thinking that. He hadn't joined the Army for glory, even
if he had been foolish enough to think that war was in
any way glorious. Other guys might have that notion, but
anything that involved a chance of being shot at didn't
seem all that appealing to Joe. He was here because of
what Dale had done, and because it was probably inevitable that they would both wind up in the service, one
way or another. But the idea of being some sort of
hero . . .

That was bull, Joe thought. Pure bull.

★   ★   ★

Having grown up in Chicago, riding trains was nothing
new for either Joe or Dale, but once they had left the city
behind and were rolling southward through Illinois, the
experience was largely a fresh one. They had taken the
train to visit relatives once in Iowa, when Joe was seven
and Dale was five, but that was the last long train trip
they had taken. Joe barely remembered it, and Dale
couldn't recall anything at all about it.

This was a troop train, filled with hundreds of young
men who had either volunteered or been drafted into the
Army. The cars were noisy and crowded. Joe had used
one of his few spare dimes to pick up an issue of *The
Shadow* at the train station newsstand before they left Chicago, but it was hard to read with such commotion going
on around him. He tried to concentrate on the story—"The
Green Terror," it was called—but he couldn't get inter-

ested in Lamont Cranston's exploits this time. He finally gave up and stuck the magazine in his bag.

Dale was sitting by the window, smoking as he watched the countryside roll past. "Are there mountains in Texas?" he asked idly.

"I don't know. Probably. But there might not be in the part we're going to." Joe dug out his orders and looked at them more closely. "This Camp Wolters is close to a town called Mineral Wells. I think I've heard of it. Some sort of health spa or something."

"Well, we're going there for our health, I guess. Say, you think it's one of those places where rich guys pay to sit around in mineral baths with good-looking dames in bathing suits?"

"I'm sure that's what the Army will have us doing," Joe said dryly.

"You never know."

A kid came through the cars selling sandwiches, apples, candy, and cigarettes from a rolling cart. Dale bought another pack of Luckies and Joe bought an apple. He ate it slowly. From the looks of things, the Army wasn't going to feed them again until they got to Texas, so he would have to make the money he had last until then.

That evening they ate sandwiches in the club car. Reuben Gilworth looked so miserable that Joe invited him to join them. Reuben accepted gratefully. As night closed down over the Midwest, the train continued rolling south toward Texas.

The trip took two days and a night, which were passed sitting up uncomfortably and snatching what little sleep they could, and stretched through Omaha, Wichita, Oklahoma City, Fort Worth, and finally Mineral Wells. It was early evening when the train reached Camp Wolters on the eastern edge of the town. Mineral Wells didn't look like a very big place, but there was one skyscraper downtown that rose eight or ten stories. To the north was a good-sized hill—more of a rocky, heavily wooded bluff, Joe thought—and stretching eastward from it and forming the northern edge of the army camp was a range of smaller hills. The camp was spread out between U.S. Highway 180 and those hills.

Dale still had the window seat. As the train slowed, Joe peered past him and saw tents almost everywhere he looked. Any place where there weren't tents, new-looking buildings of raw wood had sprung up. The camp had been here before the country started mobilizing for a possible war, so Joe was sure there were some older buildings, but he couldn't spot them in the twilight. The frantic new construction had obscured everything else.

"How long do you think we'll be here?" Dale asked.

"I have no idea. The sergeant back at Fort Sheridan made it sound like they'd send us on somewhere else from here."

"Can't be too soon to suit me," Dale muttered. "This place is really out in the sticks."

Joe didn't think Camp Wolters and Mineral Wells looked that bad, but he could understand why Dale would feel that way. Dale liked the night life, and that was something probably in short supply around here. But they were in the Army and weren't going to be going anywhere at night anyway except their barracks. Dale needed to get that idea through his head.

The train came to a stop next to a depot that looked less than six months old. At least a dozen noncommissioned officers in khaki uniforms and dark brown campaign hats were waiting on the platform. They stepped forward as one and began entering the cars. The door at the rear of the car where Joe and Dale were riding banged open, and a voice like a gravel road bellowed, "Off the train now! Move, move, move!"

Joe and Dale had already started to stand up. They grabbed their bags and joined the throng of recruits trying to disembark hurriedly from the train. They began to stack up in the bottleneck formed by the door, and the red-faced sergeant became even more livid.

"Get onto that platform! Now! Move it, you shitheads!"

Joe managed to squeeze through the press at the door with Dale right behind him. They stumbled onto the platform. Another noncom shouted, "Form up! Form up!"

Their limited experience in forming ranks at Fort Sheridan helped a little, Joe supposed. In a few minutes, the depot platform was packed with irregular lines of recruits. The sergeants stalked back and forth, trying to straighten the ranks. Harsh white light washed down from the bare lightbulbs suspended from the roof over the platform.

Joe was surprised by how warm it was. Having left Chicago in midwinter, he was used to the cold and hadn't really thought about the fact that the climate might be different in Texas. The early evening air was probably close to sixty degrees, he thought.

An officer with silver eagles on the collar of his jacket and a crossed sabers insignia on the stiff-brimmed cap he wore strolled along the platform facing the assembled recruits as one of the sergeants called, "Ten-*hut*!" Joe thought the eagles meant the man was a colonel, but he wasn't sure about that. A few minutes later, the officer confirmed that guess by saying in a loud voice, "Welcome to Camp Wolters. I'm Colonel Stockbridge. This is an Army Reception Center. Most of you men will spend only a few days here and will then be sent on to other installations for your basic training. Good luck to you all."

The sergeants saluted, and the recruits tried sloppily to follow suit. The colonel returned the salute, then nodded curtly and turned to walk into the depot building. A noncom shouted, "You will proceed immediately to the infirmary! Right face! Forraaaaard . . . *harch*!"

The men marched off the platform to the right, even though none of them had any idea where the infirmary was. They must have been going in the proper direction, however, because the sergeants didn't correct them, Joe noticed. He glanced over and saw Reuben Gilworth awkwardly trying to keep in step, without much success. He wondered if his own efforts to do it right looked as feeble and futile.

Somehow the recruits reached the large infirmary building, which was constructed of raw wood like most of the buildings in the camp. They filed inside. The lights were just as harsh as the ones at the depot. They reflected glaringly from the tile floors and the ugly green walls. In response to shouted orders from the sergeants, the men lined up again, and then one of the noncoms surprised them by bellowing, "Lower your trousers for short-arm inspection!"

Dale suppressed a groan. "Again?" he muttered, so quietly that only Joe could hear him. "We just got here!"

"I guess they want to know starting out who's got the clap," Joe hissed back. With a sigh, he reached for his belt buckle.

This had to be one of the most disconcerting feelings in the world, he thought as he stood there with his trousers and underwear down around his ankles, alongside several hundred men in the same circumstances. They stood at attention, shirttails flapping over bare buttocks, as several medical corpsmen moved along the lines and conducted the examinations. Joe kept his eyes carefully level and focused straight ahead.

When the inspection was finally over and the men were allowed to hitch up their pants again, a white-coated doctor stood in front of them and said, "I'm Captain Wallace. It's my job to get through to you knuckleheads and pussyhounds that we don't have a problem with venereal disease here at Camp Wolters, and we're not *going* to have a problem with venereal disease. Do I make myself clear?"

The recruits had already learned during their brief time in the army to shout, "Yes, sir!"

Wallace, unlike some officers, was evidently satisfied with their first response, because he didn't make them repeat it even louder. He went on, "You all know the dangers of consorting with loose women: syphilis, gonorrhea, crabs, et cetera, et cetera. Not to mention all the problems that can arise from frequenting the places where you might find those loose women. We have an excellent Military Police force here at Camp Wolters, and you don't want to have any run-ins with them, I assure you. So keep your nose clean while you're here, and chances are your pecker will stay clean, too. That's all."

The sergeants marched the newcomers to the mess hall for supper, then to barracks that were arranged in long rows along the main road through the middle of the camp. As late in the day as it was, uniforms would not be issued until the next day. The fact that they were still dressed in civilian clothing might have made some of the men feel like they were still civilians, but the sergeants quickly disabused them of that notion. These leather-lunged non-coms put Sergeants Markham and Robeson back at Fort Sheridan to shame, Joe thought. He had never heard any-one yell quite so much or quite so loudly.

His ears would just have to get used to it, he told him-self, because for now and for the foreseeable future, the Army was his home.

THIRTY

The door of the barracks slammed open what seemed like only a few minutes after Joe had stretched out on his bunk and gone to sleep. "Get up, get up, get up!" someone shouted. "On your feet, you pussies!" Eye-stinging light flooded the room as the overhead bulbs were switched on.

Joe tried not to groan as he sat up and then stumbled to his feet, wearing only his undershirt and shorts. The wood floor next to the bunk was cold. All through the barracks, the recruits were pulling themselves upright, many of them muttering and grumbling. Next to Joe, Dale ran his fingers through his tangled blond hair and yawned mightily.

A beefy master sergeant with close-cropped sandy hair under his campaign hat strode down the aisle between the rows of bunks. "I am Sergeant Bogard!" he shouted. "Not Bogart! The first one of you shitheads who makes some crack about movie stars will be whistling out the new asshole I rip for you! Remember my name—Sergeant Bogard! What's my name?"

"Sergeant Bogard!" The shouted reply didn't sound too bad for men who had just been rousted out of bed in the middle of the night, Joe thought.

"You will not be here long, but I promise you, if you cross me the time you spend here at Camp Wolters will seem like an eternity! Reveille and roll call will be in ten minutes! I want these bunks made, the barracks policed, and all of you fully dressed and in formation outside when reveille sounds! Do you understand me?"

"Yes, Sergeant Bogard!"

"Then move it!"

Bogard turned on his heel and stalked out of the barracks. Instantly, the place was controlled chaos as men scrambled to make their bunks and clean up around them, then pull on their clothes and hurry outside.

Joe and Dale made it with about a minute to spare. Joe looked around as the rest of the group came straggling out of the barracks. The sky was faintly gray to the east, but he figured it would be at least an hour before the sun was up. He had worked at early morning jobs before, so he had a pretty good idea of such things.

Everyone snapped to attention as the martial strains of "Reveille" blared tinnily from loudspeakers atop poles set along the street lined by barracks. Sergeant Bogard stepped in front of the formation, a clipboard in his hand, and began calling out names from the list on it. Up and down the street, the scene was repeated in front of each barracks building.

When Bogard came to Joe and Dale, he shouted, "Parker, Dale!"

"Here!" Dale answered.

"Parker, Joseph!"

"Here!"

Bogard looked up from his clipboard. "Are you two related?" The question was the first sign of true humanity he had displayed so far, Joe thought.

"We're brothers, Sergeant Bogard," he said.

"Good," Bogard snapped. "I was afraid for a minute you might be married."

No one in the formation laughed, but as Joe glanced around he could see several men grinning as they tried not to laugh. Bogard moved on, and Joe was glad of that. His face was already warm with embarrassment.

"Chow is in five minutes," Bogard told them when he was finished calling the roll. Everyone on his list had answered. "Left face! Forraaard *harch*!"

They marched to the mess hall, which was already noisy with conversation and the rattle of cutlery. After they had gone through the serving line and carried their trays over to one of the tables, Dale stared at his food and said, "What is this?"

"Powdered eggs and toast would be my guess," Joe said. He poked at a couple of blackened strips of some sort of meat next to the toast. "And bacon, I think."

Dale sighed. "The cuisine leaves something to be desired."

Reuben Gilworth put his tray on the table next to Joe's. "Is it okay if I sit here?" he asked.

"Sure. Help yourself, Reuben."

"Thanks." Reuben sat down, looked at the food on his plate, and sighed.

Dale said, "I'm with you, buddy. Wherever we're going, I hope they feed us better there."

A voice spoke sharply behind him. "Don't like the food, Private?"

That was the first time either of them had been addressed by their rank, Joe thought. Both of them were buck privates, as low in the Army as anyone could possibly go. And if they got in trouble right off, they might not ever progress any higher.

Dale glanced back over his shoulder at Sergeant Bogard. "It's fine, Sergeant," he said.

Sergeant Bogard leaned over and said in a quiet but menacing tone, "You'd think it was a damn feast if you'd been squatting in the mud in a trench for the past two weeks with a goddamn Boche bombardment pounding the hell out of you the whole time. Wouldn't you?"

Joe wondered if Bogard was speaking from experience. The sergeant was old enough to have been part of the American Expeditionary Force during the World War. He certainly sounded as if he knew what he was talking about.

Dale swallowed hard, then said again, "The food's fine, Sergeant. I don't have any complaints."

Bogard's teeth drew back from his lips in an angry grimace. "I say it's a goddamn feast."

Dale looked him in the eye and said distinctly, "It's a goddamn feast."

For a second, Joe saw a glitter of amusement in the sergeant's eyes. Then Bogard nodded curtly and said, "That's better. Now get yourself on the outside of that chow, Private."

Dale dug in, trying to show some enthusiasm. Joe and Reuben followed suit, but it wasn't easy. The eggs and toast were cold, and the bacon was almost charcoal. With an effort, they got the food down.

When breakfast was over, the men marched to one of the other large new buildings in the camp. A short flight of wooden steps led up to the door. They formed a long line and filed inside. The first stop was a room containing a pair of barber chairs. Army barbers in olive-drab uniforms were waiting with clippers in hand. Two at a time, the recruits were shorn of their locks.

When Dale stepped out of the chair, he ran a hand over his now extremely close-cropped hair and grimaced. "I hope I look better than you," he said to Joe, who was just standing up from the other chair. Joe figured his appearance hadn't changed all that much, since he kept his hair cut short to start with.

"Both of you look like Tyrone Power!" Sergeant Bogard said from the doorway. They hadn't seen him come in. "Move it! You still have uniforms to draw."

Joe and Dale went through a door into a much larger room where the recruits were lining up to receive their uniforms and equipment from the quartermaster. Smoking was allowed, but talking was not. Sergeants stalked up and down the line to enforce that rule.

Joe and Dale had to wait thirty minutes before they reached the long counter where the uniforms were being issued. A soldier with two stripes on the sleeves of his shirt—that would make him a corporal, Joe decided—thrust a bundle of khaki clothing across the counter and into his arms. That was followed by another bundle of socks and underwear, a zipped-up shaving kit, a hat, and finally a folded duffel bag. The stack was so tall that Joe could barely see over it.

The corporal said, "Stow your gear in your bag and then go through there to be fitted for boots and shoes." He pointed to a door.

Beside Joe, Dale asked the corporal who had issued his uniforms, "How do I know this stuff all fits?"

The corporals behind the counter who had heard the question all looked at each other and began to cackle with laughter. Dale flushed and said, "All right, all right, I get the message." He stepped back from the counter and looked at Joe. "Gimme a hand with this stuff."

They helped each other pack their uniforms and gear in the duffel bags, then followed the line through the door into the other room. When their turn came, they stepped up to where several pairs of large footprints were painted on the floor. The footprints were marked off inside to indicate the various shoe sizes.

A pair of technical sergeants were running this part of the operation. One of them told Joe, "Set that bag aside and take your shoes off, son." When Joe had done so, the sergeant pointed to a pair of metal buckets sitting on the floor next to the painted footprints. "Now pick those up and stand on the prints."

Joe didn't understand the purpose of the buckets, which were filled with sand. He picked them up, grunting with the effort to lift them. They were even heavier than they looked. He stepped onto the footprints.

"In case you're wondering," the sergeant said, "those buckets approximate the weight of the field pack you'll be carrying, Private. Carrying that much weight can change a man's shoe size."

Joe felt the muscles in his arms trembling with the effort of holding the buckets as the sergeant made a note of the size indicated by the footprints. How in the world did the Army expect to load them down with this much weight and then have them march and fight? Joe wondered.

"Okay, put the buckets down," the sergeant said. He turned to the metal shelves behind him and took down a pair of shoes and a pair of boots. "Here you go, one pair of shoes, one pair of boots. Take good care of them and they'll take care of your feet."

Joe took the shoes and boots and tucked them under his arm, then picked up his duffel bag and joined the men leaving the quartermaster's depot and heading back to the barracks. Dale caught up with him before he got there.

Sergeant Bogard was waiting at the barracks. "There are empty boxes on your bunks," he said. "Get your uniform on and pack all your personal belongings in the boxes. They'll be shipped back to your families."

"Yes, sir," Joe said, then caught his slip and added hurriedly, "I mean, yes, Sergeant Bogard."

"That's better." Bogard jerked a thumb over his shoulder at the door. "Get moving."

Joe and Dale went inside and began getting into their uniforms, stripping all the way down and pulling on the olive-drab underwear. The letters "GI" were stenciled on the items of clothing. "What's that mean?" Dale asked.

"Government Issue, I think." Joe held up a pair of odd-looking pants. "How do you get these on?"

"They're leggings. You have to wrap that bottom part around your calves."

"Since when did you become a fashion expert?"

Dale grinned. "I know all sorts of interesting things."

"Yeah, I'll bet you do," Joe muttered. *Like how to get your ass in a sling so bad that both of us wind up in the Army*.

Joe struggled into the uniform, including the hat and the shoes. By the time he and Dale were dressed, most of the other men assigned to this barracks had come in and were pulling on their uniforms. The last few recruits straggled in under their loads of clothing and gear, and they had to dress quickly because Sergeant Bogard was ready to usher them on to the next item on the day's agenda.

They were beginning to look more like soldiers now,

Joe thought as the group marched over to a large auditorium. The uniforms made a lot of difference. The hats, though, still made them look a little like a troop of Boy Scouts.

Colonel Stockbridge was waiting for them in the auditorium. When everyone was seated, he stood at a lectern and said, "I will now read the Articles of War."

The recruits had already heard the Fifty-eighth and Sixty-first Articles of War, covering desertion and absence without leave, but they discovered now that there were a great many other provisions to the code that covered military behavior. They sat and listened as the colonel read from a small book in a droning voice. At first, Joe tried to pay attention and memorize at least the subject of each article, but he soon gave up the effort. They would probably be required to memorize the articles, he thought, but not from listening to Stockbridge read them. He expected they would each be issued one of those books.

When the colonel was finished, the recruits were taken to another building divided into rooms that reminded Joe of university classrooms. There were long tables with chairs and a desk and a lectern at the front of each room. Approximately a hundred men fit into each room. When they were all seated, an officer came to the lectern and announced, "I'm Major Tomlinson. You will now be given the Army General Classification Test. The AGCT consists of one hundred and fifty multiple-choice questions covering your general knowledge. You will have forty minutes to complete the test, and you will receive one point for each correct answer. The results of this test will classify each of you in one of five possible categories. Class One will consist of the men who score at least one hundred and thirty points on the test. Class Two will include those who score between one hundred ten and one hundred twenty-nine, Class Three between ninety and one-hundred nine, and so forth and so on. The tests will now be passed out."

Corporals moved along the tables handing out test pa-

pers and pencils. Other than the uniforms, Joe thought he
might as well have been back at the University of Chicago.

When everyone had a test, Major Tomlinson called,
"Begin."

Joe picked up his pencil and went to work. The first
questions were easy—"What tool would be most appropriate for installing or removing a screw? A. Hammer. B.
Screwdriver. C. File. D. Crowbar."—but they became
somewhat harder as he went on. There were questions
covering history, biology, religion, politics, electrical theory, chemistry, economics, mechanical engineering, and
an assortment of other subjects. Joe felt like he knew most
of the correct answers, but when he glanced over at Dale,
he saw a worried frown on his brother's face. School had
always been difficult for Dale, and he had never done well
on tests, even when he knew the material.

Joe completed the test in plenty of time and went back
over it, checking his answers. Dale worked on until the
forty minutes were nearly up. He finally set his pencil
aside with a sigh, and less than a minute later, Major
Tomlinson called, "Time!" The corporals moved along the
tables, gathering up the tests and pencils.

"The results of these tests will be evaluated, and this
afternoon each of you will speak to a classification spe-
cialist, said discussion to be pursuant to the Index and
Specifications for Occupational Specialists, Army Publication AR Six-one-five-dash-twenty."

"What does that mean?" Dale asked when they were
back outside and on their way to lunch. The issuing of
uniforms and the AGCT had taken all morning.

"They're going to try to figure out what to do with us,"
Joe said.

Lunch was better than breakfast. The slices of ham and
piles of mashed potatoes and creamed corn were all rec-
ognizable as what they were supposed to be. When the
recruits were finished, they were taken to yet another
building, where they were given shots immunizing them

against smallpox, tetanus, and typhoid. From there they went to a building divided into smaller rooms. They went in individually, each man finding himself sitting across a desk from an officer in one of the rooms.

"I'm Lieutenant Bedford," the officer interviewing Joe said after he had returned Joe's salute. "Have a seat, private."

"Thank you, sir." Joe sat stiffly with his hat balanced on his knees. He didn't know if that was the proper way or not, but he thought it seemed respectful enough.

"Tell me about yourself, Parker. From Chicago, aren't you?"

"Yes, sir. Born and raised there."

"And a college man, too, I see."

"Yes, sir. The University of Chicago." Joe hesitated, then added, "I was the first one in my family to go to college."

"I'm sure your parents were very proud of you."

Ma was. Pop was too busy resenting me. He kept that to himself.

Bedford went on, "What were you studying?"

"I was an English major, sir. I hope to be a professor someday." *Or a famous novelist.*

"What about your work experience?"

"A little bit of everything, sir." Joe recited the list of jobs he'd held, from selling newspapers as a boy to clerking in Mr. Grissom's hardware store. He hesitated again, then said, "And I write stories, too."

Bedford had been listening with only polite attention, but he looked up with interest at that. "What do you mean, you write stories?"

"For magazines, sir."

"What sort of stories?"

"Mysteries, Westerns, science fiction, adventure, a little horror or weird menace every now and then . . . Anything I think I can sell."

"Oh. You write for the pulp magazines."

Joe had heard that disappointed tone before, usually

from his professors. That was why he had pretty much stopped telling any of his teachers about his writing. He said, "Yes, sir."

"Good at it, are you?"

"I've sold about fifty stories."

Bedford made a notation on the paperwork in front of him. "So you can type?"

"Yes, sir. Pretty well, in fact."

Bedford nodded. "All right, Parker, I think I have all I need. Report back to your barracks."

Joe stood up and said, "Yes, sir," then saluted.

Bedford returned the salute. "Dismissed."

I may be just a pulp writer, Joe thought as he left the building, *but I'm already learning how to be a pretty damned good saluter!*

★   ★   ★

"I told the guy I want to be a mechanic," Dale said that evening as he lay stretched out on his bunk with his hands folded behind his head. "Think they'll pay any attention to me?"

"I hope so," Joe said. "I still think they'll look at my typing skills and make me a clerk. I could work for the quartermaster and pass out uniforms."

Dale blew smoke toward the barracks ceiling. "Oh, yeah, that'd be exciting."

"I'm not here for excitement," Joe said.

"Me neither."

Joe wasn't sure Dale meant that, however. Deep down, a part of Dale probably still thought that he was just playing soldier. He might be eager for adventure.

Dale looked over at Reuben, who had taken the next bunk. "What'd you tell 'em, Reuben?"

Reuben looked a bit surprised to be asked. "I said that I used to work in a pharmacy and that I knew a little about drugs and medicine. I think they might make me a medic. That would be nice."

"Yeah," Joe agreed. He couldn't imagine Reuben Gilworth going into combat. The only less likely hero he could think of was himself.

The lights were turned off at a quarter of ten. That was all right with Joe. He was tired after getting up so early that morning. He slept soundly and, as far as he could remember, dreamlessly until just before six o'clock the next morning, when Sergeant Bogard once again barged into the barracks and announced his presence at the top of his lungs.

After breakfast, the recruits went back to the building where they had been interviewed by the classification specialists. This time, when they went into the rooms, they were greeted by different officers. A gray-haired major shook Joe's hand and passed a large envelope across the desk. "Here are your orders, soldier. Good luck."

"Thank you, sir." Joe was burning with curiosity, but the major didn't seem to want him to stand there and rip open the envelope, so he saluted instead and left the office.

Outside the building, the men were gathering to check their orders and compare assignments. Joe looked around for Dale but didn't see him, or Reuben, for that matter. With his heart pounding and his mouth dry, he slid a finger under the envelope's flap and pried it up. He took out a thick sheaf of mimeographed sheets of paper. He started reading, trying to make sense out of the lengthy military forms.

A few minutes later, a hand came down on his shoulder. "They made me a mechanic, just like I hoped," Dale said happily. "I'm going to some place called Camp Bowie here in Texas. What do your orders say, Joe?"

Joe looked up, a baffled expression on his face. "I'm going to Camp Bowie, too."

"That's great!" Suddenly, Dale frowned as he noticed Joe's expression. "What's wrong?"

"I've been assigned to the Signal Corps. I'm going to be a radioman."

"What? You've never done anything with a radio except turn one on and off!"

Joe nodded. "I know. All that stuff I told 'em about writing stories and how I can type . . . they didn't pay any attention to any of it!"

"Yeah, I guess that's the Army for you," Dale said with a shrug. "But at least we're going to the same camp. I'm glad about that."

"Yeah, me, too."

"You'll see, it'll be fine." Dale was in the unusual position of trying to cheer up his brother, and he was clearly uncomfortable with it. "Come on, let's go back to the barracks. Our train doesn't leave until tomorrow. Maybe we can get some extra sack time."

"Sure," Joe said. "Wait a minute, there's Reuben." He waved over the little recruit from Milwaukee. "What're your orders, Reuben?"

Reuben's eyes were wider than usual behind the thick glasses. "The infantry," he said hollowly. "I'm going to be in the infantry."

Well, Joe thought, there were worse things than being a radioman.

THIRTY-ONE

This was the moment Catherine had been dreading. She had never been good at saying good-bye—and she had never had to say good-bye to someone as precious to her as Adam, either.

She had come down to Union Station with him and his mother. Ruth Bergman was friendly enough toward her, but there was some unavoidable resentment in the older woman's eyes whenever she glanced toward Catherine. As far as Ruth knew, Catherine was just her son's girlfriend. A moment of farewell such as this should have been shared only with those closest to Adam.

This certainly wasn't the time or the place to tell Ruth that she and Adam actually were married, Catherine decided.

It was a raw, blustery day, but the wind just gave them a handy excuse for having red faces. Catherine tried to hold back the tears as Adam hugged her. The platform was full of young men and women embracing each other; the train that was pulled up on the tracks was bound for Charleston, South Carolina. From there, the hundreds of Marine recruits it carried would board buses for the rest of the trip to Parris Island.

"It'll be all right," Adam whispered into Catherine's ear. "I love you."

"I love you, too," she said as she held on to him. Desperation built inside her. This was not going to go well.

"I'll get a furlough when I finish basic training. I'll come see you then."

"I won't be here," she reminded him. Her own enlistment in the Naval Nurse Corps was due to begin in a week. She had no way of knowing where she might be in three months, when Adam's stint at Parris Island would be over.

"Wherever you are, I'll come there," he said.

She didn't want him to make promises that he might not be able to keep, because he would feel bad if he was unable to follow through on them. "We'll see each other again when we're meant to see each other," she said. She leaned up and kissed him, knowing that his mother was watching, but not caring.

Adam held her so tightly she couldn't breathe. She didn't care about that, either. She didn't need air as long as he was holding her. She didn't need anything except him.

A sharp sense of loss went through her as he let go of her and turned away. *Be reasonable*, Catherine told herself. *He has to say good-bye to his mother.*

Adam hugged Ruth and kissed her on the cheek. "You're sure you'll be all right?" he asked her.

"I have to be, don't I?" Ruth shook her head. "Don't worry about me, Adam. Just take care of yourself. You're doing a noble thing. You're going to help stop perhaps the most evil man the world has ever known." She held on to the lapels of his overcoat. "But you have to take care of yourself. You have to come back to me . . . and to Catherine."

The generosity of Ruth's words took Catherine by surprise. She was touched by them, and she reached out to rest her gloved fingertips on Ruth's shoulder for a moment.

"Don't worry, I'll be back," Adam said heartily. "Just as soon as we've knocked the stuffing out of Hitler."

Some people might have pointed out that the United States wasn't officially at war with Germany, Catherine thought, but she doubted if anyone here on the platform really believed that war wasn't coming, sooner or later. They might all hope that it would never come to that, but facts were facts: with the Lend-Lease program going into effect soon, the United States would be forever linked with England and the other Allies. Its illusion of neutrality was quickly fading.

Ruth kissed Adam on the cheek, looked into his eyes for a long moment, then stepped back beside Catherine as the conductor came along the platform shouting, "Booaarrdd! All aboard!"

Adam bent, picked up the small suitcase sitting on the platform at his feet, and raised his other hand in tentative farewell. Catherine was trembling with the need to throw herself forward into his arms, to hold on to him as tightly as she could and never let go until the world made sense again and war was nothing but a memory. Her eyes burned with the tears she was on the verge of shedding. She controlled herself, but just barely.

Adam turned and joined the throng of men getting onto the train. He looked back over his shoulder once at Catherine and his mother, and he called, "Good-bye! I'll see you soon! I love you!" The words were almost lost in the tumult of similar farewells being shouted up and down the platform.

Catherine felt Ruth's hand close over hers and squeeze tightly. She returned the pressure. "He'll be all right," she heard herself saying.

"Of course he will. He's my son."

With the other women and children being left behind, they stood there on the platform and watched until all the men were on the train and it had pulled out of the station and vanished in the distance.

Adam had traveled with the University of Chicago baseball team, but mostly throughout the Midwest. He had been to New York City once, when he was young and his father was still alive. The family had gone there to see relatives in Brooklyn. Adam had been jealous because he was an only child and all the other Bergman families seemed to have tons of kids, so that no one was ever without somebody to play with. He knew from hushed comments he had overheard, though, that for some reason his mother couldn't have any more children. He was it.

Maybe that was why he had always tried so hard to please her, he had thought more than once. If she was disappointed in him, there were no other children to make up for his failures.

He knew she wasn't disappointed in him now. She might not like the fact that he had joined the Marines, but she knew that unless the Nazis were stopped soon, her own mother and father back in Kiev would be in danger. Besides, once his draft notice had arrived, it was inevitable that he would be leaving to join one branch or another of the military services. It had been beyond his control.

He sat back and tried to enjoy the train ride, but it was difficult. The car was crowded and noisy. Most of the men were upset about leaving their homes and families and complained about it loudly. Others, who probably came from less pleasant circumstances, were excited about leaving Chicago, so it wasn't uncommon for snatches of boisterous laughter to burst out. Many of the men were young, even younger than Adam, and they were filled with a mixture of fear and anticipation that made them laugh nervously and brag about how many Nazis they were going to kill if and when they got a chance to get in on the fighting.

Adam hoped Catherine would be all right. He would have felt better about things if he had known she was going to be safe in Chicago. At the same time, he couldn't blame her for wanting to do her part and, of course, the chance that perhaps she could be closer to him and see him more often had played the largest part in her decision to enlist. He couldn't be upset about that, either.

He wondered how Joe and Dale were getting along in the Army. They had been gone for a week now and had no doubt gotten to wherever they would be stationed first.

Joe would make a good soldier, Adam thought. Joe was the serious sort who studied everything he tried to do so that he could do it well. Dale would never be like that. Adam knew that he and Dale probably never would have been friends if Dale hadn't been Joe's brother. Dale was just too irresponsible, too hotheaded and reckless and impulsive—and it was that impulsiveness that had gotten him and Joe into such a mess that they'd had to join the Army. It was easy to think that the draft would have gotten them eventually, but there was no way of knowing that for sure.

★　★　★

Adam dozed off somewhere along the way, even with all the hubbub around him.

He didn't wake up until something jolted heavily against his shoulder. He sat up straighter, blinked his eyes, and said, "What?"

"You say somethin' to me, buddy?"

The voice came from the seat beside him. The man sitting there earlier, when the train left Chicago, had been a skinny youngster who was trying without much success to grow a mustache. Now Adam saw that the seat was occupied by a much larger man who had bumped his shoulder as he was sitting down.

"What happened to the other guy?" Adam asked.

"That scrawny little gink?" The newcomer shook his head. "He got up to go to the can, so he lost his seat."

"Oh." The skinny youth had been a stranger to Adam, so he didn't feel compelled to defend his right to a seat.

The newcomer was short and fat, almost grossly so. He wore a cheap brown suit that was strained at the seams by his bulk. His face was red, and his almost colorless hair was cut very close to his round head. He turned slightly in the seat—as much as his size would allow him to turn—and offered his hand to Adam. "Ed Collins," he said.

Adam shook hands. Collins's grip was strong. "Adam Bergman."

Collins looked surprised. "Jewish fella, are you?"

"Yeah, that's right," Adam said, instantly and instinctively wary. "Why do you ask?"

"It's just that you don't look much like a Jew. You look more like a reg'lar fella."

Adam's jaw clenched. He wanted to get angry—and yet, Collins hadn't sounded like he was trying to provoke any sort of angry reaction. On the contrary, he seemed as if he were just trying to make friendly conversation to make the trip pass faster.

When Adam didn't say anything, Collins pressed on, not even seeming to notice the way Adam had tensed. "I'm gonna be a Marine," he said. "That where you're headed, Parris Island?"

"That's right."

"That's all the way down there in South Carolina, ain't it? I never been that far away from home before. Shit, I ain't hardly been off the farm." He dug an elbow into Adam's side and laughed. "Know what I mean?"

"Yeah, I suppose so," Adam said. He didn't like Collins and didn't want to encourage him to continue the conversation, but he didn't want to be rude, either, no matter how crude and ignorant his seatmate might be.

"What I'm hopin' is that they'll send us to Germany to kick Hitler's ass. I don't believe in all that Nazi shit. Master race, my hind foot. Hell, you're a Jew, and you seem like a good enough fella."

"Thanks," Adam said dryly.

Collins waved a pudgy hand. "No, I mean it. I like to judge a gent on what he does and how he acts, not on whether he's a Jew or a nigger or what have you. That's the American way." Collins reached inside his coat and took out a small brown bottle. "Hooch?" he asked, offering it to Adam.

"No thanks. It's going to be a long ride to South Carolina."

"That's the damn truth." Collins unscrewed the cap on the bottle and took a swig, then licked his lips and replaced the cap. "I just like to take a little pick-me-up now and then. Say, you think that boot camp's gonna be hard?"

"Probably," Adam said. He felt a momentary pang of sympathy for Collins. He wasn't in quite as good shape as he'd been during his days on the baseball team, but he still felt confident he could handle any physical challenge the Marines might throw his way. Collins, on the other hand, probably weighed close to two hundred fifty pounds, and he would be in for a lot of sweating and gasping for breath as the Marines tried to work that excess fat off of him. Adam was a little surprised that the Marines had even accepted Collins.

"My daddy was a Marine," Collins said. "Fought in the Great War at a place called Belleau Wood. The damn Germans gassed him, and he weren't never the same after that. I reckon that's another reason I got for wantin' to go over there and kill me some Krauts. I owe it to my daddy." Collins looked at Adam. "What about your daddy? Was he in the war?"

"No," Adam said. "He wasn't."

"Well, that don't mean nothin'. You got plenty of reason for joinin' up, just bein' a Jew. I read about that *Kristallnacht*, when the Nazis went around bustin' out all the Jews' windows and such. That's mighty sorry behavior, if you ask me. I never would bust out nobody's window, not even a Jew's."

Adam closed his eyes for a moment. It was becoming obvious that Ed Collins liked him and enjoyed talking to him. No matter how quickly the train got to South Carolina, it wasn't going to be soon enough to suit Adam.

THIRTY-TWO

The idea of locating a troop training center in Brownwood, Texas, had been suggested as early as 1923, but nothing had ever come of it until seventeen years later. In the summer of 1940, with a military draft imminent, the War Department knew that many more training facilities than were currently in existence would be needed. Representatives of the Brownwood Chamber of Commerce paid a visit to the commanding general of the Eighth Army Corps, the headquarters of which were located in San Antonio. These citizens informed the general that Brownwood, with its mild central-Texas climate and tens of thousands of acres of open, rolling land nearby, would make an excellent location for a military training center. The general agreed and passed the suggestion on to Washington, and on September 15, 1940, the Brownwood *Bulletin* informed its readers that their hometown had been selected by the War Department as the site of a National Guard Training Center.

With the prospect of war coming closer all the time, the War Department's plans for the newly named Camp Bowie rapidly expanded in terms of both money and land. The camp itself occupied an area of nearly 5000 acres, and a vast expanse of land south of Brownwood that totalled over 120,000 acres was leased by the government as a military reservation for purposes of maneuvers and training. In the process, the communities of Indian Creek, Elkins, and Jordan Springs were taken over so that they completely ceased to exist.

By the time the first phase of construction was completed, Camp Bowie boasted 8,149 buildings; 301,700 feet of water lines; 464,000 feet of gas lines; 725,000 feet of electric lines; 204,500 feet of sewer lines; and 52 miles of paved roads. It was practically a city unto itself and had sprung up seemingly overnight despite heavy rains during the fall of 1940 and an influx of construction and military personnel that had strained the resources of the small city of Brownwood almost to their limit.

Headquarters of the Eighth Corps were moved from San Antonio to Camp Bowie, and Brigadier General K. L. Berry was the first commanding officer there. The Thirty-sixth Infantry Division was formed in January 1941 and was the principal unit to occupy the camp, but there were also elements from the 113th Cavalry Division (transferred there from the Iowa National Guard), the Forty-fifth Division (originally from the Oklahoma National Guard), and the Second Division, Regular Army.

So when Joe and Dale Parker disembarked from the train that had rolled to a halt at the newly constructed Camp Bowie depot, they saw more soldiers than they had ever seen in one place before. Camp Bowie dwarfed Camp Wolters, both in personnel and sheer size.

"Fall in!" the sergeant who was waiting for them shouted. "Line up, you mullets!"

Well, that was far from the worst thing they had been called lately, Joe thought as he and Dale came to attention along with the other men from D Company. They had all been ordered to ride in the same car on the trip from Camp Wolters. Reuben was in D Company as well and stood in the row of men behind Joe and Dale, who uncomfortably found themselves in the front row.

The noncom who had taken charge of them walked along in front of the formation. "I am Master Sergeant Dent," he said, and instead of shouting, he spoke in a normal tone of voice. That sounded odd to Joe, who had already grown accustomed to being bellowed at by sergeants. "I'm the topkick of D Company. The CO is Lieutenant Page. D Company is referred to as Dog Company. Do you know why?"

Something about Sergeant Dent made Joe uneasy. Evidently the other men felt the same way, because none of them answered the question. Joe figured it was rhetorical anyway, and Dent proved him right by continuing, "You're known as Dog Company because that's what you are right now—dogs. Worthless mongrels. Cringing curs. If you had to face the enemy right now, you'd run away with your tails between your legs, wouldn't you?"

Again, no one answered.

Sergeant Dent turned and stalked back the other way. "But we'll do something about that, the lieutenant and I. We'll make fighting dogs out of you. By the time we're through with you, when you see the enemy you'll bare your teeth at him and growl at him. Let me hear you growl!"

The order took Joe by surprise. He stood there and didn't do anything, just like the other members of D Company. A glance over at Dale told Joe that his brother thought Sergeant Dent was nuts.

"I said, let . . . me . . . hear . . . you . . . *growl!*"

Someone somewhere behind Joe ventured a feeble, "Grrr."

Sergeant Dent slammed his right fist into his left palm with a loud smacking noise. "That's better. Again."

More men growled this time.

"Growl at the enemy!"

Joe felt like an idiot, but he growled. So did Dale. Sergeant Dent motioned for them to continue, and more and more men joined in until the platform sounded like a kennel. Joe wondered if the recruits in the other companies were laughing at them.

Dent said, "That's enough." When the growling had died away, he went on, "Sometimes you'll run into members of the other armed services, and they'll call you dogfaces or doggies. They'll mean it as an insult, but you don't have to take it that way. Take it as a compliment, because what they're telling you is that the Army are the only true sons of bitches in this man's military! Show 'em your fangs and bite 'em if you have to!"

This guy is a raving loon, Joe thought. *And he's going to teach us about going into combat?*

Sergeant Dent turned and said, "Follow me!" He went down the steps from the platform and started toward the rows of barracks nearby. He never looked back to see if the men of D Company were following him.

They were, of course.

The barracks was similar to the one at Camp Wolters, a long main room with bunks along both walls and quarters at the end for Sergeant Dent. Considering all the tents they had passed while marching to the barracks, Joe was glad D Company had an actual building to live in, even though it was of prefabricated construction, smelled of paint and fresh-cut lumber, and had unfinished inner walls with the studs exposed. Plenty of the trainees at Camp Bowie obviously had to live in tents.

D Company consisted of 110 men, split evenly between two barracks. Joe and Dale were together, of course, since the men were assigned bunks alphabetically. Reuben Gilworth was in the other barracks. Reuben was the best friend Joe had made so far in the Army, so he hoped Reuben would be okay. It was still possible for a recruit to be classified as a neuropsychiatric and discharged for the convenience of the Army. A black mark like that might well follow a man and make things difficult for him when he tried to return to civilian life.

When the men had stowed their gear in the barracks, the company assembled in the road in front of the newly constructed buildings. A slim officer in a khaki uniform with a single silver bar on each collar point and on his fore-and-aft cap strode up after Sergeant Dent had called the company to attention. The men all saluted, and the lieutenant returned it with a precise motion. "At ease," he said. "I'm First Lieutenant Norton Page, the commanding officer of D Company. You've already met Sergeant Dent. I want to welcome you to Camp Bowie. We're going to work hard here, very hard, but when the next thirteen weeks are up, you men will be soldiers. More than that, you'll be soldiers in Dog Company." Page smiled thinly. "No, I'm not going to make you growl. That's Sergeant Dent's way of greeting you. I just want to say that I won't ask you men to do anything that I can't or won't do myself. I intend to *lead* this company in every sense of the word." Page nodded, as if agreeing with himself, then continued, "Sergeant Dent will now give you your daily schedule."

Dent stepped up beside the lieutenant. "First call is 5:55 A.M.," he said. "Reveille and roll call, 6:05. Breakfast, 6:25. We'll be back here at the barracks by 6:45, then march to the site of that day's training at 7:20. Training will last from 8:00 A.M. until 5:30 P.M., with a break for chow at 12:30. Supper is at 6:20. Back in barracks at 7:00 for mail call, studying, housekeeping, what have you. Lights out at 9:45." Dent paused and took a deep breath, then went on, "Now, then, you know when you'll eat, shit, work, and sleep. Anything else you'll do on your own time, not the Army's time."

Joe felt like asking when exactly their own time was, but he knew to keep his mouth shut. The answer came next, anyway.

Lieutenant Page said, "There are chapel services on Sunday morning, and Sunday afternoon and evening are free time. A limited number of passes will be available so that you can leave the camp on Saturday night . . . *after* the first four weeks of your training. You will be required to do classroom work in basic military knowledge as well as in your specialization. You will practice close-order drill and participate in combat simulations. You will be taught to fire your rifle and expected to post qualifying scores on the rifle range. You will take part in grenade exercises and night maneuvers. You will run the obstacle course, and you will participate in hikes while carrying your full pack." Page paused again. "I know this sounds like a great deal of work and a great deal to learn. *It is.* But the purpose of this training is to keep you alive and give you the best possible chance of defeating your enemy."

Sergeant Dent stepped back up. "There is a post exchange, a store where you can buy whatever you might need in the way of cigarettes, sundries, prophylactics, et cetera. There is also a recreation hall where movies are sometimes shown and where you can play pool or read or purchase soft drinks. For the next four weeks, the PX and the rec hall will be your only sources of entertainment. Put them to good use."

"I believe that's all for now," the lieutenant said. "First thing in the morning, you'll be issued your rifles and other gear." He drew himself up straight and saluted, and the men of the company returned it, most of them relatively crisply. Joe saw Sergeant Dent watching them closely. He suspected that any of the recruits who were having trouble saluting properly would receive some individual instruction from the sergeant.

"Fall out," Dent called. "This evening will be your last chance to take it easy for a while. I suggest you make good use of it."

The men went back into the barracks. Dale threw himself on his bunk and fished out a cigarette. As he lit it, he said, "They're gonna keep us hoppin', aren't they?"

Joe sat down on his bunk and nodded. "It sounds like it, all right."

Dale looked at him, eyes narrowed, and said, "Are you sorry about this, Joe?"

"About what, being in the Army?"

"Yeah. I mean, you wouldn't be here if it wasn't for me and . . . well, you know why we're here."

Joe shrugged and looked down at the floor. "I don't know. I don't think about it that much."

"Yeah, but you could be back in Chicago right now,

going to school and writing your stories, if I hadn't been such a stupid bastard—"

"Look," Joe said, "we're here, and beating ourselves up over why is just a waste of time. There's no way of knowing what might have happened if things had been different. They might have been worse, we don't know." He hesitated, then tried to put into words some of the things he had been thinking. "Besides, we probably would have joined up sooner or later anyway. I don't think we would have been able to turn our backs on our duty."

"You mean somebody's got to put a stop to all the crap going on in Europe, and it might as well be us?"

"Yeah. I don't want to be a flag-waver, but—"

"Maybe you're right," Dale cut in. He took a drag on the Lucky and blew smoke toward the ceiling. "Just don't get all patriotic on me. I'd still rather be behind the wheel of a hot car right now."

Joe knew exactly what his brother meant. He was already starting to wonder if that recreation hall the sergeant had mentioned might have a typewriter in it. . . .

THIRTY-THREE

Catherine's heels clicked on the tile floor of the first-floor hallway in the university's administration building. She had registered for the spring semester's classes before the idea had come to her to join the Naval Nurse Corps, so now she was on her way to the registrar's office to officially withdraw and get back as much of the tuition as she could. Her father would never miss the money if she had to forfeit the whole amount, but she thought she might as well do things by the book. Besides, whether he'd miss it or not, forfeiting all the tuition would be one more grudge he would hold against her.

As she turned a corner, someone called from behind her, "Catherine?"

She stopped and turned, and saw a blond, handsome, athletic-looking young man in a brown double-breasted suit hurrying after her. "Hello, Ken," she said with a smile. "How are you?"

Kenneth Walker came up to her, slightly out of breath. "I'm fine," he said. "What do you hear from Adam and Joe and Dale?"

"Adam only left for Parris Island a couple of days ago," Catherine said. Keeping her tone of voice light and chatty cost her a considerable effort. "He's hardly had time to get there yet. Joe and Dale left last week, but I haven't heard from them. I'm sure they've been busy and they'll write when they have time."

Ken nodded. "I knew they had all enlisted, of course. To tell you the truth, there's a part of me that wishes I could have joined with them."

Why didn't you, then? Catherine stopped herself from

asking that question. There was no reason to be rude to Ken just because he was here and Adam wasn't.

She didn't know Ken all that well, but she knew he was a graduate student and a teaching assistant in the physics department. She forced a smile onto her face and asked, "How are things in the mad scientist department?"

Ken frowned and asked sharply, "Why? What have you heard?"

"Nothing, really. I didn't mean any offense, Ken," Catherine said quickly.

Ken shook his head and chuckled; rather insincerely, Catherine thought. "None taken, of course. Everything is fine."

"Well, that's good." The conversation had been a little awkward to start with, and now it was on the verge of becoming genuinely strained. Catherine said, "I have to get on to the registrar's office, but I'll let you know if I hear from Adam or Joe. If I'm still here."

A second later she regretted adding that last part, because Ken asked, "What do you mean?"

She sighed and said, "I'm leaving Chicago, too. I've joined the Naval Nurse Corps. I'm going to be a nurse."

"Well." Ken looked surprised. "I'm sure you'll make an excellent one, what with your premed courses and your background."

"That's what I thought. I've really got to go."

"All right. Good-bye, Catherine."

"Good-bye." She hurried on down the hall toward the registrar's office.

Catherine had already realized that Ken's startled reaction to her news was the most common one. Most people stopped short of asking why in the world she wanted to do such a thing as enlist in the military, but she knew they were thinking it. In the case of her father, the question had been asked loudly and in a great many variations, but it always came down to the same thing.

And it was totally unfair, she thought. Even if she hadn't been trying to stay close to Adam, what was wrong with a woman wanting to do her part? That was why women were allowed to join the Army and Navy as nurses, so that a mere matter of sex wouldn't stop a person from serving her country. But *some* people seemed to think that she had lost her mind. . . .

She paused in front of the door to the registrar's office and took a deep breath in order to calm down. She wasn't here to argue, just to fill out paperwork. And the reason she was withdrawing from the university wasn't anybody's business but her own.

★   ★   ★

Catherine's news had certainly taken him by surprise, Ken thought. He hoped he hadn't hurt her feelings by his reaction. But if she was going to be offended, she probably already was by the way he had acted so suspicious and defensive when she made that crack about mad scientists. Of course she hadn't meant anything by it; she was just making small talk.

Anyway, Ken had never been bothered personally by such comments. He had been called an egghead and worse ever since he had discovered the appeal of science. It was just that Dr. Fermi and the others, including the government men who hung around the labs in suits and fedoras and shoulder holsters, had made Ken very conscious of the need for security. That the work they were doing could have some very important—almost staggering—military implications somewhere along the line was obvious to anyone who had the scientific knowledge that Ken possessed. Those implications were nowhere near fruition, of course, and there was no way of being certain how long it might take to complete the work, but someday in the future, if everything went as Fermi and the others speculated that it might . . .

It was only natural to be jealous of something so momentous, Ken told himself. Catherine Tancred wasn't a Nazi spy. To believe that she might be would require a stretch of the imagination farther than anything Joe Parker had ever dreamed up in his pulp magazine stories. Still, she wasn't part of what Ken was doing, and he couldn't have brought himself to share it with her, even if security considerations had permitted such a thing.

He gave a little shake of his head and laughed at himself as he left the administration building and started walking toward Stagg Field and the laboratories underneath it. "You're reading a hell of a lot into one innocent question about mad scientists, old boy," he said aloud. Still shaking his head, he hurried on.

There appeared to be only one way on and off Parris Island, Adam realized as the bus pulled up in front of the main gate. The road went through the gate and then, a short distance farther on, crossed over a broad stretch of water on a narrow causeway. At the other end of the bridge was the low, sandy, brush-covered ground of the island itself, stretching off into the distance to the north and south. Parris Island didn't look like it would be worth much of anything to civilians.

Which made it the perfect place to train Marines, he supposed.

Adam's muscles were stiff from the two nights and three days he had spent on the train, sleeping only when he could doze off sitting up. That hadn't been easy due to the discomfort of the seats and the noisy surroundings. Then, when the train had finally reached Charleston, South Carolina, the Marine recruits had disembarked and immediately were ushered onto buses by sergeants in green uniforms and brown campaign hats. The ride from Charleston to Parris Island was only thirty-some-odd miles, but it had seemed longer than that to Adam. He was looking forward to an opportunity to stretch his legs.

The driver of the first bus, in which Adam rode, was a middle-aged Marine in green fatigues and a soft, billed cap. The driver spoke through the window beside him to the guards at the gate. The guards wore flattened, World War I–style helmets and carried rifles, Adam noted. They stepped back and waved the buses on through. With their engines grumbling, the buses rolled across the causeway and onto Parris Island itself.

They came to a stop in front of a large, red-brick building with the letters U.S.M.C. and the already familiar globe-and-anchor symbol of the Marine Corps on it. One of the sergeants who had greeted them at the train station in Charleston bounded onto the bus from somewhere and shouted, "Off the bus! Move it, move it, move it!"

From the seat beside Adam, Ed Collins observed, "These Marines surely do like to holler, don't they?"

During the trip from Chicago, Adam had learned to ignore Collins for the most part. All he had to do was grunt occasionally as if he were paying attention and Collins would talk happily for hours. Adam had even been able to sleep through part of the endless yammering.

But despite himself, he had learned some things about Collins and the life the young man had led on his family's farm. Collins was annoying as hell and probably a bigot to boot, but Adam had found himself almost liking him in spite of that. Almost. It certainly wouldn't bother Adam if they wound up in separate companies, though.

"Come on," Adam said to him now. "We'd better go."

With a grunt, Collins extricated himself from the tight confines of the bus seat and waddled into the aisle. Adam followed him. Wherever he went, no matter how crowded it was, Collins's bulk easily cleared a path. Adam had to give him credit for that ability, anyway. They stepped down from the bus, Adam carrying his small suitcase, Collins with a larger, more battered valise hanging from his hand.

As the men lined up beside the bus, the sergeant watched them with narrowed eyes, clearly not pleased by the slow, awkward way most of the recruits moved. Nor did he care for the sloppiness with which they formed a single line.

He looked at the clipboard he held in his left hand, then began stalking up and down in front of the men. In a loud, clear voice, he said, "You are the first, second, and third squads of Able Company, Second Marine Training Regiment. I am Gunnery Sergeant Tompkins, your drill instructor. You will refer to me as Drill Instructor." Tompkins stopped and faced them. "Now, you may think that you are Marines. You are not. Not by any stretch of the imagination. You are trainees who may someday turn into Marines, but you will not actually *be* Marines until another Marine looks you in the eye and says that you are. Do you understand?" Before the squads could reply, Tompkins called out, "Say, 'Aye, aye, Drill Instructor.' "

Obediently, the men shouted, "Aye, aye, Drill Instructor!"

"What was that?"

"Aye, aye, Drill Instructor!"

"That was mighty poor. Yes, sir, piss-poor. But I'll let it pass for the time being. Now, when you are given an order by me, you will say 'Aye, aye, Drill Instructor.' When you are given an order by an officer, you will say 'Aye, aye, sir.' When you speak of yourself, you will not use your name, because nobody gives a shit about your name. You are all recruits, and none of you is any better than the others. If someone asks you why you are here, you say 'This recruit is here to become a Marine.' That is now your sole purpose in life. Do you understand?"

Some of the men shouted, "Aye, aye, Drill Instructor!," while others slipped and called out, "Yes, sir!" Tompkins glared at those individuals, and Adam was glad he had remembered the correct response.

"Some of you will be cooks," Tompkins went on. "Some will drive trucks, some will draw maps. There is a job for everyone and everyone will have a job. But there is one job above all else that you will have if you are lucky enough to become Marines. Remember this saying: "Every man a rifleman." Remember that no matter what else you may be doing, your first job and your most important job as a Marine will be to fight the enemy and defeat the enemy! Do you understand?"

This time, everyone in the three squads shouted out, almost in unison, "Aye, aye, Drill Instructor!"

Tompkins didn't look pleased that they were already learning. In fact, his hard-planed face never changed expression as he ordered the men to march to their barracks and then led the way. As Adam walked along behind Collins, Collins turned his head and said quietly over his shoulder, "That sarge acts like one hard-assed son of a bitch."

Adam didn't say anything, but he thought that it wasn't an act. Gunnery Sergeant Tompkins really *was* one hard-assed son of a bitch.

THIRTY-FOUR

At first, basic training really *was* basic, Joe and Dale discovered during their first week at Camp Bowie. Simply getting the men of Dog Company up in the morning and marching in a reasonably crisp manner to the mess hall for breakfast proved to be a daunting task. Sergeant Dent was undaunted, however. In his quiet, yet clear and somehow menacing voice, he instructed the troops on the proper way of doing things. By the end of the week, all the members of the company were assembled on the road in front of the barracks each morning before "Reveille" sounded over the loudspeakers, and their marching, while still sloppy at times, showed distinct improvement.

Their mornings were spent in classrooms. The men were taught the chain of command, the general orders, how to recognize rank by insignia, and in general were familiarized with the Army way of doing things.

The afternoons were more enjoyable for Dale. The classroom work was too much like being back in school. A "boys only" school, of course, with really drab clothes, but it still seemed like school to him. In the afternoons, though, Sergeant Dent and the other noncoms assigned to the company began to teach them about waging war.

The first thing was the issuing of rifles. They lined up in front of the supply depot and went through single file, each man receiving an M1 rifle from a sergeant of the quartermaster corps. As Dale closed his hands around the smooth wooden stock of the weapon, he truly felt like a soldier for the first time. It didn't matter that the rifle was unloaded and that he had no ammunition for it, or that there was no bayonet attached to the barrel. The fact that the Army was giving him a rifle meant that they were putting some trust in him. That hadn't happened too often in Dale's life. To be fair, though, he thought, he had never wanted much trust, because responsibility usually went with it.

When everyone had been issued a rifle, the company assembled on the parade ground. Holding one of the M1s, Sergeant Dent stood in front of them and said, "This is the standard weapon of the United States Army infantry. The M1 Rifle, also known as the Garand. Look at it closely. Study it. It will save your life someday."

After the men had stared down at the rifles in their hands for several moments, Dent went on, "Remove the bolt, like so." He demonstrated, lifting the bolt and pulling it back so that it could be removed from the rifle's breech. When everyone had removed the bolts, Dent showed them how to replace them. "Now we will remove the magazine and I will show you how to load the weapon."

A voice from somewhere in the ranks behind Joe and Dale called out, "I don't have no ca'tridges, Sarge. How'm I gonna load it?"

For a long moment, Dent didn't say anything. He stood there silently and seemed to be breathing a bit harder than usual. Dale finally realized that the sergeant was trying not to explode with anger.

Dent succeeded. In a relatively normal tone of voice, he said, "I am well aware that you men have not been issued any ammunition. For the time being, we will merely *pretend.*"

The last word came out with a little hiss to it, as Dent said it between clenched teeth. Dale looked down and tried not to smile. The sergeant obviously prided himself on his ability to remain in control and not lose his temper. But at the same time, Dent clearly had a short fuse. It might be interesting, Dale thought, to get up a little pool on how many days it would be before the sarge completely blew his top.

★   ★   ★

Once they had their rifles, they began close-order drill.
Wearing ugly steel helmets just like the ones worn by
members of the American Expeditionary Force in The
Great War, they marched up and down the parade ground,
practicing their turns—"Leffft *face*! Riiight *face*! Abouuut
face!"—and learning the different cadences that were
shouted out by Sergeant Dent. Soon they were shouting
along with him, many of the words cheerfully obscene.

They practiced the manual of arms, too, for hours at a
time, learning what to do when Sergeant Dent bellowed,
"Preeesent . . . *harms*! Orderrr . . . *harms*!" and all the
other commands. After going through all the motions with
the heavy rifle, Dale's arms ached and sometimes trembled, reminding him of the reaction he'd felt after driving
in a race. That had been partly an emotional reaction,
however; this was pure fatigue.

One afternoon several days into camp, after a particularly long stretch on the drill field, Sergeant Dent said,
"Take five," then turned and walked off. He went to the
edge of the field where Lieutenant Page was standing and
watching, his arms crossed over his chest. While Dent and
Page were talking, the men of Dog Company gratefully
sank to the ground to rest for a few minutes. Many of
them pulled cigarettes from their shirt pockets and lit up.

Dale savored the smoke of a Lucky as he pulled it into
his lungs and then blew it out. He looked over at Joe, who
was sitting beside him, and said, "All this time in Texas,
and I haven't seen a wild Indian yet."

From behind them, a man said, "I reckon the Army's
savin' the Comanche raid for later in camp."

As Joe and Dale looked over their shoulders, Reuben
Gilworth said, "Hi, guys. Meet Nate and Otis. They're
buddies of mine."

Joe stood up, brushing off the seat of his pants as he
got to his feet. Dale remained sitting down, but he swiveled around so that he could see Reuben and the two

trainees who had come up with him. Both of the strangers were a little above medium height and had the same sort of rangy build. One was dark-complected, with black hair under his helmet. The other had removed his helmet, revealing bright red hair over a freckled face.

"Name's Nate Fowler," the dark one said as he shook hands with Joe. "This here's Otis Lawton."

"Pleased to meet you, gents," Otis said. Dale recognized his voice as the one that had pointed out to Sergeant Dent a couple of days earlier that they didn't have any ammunition for the Garands.

Dale reached up to shake hands with both men. Joe said, "You're Texans, aren't you?"

"Yep," Otis said. "Born, bred, and forever. Reuben tells us you boys're from Chicago." He shook his head. "Man, I'd like to see me a big city like that someday. Back where I grew up, the biggest town in those parts was Mobeetie."

"Where's that?" Joe asked.

"Up in the Panhandle. That's where Nate and me been cowboyin' for the past six, eight years."

Neither of the Texans looked like they were any older than Joe, so that meant they must have started working as cowboys when they were in their middle teens, Dale thought.

"I really like Western movies," Reuben said. "My favorite cowboy is Gene Autry. When you live on a ranch, is it really like it is in the movies?"

"Oh, sure," Otis said. "Me 'n' Nate, we always carry our guitars around on our saddles, and we don't never miss a chance to break into song, do we, Nate?"

"Nope," Nate said.

"And when we're not fightin' Injuns, we're havin' shoot-outs with rustlers and bank robbers and such like," Otis went on. "Why, I recollect once we had a run-in with the Cavendish gang. Ol' Butch Cavendish his ownself threw down on me and tried to ventilate me, but I grabbed my six-shooter and flung lead at him. That was one hell of a ruckus, let me tell you."

Eyes wide, Reuben said eagerly, "I'd like to hear more about it. I think I've heard of Butch Cavendish and his gang. The name sure sounds familiar."

Dale exchanged a glance with Joe. Joe had been a little excited at first by the idea of meeting a couple of genuine Texans, but he had wised up as Otis talked. Reuben, on the other hand, was still swallowing the guy's bullshit. Dale couldn't stand it anymore.

He came to his feet as he said, "Butch Cavendish sounds familiar to you because that was the name of the outlaw whose gang ambushed the Lone Ranger. Don't you ever listen to the radio?"

Reuben turned toward him, looking hurt and confused at the same time. "Cavendish, Cavendish," he said. "Yeah, I remember now." He swung back toward Otis. "Say, that *was* on the radio. What are you trying to do?"

Otis shrugged. "Just havin' a little fun, ace."

"Yeah, but I believed you."

"No offense, all right?"

"You think it's all right to make fun of me just because I'm . . . I'm not from around these parts?"

Joe put out a hand. "Let it go, Reuben. Otis didn't mean any harm."

"Yeah, but they were laughing at me, these two . . . drugstore cowboys!"

Nate Fowler said, "Don't go to talkin' like that, son. We ain't drugstore cowboys."

"No, but you're bullies." Reuben's hands clenched into fists. "I oughta—"

Dale reached out, put his arm around Reuben's shoulders, and turned him away from the Texans. This was going to turn into trouble unless somebody put a stop to it. "Like Joe said, Reuben, let it go. You don't want to take a swing at these hicks. That'll just get the sarge down on all of us."

"Dale's right, Reuben," Joe said.

"All right, all right," Reuben muttered as he looked

down at the ground. "It's just that I thought they were my buddies."

Joe moved over so that he was between Reuben and the Texans. "You guys take a hike," he said.

"I was just funnin'," Otis said. He looked angry now, too. "But if you Yankees want to make somethin' of it—"

Nate said, "Come on, Otis. Let's go."

Otis went, reluctantly. A moment later, Sergeant Dent returned to the drill field, and the men began getting up from their short break.

"I'm sorry," Reuben said to Joe and Dale. "I shouldn't let myself get so mad. My mama always said I was a holy terror when I got my dander up, so I try to never lose my temper."

Dale patted him on the shoulder. "Don't worry about it, Reuben. You handled yourself with those two yokels just fine."

"They're in my barracks, though. I'm afraid when I see them again, I'll just get mad all over again."

"No, you won't," Joe said. "You're too big a man for that."

Reuben sighed. "I guess so. Thanks for sticking up for me, fellas."

"What're friends for?" Joe said.

Reuben returned to his place in the formation, and when he was gone, Dale leaned over and said quietly to his brother, "Oh, I'll bet he's a holy terror, all right."

Joe was looking after Reuben, frowning slightly. "You never know," he said.

★   ★   ★

Joe was sitting on the steps in front of the barracks that evening, his rifle across his knees as he worked the bolt back and forth and studied the action. He had never handled a gun in his life until coming here to Camp Bowie. He found the sleek, dangerous look of the Garand somehow disturbing, yet he had to admit to himself that he was looking forward to firing it for the first time. In the meantime, he wanted to familiarize himself as much as possible with the weapon.

Boots crunched on the gravel walk in front of the building. Joe glanced up to see the two Texans who'd had the trouble with Reuben that afternoon. They stopped in front of him.

"You're Parker, aren't you?" Nate Fowler asked.

"That's right. Joe Parker. What do you want?"

Otis said, "Look, I really am sorry. I didn't mean to hurt the little fella's feelin's. Since you're his friend, we thought maybe you could tell him we don't want no hard feelin's between us."

"You could tell him yourself," Joe said.

Otis shook his head. "He won't listen to me. He just says I'll try to feed him another pack of lies."

"How do I know you won't?"

Nate took a small pouch out of the breast pocket of his uniform tunic, along with a small piece of paper, and began rolling a cigarette. "Look," he said, "most of these ol' boys here at the camp are from Texas, but there's a lot of you Yankees, too. Ever since the Army started sendin' you down here, we've been hearin' about what hicks and yokels we are, how backward we are. It gets a mite tiresome after a while. So when we run across somebody like your friend Reuben who's a little gullible, I guess we just like to get a little of our own back." Nate shrugged. "Trouble is, the one who's really the most innocent in the whole deal is the one who gets hurt."

Joe had a feeling it was unusual for Nate to make such a long speech. What Nate had said made sense, he supposed. He and Dale—especially Dale—had been guilty of jumping to conclusions about what things would be like in Texas. Reuben had just carried that attitude to an extreme. Besides, for all any of them in Chicago or Milwaukee knew, those Gene Autry movies *were* realistic.

"All right," he said. "I'll talk to Reuben and try to set him straight . . . on one condition."

"What's that?" Otis asked.

Joe set his rifle aside. "Tell me about Texas. What it's really like, I mean." He took a deep breath and plunged ahead. "You see, I write stories. Sometimes I write Westerns, so I don't guess it would hurt if I tried to learn as much about the real West as I can."

"Stories?" Otis repeated with a frown. "Like in magazines, you mean?"

"That's right. For what they call pulp magazines."

Otis let out a low, excited whistle. "You ever have any stories in *Texas Rangers* or *Thrilling Western*? Dang, I love those magazines!"

Joe grinned, surprised that he had found some common ground with these Texans. "As a matter of fact, I have. I even made Street and Smith's *Western Story*. Once."

"Scoot on over there." Otis sat down beside Joe, while Nate continued smoking the cigarette he had rolled. "Ever' time one of the boys'd pick up a new magazine in town, we'd pass it around the bunkhouse until it was fallin' apart. I read 'em all, *Western Story, Wild West Weekly, The Masked Rider* ... How does a fella get started writin' for them magazines, Parker?"

"You have to be pretty damned hard-headed," Joe said. "I've heard that Walt Coburn papered the walls of the shack he lived in with all the rejection slips he got."

"Walt Coburn? You know him?"

"Well ... no. I don't actually know any of the other pulp writers. I've just exchanged letters with some of the editors in New York."

"Listen," Otis went on excitedly, "I got all sorts of ideas for stories. Maybe I could tell you about 'em, and you could write 'em up."

Joe shrugged and said, "I, ah, don't think I'll have the time to be doing much writing for a while."

"Oh, yeah. We're in the Army. Well, hell. Maybe someday, right?" Otis slapped Joe on the back.

"We'll see," Joe said. Now that things were going better, he didn't want to insult Otis by saying that he didn't have any interest in collaborating, especially when it sounded as if he would still have to do all the work.

Nate said, "You'll talk to Reuben?"

"Sure," Joe said. These Texans weren't so bad after all, he decided. You just had to know how to get along with them.

"Thanks," Otis said as he stood up. "I want to talk to you some more about story-writin'."

"Any time," Joe said.

Otis and Nate strolled back toward their barracks. As they did so, the door opened behind Joe, and Dale stepped out. "Was that those two obnoxious Texans?" he asked.

"Yeah."

"What did those bastards want?"

"They're not that bad once you get to know them," Joe said. "They want me to patch things up with Reuben for them."

"Are you going to?" Dale sounded surprised.

Joe thought about it for a second, then nodded. "I reckon."

" 'I reckon'? *I reckon*? Oh, shit, it's contagious!"

The barracks door slammed behind Dale as he retreated.

THIRTY-FIVE

The Dells was one of the best roadhouses in the Chicago area. Three miles west of Evanston, its ballroom had seen performances by such artists as Ted Healy and Sophie Tucker, and the dance floor was often packed with couples swaying to the music of Guy Lombardo and His Royal Canadians or Fred Waring and the Pennsylvanians. The bartenders were virtuosos, the waiters were elegant, and the maitre d'hôtel was suitably snobbish. The prices were high, but most people considered that for dining, dancing, and a great floor show, the Dells couldn't be beat.

The high-stakes games in the private rooms off the ballroom weren't bad, either.

A cigarette dangled from the corner of Spencer Tancred's mouth as he came into the club with Jack Cronin. Spencer had thumbed his fedora to the back of his head, and his hands were jammed in his pockets, somewhat spoiling the lines of his expensive gray double-breasted suit. He and Cronin paused to check their hats, and Spencer let his eyes stray to the low-cut neckline of the girl's gown. The girl was a blonde who let her hair fall in front of one eye like that actress, Veronica Lake, and the creamy flesh of her breasts swelled nicely over the top of the gown. Spencer thought she was sexy as hell. He wondered if she would go out with him.

She wouldn't, of course, if she knew he had just turned eighteen the week before. But he looked older than that, and he had a phony Indiana driver's license in his billfold that said he was twenty-four years old, so what she didn't know wouldn't hurt her, he decided. He was about to put the make on her and try to get her number when Cronin grasped his arm and said, "Come on, Spence. I want you to meet this guy."

Jack Cronin was actually twenty-five; he didn't need a fake ID to get into places like the Dells. He was the older brother of a guy Spencer had known back east in boarding school. Spencer happened to be holding an IOU for five hundred bucks from Cronin's little brother, but he had been happy to tear it up on the condition that Cronin would get him into the hot spots and the hot games.

As it turned out, Spencer and Cronin had hit it off, despite the difference in their ages. Once Cronin had fixed Spencer up with the Indiana driver's license, they paid visits to all of Chicago's best nightspots. They became regulars in all the clubs and dance halls and roadhouses like the Dells. Sometimes it was tough getting away from the old man, who seemed determined to keep such close tabs on Spencer that he could never have any fun, but somehow he managed to get together with Jack Cronin a couple of times a week. They had been to the Dells before, and Spencer had emerged from the private gambling rooms a winner.

Now Cronin led him past the maitre d'hôtel and across the ballroom floor to a table where three men and three women, all expensively dressed, sat watching a smoky-voiced, redheaded female singer in a green gown so tight it looked as though the seams would burst if she took a deep breath. And she had nice breathing apparatus, too, Spencer thought, his eyes lingering on the thrust of breasts under green silk. He was so enthralled by the way she looked that he almost didn't notice how good she sounded singing "Careless."

"Spence, I want you to meet Mike Chastain," Cronin said as they reached the table.

Spencer tore his attention away from the redhead and focused it on the man who was offering a hand to him. As he shook the hand, Spencer said, "I'm pleased to meet you, Mr. Chastain."

"Call me Mike," Chastain said. He was in his thirties

and handsome with sleek dark hair. He nodded to his male companions. "This is Bud, and Lou."

A grin spread over Spencer's face. "Just like—"

Chastain held up a finely manicured hand and wiggled it back and forth. "Don't say it. They've heard it before, and they don't like it."

"Oh. Sorry. No offense meant."

"None taken," Chastain said. Obviously, he didn't mind speaking for his companions. Spencer noticed that he hadn't introduced the women. They were all gorgeous. One of them, a slender brunette, could have had bigger boobs as far as he was concerned, but overall she was okay, Spencer decided. He wouldn't kick any of them out of bed.

Of course, considering the fact that he had never actually had a woman *in* his bed, it was an easy judgment to make.

"Pull up a chair," Chastain invited. "Both of you."

"Thanks, Mike," Jack Cronin said. He sat down, and so did Spencer. Cronin leaned forward and went on, "I thought maybe we could get in your game tonight."

"You thought so, did you?" Chastain murmured. Spencer could barely hear him over the music from the orchestra and the redhead's singing. "Well, we'll see. Have a drink first, though." He signaled a waiter.

Without anyone asking Spencer what he wanted, a glass was placed in front of him a few moments later. He took a sip and managed not to flinch as the fiery bite of the liquor hit his mouth and throat and, ultimately, his stomach. "Good," he said.

Chastain asked, "What is it you do, Spence?"

"He works with me," Jack Cronin said quickly. Cronin worked in a brokerage firm on LaSalle Street, in the financial district.

"Is that so?"

"That's right," Spencer said. He hoped like hell that Chastain wouldn't ask him any questions about the stock market. All Spencer knew about the market was that it had crashed back in '29, triggering the Depression, and that it was finally starting to recover, thanks in large part to all the preparations for war that were going on—even if nobody wanted to come right out and say that the United States was getting ready to go to war.

Chastain just nodded and let the subject go, and Spencer was grateful for that. He had seven hundred dollars in his pocket, his winnings from the last couple of times he had been here, and he was ready to move up to a game with higher stakes, such as the one that, according to Jack Cronin, Mike Chastain hosted a couple of times a week.

The redheaded singer finished her number, bowed as the audience applauded enthusiastically, then left the bandstand and came out into the ballroom. Spencer was surprised when he realized that she was coming toward the table where he was sitting. The orchestra continued playing, this time a peppy version of "South of the Border."

Chastain stood up to meet the redhead, took her in his arms and kissed her. She rested her fingertips on his cheek. At that moment, Spencer would have paid any price in the world to change places with Chastain. He would have even considered trading his soul. God, she was beautiful!

One of the other girls had moved over, taking another chair so that the redhead could sit beside Chastain. "This is Karen Wells," Chastain said to Spencer. "Meet Spence."

Karen Wells held out a hand and smiled. "Pleased to meet you Spence. Are you a friend of Jack's?"

"Uh, yeah, that's right," Spencer said. Her hand was soft and smooth and cool.

"Welcome to our little circle."

"Thank you. I . . . I'm glad to be here."

Stop stumbling over your words, damn it! She's going to think you're some sort of idiot!

She was still smiling at him. "What did you think of my set?"

"It . . . it was great! You're really a great singer!"

"Thank you." Her eyes twinkled with amusement. Spencer hoped she wasn't laughing at him.

Chastain gestured toward the glasses on the table. "Drink up, gentlemen, and then we'll get to that game you're waiting for."

As Spencer picked up his glass, Karen Wells said to him, "You're playing in Mike's game?"

"That's right." Spencer downed the rest of the drink and held back a cough.

"Good luck."

"Thanks."

Karen Wells said, "You may need it."

★   ★   ★

Luck, Spencer realized an hour later, had nothing to do with it. Poker was a game of skill.

And at this table, he was so far out of his league that it wasn't funny.

He was down to about fifty bucks, out of the seven hundred he had brought tonight. Starting out, he had bet cautiously, but when he saw how the other men in the game played, he hadn't wanted to look like a piker. Especially not with Karen Wells watching.

The women had followed Spencer, Chastain, Cronin, and Bud and Lou into the luxuriously appointed private room, where they had found four more men waiting for the game to get underway. These players were older, middle-aged men with the look of success about them. Spencer figured them for bankers or businessmen, and wealthy ones at that.

Bud and Lou didn't play. Spencer had already figured out that they were probably Mike Chastain's bodyguards. A man like Chastain would certainly have bodyguards. The guy was probably at least a borderline mobster, Spencer thought. But he was friendly enough and didn't seem to mind Spencer being there.

Karen Wells and the other three beautiful women drifted around the room, nursing drinks and watching the game from time to time. Several times when Spencer looked up from his cards, he found the redhead watching him, and when she smiled at him he felt hollow inside all the way down to his toes.

Jack Cronin had lost, too, but not as much as Spencer. So had all but one of the other players. The other one, a man who had been introduced only as Frank, was running neck and neck with Chastain as the big winner for the evening. Spencer found himself wondering if Chastain might be setting the man up for a big loss. He and Cronin and the other players might not be anything but pawns in the real game Chastain was playing, window dressing to make everything look good.

Or maybe he had just seen too many movies. The fact that Chastain looked a little like Humphrey Bogart didn't help matters.

The betting went around the table, and Spencer felt that he had no choice except to raise. The hand he held wasn't bad—two pair, jacks over sevens—and he thought he might actually win this pot for a change. He tossed his remaining money into the center of the table. "See the forty and raise you ten," he said. That was the best he could do.

Chastain called when he could have raised—he had plenty of money left—and so did Frank. The other players dropped out. Holding his breath, Spencer laid his cards down. If he won, he would have enough of a bankroll to keep playing. If he lost, he was out of the game.

Chastain smiled. "Not bad, Spence, but not good enough." He had two pair as well, queens over tens. Spencer tried to keep his face emotionless as he realized he had been cleaned out.

Frank chuckled. "That beats my busted flush, too. You're good, Chastain." He sounded jovial enough about his loss, but his eyes were hard and cold. He didn't like losing, Spencer thought.

Spencer took a deep breath, blew it out in a sigh. "That's it," he said. "I'm done."

"No more for you?" Chastain asked.

Spencer gave a little laugh. "No money."

"Credit can be arranged."

Spencer had been on the other side of that offer most of the time, so he knew where it led. He shook his head. "No thanks."

Chastain shrugged. "Suit yourself. Feel free to have a drink and hang around if you want. Karen will be doing another set later."

That was reason enough in itself to stay at the Dells for a while. Spencer pushed his chair back and said, "Thanks." Chastain waved a hand as if to say it was nothing.

Spencer went over to the bar. Bud and Lou were standing there. Spencer wasn't quite sure which one of them was which, since unlike Abbott and Costello, they looked pretty much alike. One of them said, "Drink?"

"Yeah. Scotch. On the rocks."

The bodyguard poured the drink and handed it to Spencer. Sipping the Scotch, Spencer wandered back toward the table, where another hand was getting underway. He was intercepted before he got there, however, by the slender brunette. She linked her arm with his and said, "Come sit with me a while, why don't you?"

The gown she wore left her arms and shoulders bare, and he felt the warmth of her arm through his coat as it pressed against his. Even though she wasn't as well-endowed as the other girls, her shoulders were nice and smooth, and she had a faint dusting of freckles across her upper chest that Spencer found appealing. Her smile was nice, too, as were her green eyes.

"Sure," Spencer said. He felt a stirring in his groin. It was an unavoidable reaction, given the fact that he was eighteen years old and this close to a beautiful older woman.

She led him to an alcove with a padded bench seat

across it. Thick drapes were drawn over the window at the back of the alcove. They sat down, and Spencer grew harder at the way her hip pressed warmly against his. He hoped she wouldn't notice.

"They're real, you know," the brunette said.

"What's real?" Spencer asked, confused.

"Karen's bosoms. She doesn't use any padding." She laughed. "Neither do I, as I'm sure you already know."

Spencer flushed. "I, I didn't notice."

"The hell you didn't. You scoped the breasts of every woman in the place. Nothing wrong with that. Some men are breast men, others like legs or bottoms."

Spencer couldn't believe he was having this conversation. He had never talked to a woman who was so bold, so risqué, in her speech. He was incredibly thrilled.

"I think yours are . . . are very pretty," he said. He was equally shocked that he would say something so bold.

"My, aren't you the gallant one?" She laughed again, then said, "I'm Joscelyn. Joscelyn St. Clair."

That sounded like a made-up name to Spencer, but he didn't say so. He didn't want to offend this lovely creature who was sitting so close beside him and making his insides turn Immelmanns and barrel rolls. Instead, he introduced himself. "Spencer Tancred."

"Tancred," she said. "I know the name."

"My father's a doctor."

"Of course. I must have heard of him. Well, I'm pleased to meet you, Spencer Tancred." She inclined her head toward the ballroom. The strains of dance music could be faintly heard. "How are you at dancing, Spencer?"

"Okay, I guess."

"Why don't you show me?"

Spencer forgot all about his drink and his plans to watch the game for a while. All he could think about was how it would feel to glide around a dance floor with the exquisitely lovely Joscelyn St. Clair in his arms.

"Sure," he said as he came to his feet. He held out his hand, and Joscelyn took it.

From the poker table, Jack Cronin called, "Where are you two going?"

"Dancing," Spencer said over his shoulder.

"Have fun," Mike Chastain said. He smiled. "Take it easy on him, doll, he's only a kid."

Spencer felt a flash of annoyance and resentment. He wasn't a kid, and he would show them all that he wasn't. He turned to Joscelyn and pulled her into his arms. She looked startled, but she didn't pull away when he kissed her. In fact, after a moment the slight resistance he felt in her body faded away to be replaced by a soft, melting pressure that molded the two of them together. Her lips were hot and wet and sweet, and they opened to let her tongue slip through into Spencer's mouth.

She had to feel his hard-on poking against her belly, Spencer thought crazily, but she still didn't pull away. Clearly, she didn't mind.

Finally, when she broke the kiss, she smiled at Spencer and said, "You're wrong, Mike. This is no kid."

Chastain laughed. "All right. Have fun, you two. Come back any time, Spence."

Oh, he'd be back all right, Spencer thought as he led Joscelyn from the private room back into the ballroom. She came into his arms again, and they began to swoop around the dance floor in time to the music from the orchestra. Now that he had met Joscelyn, he was going to be around here a lot.

THIRTY-SIX

"This is the SCR300," the technical sergeant from the Signal Corps said as he lifted the two handheld units and displayed them to the members of the communications platoon from D Company. "Sometimes called a walkie-talkie. Under the right conditions, it has a range of up to twenty-five miles, but you'll find that its effective range is really more like five miles. It's an FM set—FM standing for frequency modulation, as opposed to AM, which stands for amplitude modulation—and has a manual tuner with a range of forty to forty-eight megacycles. If some of you don't understand what I'm talking about, don't worry. You will."

That was good, Joe thought, because so far the sarge might as well have been speaking Latin part of the time.

The communications platoon consisted of eight men—six Texans, a big Swede from Minnesota, and Joe. This was their first class together after a couple of weeks at Camp Bowie. Their combat training would continue under Sergeant Dent throughout the thirteen weeks, but from here on out, they would also be expected to learn everything there was to know about operating and maintaining the equipment they would be using as communications specialists.

The sergeant held up an even smaller unit. "This is the handie-talkie, the SCR536. It's an AM set, good only for short distances, but it has the advantage of being small and easily carried." He continued walking along behind the table on which the various radios were displayed. "As opposed to this baby—" Almost affectionately, he patted a much larger piece of apparatus. "The SCR284. They call it a portable, but it weighs two hundred and fifty pounds. You'll find it carried in a vehicle much more often than being toted around by some poor dogface." His voice hardened. "But you *will* learn to transport it manually, each and every one of you. As well as how to use it and how to fix it when it's fucked up. Any questions?"

Joe didn't think the sergeant would appreciate it if he asked why in the world the Army had decided to make a radioman out of him instead of assigning him to a job more suited to his talents, so he kept quiet. So did all the other members of the platoon.

"All right," the sergeant said after a moment. "We'll move on to the field telephones, which operate much like regular telephones through wires that you'll string from one position to another on the battlefield. Those wires are prone to being broken by enemy action, for example artillery bombardments, but when they're in place they provide a clearer connection between positions than the radios do."

Artillery bombardments? They expect us to be running around and stringing wire during artillery bombardments?

Joe tried not to think too much about that.

★ ★ ★

Dale straightened up from under the hood of the Dodge truck—or, as the Army called it, the truck, three-quarter ton, four-by-four, weapons carrier, Dodge—and wiped his hands on an oily rag. "There you go, Sarge," he said. "The compression ratio ought to be a lot better now."

Master Sergeant Henry Garmon frowned and said, "Sure about that, are you, Parker?"

"Yes, sir," Dale said.

"How do you know?"

"Well," Dale said, thinking of Harry Skinner, "I was taught how to work on engines by the best damned mechanic in the Midwest."

Master Sergeant Garmon nodded slowly. "Start it up."

Without lowering the hood, Dale got into the cab of the truck. The other members of his platoon looked on as he turned the key and then stepped on the starter. The motor ground noisily for a second, then caught. Dale fed it some gas and listened in satisfaction to the roar of response.

Through the truck's windshield, he saw Garmon make a slashing motion across his throat. Dale cut the engine, then dropped from the cab. "Well, what do you think, Sarge?"

"You're right, Parker, it sounds pretty good." Garmon bent over and picked up a ball peen hammer from the open toolbox on the ground, then straightened and reached under the hood to smash two heavy blows against the engine. Dale flinched, startled by what he had just seen.

Garmon tossed the hammer down. "Now, two pieces of shrapnel from an artillery shell have just hit the engine, knockin' it out. Make it sound that good again, Parker. And do it quick, because if you don't get the ammunition you're carryin' to the troops up on the line in a hurry, they're all gonna die." He leaned closer to Dale, and his lips pulled back from his teeth as he hissed, "You got that, asshole?"

Dale still felt a little stunned. He managed to say, "Yeah, Sarge, I got it." He gave a little shake of his head and peered under the truck's hood to see just how much damage Garmon had done. Almost immediately, he saw that the distributor cap was busted and a hose was torn off. It wasn't too bad, Dale thought as he reached for the toolbox.

Sergeant Garmon motioned for the other members of the platoon to watch what Dale was doing, then strode off about forty yards to the other side of the fenced motor pool lot. Another master sergeant was standing there smoking, a wry grin on his face.

"Still using the old hammer bit, eh, Hank?" he asked.

Garmon shrugged. "It takes 'em by surprise, makes 'em

realize they can't know what to expect once they get out in the field."

"Yeah, but you keep damaging trucks."

"My guys can fix 'em," Garmon said confidently. "I could've done a lot worse to that old Dodge and the grease monkey I got fiddlin' with it could've got it back in top-notch shape in no time."

"Good, is he?"

Garmon nodded. "Maybe the best damned natural mechanic I ever saw. But don't you dare tell him that. Trouble is, he's too cocky already. If his head swells any more, he won't be able to get it under a hood."

"You'll get him squared away. You always do."

Garmon took out a Chesterfield and lit it, squinting against the smoke as he watched Dale work under the hood of the truck. "Maybe," he muttered. "But I was thinkin' that private might be wasting his talents changin' spark plugs and settin' points."

"What do you think he should be doing, then?"

"They're still going to send us those M3 General Grants to check out for the Limeys, aren't they?"

The other sergeant laughed. "Just because the guy can fix a truck doesn't mean he can work on a tank!"

"I've got a hunch Parker can handle just about anything that runs on gasoline," Garmon said. He saw that Dale was climbing back into the cab of the truck again. "I think we're gonna find out, anyway."

The engine caught, and Garmon saw Parker grinning through the windshield at him in triumph. Master Sergeant Garmon nodded. That engine was purring like a kitten.

★   ★   ★

"So no kidding, this big dumb cracker of a master sergeant takes a hammer and whams the hell out of that engine," Dale said, the tip of the cigarette between his lips bouncing up and down as he talked. "Then he tells me to fix it and do it fast, because if I don't, a bunch of

GIs are going to get killed because of me."

"Theoretically, you mean," Joe said.

"Well, yeah, nobody was really going to get killed. But the point is, he thought I couldn't do it. Only he didn't hurt the truck's engine near enough. I had it running again in ten minutes."

Otis said, "That'd be Sergeant Garmon, right?" It was Sunday afternoon, and he, Nate, and Reuben were sitting at the table in the rec hall with Joe and Dale. All of them had open six-ounce bottles of Coca-Cola in front of them. They would have preferred something with more kick to it, but the rec hall didn't sell liquor. Brown County was dry, and that included the camp.

"Sergeant Garmon, yeah, that's him," Dale said. "A real shit-for-brains sort of guy."

Joe leaned forward. "Keep it down, okay? You don't want one of the other noncoms hearing you and telling your sarge what you said."

"I'm just stating the facts."

"Yeah, well, do it softer," Joe said.

Nate drained the last of his Coke and set the empty bottle on the table in front of him. "I could sure use a real drink," he said.

"Next Saturday they're going to start giving out passes," Reuben said. "Maybe you could get one."

"Maybe we could all get one, and go out and have us a real fandango," Otis said.

"Where's the nearest place you can buy liquor?" Dale asked.

"Legally, you mean? Not the home-brewed stuff?"

Dale shuddered. "I've heard that shit'll give you the blind staggers. No, I mean the real thing."

"That'd be Abilene," Otis said.

"Where's that?" Joe asked.

" 'Bout ninety miles northwest of here."

Dale grimaced. "How would we get there? We sure can't afford to take a cab that far on what Uncle Sam pays us."

"I got a lady friend in Bangs," Nate said. "She's got a car I reckon she'd let us borrow."

"You've got a girlfriend? The great stone face himself?"

"Don't let Nate fool you," Otis said. "He ain't much for talkin', but he's a humdinger with the gals. I hear tell a lot of 'em go for the strong, silent type."

"Yeah, Nate and Gary Cooper," Dale said. "They're two of a kind, all right."

Reuben said, "So, are we going to Abilene next Saturday to get some booze or what?"

The other four soldiers looked at him but didn't say anything. After a moment, Reuben said in exasperation, "What, I'm not supposed to like to drink, is that it?"

"You just don't strike us as the carousing type, Reuben," Joe said.

"I carouse just fine, thank you."

Otis slapped him on the shoulder. "I'll just bet you can, boss." He looked around the table. "We got a deal? We head for Abilene next Saturday and have us a whingding?"

"*If* we can all get passes," Joe said.

Dale said, "If we can't all go, I think the ones who do have passes should go on. It wouldn't be fair if they didn't."

"Remember how noble you sounded when you're the one who doesn't get a pass."

Dale grinned. "Oh, I'll get one. I've got Sergeant Garmon wrapped right around my little finger already."

★   ★   ★

Joe listened patiently as Dale spewed every obscenity and vulgarity he had ever heard before, plus a few that Joe was convinced he had just made up. When Dale stopped to take a breath, Joe said, "You know, with a vocabulary and an imagination like that, you ought to be the writer, not me."

Dale put his head in his hands. "I can't believe it," he groaned. "I'm all set for a pass, and that son of a bitch gives me this goddamn encyclopedia instead!"

Dale swatted at the manual and knocked it off his bunk, then fell back on the mattress and thin pillow. Joe reached down to pick up the thick book and read from the cover. "Technical Manual, Tank 26.8 Ton, Series M3, with British Turret, Designation: General Grant." He looked up and grinned. "26.8 tons. Sounds like weighty reading."

"Shut the hell up," Dale muttered from the bunk.

Joe reached for his tie, looped it around his neck, and began tying it. His shoes were shined, his uniform was pressed, and his fore-and-aft overseas cap was lying on his bunk, ready to be donned. He wanted to look particularly natty tonight, in case he ran into any girls in Abilene who might be impressed by a handsome young serviceman. He wished he had already made private first class; a stripe would have looked nice on his sleeve.

"Let me get this straight," he said. "We're building these tanks for the British?"

"That's what Sergeant Garmon said. Chrysler designed and built them, with help from some English guy named Dewar. Only he wants the turret to be different than what our guys think it should be, so they made some of both kinds. The British one's called the General Grant, and the American design's called the General Lee. Other than that, they're the same tank." Dale sat up before he went on, and Joe could tell that despite his brother's disappointment at not getting a pass, he was genuinely interested in what he was talking about. "The Army's sending out some of the prototypes to bases all over the country so our tank people can get a look at them. We're getting some of the General Grants. Doesn't really matter to me because the engine's the same, and that's what I'll be working on."

"They're going to teach you how to fix tanks?"

"Hell of a note, ain't it? But I figure if it's an internal combustion engine, I can work on it."

The door of the barracks opened, and Reuben, Otis, and

Nate came in. They stopped short as they saw Joe in his dress uniform and Dale still in fatigues.

"Better get a move on, Dale," Otis said. "We got a taxi coming to take us to Nate's friend's house out in Bangs."

"I'm not going," Dale said. He picked up the tank manual, which Joe had tossed back onto the bunk. "I've got to spend the whole weekend studying this, so that I can start working on tanks Monday morning."

"That's a pure-dee shame. We'll miss you, won't we, boys?"

"Sure enough," Nate said.

"Sorry, Dale," Reuben said. "We'll try not to have too much fun without you."

Joe tightened the knot on his tie and reached for his cap. "Speak for yourself, Reuben. I intend to have a great time tonight."

He settled the cap on his head, then adjusted it to a slightly rakish angle. "So long, Dale."

Dale muttered some more obscenities as the group started toward the door of the barracks, then called after them, "Don't do anything I wouldn't do!"

Considering what had happened to cause them to join the Army in the first place, Joe thought, there probably wasn't a hell of a lot that fell into that category.

THIRTY-SEVEN

The taxi was an eight-year-old Ford. Joe sat in front with the driver while Reuben, Nate, and Otis piled in the back. The highway that led to Bangs, a small town nine miles west of Brownwood, ran up a steep hill just outside of the city, and Joe twisted his head to look back at the view. He could see the smallish skyscrapers downtown, the campuses of two colleges, Howard Payne and Daniel Baker, the neat residential neighborhoods, and Camp Bowie dominating the south side of town. Beyond that, miles and miles of rolling Texas countryside were visible. It was an impressive view. Having grown up in a metropolis like Chicago, he wasn't sure if he would ever get used to such wide-open spaces as he and Dale had encountered down here. Joe could easily imagine the cowboys he had written about riding over that prairie landscape some sixty-five or seventy years earlier.

Nate's girlfriend was a nurse who had evidently just gotten home from her shift at the hospital in Brownwood, because she was still wearing her white uniform and shoes. She had taken the white cap out of her auburn hair, though. She came out of the house where the taxi dropped them, threw her arms around Nate's neck, and kissed him soundly.

When she drew back, she said, "Now tell me again why I should let you borrow my car when I'm not even invited along on this jaunt?"

"Because you love me, honey," Nate said with a grin.

"Oh, yeah, that." She gave him a quick peck on the lips. "Okay, I guess it's all right."

Nate turned to the others. "Fellas, meet Sally. Otis, you already know her."

" 'Course I do," Otis said. "Howdy, Sally."

"Hi, Otis. Keep an eye on this big lug for me tonight, will you? Don't let him get into trouble—and that includes other women."

"I'll make sure he stays on the straight and narrow," Otis said, "just like I intend to."

Sally rolled her eyes. "*Now* I'm worried." She stepped back and ran her eyes over Nate. "My, don't you look handsome in your uniform." She looked at the others. "All you boys do."

"Thanks," Joe said. "I'm Joe Parker, by the way."

"And I'm Reuben Gilworth," Reuben introduced himself.

"I'm pleased to meet you. No offense, but you both sound a little like Yankees."

Joe knew he and Reuben probably sounded a *lot* like Yankees to these Texans. He said, "I'm from Chicago and Reuben is from Milwaukee."

"Well, I'll swan. I've never been any place bigger than Fort Worth. I bet Brownwood seems like it's really out in the sticks to you boys."

"Not at all," Joe said, not mentioning that that was exactly how his brother felt about it. "I sort of like it here. Lots of space."

Sally laughed. "Texas has got plenty of that, all right." She reached in one of the pockets of her white dress and brought out a key ring. As she handed it to Nate, she said, "Now you be careful with my baby, you hear?"

"We'll bring the car back good as new," Nate promised. "But I thought I was your baby."

She laughed again and waved at him. "Go on now. Have your fun, soldier boys."

The car was a stylish '38 Chevy. Nate and Otis got in front while Joe and Reuben climbed into the backseat. They all waved at Sally as they backed out of the driveway.

"Sally seems nice," Joe said to Nate when they were back out on the highway.

"She is," Otis answered instead, resting his left arm on the back of the front seat as he turned halfway around. "She's smart as she can be and a good looker to boot. Her mama's sick, but Sally takes care of her real good. If ol' Nate here wasn't such a damnfool cowboy and didn't want to be tied down, he'd've likely married her by now."

"You best mind your own business," Nate said. "I'll get around to gettin' married when I'm damn good and ready, not before."

"See what I mean?" Otis said with a grin.

The sun had set by now. Nate flicked on the headlights. They passed a crossroads where a smaller highway angled off to the northeast. In the glare of the headlights, Joe noticed a sign with an arrow pointing that direction. The sign read CROSS PLAINS 33.

"Cross Plains is that way?" he asked.

"Yep," Otis said. "Where'd you ever hear of a wide place in the road like Cross Plains?"

"Robert E. Howard lived there."

"Who?"

"Robert E. Howard," Joe said. "A writer who had stories in *Weird Tales* all the time. He died three or four years ago, and I remember reading that he had lived in Cross Plains, Texas."

Otis snapped his fingers. "Sure, I know who you're talkin' about. He wrote those stories about Breckenridge Elkins. Dang, those are funny stories!"

"Yeah, I've read some of them." Joe shook his head. "And he came from out here in the middle of nowhere."

"Reckon a fella can be a writer just about any place, come to think of it. Me, I always figured all writers lived in New York City until I met you, Joe."

Reuben said, "You ought to write stories about being in the Army, Joe."

Joe laughed and shook his head again. "I don't think so. I don't know enough about it."

Yet, he added to himself. But maybe someday . . .

★ ★ ★

Sally's car ran well. They listened to the radio, WBAP booming in clearly through the night air from Fort Worth. Joe had never heard the music of Bob Wills and his Texas Playboys or the Light Crust Doughboys. Not all of the tunes were to his taste, but he found himself snapping his fingers along with some of them, especially "San Antonio Rose."

The drive to Abilene took a little less than two hours. They had to be back at the camp by midnight, which left them about two hours in which to celebrate their first trip away from Camp Bowie in several weeks. Nate pulled in at the first roadhouse he came to on the outskirts of Abilene, a place called the Broken Spur.

"Been here before," he said. "They got a good band, and the liquor ain't watered down too much."

Most of the other vehicles in the parking lot were pickup trucks, Joe noted as they climbed out of the Chevy. The door of the roadhouse opened and a couple of men in cowboy hats came out. The twanging strains of music came from inside the building.

Joe would have preferred visiting an old-fashioned Texas saloon, with bat-wing doors, sawdust on the floor, poker tables, dancing girls, and a slick-haired gent called the Professor playing the piano. Probably such places no longer existed, he thought, if indeed they ever had existed outside of B-movies and pulp magazines. Still, it would have been nice.

The Broken Spur would just have to do. The four of them went inside, stepping into a dim, smoky interior that seemed to be lit mostly by electric beer signs behind the bar. The room was crowded, but they had no trouble making their way to the bar. Nate ordered whiskey for all of them, with beer chasers.

The whiskey was raw and potent, Joe discovered as he sipped it and felt its fire all the way down his throat. The beer was cold and soothing, though.

"You boys from Camp Bowie?" the bartender asked over the music that came from a trio of musicians on a tiny bandstand. Two of the men played guitars, while the other sawed on a bass fiddle.

"That's right," Otis said.

The bartender squinted at them in the bad light. "Seems I ought to recognize you."

"Otis and me been in here before," Nate said, "before we joined up."

The bartender slapped a hand down on the scarred hardwood. "Hell, yeah, I remember you now. Fowler's your name, ain't it?"

"That's right," Nate said.

The bartender's eyes suddenly widened. "Oh, shit. Darrell Wingate's in here tonight. I near forgot you and him got in a fight over that gal—"

"We ain't lookin' for trouble," Nate cut in. He tossed down the rest of his drink. "We just want to do a little peaceful drinkin' and then head back to the camp."

The bartender still looked worried. "Well, maybe Darrell won't see you—"

He was interrupted again, this time by a loud voice that said, "Fowler? Nate Fowler? Is that you in that soldier boy getup, you cocksuckin' bastard?"

A brawl, Joe thought. *Oh, my God, there's going to be a real, honest-to-goodness saloon brawl!*

Nate turned slowly and confronted a burly man in work clothes. He nodded. "Howdy, Darrell. Been a while, so I'm goin' to overlook what you just said."

"Overlook this, you son of a bitch!" The man stepped toward Nate and swung a big, knobby-knuckled fist at his head.

The bartender yelled, "Hold it!" but no one paid any attention to him. A couple of women screamed, and men scrambled to get out of the way. Nate ducked easily under the roundhouse punch and stepped inside to slam a couple of short, sharp blows into his opponent's midsection. The man bent over, turning pale and gasping for breath.

That was when someone jolted heavily against Joe, knocking him aside. This second man grabbed Nate from behind and shouted, "I got him, Darrell! I'll hold him for you!"

"The hell you will!" Otis said. His fist smacked into the side of the second man's head, forcing him to let go of Nate. Then a third man tackled Otis from behind. In a matter of seconds, the area in front of the bar was a confused jumble of staggering, punching figures.

Joe and Reuben backed away, unsure of what to do. Other men, friends of Darrell Wingate, no doubt, piled into the fight, so that Nate and Otis were outnumbered more than two to one. Reuben pointed a trembling finger and said, "That's not fair!"

No, it certainly wasn't, Joe thought, and as a friend of Nate and Otis, it was beginning to look like he was going to have to get involved, whether he wanted to or not.

Reuben beat him to it. With an incoherent yell, the little soldier from Milwaukee threw himself forward and grabbed the shoulder of one of the brawlers. The man was a head taller than Reuben, but that didn't stop Reuben from hauling him around and hitting him with a left-right combination that was almost too fast for Joe's eyes to follow. The man's head jerked from side to side as the punches sledged into his jaw. His eyes rolled up in his head, and he fell to his knees before pitching forward on his face, out cold.

Joe blinked, not sure he had really seen what he thought he saw.

By that time, Reuben had tackled another man and slammed him up against the bar. Reuben began punishing him with blows to the body.

"Sol'jer boy!" somebody yelled in Joe's ear. Then he was hit from behind, a blow that caused him to stagger forward. He caught himself and twisted around to see a large man swinging a second punch at him. Instinctively, Joe ducked and struck out. He felt his fist thud into the man's chest. He bulled ahead, knowing that if one of his opponent's looping swings ever connected, it might take his head off. He would stand a better chance if he kept this fight at close quarters.

The strategy might have worked, he thought later, if the guy hadn't kneed him in the balls.

The impact in his groin sent sheets of blinding pain through him. He doubled over and felt himself falling. The floor came up and smacked him in the face, but his testicles hurt so much he barely noticed. He curled up and tried not to whimper. Feet stomped the floor around him. He would be lucky if he wasn't trampled to death, he thought.

But right at that moment, dying didn't sound so bad. If he was dead, his balls might not hurt quite so much. . . .

"Whoo-eee, Reuben! When your mama said you was a holy terror, she wasn't far wrong! You lit into those fellas like a bobcat with a cocklebur up its ass!"

"I just didn't think it was a fair fight," Reuben said from the backseat of the Chevy. His face was bruised and swollen, and one arm of his glasses was broken. The lenses themselves were all right, however, and he had taped up the broken stem with some surgical tape Nate had found in the glove compartment. A grin stretched across Reuben's battered face as he looked across at the backseat's other occupant. "We had to pitch in and help, didn't we, Joe?"

Joe was huddled in a corner of the backseat, still holding himself and rocking back and forth a little. "Yeah," he said between gritted teeth. "Had to . . . pitch in."

"I sure didn't mean for that to happen," Nate said from behind the wheel. "It sure cut our evenin' short. I'm sorry, fellas. But I didn't know Darrell Wingate would be in there. It was just pure bad luck."

"Bad luck," Joe gasped.

Otis said, "What's bad is, the gal that Nate and Darrell

fought over wasn't hardly worth it. She up and run off with some oilfield promotor from Odessa right after they'd gone to Fist City over her. Hell of a note."

"Yeah," Joe said. "Hell of a note." He hoped his voice wasn't really as high-pitched as it sounded to him.

"Well," Reuben said, "we've got a story to tell Dale anyway. He's going to be sorry he missed all the fun."

The bad thing was, Joe thought, that was probably right. Dale would have had a good time tonight.

Otis said, "Where'd you learn to fight like that, Reuben?"

Reuben shrugged. "I don't know. Something just sort of comes over me. I don't really think about what I'm doing."

"Maybe next time we won't run into a fracas like that," Nate said.

Next time? Joe thought. There wasn't going to be a next time for him. *Please, God, let my balls quit hurting, and I swear I'll never go near a place like that again.*

The Chevy rolled on across the night-dark Texas prairie, and if there was an answer to Joe's prayer, he didn't hear it.

THIRTY-EIGHT

Adam had never itched so much in his life. The sand fleas were so thick on Parris Island that they were like the grains of sand on the island's beaches, he thought as he scratched idly at the bites and waited for his turn at the rifle range. He had been here three weeks, and he figured he had been bitten at least fifty times every day. That worked out to over a thousand bites.

There probably weren't quite that many bites on him, he decided in a momentary burst of fairness—but damned near.

"Damn it, Sikorsky, don't you use those eyes of yours for anything but filling up the holes in your head? Are you totally blind?"

At the sound of Sergeant Tompkins's angry bellow, Adam looked up and saw the gunny standing over one of the recruits who had been firing from the prone position. Down at the other end of the rifle range, above the target at which the recruit had been shooting, a red flag waved back and forth in the air. The flag was known as Maggie's Drawers—Adam had no idea why—and it signified that the rifleman had not scored any hits on the target.

A clean miss was nothing unusual for Recruit Leo Sikorsky. If he hit the target with two or three of his shots, he was doing exceptionally well. Sergeant Tompkins had been riding him unmercifully ever since the first day the squad had marched over to the rifle range.

"Dang, Chopper's really catchin' hell from the gunny this time," Ed Collins said from beside Adam, where he was also waiting for his turn to fire. Despite the fact that it was winter and still cold on Parris Island, Collins's fatigues were stained with sweat. Just as Adam had figured would happen, the DIs had Collins running almost every minute of the day that he wasn't involved in some other aspect of training. They had sworn that they would get that extra weight off Collins, but so far they hadn't had much success. He had lost four pounds, that was all.

The thing about Collins was, the extra weight didn't seem to slow him down all that much, Adam reflected. When the squad was running, Collins always finished in the back of the pack, but he was never dead last. When they went through the obstacle course, he had trouble with some sections, but all of the recruits had problems with at least part of the course. Collins had been able to finish every time so far. That put him ahead of Sikorsky, who had failed to complete the course several times.

Sergeant Tompkins kicked sand at Sikorsky, causing the skinny recruit to cough and flinch and blink his eyes rapidly as the grit got in them. "You fucking feather merchant!" Tompkins screamed. "Get off my rifle range, you asshole! Get off my fucking island!"

Sikorsky probably wished that he could do exactly that, Adam thought. Some people just weren't cut out to be Marines. He wondered why Sikorsky had volunteered in the first place. Collins at least seemed like he would make it through basic training. Adam wasn't sure Sikorsky would be able to.

Sikorsky climbed awkwardly to his feet and trudged away from the firing line, holding his M1 so that the butt of its stock almost dragged on the ground. If that happened, Sergeant Tompkins would be even more livid, and Sikorsky was liable to find himself running laps around the barracks with the Garand held over his head. Silently, Adam urged Sikorsky to pick up the rifle.

Sikorsky did so, bringing the Garand to the proper position for carrying it, right hand on the grip, left under the breech just ahead of the magazine, the rifle angled slightly across the front of his body. He gave Adam and Collins a weary grin as he walked past them.

"Tough luck, Chopper," Collins said. "You'll get 'em next time."

"Thanks," Sikorsky muttered. "I doubt it, though."

That was part of the problem, Adam told himself. Sikorsky just didn't believe in himself. He was convinced before he ever started that he was going to fail. Worst of all, he blamed that attitude on being Jewish.

As one of the few Jews in the squad, Sikorsky had tried to make friends with Adam right away after they reached Parris Island. Adam had tried to like the gaunt recruit from New Jersey, but after listening for awhile to Sikorsky complain about how he never got any breaks because he was Jewish, Adam had grown tired of it. He didn't want to tell Sikorsky to go away and leave him alone, but he was afraid that sooner or later it was going to come to that.

Collins, of all people, was the closest thing to a friend that Sikorsky had in the squad. It was Collins who had hung the nickname "Chopper" on him. The moniker seemed wildly inappropriate at first to Adam, but Collins had explained that a Sikorsky was a new type of autogyro flying craft, sometimes called helicopters or choppers. "Aviation is one of my hobbies," Collins had said. "I read all I can about it."

That was another surprise, because Collins's bulk would always prevent him from even fitting into the cockpit of many airplanes. But Adam supposed that didn't mean Collins couldn't be interested in flying.

Tompkins called out, "Bergman! You're up!"

Adam went forward to the firing line. Sikorsky's target had been lowered even though it had been untouched by Sikorsky's shots, and a fresh one put in its place. Adam stretched out on the ground, positioned his elbows properly for firing from the prone position, and lowered his head so that his cheek nestled against the smooth wooden stock of the M1. He checked the rifle's sights and fired several shots so that he would have a basis for comparison to adjust them. When he was finished sighting in, he took a deep breath, settled all his attention on the target, and began firing methodically. He didn't go too fast or too slow. There was no need to rush, but at the same time he was confident enough in his ability that he didn't linger unnecessarily over his shots, either.

When he had emptied the Garand's clip, he reloaded and fired out another clip. Then the target was lowered so that his shots could be checked. In a moment, flags were waved indicating that he had hit the target with every shot and had put half a dozen in the bull's-eye.

"Good shooting, Bergman," Sergeant Tompkins said. Sikorsky was convinced that the gunny was prejudiced against Jews, but Adam had never seen any sign of bias. Tompkins had always been quick to praise him when he did well and equally quick to chew him out when he fouled up.

Fouling up was rare for Adam. His natural athletic ability had stood him in good stead so far during his training. He was able to handle the running and the calisthenics, the combat simulations and the lengthy hikes. Tompkins had dropped hints several times that someday, Adam might—just *might*—make a decent Marine.

"Thanks, Gunny," Adam said now as he stood up.

"Keep this up and you'll qualify as an expert," Tompkins said. "That's what I want, Bergman. Understand?"

"Aye, aye, Drill Instructor."

"Everybody in this squad qualifies." Tompkins looked over toward Sikorsky, who was talking to Collins and some of the other men. "Everybody!"

"Aye, aye, Drill Instructor," Adam said again, because there seemed to be no other response he could make. The gunny wasn't going to take it kindly if Sikorsky was the only recruit in the squad who didn't qualify on the rifle range.

Collins's turn to fire came up next. He waddled up to the line and grunted as he got down in the prone position. Tompkins glared at him and said, "Damn it, Collins, you sound like one of the hogs off your farm back in Indiana.

You miss 'em so much that you're trying to call 'em?"

"No, Drill Instructor," Collins said.

Tompkins stepped hard on Collins's broad buttocks. "Get that lard-ass down, you fat son of a bitch! How are you ever going to be able to crawl under barbed wire with that fat ass of yours sticking up?"

Collins swallowed hard and said, "Don't know, Drill Instructor."

"Don't know?" Tompkins echoed. "*Don't know?* I'll tell you how you're going to do it, you fucking hog! You're going to lose all that lard! You're either going to run it off or die trying!"

Adam was afraid something like that might be exactly what happened someday, but Collins just said, "Aye, aye, Drill Instructor. Permission to fire now, Drill Instructor?"

Tompkins made a gargling sound of disgust and waved a hand at Collins. "Permission to fire!"

After he had sighted in, Collins began to shoot with the same sort of unhurried efficiency that Adam had demonstrated. His shots weren't as accurate, but Adam figured that Collins would have no trouble qualifying. He might even be able to attain sharpshooter ranking, the middle level of three, above marksman but below expert.

When Collins was finished shooting he came over to join Adam, who was waiting with the rest of the squad members who had already taken their turns at the firing line. Sikorsky was there, nervously puffing on a cigarette, and he said, "Good shooting, Ed."

"Thanks, Chopper." Collins pointed at Adam with a blunt thumb. "Not as good as ol' Hawkeye here, but not bad."

"I'll never shoot as good as you, Adam," Sikorsky said.

"You might someday," Adam said, trying to suppress his impatience at Sikorsky's gloomy attitude. "It's just a matter of concentration and practice."

Sikorsky shook his head. "Nah, it's more than that. You got to have what they call the eye-hand coordination. I ain't got that." He jittered back and forth on his feet as he spoke, never still for more than a second or two. That was the way he was most of the time.

He turned to Adam and went on, "Say, they're showing a new George Raft picture at the movies tonight. You want to take it in?"

"I don't know . . ." Adam began. He wasn't sure if he was up to an entire evening of Sikorsky's company.

"Sounds good to me," Collins said. "You sure it's new, though? I thought they didn't send us any pictures more recent than *The Jazz Singer*."

"Yeah, it's new," Sikorsky replied, not even catching Collins's sarcasm. "A gangster picture, I think. Say, Adam, you ever wonder why there aren't any Jewish gangsters?"

"You never heard of Meyer Lansky?"

"Who's that?"

"He's in organized crime," Adam explained patiently. "The Mafia."

"And he's a Jew?"

"That's right."

"Well, will wonders never cease? The Italians are tolerant enough to let a poor Jewish boy work for them. And for this we should be thankful?"

There was no winning with Sikorsky when it came to this subject. Adam knew that, so he didn't bother arguing. Instead, he said, "I think I'll pass on the movie. I ought to stay in the barracks and study."

"What for?" Sikorsky said. "You're already the best Marine on Parris Island."

"Don't call me a Marine," Adam said sharply. "Not yet."

"The best recruit in training, then. Hell, Gunny Tompkins loves you, even if you are Jewish."

Collins said, "George Raft don't have an Eye-talian name. How come he plays gangsters all the time?"

Adam left the two of them discussing the Mafia and walked over to where he had a better view of the firing range. The squad was almost through for the day.

Three weeks down, he thought, and ten to go. And then he would be sent where he could do some good in the world.

He scratched a sand flea bite and thought about Catherine, wondering what she was doing right now. In San Diego, it was three hours earlier than here at Parris Island. . . .

THIRTY-NINE

Dear Adam, Catherine wrote, *the training here hasn't been too hard so far. The other girls are nice, and the nurses who are our instructors have taught us a lot. And you wouldn't believe how pretty San Diego is! The weather is so warm, even though it's still winter. You can even see the ocean from the upper floors of the naval hospital.*

She stopped, laid the fountain pen aside, and read what she had written so far. It was nice and chatty, she thought. Her hand came down on the paper and crumpled it in disgust. She dropped the ball of paper in the wastebasket next to the small desk which was one of only three items of furniture, along with the chair and the bed, on her side of the tiny room.

Why couldn't she write what she really wanted to write to Adam? *I love you and I miss you and I want to be with you and I need to feel you inside me so bad . . .*

Yeah, that would really make him feel better there on Parris Island, she told herself sternly. Get him all sexed up, that would certainly make basic training pass faster for him.

But it was on her mind all the time these days. There was nothing wrong with that. He was her husband and she loved him, and if he walked into the room this very minute she would tear his clothes off and throw him down on the narrow bed and have her way with him at least a dozen times, in every position she could think of.

"Shoot," Catherine muttered. This wasn't helping a bit. Maybe she should try to write today's letter to him later.

She had written every day since he'd sent her his address at Parris Island, except for the two days she had spent on the train going from Chicago to San Diego. She was determined to continue writing every day as long as she could. She had to do everything possible to keep the lifeline intact between her and Adam, to keep their bond strong.

It didn't help that they had the entire continent between them. Catherine had been upset when she found out that her training would take place at the naval hospital in San Diego, California. That sounded almost as far away as Mars to her. She had joined the Nurse Corps in hopes of being closer to Adam, not farther away.

But she told herself that this was just temporary. Once she was finished with her training, surely she would be sent to the same part of the world as the Marines, since they relied on naval hospitals and personnel for their medical care. It was enough that she and Adam were separated by the whole country for the time being. She didn't believe that Fate could be so cruel as to put half a world between them.

The door opened, and Catherine's roommate came in. Margery Mitchell—"Call me Missy!" she had announced the day they met with what Catherine had come to know was her customary enthusiasm—flung herself down on the bed on her side of the room and declared, "If I never see that old hag's face again, it'll be too darned soon!"

Catherine turned halfway around in her chair. "You mean Commander Stowe?"

"That is exactly the hag I mean!" Missy sat up and ran her fingers through her short, dark, curly hair. "I can't do anything to please her! I try and I try and I try, and she still says I'm doing everything wrong!"

"She's pretty demanding, all right," Catherine agreed. "From what I've seen, though, nurses get pretty set in their ways when they've been doing it for a long time."

Missy sniffed. "I don't think she ever does it, that's her problem."

"That's not what I meant—" Catherine began.

Missy held up a hand to stop her. "I know what you meant," she said. "But I still say Commander Stowe wouldn't be so mean if she had a boyfriend." She leaned forward and continued avidly, "I mean, you're married, Catherine. Don't you miss . . . well, you know, doing it . . . something awful?"

Catherine shrugged, not wanting to tell her roommate that she had just been struggling with those very feelings as she tried to write to Adam. "I try not to think about it."

"I don't see how you can keep from thinking about it. I miss Chuck so bad I can't hardly stand it, and he and I weren't even, you know, doing the deed. But I'd give almost anything if I could kiss his sweet little sugar lips for awhile."

Catherine turned back to the desk. Missy could be a little much sometimes, and right now she didn't feel like listening to the other girl gush about her devoted boyfriend Chuck. She picked up the fountain pen and wrote *Dear Adam.*

"Writing to your hubby?"

"That's right."

"I'll bet he's lonely there all by himself at Parris Island."

"He's hardly all by himself. There are thousands and thousands of other Marines there."

Catherine heard the bedsprings creak and knew that Missy had lain back. "Thousands and thousands of Marines," Missy repeated. "Doesn't that just sound yummy?"

Catherine put the cap on the pen, opened the single drawer in the desk, and placed the pen and the sheets of stationery in it. As she closed it, she stood up. "I think I'll go for a walk," she said.

"I'd go with you," Missy said, "but I'm really pooped. Maybe another time, okay?"

Catherine didn't recall asking Missy to go with her. In fact, solitude was what she was after at the moment, as much as solitude could be achieved on the sprawling naval base. "Sure," she said, not wanting to hurt Missy's feelings by telling the truth. She picked up a sweater from her bunk and shrugged into it as she left the room in the nurse's barracks.

She heard a lot of laughter and talk from the other rooms as she walked down the hall and then went down the stairs from the third floor. She walked outside and felt the cool breeze blowing off the ocean. The sun was almost down, and the warmth of the day would quickly dissipate. The sweater would feel good by the time she got back from her walk.

The barracks was part of the massive complex of white-painted buildings that formed the naval hospital campus. Catherine saw white-uniformed sailors hurrying here and there, as well as doctors in officers' uniforms and nurses in the standard white blouses and skirts, white hose and low-heeled shoes. The only things that separated them from civilian nurses were the naval insignia pinned to their blouses and caps.

She walked past a palm tree growing beside the concrete path she was following and thought once again how odd it was to find herself in Southern California. She had never visited here, had never even given any thought to coming here. It had taken the Navy to send her to what some regarded as a sunny paradise. To Catherine, though, any place, no matter how beautiful, seemed empty and sterile if Adam wasn't there.

Her mother had been quite upset when she found out that Catherine was being sent to the West Coast. Elenore Tancred's normally stoic reserve had given way, and there had been a considerable amount of crying and hugging and carrying on. Not on the part of her father, though. By that, time, Dr. Gerald Tancred had stopped arguing. He knew that, for once in his life, he was faced with a situation in which he had no power, whether he liked it or not.

So he had just looked stonily at his wife and daughter, both of whom were sobbing, and said, "For God's sake, caterwauling won't help anything. Elenore, stop that! Catherine has made her decision. Now she must live with it."

"But . . . but she's going so far away!" Catherine's mother had said.

"And it was her own choice," Tancred said. "She has no one to blame but herself for acting so rashly."

"Aren't you even going to miss me, Daddy?" Catherine had asked.

"The way you've been acting lately, not particularly. You've been moping around about that Bergman boy so much that you don't even seem like my daughter anymore."

Those words had hurt at the time, and as Catherine recalled them now, they still hurt. Her father had never been an overly affectionate man; she was used to that. But he had acted as if he would be just as glad to see her gone.

Well, she was gone, all right. She was two thousand miles or more from Chicago. She wouldn't see her parents again for months. And in the weeks she had been gone already, her father had not written once. Thank goodness her mother and Spencer wrote to her, or she would have felt completely cut off from her family.

Spencer's letters weren't very long, but she didn't blame him for that. He was busy with his jobs—he couldn't seem to stick with one for very long—and of course he had his social life to attend to. He had mentioned a girl named Joscelyn and hinted that he was seeing her fairly regularly. He promised he would send Catherine a picture of her whenever he could, but she didn't really need a photograph to know what the girl probably looked like: some fifteen-year-old bobby-soxer with braces on her teeth, more than likely. Catherine hoped Spencer enjoyed his little romance, but it seemed so . . . so *juvenile* compared to what she and Adam had together.

★   ★   ★

Joscelyn lifted her head from Spencer's groin, licked her lips, and said, "Anybody else ever do *that* for you, baby?"

His back was still arched and his hands were tightly clenched in the sheets of her bed. His pulse was pounding so hard it felt as though his head was going to explode from the pressure in his veins. For a moment, he couldn't seem to get his breath. Then, slowly, he relaxed. Joscelyn slid up beside him, her naked skin feeling like velvet where it glided over his.

He wasn't going to tell her that *everything* they did together in bed was new to him. He was still amazed and stunned that she had brought him back here to her room tonight, but even so, he had his wits about him enough to realize that he shouldn't let her know he had been totally inexperienced before now.

"Man, that was something!" he said, still a little breathless.

She leaned over him and kissed him hard on the mouth, then rolled onto the pillow next to him and spread her legs. "Now me."

"What?"

"It's my turn. Do to me what I did to you."

Spencer felt confused. He had heard talk at school about girls who would do a guy with their mouth, but nobody had ever talked about it being the other way around. The idea sort of appealed to him, but at the same time it made him a little queasy. "You mean . . . ?"

"I mean get your head down there and get busy, buster. Fair's fair, you know."

Spencer sat up and scratched his head. "Yeah, I guess so." She had a point, he told himself. And as he bent over and studied the layout, he found himself getting more interested. What the hell, it was a little perverted, but he didn't mind.

Besides, Joscelyn was so damned beautiful. How could he have ever felt that she didn't quite stack up to Karen Wells and the other girls at the Dells?

He couldn't afford to sit in on Mike Chastain's poker

game all the time, of course. But in the weeks that had passed since Jack Cronin first took him to the roadhouse, he felt as though he had become part of the regular group, one of the insiders who could be considered a pal of Chastain's. That was a great feeling. A little dangerous, maybe, because Spencer was still convinced Chastain was a mobster, but great anyway.

And there was Joscelyn, who made it all even better. She was always at the roadhouse when he was there, and they danced and drank together, and sometimes when they sat in a darkened booth they kissed. The last time they were together like that, Spencer had even worked up the courage to feel her up. She hadn't seemed to mind at all when his hand closed over her breast. She wasn't wearing a bra under the evening gown, and through the silk of the garment he had felt her nipple hardening against his palm. The reaction had encouraged him, and probably he would have tried to go even farther tonight.

Joscelyn had taken that decision out of his hands by declaring right off the bat that he was coming back to her place for a drink. Chastain had smiled faintly and lifted his hand, as if he were a priest blessing them, and Cronin had smirked as Joscelyn took Spencer's hand and led him toward the club's front door. Bud and Lou had been their usual expressionless selves.

Only Karen Wells had looked a little concerned when Spencer glanced back at the table on the way out.

He forgot all about Karen in a hurry once he was in Joscelyn's little roadster, sitting close beside her as she drove. She pulled up the skirt of her gown, and the street-lights they passed cast fleeting glows over the smooth flesh of her calves. She kept one hand on the wheel, but when she wasn't shifting gears, the other hand was on Spencer's left thigh, kneading it through his trousers and working its way tantalizingly higher and higher.

By the time they got to her place in an apartment house on the north side, he was ready to pop. But he hadn't. With an effort of will, he had controlled himself until they were inside. She didn't turn on any lights. She just led him into her bedroom and pushed the curtains back so that the glow of the city illuminated her body as she shrugged out of the gown and let it fall around her feet. The drink that had been the excuse for them coming here wasn't even mentioned.

The first time had been fast, of course. He was too excited to hold off for very long after he had plunged himself into her body. And then, he was sorry to say, he had dozed off. But he woke up quickly enough when she took him in her mouth, and when he opened his eyes he saw that she had drawn the curtains and turned on a small lamp on a bedside table. Its soft yellow light made her bare skin tawny. She was gorgeous.

Now he knelt between her widespread thighs and began doing what she had asked him to do. It wasn't too bad, he decided after a few moments, and from the way she was breathing harder and moving her legs back and forth so that her thighs pressed against his ears, he supposed he was doing it right. She said, "You've got . . . a natural talent . . . kiddo," and gripped his head with her fingers. Moments later, she started to shudder and cry out.

Afterward, while they were lying nestled together under the covers, he said, "We're going to do this again, aren't we?" He didn't know what he would do if she said no. He would be devastated. He didn't know if he could go on living without it.

"Of course we are, sweetie," Joscelyn said. "All the time."

FORTY

The time which had passed so slowly at first went more and more quickly as Joe and Dale continued their training at Camp Bowie. Winter drew to a close, and spring in Texas arrived with a series of violent storms. Joe had seen thunderstorms in Chicago, but somehow these disturbances, with their crashes and peals of thunder, tongues of brilliant lightning that lit up the night like day, and sheets of blinding, pouring rain seemed more elemental to him.

"Wait'll you see your first twister," Otis said one evening when they were all sitting in the barracks playing cards and listening to a storm rage outside. "You never saw the like. Back thirty-some-odd years ago, a cyclone come a-roarin' along and hit a little town southeast of here called Zephyr. Practically blew the whole damn town away, it did."

Dale shuffled the cards. "I can live without that, thanks. Those twisters of yours can just stay away."

Joe said, "We have tornadoes in the Midwest, too, you know."

"Not like the ones down here," Otis said.

Joe just nodded. He had already gotten used to the idea that to these Texans, everything was bigger and better—or worse, as the case might be—in Texas.

His radio classes had gone fairly well. He still had some trouble understanding the concepts behind broadcast theory, but he could operate any of the dozen or so units that his platoon had been trained on, and operate them well. He also had that stripe on his sleeve, having been promoted to private first class after a particularly impressive showing during an unarmed combat drill. Joe wasn't sure what had been going on with him that day—maybe all the training and exercising and drilling was finally having an effect—but Sergeant Dent had been impressed, and Lieutenant Page had concurred that it was time to buck Parker, Joseph, Private, up to the next rank.

Dale's fortunes had run along similar lines. The M3 General Grant tanks had arrived at the camp, and Sergeant Garmon had put Dale to work on them immediately. After a couple of weeks of ending each day coated with a fine covering of grease, Dale felt like he knew the tank's engine inside and out. The nine-cylinder radial engine, designated R975 EC2, air-cooled and operating on regular gasoline, sat underneath the rear deck of the M3, and hull doors swung up and out to give Dale and the other mechanics access to it.

A few days after the violent thunderstorm, while a lot of the camp was bogged down in mud, Sergeant Garmon surprised Dale by asking, "How'd you like to get your hands on the controls of this thing, Parker?"

Dale's eyes widened. "You mean it, Sarge?"

Garmon shrugged. "You've been up to your elbows in the engine. I thought maybe you should get an idea what it's runnin'."

"Yes, sir—I mean, Sarge." Dale started scrambling up the side of the tank, which was parked on the macadam pavement of the motor pool parking lot. He glanced at the other recruits and noted to his satisfaction that they looked jealous.

The hatch on top of the turret was open. Dale had studied the technical manual for the M3 enough so that he knew what to expect as he climbed down into the crew compartment, using the steel rungs welded to the side of the turret. He dropped into the driver's seat at the left front of the crew compartment.

From the hatch above him, Sergeant Garmon called out, "Do you know what you're doin', Parker?"

"Yeah, Sarge." Dale's eyes swept over the instrument

panel, picking out the ignition switch and starter from the array of gauges and dials and switches. He hit the fuel primer, which was in the upper center portion of the panel, to send gasoline to the cylinders in the engine. He flipped on the ignition switch, then pressed the starter.

The engine started with more of a rumble than a roar. Dale looked out the vision port directly in front of him. He put his foot on the accelerator pedal, ignoring the hand throttle lever to his right next to the gearshift lever. He knew he would be more comfortable giving the tank gas with his foot rather than with the hand throttle. He checked the oil pressure and oil temperature gauges, then the voltmeter and ammeter. All the needles were in their normal ranges. He released the parking brake on the left. Two steering levers with rubber grips jutted up from the floor, one on each side of the driver's seat. Pulling back on either of the steering levers slowed the track on that side, causing the tank to turn in that direction; pulling back on both at the same time would bring the tank to a stop. Dale noticed the triggerlike switches on each of the rubber grips. Triggers were exactly what they were. When depressed, they fired the two machine guns mounted on the front of the tank. Those guns were unloaded now, of course, but just to be on the safe side, Dale told himself to be careful and avoid touching the switches.

Through the vision slot, Dale spotted Sergeant Garmon, who had climbed down from the turret and was now standing in front of the tank. Garmon lifted both thumbs to indicate that everyone was cleared out from around the tank, then moved out of the way himself. Dale put his left hand on the steering lever on that side, pressed the clutch pedal with his left foot, and put his right hand on the gearshift lever. He shifted into first, then moved his right hand to the right steering lever as his right foot fed gas to the engine.

The tank lurched forward.

Dale had to restrain himself to keep from whooping in glee. Being in control of the Ford's powerful engine when he was racing had been a kick; having as much power as was contained in this General Grant tank was even more thrilling. No speed was involved in this sensation. The M3 crept forward in first gear so slowly that a child could have outrun it easily. But Dale didn't care about the speed. What had his pulse racing was the sense of awesome invulnerability. He leaned forward, failing to notice as he did so that he had also moved the left steering lever.

Suddenly, the tank began to swing to the left. Dale wasn't aware of the turn until he saw the Texas landscape moving sideways in the vision slot. A fence abruptly loomed up in front of him.

He couldn't hear his own yell of alarm over the noise of the tank's engine as he tried to figure out what to do. His foot lifted from the accelerator and stabbed for the brake pedal, but there was no foot brake. Instead, he needed to be hauling back on the steering levers, but in his excitement his mind had gone blank on the procedures he had read about in the manual. He shoved the left steering lever forward, hoping that would turn the tank away from the fence.

The tank turned, but not sharply enough or soon enough. Its momentum carried it into the fence. Wires snapped like strings under the impact as the tank lumbered through the fence. Dale felt a jolt as the massive armored vehicle left the smooth pavement and began to churn over the muddy ground. Finally, his eyes happened to fasten on the fuel cutoff switch. He lunged toward it and slapped it down, killing the supply of gasoline to the engine. The engine sputtered and died, and the tank shuddered to a halt.

For a moment, there was only an eerie silence inside the tank's crew compartment after the rumble of the engine faded away. Then, through the open turret above him, Dale heard shouting. Footsteps thudded on the tank's armored decking as someone clambered onto it. Sergeant Garmon practically screamed down through the turret, "Parker, have you lost your goddamn mind?"

Dale twisted in the driver's seat and looked up so that he could see the sergeant's angry face framed in the opening at the top of the turret. "Sarge, I'm sorry," he said. "I don't know how it got away from me—"

"Get out of there!" Garmon bellowed. "Get your ass out of this tank!"

Dale grabbed the steel rungs and scrambled up through the hatch. As he climbed out onto the turret, he saw that the M3 had crashed completely through the fence and into the field bordering the motor pool lot. Its treads were bogged down in the sticky Texas mud.

"I never meant for this to happen, Sarge—" he began, but once again Garmon interrupted him.

"Do you know what you've done, Parker? You've gotten this tank stuck in the mud! How the hell are we goin' to get it out of here?"

"Well, Sarge, I think maybe the engine's strong enough to pull itself out of the mud. We just need to put it in reverse, maybe rock it a little—"

"Rock it a little! What the hell do you think it is, a baby?" Without giving Dale a chance to respond, Garmon leaned closer and went on, "That's exactly what it is, a big armored baby that the United States government gave to us to take care of, and what did we do? What did *you* do? You crashed it through a fence!"

The incident had drawn the attention not only of the rest of the motor pool soldiers, but also some of the brass. Dale noticed a couple of officers jogging across the parking lot, and he pointed them out to Garmon with a jerk of his chin and an "Uh, Sarge . . ."

Garmon swung around and came to attention as best he could perched atop the tank as the officers stopped at the edge of the parking lot. They stood at the new gap in the fence and stared at the bogged-down tank. Garmon snapped a salute, as did the other enlisted men. The officers returned it distractedly, and then one of them asked, "Sergeant, what happened here?"

"Just a little accident, sir," Garmon said.

"We can see that," the other officer said dryly. "Who was driving that tank?"

Dale said, "I was, sir."

"And who are you?"

"Parker, sir, Private Dale Parker."

"Well, Private Parker, who gave you permission to drive the tank?"

Dale forced himself not to even glance toward Garmon. "No one, sir. We've been working on the engine, and I was in the crew compartment checking some of the gauges when I must have accidentally started it moving."

Garmon and all the other enlisted men knew that was a lie. The question now was whether or not they would back up Dale's story. Dale wasn't quite sure why he had lied. He could have passed the buck easily and blamed the whole fiasco on Garmon, who had put an unqualified man at the controls of the General Grant.

"Is that what happened, Sergeant?" one of the officers asked.

Garmon hesitated, then said, "Yes, sir."

Both officers nodded. One of them said, "Can you get that tank out of there?"

"I think so, yes, sir."

"Which is it?"

"Yes, sir," Garmon said. "We'll get the tank out."

"Very good. Carry on. And Parker, you be more careful next time."

"Yes, sir," Dale said. "I will."

The officers started back toward the motor pool building. Garmon waited until they were out of earshot, then turned to Dale and glowered at him. "Don't think this means I owe you a damn thing, Parker."

"I don't, Sarge. I just wanted a chance to try to get this tank out of the mud. I think I can handle it better now that I know what I'm doing."

Garmon hesitated, and his mouth pulled in a grimace. "All right," he said abruptly. "Get down there, and let's see what you can do."

In the end, it took all of the tank's power, plus a steel cable attached to a three-quarter-ton trunk, to pull the M3 out of the mud. But once all the sticky gunk had been washed off its treads, it was as good as new.

"Sarge, I was wondering," Dale said to Garmon once the tank was free of the mud, "how do I go about signing up to drive one of these things?"

"You mean transfer to the armored cavalry?" Garmon shook his head. "You're a pain in the ass, Parker, but you're a good mechanic. You're goin' to stay right here where I can get some use out of you."

Dale tried to hide his disappointment. "I just thought maybe I could—"

"I know what you thought. But it's not goin' to do you any good. We're just familiarizin' ourselves with these vehicles on a contingency basis, as well as testin' them out for the British. They're all goin' to the Limeys, that's why they've got the British turret on 'em."

"Okay. But one of these days . . ."

"One of these days you'll wise up to the fact that the Army tells you what to do, Parker, not the other way around."

That was true enough, Dale thought, but he had felt the same thrill today in the driver's seat of the M3 as he had experienced the first time he sat behind the wheel of the Ford at the starting line on a racetrack. He looked at the massive tank and swore to himself that, sooner or later, he would drive one of them for real.

FORTY-ONE

Joe spent as much time as possible with Otis Lawton and
Nate Fowler, talking about the time they had spent as
cowboys in the Texas Panhandle and other parts of the
Lone Star State. Otis did most of the talking, since Nate
was as laconic as ever. Joe enjoyed picking their brains
about the West. He had the city boy's fascination for such
things as horses and cattle and roping and riding. One
evening during free time as the end of basic training drew
near, Joe asked the two Texans if they could teach him
to twirl a lasso like the late Will Rogers.

"Naw, we never went in for any fancy rope tricks like
ol' Will," Otis said. "We were always workin' cowboys,
not entertainers. Not that Will couldn't do some pretty
fair cowboyin' himself. He started out as a top hand on a
workin' ranch up there in Oklahoma, you know."

"Well, then, what *can* you teach me?" Joe persisted.

Nate said, "To ride a horse."

"What?"

Otis grinned. "Say, that's a mighty fine idea. We'll
teach you and Dale and Reuben how to ride."

Joe said, "I don't know. I'm sure not sure that's a
good idea." He wasn't afraid of a lasso, but a real live
horse . . . ? A *big*, real live horse? That was an entirely
different matter.

"What's wrong?" Otis asked. "Didn't you never go ridin' in one o' them big-city parks?"

"Horseback riding was for rich people on the North
Side," Joe said. "My family was just barely scraping by."

"Well, you can still learn," Otis said. "We'll just borrow us a couple of horses from the cavalry stables, right, Nate?"

Nate nodded silently and solemnly.

Joe hoped he didn't sound too cowardly as he said, "I'm still not sure. We'd better go see what Dale and Reuben think about this idea."

A few minutes later, they found Dale and Reuben in the rec hall. As soon as Otis had explained the plan, Dale said excitedly, "Sure. Sounds like fun."

Joe rolled his eyes. Of course he should have known that Dale would go along with almost anything that promised a little excitement. Surely Reuben wouldn't think it was a good idea, though.

"Great," Reuben said. "Count me in, boys."

That had been equally inevitable, Joe decided. Reuben was still unsure of himself and wanted to fit in, even if it meant risking his neck by climbing up onto the back of some wild beast. . . .

"When are we going to do this?" Dale asked.

Otis shrugged. "No time like the present."

"Tonight?" Joe said. "Gee, I'm not sure . . ."

"Come on, Joe," Dale said. "Take a chance for once in your life."

Joe refrained from pointing out that enlisting in the Army had been a pretty big gamble in itself, and he probably wouldn't have done that if Dale hadn't gotten himself in such trouble with Victor Mason. After a moment, he sighed and nodded. "All right, if we're going to do this, let's get it over with."

Otis clapped him on the back. "Thattaboy!"

The five of them left the rec hall and started walking across the camp toward the cavalry stables. Camp Bowie had only a small cavalry force, most of them members of the Military Police, and only a few dozen horses were kept in the stables. The closer Joe and the others got to the long building with the corral behind it, the more nervous he became. He was certain this was not a good idea.

Dale, Reuben, Otis, and Nate were all quite excited,

however. When Joe said quietly, "If we get caught, they'll throw us all in the stockade," Otis waved off that worry.

"Nate and me know all the wranglers. They won't give us no trouble." He paused, then added, "That's what the Army should've made the two of us, 'stead of sendin' us to the infantry. It's a hell of a note when they take two of the best cowboys in Texas and make *foot* soldiers out of 'em."

Joe couldn't argue with that.

A dim light was burning inside the stables. Otis eased open one of the small doors and called, "Hank? You in there?"

A moment later the door was opened wider, and a scrawny, bald-headed man peered out at them. "Who's that?" he asked. "Otis, is that you?"

"Yeah, it's me, Hank," Otis told him. "I got some fellas out here who want to go for a little ride."

The man called Hank blinked at them. Joe noted that he wore a master sergeant's stripes on his sleeve. "Four months short o' retirement and you want me to let some boys in here who don't have no business bein' here? You tryin' to get me kicked out of the Army, boy?"

"Hell, no, Hank," Otis said. "You're the only one here, ain't you?"

"Ever'body with any sense is in bed, and that's where you oughta be."

"You see, nobody's goin' to know about it except us," Otis argued. "Come on, Hank, what's it gonna hurt?"

"Oh, all right," Hank said with a sigh. He pushed the door open even farther. "Come on in. But be mighty damned quiet about it."

They filed into the stable, and Hank shut the door behind them. The smells of hay, sweat, and horse manure filled the air. Joe had written about such things in his Western stories, but this was the first time he had ever experienced them for himself. The smell was strong, but not entirely unpleasant.

The middle-aged noncom led them down a wide, hard-packed dirt aisle that ran between two rows of wooden stalls. Only one bare lightbulb was burning. Hank turned toward the visitors and said, "You can saddle up a couple of mounts and take 'em out in the corral. A couple of turns around apiece, and that's it. No more."

"All right," Otis said. "That sound okay to you boys?"

"Sure," Dale said, and Reuben nodded. Joe nodded, too, but even two turns around the corral on horseback sounded like a lot to him, especially since he had looked into some of the stalls and seen how big the horses were.

"Reckon you'd better give us your gentlest mounts," Otis said, and Hank indicated a couple of stalls. Otis and Nate went into the tack room, emerged with saddles and harnesses, and went into the stalls to get the gear on the horses. When the animals were saddled, they led them out, and Joe got an even better look at them.

One of the horses was a tall, muscular animal with a glossy reddish coat. The other was a bit shorter and more rangy, mouse-colored with a dark stripe down its back. Otis was leading that horse. He patted its shoulder and grinned at Joe. "This here lineback dun is the horse for you, Joe," he said.

Joe nodded nervously. "Whatever you say. I'm no judge of horseflesh."

"I am," Otis said, "and both of these are good animals." He looked at Hank. "You sure they're both gentle?"

"Gentle as rain in the springtime," Hank said.

Joe recalled the storms that had rolled through the area several weeks earlier and wasn't sure how gentle rain in the springtime really was.

Everyone walked out into the large corral behind the stable. Nate motioned Dale over to the big reddish horse. "Put your foot here," he said, pointing to the stirrup on the horse's left side. "Hang on to the saddle, step up, and swing your other leg over."

"It's easier with a cowboy's saddle," Otis commented. "These army saddles ain't got saddlehorns to grab hold of. You'll just have to make do."

Dale followed Nate's instructions and swung up into the saddle. He shifted around slightly, and Joe could tell that he was nervous despite his bravado and his eagerness to do this. "Mount up, Joe," Dale said. "It's great."

Otis said, "Just do like Dale did. Foot in the stirrup and step up."

Joe's heart was pounding heavily in his chest. He moved closer to the horse and reached out to tentatively pat its shoulder, as Otis had done. The horse swung its head around, and Joe jumped back.

"Nothing to be afraid of," Otis said. "You got to show the horse that you're in charge."

Joe took a deep breath. He held the stirrup and lifted his left foot. He worked his boot into the stirrup until it felt relatively secure, then grabbed hold of the front and back of the saddle. He pulled himself up and brought his right leg up and over the horse's back. The horse moved a little as Joe's weight came down on the saddle. Joe grabbed the front of the saddle with both hands. When the horse was still again, he managed to get his right foot in the stirrup on that side.

Otis and Nate were holding the bridles. They handed the reins up to Joe and Dale. "Hang on to these," Otis said. "Not too tight, now. When we let go, just bump your heels against their flanks, and they'll walk for you."

"Okay," Dale said. "I'm ready."

"Joe?"

"I . . . I guess." He wished he had insisted that Reuben go first.

"Let 'er rip," Nate said as he let go of the bridle on Dale's horse. Otis let go at the same time, and they both stepped back.

Joe took off for the moon like there was a rocket under him.

He yelled as the horse arched its back and leaped straight up in the air. He couldn't help it. His knees clamped against the horse's flanks, and his hands tightened on the reins, pulling back hard on the horse's head.

The animal kept bucking and jumping and twisting. Joe yelled incoherently. He thought other people were shouting, too, but he couldn't be sure of that. From the corner of his eye he caught a glimpse of Dale sitting on top of the other horse, and it was going crazy, too.

Joe held on for dear life. It was all he could do.

Finally, after what seemed like an hour on top of the crazed horse but was probably less than a minute, Otis succeeded in grabbing the bridle and bringing it back under control. On the other side of the corral, Nate had hold of the other horse's harness and was talking softly to it. Reuben stood to one side, eyes wide with amazement and fear behind his glasses, and Hank stood beside him, cackling with laughter and clapping his hands together.

"You boys are good!" he called to Joe and Dale. "I figured you'd get thrown right off, but instead you stayed on just fine."

Joe slid down off the horse while Otis held it. His legs were shaking so hard that he almost fell when he hit the ground. Anger helped hold him up, though, and he turned toward Hank to say, "You knew that was going to happen?"

"Why, sure. When Otis said he wanted horses that were gentle, I figured he really meant he wanted to teach you boys a lesson. So I picked out a couple of good buckers."

Sheepishly, Otis said, "Actually, Hank, I really wanted some gentle mounts for these boys. They never rode a horse before."

Hank frowned. "You mean you wasn't playin' a trick on these Yankees?"

"Nope," Nate said.

"Well, hell." Hank scratched his bald head. "Reckon I owe you boys an apology."

Dale had managed to get down from his mount. He started toward Hank, furious at the trick that had been played on them. "You old coot—!"

Joe moved in front of him and grabbed him. "Hold on, Dale," he said. Strength was coming back into Joe's legs now, and he was able to hold his brother back. "The guy's a master sergeant. You take a swing at him and you'll be in big trouble."

"But . . . but he could've got us killed!"

Joe was all too aware of that. He still had a sick, hollow feeling in the pit of his stomach. "I know."

"We're sorry, fellas," Otis said. "But you know, that was some damn good ridin' you just did."

"We could've gotten killed!" Dale said again.

"Yeah, but you didn't get bucked off. You stayed in the saddle damn near as good as some real cowboys I've seen. I reckon you must have a natural talent for bronco bustin'."

"Ought to try it again," Nate said.

Joe looked around the camp. It was quiet and peaceful under the springtime Texas sky. He would have thought that all the shouting would bring some sentries, but maybe the commotion hadn't been as loud as it seemed at the time.

"I don't think so," he said. "We were lucky once. We might not be so lucky next time."

Reuben spoke up. "I didn't get to try it."

The others looked at him. "You saw what happened to Joe and Dale, Reuben," Otis said. "We'll find you a gentler horse. Won't we, Hank?"

"Sure," the sergeant said, bobbing his bald head up and down.

Reuben pointed at the horse Joe had been riding. "I want that one."

"No, you don't, Reuben," Otis said.

Reuben nodded. "Yes, I do. I can handle it."

Dale turned toward the horse he had ridden. "Hell, if Reuben's going up, I'm going to try it again."

"You sure about that?" Nate asked.

"Damn right."

"You're both crazy," Joe said.

Dale looked at him. "You're the one who wrote all those Western stories without ever being on a horse.

You're the one who wanted to learn all about being a cowboy."

"Yeah, but—"

Dale shrugged and reached for the reins. "Suit yourself. I'm getting back in the saddle."

"You and Gene Autry," Joe muttered under his breath. Then he said, "All right, all right. Wait a minute, Reuben." He stepped past Reuben and took the reins from Otis. "Get your own horse."

"You boys are crazy," Hank said.

Joe looked back and shook his head. "Nope. We're plumb loco."

FORTY-TWO

Congress had finally passed the Lend-Lease Bill on March 11, 1941, after months of sometimes rancorous debate between the isolationist and interventionist factions and, under the terms of the bill, Great Britain was to receive seven billion dollars worth of supplies by the end of June. Part of that would be the M3 General Grant tanks. Dale was going to miss the massive armored vehicles when they were gone. He had spent as much time as Sergeant Garmon would allow at the controls, and by the end of April he could handle the tanks about as well as any of the members of the armored cavalry division whose job it actually was to drive them. At least, that was Dale's opinion, and from what Joe had seen of his brother's ability, it was correct.

Joe had spent some time working on the tanks, too, but not on the engines as Dale had done. The communications platoon had installed SCR508 transceivers in a couple of the General Grants, replacing the standard British Wireless Sets which had been installed in them at the factory. In addition to the SCR508, the tanks were also equipped with an Interphone system which would allow the five members of the crew to talk directly to each other by way of microphones and earphones. In the noisy interior of the crew compartment, the extra amplification of the Interphone system was necessary for everyone to be heard.

For a week during basic training, Joe and Dale and the other men from Camp Bowie had participated in extensive maneuvers in Louisiana with trainees from other camps across the South. They had ridden from Brownwood to Camp Polk in trucks, a long, butt-numbing ride on the bench seats in the backs of the trucks. Once at their destination, they had splashed around in the swamps for several days in full gear, and Joe had been utterly miserable. Their meals were cold C rations—canned meat or hash, fruit (usually peaches or pears), vegetables (carrots, peas, or green beans), and a biscuit that was usually dry and hard. They slept on shelter halves spread out on the ground; the canvas failed to keep out the moisture, so everyone was wet and muddy most of the time. Days were spent in long hikes carrying full fifty-pound packs. When they should have been sleeping, they were crawling around in night combat exercises. Luckily, the weather was still cool enough so that the snakes weren't crawling as much as they would be later in the year, it was explained to the troops, but they were still warned to be constantly on the lookout for coral snakes, the most venomous reptile in North America.

Before the maneuvers in Louisiana, Joe wouldn't have believed he could be so glad to see Camp Bowie again. It was like coming home when the trucks rolled up to the barracks.

A couple of days before basic training was scheduled to be over, Joe and Dale received word that they were to report to the company commander's office. Lieutenant Page's office was located in a small, pre-fab building next to the pair of barracks that housed D Company. The lieutenant's aide, a corporal, showed Joe and Dale into his office.

They saluted, the movements crisp, precise, and instinctive by this time, and when Page had returned the salutes, he said, "At ease. Have a seat, men."

Two straight chairs were placed squarely in front of the lieutenant's desk. Joe and Dale sat down in them.

Page got right to the point. He put his hand on a stack of documents and said, "I've been preparing the orders for the company. You're all entitled to a two-week leave in transit before you report to your next post. Sergeant Dent tells me that neither of you want to take that leave."

The lieutenant stopped and seemed to be waiting for some sort of response. Joe and Dale glanced at each other, and Joe said, "That's correct, sir."

"You don't want to go home? Back to, where was it, Chicago?"

"That's correct, sir," Joe said again.

"Why not? Trouble at home? Most recruits want to see their folks after thirteen weeks of basic training."

Joe *did* want to see his mother again, and he knew Dale felt the same way. He wouldn't have even minded listening to his father complain for a while. But the letters they had received from their mother—their father never wrote—had made it plain that their enlistment in the army had had the desired effect. The Parker family's credit had been restored, and Victor Mason hadn't made any other moves against them in retaliation for Dale's affair with his wife. Mason had evidently kept his word, and Joe and Dale wanted to keep theirs by not returning to Chicago.

The story was too long and complicated, not to mention sordid, to explain to Lieutenant Page. Joe said, "No, sir, no trouble at home." That would remain true, he hoped, as long as he and Dale stayed away. "We're just anxious to get on to our next assignment."

Page looked as if he wasn't sure whether to believe that or not, but after a moment he grunted and said, "In that case, I may have something that will interest you. The Army is looking for volunteers for a special operation."

A special operation. That phrase caught Joe's interest, all right. It sounded like some sort of secret assignment, the sort of mission that Captain Combat or the Lone Eagle or G-8 went on. But those only happened in pulp magazine stories, didn't they?

Joe glanced over at his brother. Dale shrugged and nodded, and Joe said, "Yes, sir, we'd like to hear about it."

"Both of you are familiar with the M3 tanks? The General Grants?"

Dale sat up straighter, and this time he was the one who answered the lieutenant. "Yes, sir. Quite familiar."

"As you probably know, the United States will be shipping quite a few of those tanks to the British Army in the near future as part of the Lend-Lease program. That was the idea all along, of course, when that fellow came over here from England and helped our boys design them. We just had to wait for Congress to finally get around to passing the bill—" Page stopped short and held up a hand, palm out. "Forget I said that last part. I meant no disrespect for our Congress."

"Of course not, sir," Joe said quickly.

"At any rate, the tanks are going to England, and we'll be sending some men along with them to make certain they get there all right, as well as to check out the British soldiers who will be operating the tanks. Have to make sure they know what they're doing, since our men are the ones who have all the hands-on experience so far."

Joe felt his pulse beginning to speed up. He said, "Are you asking us if we'd like to volunteer to be part of the American force accompanying the tanks, sir?"

"That's exactly what I'm asking you, Private. What do you say?"

Joe would have liked to think it over for a minute. As it was, several thoughts flashed through his mind. Such an assignment would get them so far away from Chicago that they would never have to worry about Victor Mason again. And they would get to travel to England, something it was doubtful either of them would have ever been able to do had it not been for the Army and the war.

But the war was a definite concern. All the time that the Nazis had been bombing London and several other English cities, their U-boats had also been prowling the waters of both the North and the South Atlantic. Scores of British merchant ships and warships had been sent to the bottom of the ocean. The German sea wolves were ruthless and unrelenting in their quest to control the Atlantic. If Joe and Dale went with the tanks, they would have to take their chances in a British convoy.

Before Joe could give voice to any of those pros and

cons or even think them through fully, Dale said, "We'll do it."

Page looked at Joe. "What do you say, Private?"

There was nothing else Joe could say now. He nodded and said, "We volunteer, sir."

Page looked pleased. "Very well. You'll begin Preparation for Overseas Movement immediately. As of today, you are detached from D Company, Thirty-sixth Infantry Division, and transferred to the Army Services Force. You are entitled to a pre-embarkation furlough of ten days—" He glanced up at them. "I don't suppose you want that one, either?"

"No, sir," Joe and Dale said together.

"Good. Probably better that you stay with those tanks. You and the men with you will be responsible for getting them safely to England."

Dale asked, "Does that mean if the Krauts sink the boat on the way there, we'll be in trouble?"

Page opened his mouth to give Dale a serious answer, then stopped before he said anything. He looked coldly at Dale for a moment, then abruptly chuckled. "Yes, Private Parker. You'll be in a world of trouble if the Krauts sink your boat."

"Just wanted to make sure I was clear on that, sir."

"All right," the lieutenant went on. "Your POE is New Orleans. Staging area is Camp Planche. You're to report there with the M3s as soon as we can arrange transport for them. That may require several weeks, which means you will remain here at Camp Bowie even though the other members of your former company will be moving on."

Joe nodded. "We understand that, sir."

Page leaned back in his chair and said casually, "That'll give you even more time to familiarize yourself with the Grants." He looked at Dale. "By the way, I've heard that you've actually driven some of the tanks, Private."

Dale swallowed, and Joe knew he was debating how

much of the truth to tell this officer. After a moment, Dale said, "Yes, sir."

Page didn't seem upset by the admission. He said, "Sergeant Garmon tells me that you're an excellent mechanic. You'll probably have to teach those Tommies everything you know once you get over there."

"That would be all right, sir. Whatever I can do to help."

"You're already doing it. I got the feeling that Sergeant Garmon didn't want to take those tanks to England without you."

Dale's eyebrows lifted in surprise. "Sergeant Garmon is going?" A second later he remembered to add, "Sir."

"That's right. He'll be in charge of the detail from here at Camp Bowie. The overall commander of the mission is an officer named Hoffman. Captain Hoffman from Fort Bragg. But you don't have to worry about that. Just take care of the tanks. That'll be all."

Joe came to his feet and saluted. Dale followed suit, only a split second slower than his brother. They walked out of the office, and as they emerged from the building, they saw Sergeant Garmon standing nearby with his arms folded. He gave Joe and Dale a level stare from under the brim of his brown felt hat and said, "Well?"

"Well what, Sarge?" Dale asked.

"You know damned well what I want to know," Garmon snapped. "Are you two goin' with those tanks to England?"

"We volunteered," Joe said. "We're being transferred to the Army Service Force."

Garmon grunted. "Welcome to the club." He uncrossed his arms and unexpectedly offered his hand to Dale. "I'm glad you'll be goin' along, Parker."

"Thanks, Sarge," Dale said as he shook hands with the sergeant.

Garmon nodded at Joe. "You, too, Parker. I hear you're a whiz with radios. How's about we call you Sparks?"

Joe tried not to wince. So far, he had successfully avoided being saddled with the nickname usually given to radiomen. Now his luck had run out.

"Whatever you say, Sarge," he said.

FORTY-THREE

Adam rubbed the soft cloth over the stock of the M1 rifle as he sat on his bunk in his skivvies, his legs stretched out in front of him. He had carried this rifle for the past thirteen weeks, had disassembled and assembled the Garand so many times that he could have performed the task blindfolded or in the dark. The smooth wood of the stock felt good against his cheek when he brought the weapon to his shoulder to aim it on the firing range. Earlier this week, the final week of his Marine Corps basic training here on Parris Island, he had scored 145 points during qualifying, only five points shy of a perfect score. He had not only qualified but had earned the right to wear an expert's ribbon.

So why, he asked himself, had the Marine Corps in its infinite wisdom seen fit to take the rifle out of his hands and replace it with a shovel? Why, he thought bitterly as he polished the Garand, was he being sent to some Godforsaken speck of ground in the Pacific Ocean instead of to Europe where he might actually accomplish something, might do some good for the world?

Who the hell had ever heard of Wake Island anyway?

Ed and Leo came out of the head adjusting their field scarves. Both were dressed in green Class A uniforms and were wearing fore-and-aft overseas caps. A few weeks earlier, Adam would have been surprised to hear that Leo Sikorsky would actually make it all the way through basic, but the skinny recruit from New Jersey had managed somehow. Adam and Ed Collins had both worked with Leo on his marksmanship, spending as many extra hours on the firing range with him as they could, and when the final qualifying had taken place, Leo had shot well enough to make it. Just barely, but well enough. He had survived the obstacle course, the five-mile runs, the thirty-mile hikes, and now there was actually a little muscle on those slender arms and legs. To Sergeant Tompkins, Leo was still a fucking feather merchant, but whether the sergeant liked it or not, Leo "Chopper" Sikorsky was about to become a Marine.

In thirteen weeks, Ed Collins had lost fifteen pounds, enough so that his uniform fit a little better. He still bulged enough to make the seams look threatened in places. Adam suspected that at least some of Ed's weight would come right back once the daily grind of basic training was over. Ed had performed well in basic training, finishing around the middle of the pack in all the exercises. He was still vulgar, crude, poorly educated, bigoted, and ignorant—and despite all that, Adam had come to consider him a friend.

After all, in a matter of days, they could both call themselves Marines.

Ed's cheek bulged with chewing tobacco. He shifted it to the other cheek and said around the wad, "You ain't changed your mind about havin' a drink with us, Adam?"

"No, you two go ahead," Adam said. "I think I'll just stay here in the barracks tonight."

"Hey, you got no reason to mope around," Leo said. "You're going to a tropical paradise, man. Where Ed and I are headed, I'm going to freeze my ass off."

Ed chuckled. "Chopper ain't quite as well insulated as me, I guess."

Like everyone else in the First Training Battalion, they had received their orders today and knew where they would be going when their time at Parris Island was completed. Ed and Leo were part of a contingent of troops bound for Greenland. The vast, icy island in the far northern Atlantic was owned by Denmark, but until just a few days earlier it had been occupied by German soldiers who had set up several weather stations there. Those Germans had left hurriedly when a much larger force of American Marines had landed. There hadn't been a battle, but just the fact that the Marines now held territory from which the Germans had fled made it seem like a victory. Ed and Leo would be among the reinforcements whose job it would be to see that the Nazis didn't try to reclaim Greenland.

Adam, on the other hand, had been designated a replacement for the First Defense Battalion. Adam had had no idea what that meant, so he had asked and been told that the First Defense Battalion was currently stationed on Wake Island in the Pacific Ocean, due west of the Hawaiian Islands. The men of the First, aided by a civilian construction crew, were building a naval air station on Wake.

Adam had almost told the captain who had given him his orders where he could put them. The very idea of going halfway around the world to build runways and hangars when over in Europe that little madman from Austria was sweeping up whole countries and leaving nothing but death and destruction behind him . . . It had come close to being more than Adam could stand.

But he was a Marine, or the next thing to one, anyway, and his time at Parris Island had already taught him that Marines went where they were told to go and did what they were told to do, so instead he had gritted his teeth and said, "Aye, aye, sir."

He didn't have to like it, though, and he didn't feel like going over to the slop chute with Ed and Leo and getting drunk tonight.

"Sure you don't wanna come with?" Leo asked one final time.

Adam shook his head. "You guys go on and have fun."

"Okay," Ed said. "Come on, Chopper. I'm gonna drink you under the table, boy, even if you do have a hollow leg."

"What do you mean by that?"

"Hell, it's just an old sayin'. When I was a boy, my

folks always told me I must have a hollow leg 'cause I'd eat so much."

"Oh," Leo said. "I thought it was some sort of comment about me being Jewish."

"Shoot, no. If I'd wanted to do that, I'd'a said somethin' about what they did to your poor tallywhacker when you was just a little tyke."

Leo bristled. "What?"

"Tyke, Chopper. I said tyke."

They were still squabbling good-naturedly as they left the barracks. Despite the air of gloom that had come over him, Adam couldn't help but grin a little and shake his head as his friends walked out.

A few minutes later the company clerk, a corporal named Davis, came in and said, "Mail call!" The men who were still in the barracks gathered around him as he opened the canvas pouch he carried. Adam set the Garand aside carefully and left it lying on his bunk as he stood up and went over to see if any letters from Catherine had arrived.

"Bergman!" Davis called a few moments later, holding up a pair of envelopes. Adam said, "Here," and reached out and took them. His heart seemed to give a little jump when he recognized the handwriting on the first of the envelopes. Reading Catherine's letters was one of the things that had kept him going during basic training. The other letter, he saw with less excitement but still a sense of satisfaction, was from his mother.

He went back to his bunk and sat down, then slid his finger under the flap of the envelope from Catherine and carefully pried it loose. He took out a single sheet of thin paper and unfolded it. Even though Catherine didn't use fancy perfumed stationery, he seemed to catch a hint of her scent as he opened the letter and held it up to read.

My darling Adam,
I'm afraid I have news that isn't very good. I've found out where I'm going to be assigned. I was

hoping so much that I would be sent somewhere in Europe so I could be close to you, but next week I'll be leaving for the U.S. naval hospital at Pearl Harbor, in the Hawaiian Islands.

Adam caught his breath, unsure whether to believe in this stroke of good fortune or not. Catherine had no way of knowing that they were both on their way to the Pacific. The replacements for the First Defense Battalion would be routed through Pearl Harbor on their way to Wake Island. Adam's heart began to pound harder. With any luck he could see her again, could hold his wife in his arms once more—!

Maybe Fate hadn't turned its back on him after all.

He finished reading Catherine's letter, which was full of chatty details about her training and her fellow nurses. It closed with *All my love forever, your darling, Catherine.* Adam carefully folded the letter and then slipped it back in its envelope. He would add it to the stack of them he kept in his duffel bag with a string tied around them.

Turning his attention to his mother's letter, he opened it and began to read, enjoying her comments about what was going on in Chicago. She was saving newspaper clippings about the Cubs' spring training games, she said, and she would send a bundle of them to him when she had a few more.

He was halfway down the page when he started to frown. *I have had a letter from your grandparents in Kiev,* he read, *and they say that Commissar Stalin claims to have no fear of an invasion from Germany. I'm afraid that if the Nazis come, no one will be ready for them.*

Not if, Adam thought, but when. For years now, Hitler had been talking about the need for *lebensraum*—living room—to the east of Germany. With all of eastern Europe now under his control, he wasn't going to pass up the opportunity to attack Russia, even though Hitler and Stalin had signed a nonaggression pact.

Stalin was a fool, Adam told himself bitterly. The

Ukraine was a plum ripe for picking, and Adam was willing to bet Hitler's greedy fingers would soon be reaching for it.

And what would *he* be doing while that was going on? Sitting on Wake Island, surrounded by thousands of miles of ocean. The only good thing Adam could say about that was that Pearl Harbor was in the same ocean. . . .

★   ★   ★

San Diego had been nice, but Hawaii . . . well, this was *really* a tropical paradise, Catherine thought the first time she saw the palm trees and the white sandy beaches and felt the warm breeze blowing in her face. She could have almost closed her eyes and imagined she was a honeymooner standing at the railing of a cruise ship with her new husband, rather than being aboard the U.S.S. *Larsen*, the Navy cutter that had brought a fresh supply of medical personnel for the hospital at the Pearl Harbor naval base.

But the *Larsen* wasn't a cruise ship, of course, and Catherine wasn't a honeymooner. Her beloved husband was thousands of miles away and soon would no doubt be even farther from her, perhaps as much as half a world. She hadn't heard from Adam since she had written to him about her assignment. If he had replied to her letter, it hadn't caught up to her yet. Maybe it would be waiting for her at Pearl Harbor, she thought.

"This is really something, isn't it?" Missy Mitchell said from beside her.

Catherine nodded. "It's beautiful," she said.

They had steamed past the famous Diamond Head, the rugged promontory that jutted out from the island of Oahu just east of Waikiki Beach and the city of Honolulu. Farther west was the inlet that led into Pearl Harbor itself. As the *Larsen* moved northward up this waterway past Iroquois Point, Catherine could look to the right and see Hickam Field, the Army Air Corps base. To the left was Ewa Airfield, the headquarters of the local Marine Aviation Group. Up ahead, the inlet widened out into the harbor itself, with Ford Island in the center surrounded by smaller bays known as the West, Middle, East, and Southeast Lochs. Catherine knew the names only because she had gotten her hands on an official U.S. Navy map back in San Diego and studied it. That had helped to pass the time.

Missy pointed. "Isn't that the Navy Hospital?"

Catherine looked in the direction her friend was indicating. She saw an L-shaped building on the east side of the channel, several stories high and made out of white stucco. There were palm trees and winding concrete walks on the grounds around it. Catherine nodded. "That's it, all right. I remember Commander Stowe describing it to us."

"Don't even mention her name," Missy said fervently. "I'm just glad she's still back in San Diego making life miserable for somebody else for a change."

"The head nurse here could be just as bad or worse," Catherine pointed out.

Missy shook her head. "Not possible."

Catherine turned her attention back to the harbor. There were ships everywhere, anchored along the shores of Ford Island and in the lochs. On shore, the vast complex of runways, hangars, warehouses, barracks, offices, and everything else that made up the headquarters of the Pacific Fleet stretched almost as far as the eye could see. Pearl Harbor was a busy place.

Catherine hoped that she would stay busy, too. If she had plenty of work to do, she wouldn't have as much time to think about how badly she missed Adam.

So far, Catherine had enjoyed her training. Her medical background had made it relatively easy, although she had sensed that Commander Stowe had held it against her that she was the daughter of a successful physician. The premed courses she had taken at the University of Chicago had certainly come in handy, too. Commander Stowe sometimes referred to her rather caustically as "the college girl," but Catherine hadn't let that bother her. After growing up around her father, she was used to cutting remarks. When it came to high-handedness and arrogance, the commander was a rank amateur compared to Dr. Gerald Tancred.

Still, Catherine was glad that her training was over. She was ready to get to work. If she couldn't be with Adam, at least she could be accomplishing something here at Pearl Harbor.

The next hour was hectic as the *Larsen* docked and the nurses went ashore and reported in at the hospital, which was within easy walking distance. What Catherine had at first taken to be concrete walks were actually paved with crushed sea shells, she discovered. As she and Missy and the other nurses headed toward the hospital building, they were aware of the approving glances sent in their direction by the sailors who were busy with various tasks on shore. There were even a few wolf whistles from the more daring young men.

Missy laughed. "I'm glad I'm single," she said to Catherine. "I'm going to enjoy all this male attention."

"What about Chuck?"

"Rats. Did you have to remind me?"

Missy was just joking, but she probably would be very popular among the sailors, Catherine thought. Her short dark hair and tanned skin were set off well by the white navy uniform. She would probably be swarmed by suitors in no time. Catherine felt a pang of sympathy for the far-distant Chuck. Missy was going to have a difficult time staying faithful to him, she thought.

She, on the other hand, would have no problems in that regard herself. Adam wasn't just her boyfriend, he was her husband, and that made things entirely different.

The new nurses were met at the hospital by a woman in her late thirties with light brown hair. "I'm Lieutenant Commander Miles," she said. "Follow me, and I'll take you to your quarters. You'll need to have your orders ready, so that quarters can be assigned to you."

Lieutenant Commander Miles led them to a group of

bungalows that reminded Catherine of a tourist resort. She had to give the Navy credit, she thought with a wry smile. Cute little cabins surrounded by palm trees and sandy beaches. She had always thought that the military would be a hard life, but so far . . .

Catherine and Missy weren't going to be roommates again, they discovered when their quarters were assigned to them. Mitchell came first in the alphabet, so Missy drew her assignment first. She would be sharing a bungalow with two other nurses. She shrugged helplessly at Catherine and waved, then carried her bag into the little cabin.

When Catherine's turn came, she found herself assigned to a bungalow with two nurses named Sutherland and Tabor. She knew both of them relatively well and didn't think there would be any problems with the three of them getting along.

Lieutenant Commander Miles started to hand Catherine's orders back to her, then stopped and looked again at the mimeographed sheets. "Tancred," she said. "An unusual name."

It was German, but Catherine didn't explain that. She just waited to see what the lieutenant commander wanted.

"I remember now." Miles reached in one of the pockets of her uniform and brought out an envelope. "This came for you this morning. I'd seen your name on the list of nurses we were expecting, so I thought I'd deliver it to you personally." She smiled. "Forwarded from San Diego, and it still beat you here. You must be a lucky woman, Nurse Tancred."

Catherine felt her pulse skip a beat as she recognized Adam's writing on the envelope. She took it and said, "Thank you, ma'am."

"Aren't you going to read it?"

Catherine would have preferred to wait until she was alone, but Lieutenant Commander Miles seemed to want her to go ahead and open the letter. Carefully, she did so and slid out the folded sheet of paper inside. She began to read, and suddenly her heart wasn't skipping beats any-more. Instead it was racing so fast she felt light-headed.

"Good news?" the lieutenant commander asked.

"Yes, ma'am," Catherine heard herself saying. "Very good news."

FORTY-FOUR

The couple of weeks that Joe and Dale had figured they would remain at Camp Bowie after their formal basic training was over stretched into more than a month. With the massive buildup that was going on in the military all across the country, it was almost summer before the Army found enough trucks to transport the M3 General Grant tanks and the detachment from the Army Service Force to their Point of Embarkation; New Orleans, Louisiana.

It had been hard saying good-bye to Reuben Gilworth, Otis Lawton, and Nate Fowler. All three of them were moving on for advanced infantry training at Fort Benning, Georgia. After the rocky beginning, they had all become good friends, and Joe and Dale were going to miss the two Texans and the shy young man from Milwaukee.

"You boys keep your asses down over there in England," Otis said on the last night before he and Nate and Reuben left Camp Bowie. "I hear tell ol' Hitler's still bombin' 'em pretty good over there."

"Yeah, London's still under the Blitz," Reuben said. "Be careful."

"We intend to be," Joe said. "But you guys are the ones who have to worry. Fort Benning is supposed to be tough."

"Aw, we can handle it," Otis said with a wave of his hand. "We'll just do whatever Reuben does."

Reuben flushed with embarrassment, but to tell the truth, he had turned out to be a good recruit. Despite his mild appearance and demeanor, he was a better shot with the Garand than either Joe or Dale, and he had outdone them in the hand-to-hand combat classes, the obstacle course, and virtually every other test of a soldier's skills.

Still, Joe worried about Reuben once he was gone from Camp Bowie. Reuben just had that quality about him that made other people concerned for him.

With basic training completed, Joe and Dale were able to concentrate on preparing for their new assignment. While they and the other members of the detachment were waiting for transportation, they spent their days studying and working on the M3 tanks. By the time the trucks arrived to take them to Louisiana in early June of 1941, Dale knew every bolt and rivet in the tank's structure, and Joe was an expert on the SCR508. Of course, it was possible that once the tanks were in the hands of the British Army, the American transceivers would be ripped out and replaced with British Wireless Sets, but that was their decision, Joe told himself. His job was to make sure the radios were in good working order when the tanks were turned over to their new owners and provide any instructions or assistance the British might request.

After the misery he had endured in Louisiana during the maneuvers a couple of months earlier, Joe had no desire to go back to the place, but at least they wouldn't be there for very long, he hoped. And they would be using Camp Planche, near New Orleans, as their staging area, rather than the swamps of Camp Polk. When the long line of trucks rolled out of Camp Bowie carrying the tanks and the men who were going with them, Joe felt a twinge of regret to be leaving the camp.

He and Dale were sitting side by side in the back of one of the trucks, on a bench that was already hard and uncomfortable even though the trip had just started. As the truck bounced along, Dale lit a cigarette and glanced over at his brother. "Oh, hell," he said in disgust. "You're not feeling homesick for this place already, are you?"

Joe shrugged. The canvas sides of the truck were rolled up, so he could see the sprawling camp and the town of Brownwood, and the rolling countryside around them. "It really wasn't that bad," he said.

"They could put you in Sing Sing and when you left you'd feel nostalgic about it."

"So I get used to a place and I don't like change. There's no crime in that."

Dale blew out a cloud of smoke. The truck was picking up speed, and the wind caught the smoke and whipped it away. "Not me, brother. I'd rather be headed for someplace new, someplace I've never been where I can do things I've never done."

Joe thought about the destination for which they were bound and said, "You're about to get your wish."

★   ★   ★

The heavily loaded trucks could not make much speed, so it took three days for the convoy to reach Camp Planche. Once there, the men of the detachment were informed that there would be another wait while the British ships that would carry the tanks to England steamed to New Orleans.

The time spent waiting was put to use in giving the tanks a good going-over to make sure nothing had happened to them during the trip from Texas. There were also a couple of British naval officers on detached duty at Camp Planche, and they spent several days instructing the Americans on the ins and outs of travel by British transport ship. The Army Service Force detachment, led by Captain Hoffman and Sergeant Garmon, met in a classroom and listened to the British officers as they went point by point through a diagram of a typical British vessel.

Then there were the "Abandon Ship" drills, carried out in a barracks that had been turned into a makeshift mockup of a British ship. With klaxons wailing loudly in their ears, the Americans rolled out of their bunks, secured their life vests, and clattered up and down ladders that took the place of the ladders on a ship. These drills were usually carried out in pitch blackness, just like the real thing might well be if a ship was torpedoed by a Nazi U-boat.

The thought of such things was enough to make a cold, queasy feeling grip Joe's stomach. He had grown up next to Lake Michigan, which was large enough to seem like an ocean to a kid, but now they were talking about the real thing. The briny deep. Davy Jones's locker. The same angry sea that had claimed the supposedly unsinkable ocean liner *Titanic*.

What the hell had he been thinking when he volunteered for this mission? It was all Dale's fault for speaking up so quickly and telling Lieutenant Page that they would do it.

And where would they be now, he asked himself, if they had not volunteered? Probably at Fort Benning with Reuben and Otis and Nate, but that would have been just a temporary respite, Joe told himself. If the United States got into the war, as looked inevitable, it would be overseas. He would have wound up on a boat sooner or later, a boat subject to being stalked by those Nazi sea wolves.

Still, the thought of all that cold, dark water . . .

Joe was almost relieved when the British ships finally docked in New Orleans and he was busy again. Anything to keep his mind off what might be a watery grave.

The tanks rolled up broad ramps into the cargo holds of the massive H.M.S. *Starks*, the biggest ship Joe had ever seen. Its gray metal sides towered above the docks on which Joe and Dale and the other Americans stood to watch the tanks being loaded. Captain Hoffman, a tall, slender man with a thin mustache, who had a habit of carrying a swagger stick that made him look more British than some of the actual British officers, supervised the loading along with the captain of the *Starks*, a short, broad man with thinning, rust-colored hair under his cap.

The convoy would consist of eight transport ships and a dozen heavily armed corvettes that would provide an escort. The transport ships carried a considerable amount of armament, too. Joe saw several cannon and quite a few machine gun emplacements on each of the vessels.

The tanks were not the only American-produced goods

bound for England. The transports would be filled with food, medical supplies, weapons and ammunition, aviation gas, construction materials such as rubber and sheet metal and lumber, radios, navigation equipment, anything and everything that might come in handy as the British tried to defend themselves against the Nazi onslaught. These shipments were some of the first under the Lend-Lease program, and Joe had heard that President Roosevelt had ordered the U.S. Navy to extend its patrols in the North and South Atlantic. The American naval vessels weren't looking for a fight, and they were under orders not to fire unless fired upon, but they could provide some extra sets of eyes and ears for the British convoys. If German U-boats were sighted, the news would be relayed immediately to the British.

It appeared to Joe that the president was almost trying to provoke the Germans into starting something with the United States. Hitler was already frothing at the mouth about Lend-Lease, calling the program an act of blatant aggression and warmongering on the part of the United States. By expanding the Navy's role in protecting the British convoys, Roosevelt was clearly sending a message to Berlin.

And it was a message the Nazis were going to answer sooner or later. Joe was certain of that. He just hoped they would wait until he and Dale and the General Grant tanks were safely in England.

Once the tanks and all the other supplies were loaded, the troops were allowed to board. "Get up those ramps!" Sergeant Garmon called. Joe and Dale swung their duffel bags over their shoulders and joined the line of men trudging up the ramps and through doors that opened into the bowels of the *Starks*. British sailors in round caps and bloused leggings showed them to their quarters. Dale paused just inside the door of the compartment and slowly lowered his duffel bag to the iron deck at his feet. "Home sweet home," Joe heard him mutter.

It was pretty bleak, all right. The compartment was long

and narrow, with rows of canvas and metal-frame bunks along each side. Each bunk was six feet long and two feet wide. They were stacked six high on each bulkhead with only two feet separating them. A man would have to slide in and, unless he was extremely thin, not even think about turning over while he was trying to sleep.

Joe turned to Sergeant Garmon and asked, "Sarge, just how long is this trip supposed to take?"

Garmon didn't look too happy with the accommodations himself. "Don't ask me, Parker," he said. "I'm sure the British'll get us over there as fast as they can. They're hurtin' for those tanks and all those other goods we're sendin' 'em."

A British officer came into the compartment, followed by Captain Hoffman. The Americans saluted both of them, then Hoffman said, "At ease. Major Wilton wants to say a few words to you men."

"Thank you, Captain," the Englishman said. He turned to the Army Service Force detachment and went on, "On behalf of the Royal Navy, I want to welcome you gentlemen. I wish we could offer you a bit more luxurious quarters, but we all must make sacrifices. Actually, this isn't too bad. You won't be sleeping in shifts. Each man's bunk will be his own for the duration of the voyage, so you won't have to worry about what sort of visitors another fellow might leave behind." Wilton pointed. "The loo is through there, and the enlisted men's mess is beyond it. There is also a small wardroom where you may spend your free time. I assure you that we shall take the best care of you we possibly can and will complete the Atlantic crossing as soon as possible. Our expected arrival in Liverpool is three weeks from now."

Joe suppressed a groan of dismay, and as he looked around he could tell that the other members of the detachment weren't very happy, either. Three weeks in this closed-up metal compartment? He hadn't realized until now that he must have a touch of claustrophobia. Already he wanted to get outside and see the sky again.

"You'll be allowed to go up on deck during certain times and under certain weather conditions," Major Wilton went on. "Until we are underway, however, we ask that you remain here in your quarters. An announcement will be made when you can go topside."

Well, that was a small consolation, Joe thought. They wouldn't be trapped here belowdecks for the entire voyage. Maybe it wouldn't be too bad.

He wondered suddenly if he had a tendency toward seasickness, too.

FORTY-FIVE

As Adam came down the gangplank from the U.S.S. *Nelson*, he had never been happier to leave a place in his life. For most of the week since the ship had steamed away from the naval base at San Diego, bound for Pearl Harbor, he had been sick as a dog. He had been out sailing on Lake Michigan in pleasure craft, but that was nothing like being a passenger on an oceangoing vessel like the *Nelson*. He had spent a lot of the voyage hanging his head over the railing, like many of the other Marines who had been designated replacement troops for the First Defense Battalion on Wake Island.

But now the ship had finally arrived at Pearl Harbor, and Adam was ready to see in person the woman whose image he had held in his mind for so long. Thinking about Catherine was probably the only thing that had gotten him through the miserable trip from San Diego.

He had changed into green Class A's and had his expert's ribbon pinned to his blouse. His field scarf was tied perfectly, and his fore-and-aft cap was aligned at a rakish angle. His time at Parris Island had left him in the best shape of his life, and although he felt a bit wan after the days of seasickness aboard ship, he knew he would bounce back quickly. His Garand was slung over his shoulder, and he carried his duffel bag in his left hand as he walked ashore. The solid ground underneath his feet felt wonderful.

He looked around for Catherine. He had written her from San Diego and let her know the expected arrival date of the transport. The letter had gone out in a PBY and would have been here days ago. So she should have been waiting for him. He didn't see her, though. Quite a few nurses, no doubt ones who were off duty, had turned out to welcome the Marines who were arriving at Pearl, but the only one who mattered to Adam didn't appear to be among them.

One of the nurses, a tall, good-looking girl with short dark hair, waved a hand over her head and called, "Adam? Adam Bergman?"

Surprised to hear his name coming from a woman he didn't know, Adam frowned and started toward her. As he came up to her he said, "I'm Adam Bergman."

She offered her hand. "I'm Missy Mitchell, Catherine's friend. I'm sure she's told you all about me."

Adam didn't recall Catherine ever mentioning anyone named Missy in her letters, but he smiled and said, "Sure," as he shook hands with her. "Where's Catherine?"

"She sent me to meet you. There's been a little accident—"

He still had hold of Missy's hand, and she winced as he involuntarily squeezed harder. "Is Catherine all right?" he asked anxiously.

Missy extracted her hand from Adam's grip, and he muttered an apology as he realized what he had done. She said, "Don't worry, Catherine's fine. She just had to work. You see, a lieutenant commander and his wife were involved in a little car wreck earlier today, but the lieutenant commander's wife is pregnant and the accident seems to have sent her into labor. Catherine's helping out in the delivery room."

"Oh." Adam felt a huge wave of relief wash over him. For a second, he had been afraid that Catherine was hurt.

"Come on. I'll take you to her place. You *do* have liberty, don't you?"

"Until tomorrow at oh-eight hundred. We have to be back on the ship by then."

"That's not very long." Missy grinned. "But I'm sure the two of you will make good use of the time."

Adam felt his face getting warm. He had thought all

sorts of things about Catherine during the infernally long time they had been apart—but he had to admit that he had thought more about the act of love than anything else.

"Come on," Missy said. "That's my jeep over there."

"How'd you manage to get your hands on a jeep?" Adam asked as he carried his bag over to the blocky little truck, one-quarter-ton, four by four, and put it in the back behind the seats.

Missy slipped behind the wheel. "Oh, I'm a good little scrounger. I just bat these baby blues at those poor fellas in the motor pool, and they give me whatever I want. It's the same wherever I go."

Adam couldn't help but laugh. He felt an instinctive liking for Missy Mitchell. "I'll just bet it is."

Missy started the jeep and put it in gear, and they took off with a spray of gravel from the parking lot. The road she followed was lined with palm and ironwood trees. The dozens of ships anchored here, and the buildings of the naval base and the two adjacent airfields dominated the landscape, but there were pockets of great beauty as well. In only a few minutes, Missy brought the jeep to a stop in front of a bungalow in a long line of similar bungalows.

"This is where the nurses live?" Adam asked.

"Nice, isn't it? Pearl Harbor is considered one of the best duties in the Nurse Corps; you don't have to be here very long to understand why."

Adam carried his gear up the short walk to the cottage. The screen door opened before he got there, and two young women stepped out onto the postage-stamp-sized porch. Both of them wore civilian clothes, and both were very attractive. One wore glasses and had red hair parted down the middle, while the other was a striking brunette.

"Hello, Adam," the redhead said. "I'm Billie Tabor. This is Alice Sutherland. We're Catherine's roommates."

"Glad to meet you," Adam said with a nod.

"You don't have to worry," Alice said. "We're on our way out for the evening. Catherine should be here soon, and you two will have the place to yourselves."

"All night," Billie added. "We're going to a party on the beach that won't be over until morning."

"Sounds like fun," Adam said.

"Not as much fun as you'll be having, I'm afraid," Alice said with a laugh.

Adam blushed again. Did everybody on the whole blasted island know what he was going to be doing tonight? And did they all have to take so much pleasure in it?

Another jeep came along the road and stopped in front of the bungalow. Adam turned and felt his heart leap as he saw Catherine climbing out of the little vehicle. "Thanks, Spud," she called to the sailor behind the wheel, then turned toward the bungalow. She was dressed in her nurse's uniform and had obviously come here straight from the hospital. She looked a little tired, as if she had just pulled a long shift, but that weariness vanished instantly as she spotted Adam standing on the porch with her friends.

"Adam!" she cried, her voice breaking a little.

"That's our cue to exit, girls," Missy said. She ushered Billie and Alice off the porch, and as they passed Catherine, she leaned over and whispered something to her. Catherine barely paid any attention to her. She began taking slow steps up the walk toward the bungalow. Adam was going to wait for her, but he couldn't make himself do that. He rushed off the porch to meet her and swept her into his arms. His lips came down on hers.

The kiss went on forever, and when it finally ended, Catherine pressed her face against his shoulder and said brokenly, "I was afraid I'd never see you again."

"I'm here," Adam said as he held her. "You knew I was coming."

"I was afraid something would happen. Oh, Adam . . ."

He stroked her hair and said quietly, "It's all right. It's all right."

And until 0800 tomorrow, it would be.

★ ★ ★

Catherine had lost track of how many times she had reached an orgasm. She cradled Adam's limp manhood in her hand and said, "Poor baby. Did we break it?"

His chest was rising and falling rapidly as he tried to catch his breath. "My God," he said. "Were you . . . were you always this insatiable?"

"Well, it's been a long time."

"Yes, but I thought I'd be the one to ravish you, instead of the other way around."

"We're ravishing each other." Catherine felt a stirring against her palm. "Oh, it's not broken after all!"

Adam groaned. "Have pity on a poor mortal male!"

"No," Catherine said as she swung her hips over his and lowered them. "Not one bit."

★ ★ ★

"The Hawaiians have something called a luau," Catherine said. "It's a big feast with a roast pig and everything. If I'd had time I would have tried to fix one for you, but we've been working a lot of hours at the hospital."

"Roast pig?" Adam said as he cut off another bite of the steak Catherine had cooked in the bungalow's tiny kitchen.

She put her hand to her mouth and said, "Oh. Adam, I'm sorry, I didn't mean any offense—"

He laughed. "Forget it. I doubt if there's a rabbi within hearing distance. And if there is, he certainly got an earful earlier. Did you always make so much noise in bed?"

"Gee, none of the other fellas complain."

Adam laughed again and shook his head. He wanted to reach across the table and pull Catherine out of her chair and plop her down in his lap and kiss her, but if he did that, the rest of the meal she had fixed would go to waste. He would just have to wait.

Night had fallen, and after they finished eating they

went outside. The beach was only a couple hundred yards away. They walked over to it, slipped their shoes off, and strolled along the sand holding hands. Adam felt more at peace than he had in months. If he had been able to shove the thought of what was waiting for him the next morning out of his mind, the moment would have been perfect.

But he couldn't. The 0800 deadline loomed over them like the black, star-dotted sky.

"I wish this night would never end," Catherine said.

"Me, too. I'm trying not to think about it—"

"Me, too."

"But we have to face it. Who knows when we'll be together again?"

Catherine shook her head. "No," she said stubbornly. "I *don't* have to face it. Not now."

"Well, look at it this way. When I'm relieved from Wake Island, Pearl Harbor is probably where the Marines will send me on the way to my next assignment."

"How far is Wake Island from here?"

Adam shrugged. "I don't know. A thousand miles or so?"

"There are planes flying back and forth from here to there. Maybe you can catch a ride on one of them sometimes, like for a weekend."

Adam wasn't sure how likely that was. The Marine Corps wasn't noted for trying to accommodate the love lives of its enlisted men. But he said, "Maybe." No point would be served by disillusioning her.

"It could all work out just fine for us," Catherine said.

"Sure it could."

"It could be a lot worse."

"Yeah."

"You could have been sent to Europe, like we thought you would be. Then we'd really be far apart."

"I was pretty upset when I found out I'd been assigned to Wake. Then that same day your letter came, telling me that you were here at Pearl Harbor, and I knew then I'd get a chance to see you again. That made all the difference in the world."

"Yes," she said, "it did."

They stopped and faced each other and linked their other hands. Adam leaned down and rested his lips lightly on hers. The tips of Catherine's breasts touched his chest through the lightweight shirt he was wearing. There was no bra under her shirt, and he could feel the hardness of her nipples. They stood there like that for long minutes, holding hands and brushing against each other tantalizingly. Tasting each other's mouths, breathing each other's breath. They had no idea how much time had passed until the long, slow, ponderous waves of the Pacific began to lap at their bare feet as the tide came in. Adam broke the kiss and whispered, "We'd better get back."

"Oh, yes," Catherine said urgently.

★   ★   ★

At 0730, he slipped out of bed and quietly pulled on his clothes. Catherine was sound asleep, lying naked on her belly on top of the tangled sheets. Adam let his eyes play over her silky skin, trying to memorize every inch of her body. He had to fill up his senses with her now, so that she would last in his memory during the weeks or months they were apart. He knew he should wake her before he left, and he knew she would be angry when she found him gone, and he knew he would feel guilty about it later.

But he wanted to remember her this way. The tranquil beauty of this moment could never be exactly duplicated. He moved silently around the bed and saw the faint smile that curved Catherine's lips, and he murmured, "Thank you, God."

Then he left as quickly and quietly as he possibly could, before his heart could break completely.

★   ★   ★

Billie Tabor thought she heard crying coming from the bathroom as she walked into the bungalow. She decided she had been wrong about that when Catherine emerged from the bathroom a moment later brushing her hair. Catherine was dressed in her uniform, and her face was calm and composed.

"You'd better hurry," she said to Billie, "or you'll be late. Where's Alice?"

Billie ran her fingers through her hair and made a face as she felt the sand and grit left there from the beach party. She hoped she'd have time to wash it. "She'll be along in a minute," she said in answer to Catherine's question. "I guess your hubby got back to his ship all right?"

"I don't know," Catherine said. "He wasn't here when I woke up this morning."

"Wasn't—? You mean he just left without saying good-bye?" As soon as the words were out of her mouth, Billie was sorry she had said them. They had to hurt.

But Catherine just said, "I suppose so."

"The two of you didn't, uh, have a fight or anything, did you?" Billie knew it wasn't really any of her business, but she liked Catherine and didn't want to think that Adam had hurt her somehow.

"No, of course not. It was a very pleasant evening." Catherine reached for her purse, picked it up, took two steps toward the door, dropped the purse, fell to her knees, and put her face in her hands as she began to cry. Her body shook with the intensity of the sobs as Billie hurried over to her.

Billie put her arms around Catherine and held her. "It's okay," she said. "It's okay to cry."

"N-No, it's not," Catherine said. "We'll be late."

"It doesn't matter. It really doesn't."

"He . . . he's such a son of a bitch."

"And you love him more than life itself, don't you?"

Catherine laughed a little through her tears. "Yeah. Oh, yeah."

"He'll be back."

Catherine nodded. "He'd better be. . . ."

FORTY-SIX

It just wasn't fair, Joe thought as he made his way back to his bunk from the head. Dale had never been to sea, either, so why wasn't he miserably sick, too?

"At it again, huh?" Dale asked from the bunk just above Joe's. He was lying on his back reading an issue of *Whiz Comics*, holding the comic book at an angle to catch the light from the wire-shrouded bulb on the ceiling of the compartment.

Joe tried not to moan as he slid into his bunk. "Shut up," he said instead. He laid his head on the thin pillow, and that helped for a moment until he made the mistake of closing his eyes. The darkness just exaggerated the motion of the ship and made Joe's stomach lurch again. He opened his eyes and concentrated on the rivets on the bottom of the bunk above him, and slowly the sick feeling faded somewhat.

"You'll get used to it," Dale said. "It took me a while to get my sea legs."

"You had your sea legs in an hour, while the rest of us were still hanging over the rail," Joe said.

"What can I say? I have good balance and equilibrium."

"Where'd you learn a two-bit word like that, from Captain Marvel?"

"Oh, so now the guy who writes for the pulps is making fun of comic books?"

"Shut up," Joe said again. He felt too bad to argue. Maybe if he could sleep for a while, he'd feel better . . .

An alarm began to sound. Dale tossed aside his comic book, swung his legs out of the bunk, and dropped to the deck. "That's general quarters," he said.

"We're in the U.S. Army, not the British Navy," Joe said. "We don't have to answer that."

"Yes, we do. Come on. Maybe there's a Kraut submarine out there, and we'll get to see it."

Joe thought Dale sounded like a little kid talking about catching a glimpse of Santa Claus on Christmas Eve. It would be just fine with Joe if all the German U-boats in the ocean stayed well away from the H.M.S. *Starks*. Still, he knew Dale was right. On the off chance that there was some real trouble, it would be better to be abovedecks helping out instead of waiting here deep inside the ship. It was probably just a drill, though, Joe told himself. The British Navy seemed to love drills.

The other members of the ASF detachment who were in the compartment joined Joe and Dale in hurrying up three decks and through a hatchway onto the main deck of the *Starks*. As he emerged from the companionway, Joe forgot about being seasick. Several airplanes were flying over the ship, and the thought that they might be German bombers drove every other thought out of Joe's brain.

A moment later he relaxed as he saw the markings on the planes. He was far from an expert spotter and had trouble identifying aircraft from their silhouettes, but he didn't have any problem seeing the United States flag painted on the fuselages of these planes.

A nearby British sailor, seeing the American soldiers hustle out on deck, grinned and called, "You Yanks might as well go back below. It's just a joint bombing exercise with your Air Corps."

Joe saw water splash high in the air to starboard as one of the planes overhead dropped its mock bombs. The *Starks* and the other vessels in the convoy began to weave back and forth as they cut through the waves of the Gulf of Mexico, somewhere off the west coast of Florida.

Joe said to the British sailor, "I know those bombs aren't real, but couldn't they still do some damage if they hit the ship?"

"Right. That's why we don't let them hit us."

Joe couldn't argue with the logic of that, maddening though it was. Practice was good, he told himself. If those really had been German planes up there dropping real bombs, he definitely would have wanted the officers and crew of the *Starks* to know what they were doing.

"Hey," Dale said to the sailor, "do you know if there are any real Kraut planes or subs around here?"

"Don't you worry, lad. You'll probably be seeing the real thing soon enough."

That was exactly what Joe *was* worried about.

Several American cruisers accompanied the British convoy across the Gulf of Mexico, through the ninety-mile-wide gap between Key West, Florida, and the island of Cuba, and up the East Coast. Once they were out of the Gulf and into the Atlantic, the risk of encountering German U-boats increased substantially, at least according to the scuttlebutt that Joe heard. Eventually the convoy began to veer in a more easterly direction as it entered one of the main shipping lanes between the United States and England. The American cruisers sent them on their way with semaphore flags waving that indicated wishes of good luck.

It had taken the convoy a week to reach this point in the voyage. From what Major Wilton had said, that meant another two weeks would be required to reach Liverpool. By now Joe's seasickness had settled down quite a bit. Dale had been right—it just took a little time for a guy to get his sea legs. Dale was lucky that he had adjusted so quickly.

Joe had heard about people taking ocean cruises, but to be honest, he didn't see the appeal in it. The ocean was boring, just mile after mile after mile of blue-green waves. Of course, if he had been on a luxury liner, he supposed it would be different. There would be things to do on a ship like that. Here on the *Starks*, since the Americans were just passengers, they had nothing to do to pass the time except going over everything they had learned about the M3 tanks.

One day, as he was sitting in the wardroom, Joe was surprised to hear a sound that was very familiar to him—the pecking of typewriter keys. He went down the narrow companionway to another compartment and found a British sailor sitting at a small desk, typing rapidly. The sailor glanced up, nodded pleasantly enough, and said, "Hello, Yank. You're not supposed to be here, you know."

"Sorry," Joe said. "I just heard the typing."

"Bothering you, is it?"

"As a matter of fact, no. I sort of missed the sound of it." Several times during basic training at Camp Bowie, he had toyed with the idea of trying to find a typewriter and starting a story, but he had always been either too busy or too tired to make the effort. Now he was neither. "Is this machine just for official use?"

"I'm typing up some reports for the captain, if that's what you're asking."

"Actually, I was wondering if I could maybe use it sometimes, when it's not being used for anything else. I, uh, I'm a writer."

The sailor grinned. "Like Sapper or Edgar Wallace?"

"Well, yeah, I guess."

The sailor rolled the piece of paper out of the typewriter and added it to a stack of others. He picked up the whole stack, tapped it on the desk to straighten it, and stood up. "Be my guest," he said. "There's paper in the drawer underneath. But if anybody catches you wasting Royal Navy supplies, I don't know a thing about it, got me?"

"Sure," Joe agreed. "I just saw the typewriter sitting here and helped myself to it."

"That's right. But if you write something good, you got to promise to let me read it."

"Sure." Joe stepped aside and let the sailor pass through the hatchway. He went into the office and sat down in front of the typewriter. With practiced ease, he took a sheet of blank paper from the drawer and rolled it into the machine. It was a British model, a brand he'd never heard of, and definitely old-fashioned. But a typewriter was a typewriter, Joe told himself as he centered the carriage and poised his fingers over the keys.

He felt a second of suffocating panic as nothing came to him. His mind was completely blank. Then, without really thinking about it, he typed quickly:

LAST OF THE SEA DOGS
by Joseph Parker

Considering where he was, a pirate story seemed highly appropriate. If he could finish it by the time the ship reached England, he could send the manuscript to his mother and have her submit it to *Argosy* or *Adventure*. His shoulders hunched forward a little as he began to type rapidly and accurately.

The sea was smooth as glass and the sun was a hot, brassy ball in the sky as Captain Adam Rutledge shouted to the gunner, "Fire!"

★　★　★

That night, soon after the evening mess, general quarters suddenly sounded from the ship's loudspeakers. Dale was in the wardroom playing cards, while Joe had slipped back into the tiny office to try to add a few more pages to his manuscript. As klaxons began to blare, Joe thought that this wasn't a drill; it was possible, of course, that the Royal Navy could have some sort of night exercise planned, but every instinct in his body told him it was the real thing. He ripped the paper out of the typewriter, grabbed up the other pages of the story, and ran down the aisle in the center of the sleeping compartment to stuff the pages under the mattress on his bunk. They would be as safe there as anywhere, he thought.

Dale hurried up. "What do you think?" he asked excitedly. "Are we finally going to see some action?"

"I hope not," Joe said fervently. Along with the other members of the detachment, they started toward the ladder that would take them to the upper decks.

This time, however, their way was abruptly blocked by a burly British sailor who came down the ladder. "You lads stay where you are!" he called. "You're restricted to quarters until the alert is over."

"What's going on?" one of the Americans asked, putting into words what all of them wanted to know.

"We made an asdic contact, I suspect," the Englishman said. "The entire convoy is on alert."

"What'd you say about your ass and your dick?" another soldier asked, prompting laughter from most of the ASF detachment. "You mean all the stories about you Limeys are true?"

The English sailor clenched his fists angrily, but his devotion to duty kept him from starting a fight. However, he growled, "I'll remember you, Yank."

Joe knew that an asdic machine was some sort of underwater listening device that could warn ships of the nearby presence of a submarine. He was certain now that somewhere out there under the night-black waters of the Atlantic, a German U-boat was stalking the convoy.

Faintly, he heard a couple of heavy reports and felt a tiny shiver in the deck under his feet. The other Americans heard and felt the explosions, and they immediately stopped laughing and turned sober. Joe looked over at Dale and saw that his brother was frowning now. "What was that?" Dale asked.

The Englishman heard the question and replied, "Depth bombs. Our lads are trying to chase off the German buggers."

There was another *whump!*, louder and closer this time. One of the soldiers yelped, "Shit! That sounded like a bomb!"

"A torpedo going off, rather. It must have struck one of the other ships in the convoy."

"How do you know it didn't hit us?" A note of panic edged into the question. "We could be sinking!"

"If we'd been torpedoed, you'd know it," the sailor said. "That explosion was several hundred yards away."

"But a Kraut sub carries more than one torpedo, doesn't it?" Dale said.

"Yes, certainly." The sailor paused as more depth bombs exploded in the distance. "You'd better keep your fingers crossed, as you Yanks say."

Joe swallowed hard, but it didn't ease the pounding in his head. The claustrophobia he hadn't even known he had before starting on this voyage came back strong. He wanted to yell, to pound on the walls, to run up the ladders until he reached the open air so that he could take his chances on deck. The thought of being trapped down here if the ship should happen to be struck by a torpedo was almost too much for him to bear. If the hull was breached, the cold water would rush in and fill the compartment, and he and all the others would be left to drown like rats. He could imagine fighting against the frigid grip of the water as it rose higher and higher, fighting to pull in a breath as the air pocket grew smaller and smaller . . .

"You gonna be sick, Joe?" Dale asked. "You look a little green."

Joe swallowed again and wiped the back of his hand across his mouth. "No, I'm not gonna be sick," he said, as if saying it might make it true. Sure he was scared; as he looked around him, he saw that all the other men in the compartment were afraid, too. Some of them were chattering excitedly in an attempt to cover it up, while others stood silently. One man's lips were moving without him saying anything, and it took Joe a second to recognize that he was reciting the Twenty-third Psalm to himself.

The valley of the shadow of death . . . That was where

they all were right now, Joe thought. Even Dale's excitement had faded, and he licked his lips nervously before he said, "Kinda rough, ain't it?"

"Yeah," Joe said hollowly. "Kind of rough."

FORTY-SEVEN

Joe supposed that to most people, Liverpool wasn't a very pretty town. He had never seen a more welcome sight, though. The relief that went through him as the H.M.S. *Starks* slid up the River Mersey and into its anchorage by the docks left him a little limp.

"Well, we made it," Dale said from beside him at the ship's rail.

Joe nodded. "We made it."

Not everyone who had been part of the convoy could say that. One of the transport ships had been sunk during the encounter with the German U-boat. The ship had taken a couple of torpedoes but fortunately had not been carrying any volatile cargo. If the holds had been full of ammunition or fuel oil or aviation gas, the ship would have probably been blown to bits by the resulting explosion. As it was, the cargo was mostly rubber, and though it would burn, it wouldn't blow up. The ship had gone down slowly enough so that many of the crew had been able to abandon it successfully, and rescue boats from the other transports and the corvettes had plucked most of them out of the water. Still, over eighty men had died in the attack, and the U-boat had avoided all the depth bombs and slipped away, its bloody work done.

Then, just a couple of days before the convoy's arrival in England, a German Focke-Wulf long-range bomber had attacked it. Antiaircraft fire—"Archie," Joe heard the British sailors call it—had scored a hit on the plane and sent it spinning in a fiery dive into the ocean, but not before it had successfully dropped a couple of bombs on one of the corvettes in the escort. One bomb had landed on the corvette's bridge, obliterating it in an instant. A second later, the second bomb had gone down the stack and into the boilers, and when it exploded it ripped the corvette in half.

Joe and Dale had seen that happen. Unlike the submarine attack, the Americans were already on deck when the Focke-Wulf came barreling down out of the clouds. There had been no time to hustle them below. Joe and Dale and the other men had stood there gripping the rail tightly while, a few yards away, one of the transport's antiaircraft guns fired at the German bomber. The Archie rounds burst high in the sky with a *crump!* sound, sending out puffs of black smoke along with their deadly shrapnel.

The corvette was a quarter of a mile away when it exploded and broke in two, but the concussion from the blast reached the *Starks*. Some of the Americans cursed, while others cried. Joe just stared across the water at the flaming wreckage with an enormous lump in his throat. Debris thrown high in the air came splashing back down into the ocean between the transport and the destroyed corvette.

"All those men . . ." Dale had muttered.

Joe had nodded. "Yeah." He knew that his brother now realized this wasn't a game. Dale would probably never again eagerly anticipate an encounter with the enemy.

Now, as the convoy reached Liverpool and Joe could finally breathe a little easier, he knew there was no doubt in his mind: whether the United States was officially at war or not, the Nazis were the enemy. If some of the isolationists back home had to make an Atlantic crossing a few times, they would change their tune in a hurry.

Captain Hoffman, Sergeant Garmon, and the other officers and noncoms from the ASF detachment supervised the unloading of the M3 tanks. The General Grants rolled down ramps to the docks under their own power. Every day during the trip, the tanks' engines had been started and run for a short time to keep them in good working order. The men of the detachment followed the tanks off the transport, turned out in fresh uniforms and overseas caps. Joe supposed they would be housed at some British Army base while they were teaching their opposite numbers everything there was to know about the tanks.

Sergeant Garmon surprised them by gathering the men who had come with him from Texas and saying, "You boys each have a three-day pass. Be back here Thursday mornin' at oh-six-thirty."

"What's that, Sarge?" Dale asked. "You're turning us loose in England?"

"Hell of a note, ain't it?" Garmon shook his head. "It ain't my idea, that's for sure. There's some sort of wranglin' goin' on between the British brass about what they're goin' to do with all these tanks, and until they get it straightened out, they don't need us."

"But . . . where are we supposed to go?" one of the soldiers asked.

"The British have set aside quarters for us at one of their training bases not far from here. Major Wilton said that a lorry will be goin' over there in about an hour, if anybody wants a ride."

"What the hell's a lorry?"

Joe said, "It's what the British call a truck."

Garmon looked at him. "You know a lot about England, do you Parker?"

"No, sir," Joe said quickly. He didn't want to be "volunteered" as an expert on things British. Most of his knowledge came from reading pulp stories and Agatha Christie novels.

"Anyway," Garmon went on, "you can stay at the base or you can find someplace to stay here in Liverpool. They tell me our money's good over here, at least for most things."

"What about the whores?" one of the men asked. "Do they take American money?"

"Damn it, you'd better remember those hygiene films," Garmon said without answering the question. "I don't want anybody comin' down with a case of British crabs."

The meeting broke up with some of the soldiers deciding to ride over to the British base, but most of the men opted to explore Liverpool. Joe had another idea.

"Why don't we go to London and see if we can find Arthur?" he asked Dale.

"Arthur? You mean Arthur Yates?"

"Remember, he withdrew from the university last fall and came home because of the bombing."

"Yeah, well, I hear the Krauts are still bombing London," Dale pointed out. "I'm not sure I want to go visiting while that's going on."

"Come on," Joe said. "Don't you want to see Arthur?"

"He was your pal, not mine."

"Well, then, don't you want to see London? It's one of the most historic cities in the world!"

"I don't know . . ."

It wasn't like Dale to hold back from anything that had the faintest prospect of excitement. Obviously, the battles that had taken place during the voyage over here had affected him, at least to a certain extent.

"I'd really like to go," Joe said. He knew that as frightened as he had been at sea, he should have been equally nervous about exposing himself to the dangers of the Blitz, but he wanted to see Arthur again and he knew he might not ever have another chance to visit London.

"Okay," Dale said. "If we can find a way to get there, I guess we can go. Besides, from the looks of some of the buildings around here—what's left of them, anyway—the Krauts have been doing some bombing here, too."

"Great!" Joe hefted his duffel bag. "Let's find out where the train station is."

★　★　★

Getting from Liverpool to London proved to be more difficult than Joe had thought it would be. They were told at the train station that it would be a couple of days before they could get seats on any train bound for London. Under the Blitz, travel had been greatly restricted, and open berths were at a premium.

"We don't *have* a couple of days," Joe told the clerk. "We only have three-day passes. How long does it take to get from here to London by train?"

"Eight hours—and that's *if* there are no delays," the clerk said. "These days, you'd best count on it taking ten or twelve hours."

"Well, that's it," Dale said. "We just can't get there and back in time."

Joe sighed. "I guess not. We might as well go back to the docks and see if we can catch a ride over to that British base."

They picked up their duffel bags and turned away from the window, only to stop as they found themselves confronted by a middle-aged man and woman. "You're Yanks, aren't you?" the man asked.

"Uh, yes, sir," Joe said.

The man and woman beamed at them. "American soldiers, come to give us a hand with disposing of old Uncle Adolf?" the man said.

"We're over here with some tanks that are being delivered as part of the Lend-Lease program." Joe thought the couple looked friendly, but he couldn't figure out what they wanted with him and Dale.

"Here you go, then." The man reached inside his coat and took a pair of folded papers from a pocket. "Round-trip tickets to London."

"The train leaves in twenty minutes," the woman added helpfully.

Joe didn't reach for the tickets, even though the man extended them toward him. "It's not that we don't appreciate the offer, but I don't understand . . ."

"Nothing to understand," the man said briskly. "You've come over here to help us, and now we want to help you. Don't we, Alice?"

The woman nodded and smiled.

"You see, we overheard you talking about your dilemma with the clerk, and we decided straight off that you ought to have these tickets. Got friends in London, do you?"

"Yes, sir," Joe admitted. "A friend we went to school with in the States."

"Excellent! I just hope he hasn't fallen victim to the Blitz."

"I got a letter from him about a month ago," Joe said. "He was all right then."

"Well, then, perhaps he still is. The bombing hasn't been as bad lately, you know. I suspect the bloody Nazis have figured out that they're not going to be able to pound us into submission." The man thrust the tickets toward Joe again. "Please, take them, with our thanks for everything you lads are doing for us."

"Well . . ."

Dale reached out and took the tickets. "Thanks."

"We may not be doing you a favor, you know. Never can tell when the bombing will get worse again."

"I guess we'll just have to take our chances," Joe said. "It's not really safe anywhere, is it?"

The woman sighed, and the man shook his head. "Not these days, no, it isn't, lad."

"Thank you for the tickets," Joe said. "Now, where's the platform for this train . . . ?"

The man took his arm. "I'll show you."

A few minutes later, Joe and Dale had climbed onto the train, accompanied by the middle-aged British couple. The woman pressed a small basket of fruit into Dale's hands. "We were going to take this with us for the trip, but you two lads should have it," she said. "Fresh fruit's a bit of a rarity, you know."

Joe suspected it was more than rare. In a war-ravaged country such as England, it was almost worth its weight in gold. "Thank you again," he said. "But we don't even know your names."

The man waved a hand. "Names don't really matter at

a time like this, do they? It's enough to know that we're all allies and friends."

Joe nodded. "I suppose so." He followed the couple to the door of the car and waited until they had stepped out onto the platform. A conductor was coming along, waving all the passengers inside since the train was about to pull out. Joe extended his hand and shook with the man, then the woman, thanking them once again for their generosity. "Will you be able to get to London later?" he asked.

"Oh, yes, in a few days, never you worry," the man said. He took hold of his wife's hand. "I'll just wire the mortuary. I'm sure they won't mind hanging on to our boy's casket for a bit."

FORTY-EIGHT

"Casket? Are you sure he said casket?"

Joe leaned back against the narrow bench seat on his side of the compartment and sighed. "He said casket. I figure that they had a grown son who was living in London. Something happened to him—he got sick and died, or was killed in the bombing—and they were going to get his body and bring him back home to bury him."

Dale said, "So instead of doing that, they gave their tickets to a couple of complete strangers. Foreigners, at that."

Joe shrugged. "You heard what they said. They're grateful to us for trying to help out. I guess the British felt like it was them against the whole world until the United States started pitching in."

"Maybe. But they still shouldn't have given up their tickets."

"I tried to tell them that, but it was too late. The train was already moving."

Dale shook his head. "I guess all we can do is go on to London, so their sacrifice won't have been for nothing."

"Yeah." Still, Joe knew that his last sight of the English couple would haunt him. They had looked so lost and alone, standing there like that on the platform. They had to wonder what had gone wrong with their world.

★　★　★

Joe and Dale didn't see much of the English countryside on their way to London. The train had rolled out of the Liverpool station not long before dusk, so most of the trip took place during the night. As the clerk had predicted, the train ran behind schedule. The journey across England took more than twelve hours. It was dawn the next morning before the train reached Paddington Station in London's West End.

"How are we going to find Arthur's house?" Dale asked as he and Joe left the train and made their way through the crowd that thronged the station's platform. People stood eight or ten deep, hoping to get a seat on a train that would take them out of London.

"I've got the address. Maybe we can hail a cab and have it take us there."

Only there weren't any cabs, they discovered as they left the station. The streets weren't empty, but neither were they busy. Many of the buildings in the neighborhood showed damage from the Blitz. Some of them were little more than bombed-out husks. Naturally, centers of transportation would make good targets for the German bombers, Joe thought. He was a little surprised that the train station was still standing.

People were still going about their business, however, despite the terrible damage that had been inflicted on the city. A few yards from the entrance to the train station, a wooden kiosk was set up and filled with newspapers, magazines, and books. A short, slender man in a plaid cap was running it. Joe and Dale went over to him, and Joe said, "Excuse me, do you know where we could find a cab?"

"A taxicab, you mean?" the man asked.

"That's right."

"They've been commandeered by the fire department, most of 'em. One still comes by 'ere ever' now an' then," the man said. "Ya just got to keep yer eyes open."

That could take a long time, Joe decided. He said, "Is there a bus, then?"

"Where is it ye're tryin' to go, Yanks?"

"To Kensington Road," Joe said, remembering the address from Arthur's letters.

The newsstand proprietor pointed to the south. "That way about a mile, beyond Kensington Gardens. Ye can prob'ly walk it faster'n ye can find a cab."

"A mile?" Dale said. "That's a long way."

"Not for a couple o' 'ealthy young Yanks such as yerselves. Ye'll do it in no time."

Joe looked at Dale and shrugged. "We hiked thirty miles back at Camp Bowie with full packs. We might as well start in that direction, I guess. If we see a cab along the way, we can hail it then."

"Yeah, I suppose you're right."

"Thanks," Joe said to the Englishman.

They started walking, carrying their duffel bags. The damage from the German bombing seemed to be worst in the center of the city, but it was widespread. Most of the windows in the buildings they passed had been blown out. The panes of glass that remained were crisscrossed with tape so that they wouldn't fall out and shatter. Sandbags were piled around many of the doorways. Joe and Dale couldn't follow a straight path because some streets were so choked with rubble from collapsed buildings that they were closed off. Joe hoped that their zigzagging back and forth wouldn't get them hopelessly lost.

In the distance to the east, along the Thames, Joe could see some of the landmarks that made London such a famous, historic city: the Houses of Parliament, St. Paul's Cathedral, the Tower of London, even a glimpse of the Tower Bridge itself. Tendrils of smoke rose here and there across the city, many of them in the heavily hit East End. Some of the fires started by the Blitz were probably still burning, Joe thought. It would be years, perhaps decades, before all the damage done by the German bombing raids was undone. And first, of course, before the real restoration of London could begin, the Nazis had to be defeated.

They passed an open, grassy area that Joe supposed was Kensington Gardens. To his surprise, a flock of sheep was grazing there, tended by an elderly shepherd in a tweed coat and cap. The old man gave them a friendly nod and called, "Good day, Yanks."

Joe pointed ahead to the boulevard at the southern edge of the park and asked, "Is that Kensington Road?"

"Aye. Are ye lookin' for somebody in particular?"

"The Yates family."

"I know them. Go down there and turn right. It'll be about three blocks then, on your left."

"Thank you," Joe said.

"How's the bombing been lately?" Dale asked the old man.

The shepherd said, "Haven't ye heard? The bloody Boche have given up. They know they can't beat us."

The destruction Joe and Dale had seen didn't look like the Germans had given up. But they hoped the old man was right. Obviously, London had suffered tremendously during the Blitz. The city deserved a break.

The Yates house turned out to be a three-story brick-and-frame structure behind a black wrought-iron fence and a small garden. Part of the upper floor looked as if it had been heavily damaged by fire. Some of the original roof was gone and had been replaced by new boards with no shingles on them. Other holes were patched more crudely with tarpaper. For the most part, though, the house seemed solid enough, and it was clearly the home of a well-to-do family. That came as no surprise to Joe. He had known that Arthur's family had money, otherwise they would not have been able to send him to college in the United States. Arthur's father had been an officer in the British Foreign Service when he met Arthur's mother in Washington, D.C., and had assumed some other government post upon returning to England some years earlier, but Joe recalled Arthur mentioning that his grandfather had been a very successful banker.

"This is the place," Joe said.

"Your buddy Arthur's going to be surprised to see us," Dale said.

"Probably. But there was no chance to write him and

let him know we were coming. We didn't know we'd get that pass once we got to Liverpool."

Joe opened the gate and led the way up a short walk through the garden. There was no porch, only a small step at the front door. He stood on it and pressed the buzzer.

A few moments went past, then a middle-aged maid opened the door. Her eyes widened slightly at the sight of two American G.I.s standing on the doorstep. Joe took off his overseas cap, smiled pleasantly, and said, "Pardon me, ma'am, but is this where Arthur Yates lives?"

"Arthur?" the maid echoed. "You mean young Master Arthur?"

"About our age, yes, ma'am. We're friends of his from the States. We went to college with him."

A woman's voice called from somewhere in the house, "Who is it, Edith?"

The maid turned her head and replied, "Two young American gentlemen, mum. They're asking about Master Arthur."

Joe heard the brisk clicking of heels on tile as the other woman came up behind the maid. The maid moved aside. The woman who took her place in the doorway was in her late forties, with gray streaks in her blond hair, but still rather attractive. She smiled and said, "Are you friends of Arthur's?" Her voice contained a trace of a British accent, but she also sounded almost American. Joe guessed she was Arthur's mother.

"That's right, ma'am," he said. "I'm Joe Parker, and this is my brother Dale."

"Joe!" the woman exclaimed. "I've heard Arthur speak of you many times. Come in, come in. I'm his mother, Rosemary."

"Pleased to meet you, Mrs. Yates," Joe said as he and Dale stepped into the house. The air smelled faintly of old smoke, and Joe knew the scent lingered from the fire that had damaged the upper floor.

"Please, call me Rosemary." She lowered her voice slightly and went on, "I like to be reminded from time to time that things are a bit more egalitarian in America. It's a reminder of home. And since you boys are Americans, and soldiers at that . . ."

"All right, Rosemary," Joe said. "Is Arthur home?"

She hesitated, just for a second but long enough for Joe to recognize it. "He's here," she said. "He's in his room, on the second floor. Why don't you go on up and knock? It's the third door on the right."

"Thanks," Joe said. "I hope it'll be a nice surprise for him to see us."

Rosemary just smiled but didn't say anything.

Joe and Dale started up the stairs. The house was rather dark and stuffy, but well furnished. Paintings of pastoral English landscapes adorned the walls of the staircase that wound up to the second floor. When they reached the landing, Joe and Dale went down the hall to the third door on the right. Joe knocked softly on it, not quite sure why he had the urge to be quiet. It probably had to do with the hush that seemed to hang over the house, he decided.

"Come," someone called from inside. Arthur sounded a little reedy and strained, but Joe didn't have any trouble recognizing his voice. He turned the knob and opened the door.

Thick curtains were drawn over the windows, shutting out nearly all the light. Joe frowned. Why would Arthur be sitting in here in the dark?

"What do you want now, Mother?" Arthur asked. His tone was full of weariness. He sounded worse than Joe had thought at first.

"It's not your mother, Arthur," he said. His eyes tried to adjust to the gloom. He could make out the shape of a bed, and on the other side of the room was a fireplace, unlit now, in June. An armchair sat in front of the fireplace.

A figure rose sharply from the chair and turned toward the door. "Who's that?" Arthur said. He lifted a hand tentatively, as if he were frightened.

"It's Joe, Arthur. Joe Parker."

"Joe . . . ? From America?"

"That's right. My brother Dale is here with me."

From beside Joe, Dale said quietly, "Something's wrong with him."

Joe was starting to get the same idea. He said, "Hello, Arthur. It's good to see you."

Arthur laughed hollowly. He stepped forward awkwardly, groping for the back of the chair. "I wish I could say the same, Joe," he said, and then he moved into the light from the corridor. Joe saw the smoked glasses over his eyes.

"Geez," Dale said. "He's—"

Dale stopped short, but Arthur finished the sentence from him. "Blind, I believe you were about to say. Poor old Arthur is blind. That's absolutely correct."

"What . . . what happened?" Joe forced out.

"What else? The Blitz." Arthur kept one hand on the chair for balance and pointed up toward the ceiling with the thumb of his other hand. "You saw the roof? An incendiary bomb during the last big raid a few weeks ago. I was trying to help put out the blaze when a beam fell and hit me in the face. My eyes were badly burned. Rotten luck, eh?"

"Arthur, I . . . I'm sorry."

"Don't be," Arthur said curtly. "The shape the world's in now, who wants to see the bloody thing anyway?" He lifted a trembling hand and pressed the fingertips to his forehead for a moment, then went on, "But I'm being impolite. Come in, find a lamp if you can, and tell me what in heaven's name brings you two lads to London?"

"We're, ah, in the Army now," Joe said as he turned on the gas in a lamp that was mounted in a wall sconce near the bed. The yellow glow filled the room and showed him just how gaunt and haggard Arthur had become. Arthur had always been slender, but he hadn't gotten in such bad shape in just the few weeks since the fire that had cost him his eyesight, Joe thought.

"Oh, yes, you wrote and told me about your military adventures. Conscripted, were you?"

"No, we joined up on our own," Dale said. He glanced at Joe and gave a small shake of his head. Joe understood. Dale didn't want them going into the real reasons behind their enlistment.

"And you've been sent here by the Army?"

"We came over with some tanks that are going to the British Army as part of the Lend-Lease program," Joe explained. "We got a three-day pass when the convoy reached Liverpool."

"So you ran the gauntlet of the North Atlantic. See any action?"

"The convoy lost a transport to a submarine and then a German bomber sank one of the corvettes," Joe said. "That was more than enough action for me."

"Quite. More action than I'll ever see, eh?"

Joe didn't know what to say to that. He looked at Dale, and Dale just shrugged.

"I was going to join the Army, you know," Arthur went on. "Thought I would go to North Africa and help with the fight against Rommel. My father talked me out of it. Said he would secure a position for me in the War Ministry. Under-under-secretary in charge of battlefield latrine supplies or some such. Now I'm not even good for that." The bitterness in his voice was so sharp that Joe winced.

"I'm sorry, Arthur," he said. "I wish there was something we could do. . . ."

"I wanted to do something," Arthur said. "When I came home, after Evelyn died, I wanted to do something, too. That's why I planned to enlist. Now I'm just . . . useless."

"Who's Evelyn?" Dale asked, not seeing the shake of Joe's head in time to stop the question.

"A girl. A good friend. I grew up knowing her. We had thought that perhaps someday . . . when I was back from college, and when the Germans were no longer a threat . . . that we might . . . might be married—"

Arthur seemed to crumble. He bent at the waist, and it

took both hands on the back of the armchair to keep him from falling. Joe hurried forward to take his arm.

"Let go of me!" Arthur cried as he jerked away. "Bloody Yanks! If you'd helped us stand up to Hitler a year ago, Evelyn might still be alive!"

Joe recalled what Arthur had told him back in Chicago, just before he withdrew from the university and came home. Arthur had mentioned the death of a friend but then, clearly, Evelyn had been more than just a friend.

"I'm sorry, Arthur, I really am."

Arthur let go of the chair and stumbled toward the bed. He bumped into one of the posts on the footboard and clutched it. "Why don't you get the hell out of here?" he said. "You may have come to help the rest of the British, but there's not a damned thing you can do for me now. Just get out."

"Arthur, I really wish—"

Dale put a hand on Joe's arm. "Come on. He doesn't want us here."

"That's bloody right."

"Okay," Joe said. "But if there's ever anything we can do—"

"Do you have a gun?"

The question took Joe by surprise. "Not with me."

"Then you can't shoot me and put me out of my sodding misery, now can you? There's nothing else I want from you."

Dale tugged on Joe's arm. "Let's go."

Reluctantly, Joe let Dale lead him out into the hallway. He shut the door quietly behind them, unable to get the tortured image of Arthur's face out of his mind. When they turned toward the landing, they found Rosemary Yates standing at the top of the stairs.

"It didn't go well, did it?" she asked.

Joe shook his head. "He wasn't glad to see—I mean, he wasn't happy that we'd come to visit him."

"I know what you mean. It's hard to think of him as being blind. It's so unfair. He had been in such bad shape for so long, ever since Evelyn was killed in the bombing—He told you about her?"

Joe nodded.

Rosemary sighed. "He loved her. And once she was gone, he didn't see much reason for going on himself. Then there was the fire . . . and he lost . . . he lost . . ."

She began to cry, lifting her hands and putting them over her face.

"I'm sorry, Mrs. Yates," Joe said. "We shouldn't have come here today. We had no idea what had happened. And Arthur never said anything about Evelyn in his letters."

Rosemary lowered her hands and said, "He wouldn't. He tried to keep all the pain inside. It ate away at him, but he was determined to keep it all for himself."

Dale said, "We'd better go."

"You're welcome to stay . . ." Rosemary began.

Joe shook his head and said, "We've got to get back to our unit. And it's not that easy traveling across England right now."

"No, I daresay it's not." She wiped her eyes. "Thank you for coming."

"We just upset him."

"Yes, but he needed a reminder that there's a world beyond this house. The doctors say that his blindness may not be permanent, you know. His sight could come back to him someday. Even if it doesn't, there are still things he could do to help . . . Well, I don't expect the war will be over any time soon. Perhaps Arthur will yet get his chance."

"No," Joe said. "It won't be over soon."

By the time they had walked back across Kensington Gardens and returned to Paddington Station, some of the shock and horror that Joe had felt in that dark room on the second floor of the Yates house had faded. It had been replaced, however, by something just as strong.

Anger.

He stopped on the sidewalk in front of the station entrance and said, "Look at this." He swept a hand around him.

"What?" Dale asked.

"That, for instance." Joe pointed across the street at what remained of a bookshop. A German bomb had blasted it out of existence, so that only the shell of the building remained. The sign that had once hung above the doorway now dangled askew over the blank hole where the door had been.

"Or there."

This time Joe pointed at a bakery, which was somehow still in business even though half of the front wall had collapsed. A pile of sandbags rose where the wall had been.

"Or over there."

There was nothing left to indicate what this building had housed, only a pile of rubble with an old man awkwardly clambering over it and picking through the debris. Had the old man owned whatever business had been destroyed, Joe wondered, or was he just a scavenger?

"Yeah, the Krauts have bombed the hell out of the place," Dale said. "I get it, Joe. I'm sorry. I'm sorry as hell about Arthur, too . . . though I'm not sure he should've made that crack about us not helping in time. What could we have done?"

Joe shook his head. "I don't know. But I know what we can do now." He took a deep breath. "We can settle the score. We can make sure the Nazis don't ever do anything like this again."

"Now you're talking," Dale said with a grin. "We'll get the Dirty Gerrys, or whatever it is they call 'em over here."

"Damn it, I'm serious, Dale."

Dale reached up and rubbed a hand across his mouth, then said quietly, "So am I. You know me, Joe, I have to joke around about stuff. But I know what you mean. Those tanks we brought over here, they'll help the British get some of their own back against Hitler's boys, won't they?"

"I hope so," Joe said.

Dale clapped a hand on Joe's shoulder. "So let's get back and start teaching the Tommies how to use 'em."

Joe nodded and they went into Paddington Station, leaving the destruction behind them for the moment.

But both of them knew they would never forget what they had seen in London today.

FORTY-NINE

When the doorbell rang, Spencer called, "I'll get it." He was the closest anyway, since he happened to be in the foyer. His mother was in the parlor, reading after dinner while Guy Lombardo played softly on the Philco, and his father had retreated to his library, as usual. Spencer went to the door, opened it, and looked out into a warm, late-summer evening.

Joscelyn St. Clair stood on the doorstep of the Tancred home.

Spencer stiffened in surprise. Joscelyn looked gorgeous in a lightweight summer dress and a wide-brimmed straw hat with a white ribbon around it. She smiled and said, "What's the matter, honey? Aren't you going to invite me in?"

"How . . . how did you . . ."

"Find out where you live? That wasn't hard. How about it, baby? Going to introduce me to your folks?"

Spencer stepped out onto the porch and pulled the door closed behind him. For a second he had thought about doing exactly what Joscelyn suggested. After all, she was a beautiful, well-dressed young woman, certainly nothing to be ashamed of.

But she was also five years older than he was, and there was a hardness around her eyes and mouth that said her true age was infinitely older than that. She was a roadhouse girl, plain and simple, and even though Spencer told himself he wasn't ashamed of his relationship with her, he wasn't quite ready to spring her on his parents with no warning.

"Listen, I'm not sure this is a good idea—" he began.

"I've been trying to call you. Don't you ever answer the phone?"

So that explained those mysterious calls over the past couple of days. Several times, his mother or father had answered the phone, only to find no one on the other end of the line. Spencer told himself he should be grateful Joscelyn hadn't just asked to speak to him.

"So I came to see you instead," she went on. "We have to talk."

"Not here." He looked around, a little wildly, and his eyes fastened on an array of bright lights several blocks away. "The pier," he said, pointing. "I'll meet you on the pier in ten minutes."

Joscelyn's mouth got harder, and for a moment he thought she was going to be unreasonable and refuse. But then she said, "All right. Ten minutes. But don't be any longer than that, or I'll be back here ringing your doorbell again."

"I'll be there," Spencer promised. He ducked back inside the house.

"Who was at the door, dear?" his mother called from the parlor.

"Just a, uh, buddy of mine. I'm going to walk down to the pier with him."

"Don't be out late."

"I won't," he said as he put on his fedora. He hoped this wouldn't take long at all.

A band was playing in the covered ballroom at the foot of the amusement pier. Couples swayed together to the music under the light of Japanese lanterns that hung from the ceiling. Spencer didn't see Joscelyn as he made his way through the ballroom to the pier itself, but as he walked out onto the thick planks, he spotted her at one of the tables, drinking a bottle of beer. He went over to her. "Joscelyn."

She didn't look up at him. "Sit down, Spencer."

She usually still called him Spence. It wasn't a good sign that she was using his real name, he thought. "Why don't I go get a beer?" he suggested. He was underage, but the phony ID he carried made that a moot point.

"Sit down," Joscelyn said again. "We have to talk."

She's breaking up with me. Oh, Lord, she's decided she doesn't want to see me anymore! Spencer wasn't sure if he could stand that.

Nervously, he pulled out one of the other chairs at the table and sat down. Joscelyn took another pull on the beer bottle and then set it down on the table with a thump. "I'm pregnant," she said.

"What?" The meaning of her words didn't fully penetrate Spencer's brain.

"I said, I'm pregnant. Knocked up. A bun in the oven." She finally looked at him coldly. "What the hell don't you understand about that?"

Spencer's head was spinning now. He had envisioned all sorts of problems, the most dire of which was that Joscelyn didn't want to see him anymore, but he hadn't even considered the possibility that she might be pregnant. He said, "But . . . but how . . . ?"

"Offhand I'd say it was all that fucking we did."

Spencer glanced around. He didn't mind her talking dirty when they were alone. In fact, he sort of liked it. But out here in public, she could at least try to be a lady.

He took a couple of deep breaths in hopes that they would calm down his racing pulse. They didn't. He said, "Are you sure?"

She nodded. "Positive. I've been to a doctor. Of course, he's just an old rummy Mike keeps around to patch up the boys when they get bullet holes in them, but he's still a doctor."

Spencer put his hands flat on the table and tried not to moan. This was a real problem. If he had hesitated to introduce Joscelyn to his parents when he thought she was just his girlfriend, how was he going to manage now that he knew she was going to be the mother of his child? And his . . . *wife*?

There was no way around it. He had to do the right

thing, the only thing. He drew in another breath and then said, "Joscelyn, will you marry me?"

She looked at him in astonishment and said, "Fuck, no."

Again, Spencer was left speechless and confused for a moment. When he was able to speak again, he said, "But I thought . . . I mean I just assumed . . . don't you want to . . . you can't just—"

"Shut up that babbling and listen to me." She leaned forward. "I'll be damned if I'm going to marry some dumb kid and get stuck with his puking brat. We had a few laughs together, but that was it. I never wanted anything more."

"But . . . but you're pregnant."

"Not for long. I told you, Mike's got an old rummy on the payroll who can take care of things like that. All you have to do is fork over some dough."

Spencer had heard vaguely about such sordid arrangements, but he didn't know much about them. He didn't *want* to know. All he was certain of was that the whole business felt wrong.

"You don't have to do that," he said. "I told you, I'll marry you—"

"And I told you, I don't want to get married! And I don't want to have this kid!" Joscelyn reached across the table, and her fingernails dug painfully into his arm as she clutched at him. "Just give me the money to have it taken care of, and you'll never see me again. It's as simple as that."

Spencer didn't think it was simple at all. He had never run into anything quite so complicated, in fact. But he supposed he had to be practical. After all, he couldn't force Joscelyn to marry him if she didn't want to. "How . . . how much?"

She sat back and shrugged. "A couple of grand ought to take care of it."

His eyes widened. "Two thousand dollars? You'll have to pay the doctor that much?"

"Hey, I deserve something, too, don't I? You've got me in a hell of a fix, you know that?"

"I didn't mean to," Spencer said miserably. "I never intended for you to get . . . well, you know. I don't understand it. We . . . we took precautions . . ."

Joscelyn shrugged again. "Accidents happen. Now, are you going to cough it up or what?"

"I'll get the money," Spencer heard himself say. "Somehow."

She nodded. "Okay. Meet me here with it tomorrow night."

"Tomorrow night! So soon? I don't know if I can—"

"Figure out a way," she said coldly. "Otherwise, I'll go ask your father for some advice. He's a doctor, too, isn't he?"

Spencer held up his hands in surrender. "No! Don't go anywhere near my father."

"Why, you think he might want a piece, too? Like father, like son?"

God, how had he ever deluded himself into thinking this crude, crass woman was sophisticated and beautiful? Feeling sick to his stomach, he said, "I'll get the money, and I'll be here. Just stay away from my family."

"Sure. As long as I can count on you."

"You can count on me."

Joscelyn stood up. "All right, then. I'll see you tomorrow night."

She walked along the pier toward the ballroom, and as much as he hated himself for doing it, Spencer followed the sway of her hips with his eyes. The pregnancy wasn't showing yet, and she was as sensuous and exciting as she had ever been.

He tore his eyes away from her and stared out over the dark surface of the lake, trying desperately to figure out what he was going to do next.

★ ★ ★

The next night she was where she had said she would be, at the very same table, in fact. This time she wore a smart blue hat on her short brunette hair, and she looked a little bored when Spencer first saw her. That changed instantly when she noticed him coming toward her.

As he sat down, she leaned toward him and asked avidly, "Do you have it?"

He took a folded manila envelope from his pocket and placed it on the table. "It's all there," he said.

Joscelyn started to grab for it eagerly, then stopped and tried to regain some dignity by picking up the envelope slowly and deliberately. She unfastened the clasp and lifted the flap to look inside. With a satisfied nod, she asked, "Do I need to count it?"

"I said it's all there," Spencer repeated wearily.

"Where did you get it?"

Over the past twenty-four hours, his fear and confusion and sorrow had shifted and coalesced into a cold anger. "It doesn't really matter to you where I got it, does it?" he asked.

Joscelyn shook her head. "Not as long as it's not phony."

"Oh, the money's real enough, I assure you."

"Trying to sound real grown-up, aren't you? You don't like it that you're really just a stupid kid."

He felt a tremble go through his muscles. He forced himself to ignore her insults and said, "I guess that does it. There's no need for us to ever see each other again, is there?"

"No, I suppose not." Joscelyn hesitated, then said, "Not unless you want to get together again some time. I got to hand it to you, Spence—for somebody who was new at it, you eat pussy like a pro."

He pressed his shaking hands against the table and stood up quickly. He started to turn away, but he stopped and looked back at her. "Joscelyn's not your real name, is it? You just made it up."

"Think it's too classy for a tramp like me?"

"That's right."

"Well, it just so happens it's my real name. So that just goes to show you, I guess, that you can't ever really tell what somebody's like until you get to know 'em." She slipped the envelope full of money into her purse. "So long, kid."

This time Spencer managed to turn and walk off. His anger had deserted him, too. Now he was just numb and a little sick. He couldn't believe he had sunk so low.

At least things couldn't get any worse.

His father was waiting for him when he got home.

Spencer let himself in the side door, then stopped short at the sight of his father standing, arms crossed, in the short hallway. "Spencer," Dr. Gerald Tancred said.

Instantly, all of Spencer's nerves were alert. The tone of his father's voice told him that something was terribly wrong. Dr. Tancred always sounded harsh and impatient, but this was different. This was the apocalypse.

"Pop?" Spencer ventured.

"Mrs. Lowell called me this evening."

Spencer's heart began to thud heavily. Mrs. Lowell was his father's receptionist and bookkeeper at his medical office.

"She said you came to the office today while I was at the hospital."

"Yeah, I . . . I'd forgotten your schedule for today. Sorry I missed you."

"Mrs. Lowell said you waited for me for quite a while."

Spencer swallowed. "Like I said, I forgot you wouldn't be there. I . . . I thought you were just with a patient."

"Mrs. Lowell told you I was at the hospital."

"She did? I must not have heard her."

Dr. Tancred came a step closer. "You were alone in my private office."

"Well, yeah . . ."

"And you know where I keep the petty cash." It was a statement, not a question.

"Wait just a darned minute," Spencer said. Maybe a little righteous anger would throw his father off the track. "What are you saying, Pop? That I got into your money stash?"

"Petty cash" wasn't really a good enough term to describe the money Dr. Tancred kept in the office, Spencer knew. His father had never fully trusted banks ever since the Crash of '29, so he kept quite a bit of cash on hand, not only at his office but at home, too.

"Mrs. Lowell counted the money this evening, after I had come home. She did not want to accuse you without proof. After all, you are the son of her employer. But over seven hundred and fifty dollars is gone from the office, and you are the only one who could have taken it."

"That's crazy!" Spencer burst out. "I wouldn't steal from you, Pop. You know that. Did . . . did you ever think that maybe Mrs. Lowell took the money herself, and she's just trying to put the blame on me?"

Dr. Tancred shook his head. "No. She would not do such a thing. She has been with me for years."

"What about me?" Spencer asked miserably. "Haven't I been with you for years? Eighteen years, to be precise!"

The doctor waved a hand impatiently. "It is not the same thing."

"Yes it is! You'd trust her word before you'd trust mine! Your own son, and you don't trust me!"

"Not since you began gambling. And not since I came home and found that someone has pilfered from my funds here as well. And *that* could not have been Mrs. Lowell, since she has not been here."

Spencer sagged. His father had him. He had known taking the money was a risk, but he couldn't chance Joscelyn coming to see his parents. He'd had to pay her off. So he had run the risk, and under normal circumstances, it might have been weeks or months before his father discovered the missing money.

But these weren't normal circumstances, and Spencer could see now that he had been doomed to failure from the start. He just wasn't slick enough to carry off something like this.

He looked at his father, and his chin came up defiantly. "I'm sorry, Pop. I didn't have any choice—"

Dr. Tancred hit him.

It wasn't a slap, but a full-fledged punch to the jaw instead. "Thief!" Tancred shouted. "No-good thief! You are no son of mine!" German curses tumbled from his lips along with droplets of spittle.

Spencer was so shocked that he didn't even defend himself as his father hit him again. The second blow knocked him back heavily against the wall of the corridor. He staggered and bumped hard into a small table. The lamp that was on it crashed to the floor and shattered into a million pieces.

Still cursing, Dr. Tancred grabbed Spencer's shirt and held him tightly. He began to slap Spencer across the face, back and forth. Spencer took it, tasting blood in his mouth and not caring. He had it coming to him.

Then something welled up inside him, and he threw himself forward with an incoherent yell. He crashed into his father and wrapped his arms around him. Both of them went down, sprawling on the carpet runner in the hallway.

Spencer started punching at his father, wild, futile blows that missed most of the time. Dr. Tancred tried to shove him off. Gradually, Spencer became aware that someone was screaming. Hands tugged at him. He let himself fall to the side and looked up at his mother. She was crying, her face twisted and covered with tears. "Stop it, stop it, stop it," she was saying. "Both of you, stop it!"

Spencer rolled over, got his hands and knees under him, and pushed himself to his feet. His father got up, too, and started toward him. Spencer put out a hand. "It's over," he said. Blood ran from his nose into his mouth and made his voice hoarse.

Tancred was trembling violently. "Get out," he said.

"Get out of this house and never come back."

"No!" his wife cried. "He is our son!"

"He is a thief, and no son of mine!" Tancred thundered. He pointed a shaking finger at Spencer. "Leave here now, or I will call the police. You will go to jail, do you hear me, you thief? You steal my money to pay off your filthy gambling debts, you are no son of mine!"

Spencer wiped the back of his hand across his nose and mouth and saw the bright blood on it. "Think what you want, old man," he said. He was damned if he was going to explain, especially now.

"Spencer!" his mother screamed as he turned toward the door.

"Let him go! Let the thief go! He is disowned!"

"Spencer . . ."

The ragged sob that escaped from his mother almost made him turn back. Almost. But he pushed on out of the house, unsure of where he was going, knowing only that anywhere had to be better than here.

He had reached Lakeshore Drive when a cab pulled to a stop at the curb. The back door opened, and a husky, familiar voice called, "Spence?"

What now? What else could go wrong with his life? He turned toward the street and saw Karen Wells getting out of the taxi. He was shocked to see her. She looked elegant as always, and he hated for her to see him all bloody and messed up like this.

"Hi, Karen," he managed to say. He even forced a grin onto his bruised face. "What are you doing here?"

"Looking for you," she said.

He frowned. "Why?" They had been friendly enough at the roadhouse, but certainly never close. She was so far out of his league it wasn't funny.

"I heard Joscelyn talking to one of the other girls about you."

"Oh." Spencer wanted to squirm with embarrassment. "Honest, Karen, I never meant to get her . . . well, in the family way."

Karen stepped closer to him and took a handkerchief from her purse. "Here, your nose is bleeding. Did you get in a fight with somebody?"

She knew the worst of it already, he thought, so she might as well know the rest. "With my father."

"Your father? You mean you were slugging each other?"

"Yeah. Pretty dumb, huh? He figured out that I stole the money from him to pay off Joscelyn, and he threw me out of the house. I can't ever go back."

He hadn't taken the handkerchief from her, so she used it herself to dab at the blood oozing from his nose. "You're going to ruin that handkerchief," he told her.

"I don't care. I can afford another one. Look, Spence, there's something you've got to know. That money you paid Joscelyn . . ."

"To get rid of the baby," he said bleakly.

"That's not what it was for. She bilked you, Spence. There isn't a baby."

He gave a little shake of his head. "What?"

"There is no baby. Joscelyn's not pregnant. She never was. She just lied to you and tricked you out of that two grand." Karen made him take the handkerchief, then reached back into her purse. "And I'm here to give it back to you."

"You took the money away from her?" Spencer couldn't believe she would do that for him. "Why?"

"Well, actually, I didn't. This is my money. But you can give it back to your dad, and he'll never know the difference."

Spencer pushed the bills aside. "No. I can't do that."

"Sure you can."

"You want to bail me out just out of the goodness of your heart?" He laughed hollowly. "After the past couple of nights, I'm not sure I believe in that anymore."

"Look," Karen said sharply. "I hang out with some pretty hard cases. I'm a hard case myself. But I don't like what Joscelyn did, okay? Just take the cash and get back in your family's good graces."

Stubbornly, Spencer shook his head. "I can't do it. My father said too many things . . . I just can't do it. Besides, him and me . . . we just don't see eye to eye on anything." He wiped away some more of the blood from his nose. "It's time I got out of there."

"Where will you go if you don't go home?" Karen gestured toward the cab. "I can take you anywhere you want to go."

"Thanks. I'll take you up on that offer."

"Come on." She took hold of his arm and helped him into the cab. "Now, where is it you want to go?"

The door of the cab closed, and it pulled away from the curb and rolled off into the night.

FIFTY

Summer turned to fall, and winter was on the horizon, although it was difficult to tell much about the seasons from the weather on Oahu. After growing up in Chicago, Catherine had a hard time getting used to the fact that it was November and the sun still shone nearly every day, with temperatures in the seventies. Where were the thick gray clouds, the snow, the sleet, the icy winds? Plenty of times back home, she had complained about the harsh winters, but now she found herself actually missing the bad weather.

But not nearly as much as she missed Adam. Since he had gone to Wake Island, he had not been able to get back to Pearl Harbor, even on a weekend pass.

Supply planes traveled back and forth between Pearl and Wake on a fairly regular basis, the big PBYs known as flying boats, and Catherine managed to get a letter out to Adam on every one of them. These back-channel communications were faster and more reliable than the regular mail. She knew many of the pilots, even though most of them were Marines rather than Navy aviators. They flew in and out of Ewa Airfield, across the main channel, but there was only a dispensary over there. For any major medical care, they had to come to the Naval Hospital where she worked, so she had become acquainted with many of the fliers, along with their families. It was hard for the pilots to turn down a request from a woman who gave their kids vaccinations and treated their sore throats.

Adam wrote back, too, but not as regularly. Of course, he was busy, Catherine told herself, and besides he had never been a particularly prolific correspondent. Accord-

ing to his letters, things were going all right on Wake
Island. Together with the civilian construction crew, the
Marines were making good progress at turning the island
into an air station where U.S. military planes could land
and refuel. Beginning in 1935, Pan American Airways had
used Wake for that very purpose, landing its commercial
flights there on the long jaunt across the Pacific, and the
airline had even built a hotel there.

Adam was worried, though, about how the war was
going on the other side of the world. As everyone had
expected, Germany had invaded Russia back in June, and
the unprepared Russian Army had not been able to put up
much resistance as the Wehrmacht swept through the
Ukraine. The Germans had taken Kiev, where Ruth Bergman's parents still lived, and nothing had been heard from
Adam's grandparents since that time. He feared the worst.

Catherine had heard from Joe and Dale Parker, too.
From Joe, actually, since Dale was even less inclined to
write letters than Adam was. They were both in England,
having gone over there to help deliver some tanks to the
British Army. They were staying for the time being to
help their British counterparts learn how to operate the
armored vehicles. Catherine could tell from the letters that
Joe was trying to sound chatty and cheerful, but he mentioned that the convoy in which they had crossed the Atlantic was attacked a couple of times by the Germans, and
two of the ships had been sunk. That must have been a
pretty harrowing experience, Catherine thought.

Joe's letters told her what had happened to Arthur Yates,
too, and Catherine's heart went out to the young Englishman. She hadn't been as close to Arthur as Joe was, but she
had liked him and hated to hear about him losing both his
eyesight and the woman he wanted to marry.

Some mornings, Catherine woke up and thought the
war in Europe must have been just a long, horrible dream,
and now it would go away as all nightmares must. But it
didn't go away, and from what she read in the newspapers
and heard around the hospital, the United States was edg-

ing closer and closer to taking an active part in the war. There was certainly a sense of heightened anxiety around all the military bases on Oahu. The Japanese had been rattling their sabers for quite some time, and Catherine had heard several rumors about how they were on the verge of invading the Philippines.

Her main worry, though, was her brother Spencer. She hadn't heard from him in several months, and when she asked about him in her letters home, her mother pointedly avoided answering her questions. It was as if Spencer had dropped off the face of the earth. If she had been able to, Catherine would have gone home and demanded some answers, but of course that was out of the question. Her duty kept her here at Pearl Harbor.

She was coming out of the burn ward one day when she saw Billie Tabor coming toward her. Billie said, "Catherine, there's somebody down in the lobby looking for you."

"Who is it?"

"A second lieutenant. He's wearing wings."

One of the pilots, Catherine thought. Probably one that she knew who was taking off for Wake with a supply plane and wanted to ask if she had a letter for Adam. She said, "Thanks, Billie."

"He's really cute. You're going to have to introduce me to him."

"Sure, come along."

They walked together down the stairs to the hospital's main lobby. Catherine spotted a young man in Navy whites standing near the entrance with his back toward her, watching the ship traffic in the channel through the glass doors. He was carrying his cap, and his blond hair was cut extremely short. Catherine started toward him, and he must have heard her footsteps approaching because he turned around.

Catherine's heart seemed to stop beating, and her breath froze in her throat.

"Hello, sis," Spencer said.

Catherine's stunned recognition of her brother lasted only a couple of seconds, then she cried out, "Spencer!" and hurried forward to throw her arms around him. She hugged him tightly. He gave her an awkward pat on the back, evidently a little embarrassed by the enthusiastic welcome he was getting.

She finally stepped back and put her hands on his shoulders as she looked him over, top to bottom. He was quite handsome in his uniform, and Billie had been right about something else—he was wearing aviator's wings pinned to his shirt.

"What in the world are you doing here?" Catherine asked.

"Isn't it obvious? I've joined the Navy, and I'm a pilot now. I've been to flight school and everything." Spencer grinned. "I've been assigned to the *Enterprise*. I'm supposed to meet her here when she gets back into port next week. Until then I'll be staying at the BOQ, I guess."

Catherine shook her head. "I never would have believed it. Were you drafted?"

"Signed up on my own."

A frown suddenly touched Catherine's face. "It was Dad, wasn't it? Something happened—"

"I really don't want to talk about that. It's a long, ugly story. I'm surprised Mom hasn't told you all about it in her letters."

"She won't even mention you." Catherine winced. "I'm sorry. That must sound terrible."

Spencer shrugged. "Pop's probably censoring her. He kicked me out, you know. Disowned me." He waved the hand holding the cap and laughed a little hollowly. "But hey, I said I didn't want to talk about it, and that's just what I'm doing." He glanced past Catherine's shoulder. "I'd much rather you introduce me to this lovely creature who's standing here waiting to make my acquaintance. She was very helpful to me earlier, by the way."

Catherine turned and beckoned Billie forward. "Spencer, this is Nurse Billie Tabor. Billie, my little brother Spencer."

He shook hands with Billie and said, "Nice to meet you, Nurse Tabor."

"Likewise, Lieutenant Tancred."

"Would you by any chance be free for dinner tonight?"

Billie looked a little surprised, then she grinned at Catherine and said, "He certainly doesn't waste any time, does he?"

"That's my little brother, Johnny-on-the-spot," Catherine said.

Billie turned back to Spencer and said, "As a matter of fact, I'd love to have dinner with you, Lieutenant, but don't you think you ought to spend some time with your sister first?"

"Well, how about both of you have dinner with me?" Spencer suggested. "And if you know any other beautiful nurses, invite them along, too."

Billie glanced at Catherine again. "Alice is okay," she said quickly, "but let's don't ask Missy to come along."

"Why not?"

"Alice and I have a sort of agreement." Billie stepped over next to Spencer and linked her arm with his. "Since I saw Spencer first, she won't move in on him. But I don't trust Missy."

Spencer grinned broadly, clearly enjoying the idea that these Navy nurses who worked with his sister might be rivals for his attention.

"Don't let your head swell too much," Catherine told him. "That nice new officer's cap of yours won't fit."

"Just tell me where and when to pick you up," Spencer said.

Catherine gave him directions to the cottage where she and Billie and Alice lived. "Come by about six-thirty. I want to hear about everything back home." She added, "And I do mean everything."

Spencer just shrugged. Catherine knew she would be doing well to get any of the details out of him concerning the reasons he had enlisted in the Navy. Maybe she ought to just mind her own business, she told herself. It was enough that Spencer was here, and that evidently he had turned his life around.

"I'll see you later," he said after giving Catherine another hug. "I ought to go check in at the BOQ."

"All right." She patted him affectionately on the arm. He said good-bye to Billie and then turned to stride out of the hospital lobby.

"He's a dreamboat," Billie said when Spencer was gone.

"He does look good in a uniform, for a bratty little brother," Catherine admitted.

"He doesn't have any deep, dark secrets I should know about, does he?"

"I don't know," Catherine answered honestly.

★ ★ ★

Alice respected the "no poaching" agreement she had with Billie, so it was the redhead who went walking on the beach with Spencer that night after the four of them had dined at a little restaurant in Honolulu. Catherine figured that nothing happened between them except maybe a kiss or two, but Billie was definitely attracted to Spencer. The feeling seemed to be mutual.

Catherine saw her brother several times over the next week. He came to supper at the nurses' cottage a couple of times, and on Saturday night, the four of them went to the movies in Honolulu. The picture was *The Long Voyage Home*, with John Wayne, a story about a Merchant Marine steamer in the South Pacific. The palm tree-laden sets reminded Catherine of the beaches here on Oahu. Spencer and Billie seemed to enjoy the film, too. Of course, they were more interested in each other than in the movie. . . .

They took a cab back to the naval base. The driver was a talkative Hawaiian who seemed to know more than he should about the war alert that had been issued from Washington a few days earlier. Word of such things always got around, though, because for all its sprawling size, Pearl Harbor was like a small community with a very effective grapevine for gossip. That inevitably spread to Honolulu and the surrounding area.

The base was lit up brilliantly. All of the Pacific Fleet's battleships were docked at Pearl at the moment, which was something of a rarity. The *Pennsylvania* was in Drydock Number One, while the other battlewagons were lined up along the southeast shore of Ford Island. The *Enterprise* and the other aircraft carriers were all out at sea, also a bit unusual, but the *Enterprise* was due back soon, so Spencer could report for his new duty.

The cab drew up in front of the cottage. Catherine and Alice got out first, followed by Spencer and Billie. The two of them lagged behind while Catherine and Alice went inside, and Catherine knew they were going to stand on the porch and neck for a while before Spencer took the cab over to the ferry landing. The Bachelor Officers Quarters, both old and new, were located on Ford Island, so Spencer would have to catch a ferry over there. Catherine snapped off the porch light as she went inside so that her brother and Billie would have some privacy.

She had changed into a nightgown and robe and was getting a glass of milk out of the refrigerator in the little kitchen when Billie and Spencer came into the front room. Catherine eased the refrigerator door shut so the light would go out. Spencer and Billie were holding hands, and they let go of each other reluctantly. "Good night," Billie said.

"Good night." Spencer kissed her again, quickly, and then Billie went into her bedroom and closed the door.

Spencer was turning toward the front door when Catherine stepped into the doorway from the kitchen. "Hey," she said softly.

He stopped and turned back to grin at her. "Hi, Sis. I thought you were going to bed."

"I am. I just wanted a little milk first." Catherine came into the room. "You never did tell me about what happened at home."

He started shaking his head. "It's nothing I want to talk about—"

She held up a hand to stop him. "That's all right. I just want to say that from everything I can see, you've grown up some, little brother. I was about to warn you not to hurt Billie, but I don't think I have to worry about that."

"She's a swell kid. I really like her. I won't do anything to hurt her, Catherine."

"Okay." Catherine leaned closer to him and kissed him on the cheek. "Good night, Spencer."

" 'Night, sis." He went out the door, then paused on the step and looked back at her. "Hey, why don't we have a picnic tomorrow afternoon? Might be our last chance before I go sailing off on the *Enterprise.*"

"Sounds like a good idea," Catherine told him. "I've got the early duty in the morning, but I'm off tomorrow afternoon."

"One o'clock?"

"That'll be fine."

"I'll be by for you and Billie and Alice." He lifted a hand in farewell and walked back out to the cab. Catherine watched him go, the moonlight shining brightly on his white uniform. She thought she heard him whistling happily as he left.

FIFTY-ONE

Catherine was on duty at the hospital the next morning at six o'clock. She spent the first part of her shift checking on patients, taking vital signs, dispensing medication to those who were supposed to have it. By the time she had done that, it was nearly seven. Then one of the doctors asked her to come with him on rounds. Some of the doctors had found out that she was a pre-med major in college and planned to eventually become a physician herself, and they went out of their way to point out things to her that might be helpful later on in her career. Others found the idea humorous and liked to make snide little comments about it, but Catherine had trained herself to ignore them. This morning, the major she accompanied on rounds was both friendly and helpful.

It was ten minutes until eight when she walked up to the lounge on the third floor and poured herself a cup of coffee. Several other nurses were in the lounge, but Catherine just nodded pleasantly to them and carried her coffee over to the window that looked out to the northeast, along Battleship Row. She thought for a moment about Adam, then when her longing to see him again threatened to grow too strong, she forced her mind onto other subjects. She wondered what would be good to take in the picnic basket that afternoon.

She didn't notice the planes in the sky until they were close to the base, coming in quickly. Some of the planes veered off suddenly to the south, but the others raced on toward Pearl Harbor. Catherine was no expert on aircraft, but she had seen enough planes taking off and landing at Hickam and Ewa that something immediately struck her as odd about these. After a moment she realized that their landing gear was fixed, rather than retractable.

Then the closest planes banked slightly, and she saw the bright orange ball of the rising sun painted on their fuselages.

An explosion sounded in the distance, and the floor vibrated slightly under her feet. Catherine dropped her cup. It shattered on the floor, splashing hot coffee around her ankles, but she didn't notice that. She leaned forward toward the glass of the window and whispered, "Oh, no."

Water plumed high in the air from an explosion along the shore of Ford Island, where the battleships were moored. White smoke billowed up from somewhere on the island itself. Catherine saw another plane swoop low over the water, this one coming in from the northwest. They were all around, she realized. She looked past Drydock Number One and along Pier 1010, on the southeastern shore of the main channel. Something was moving through the water toward the two ships docked at 1010, the minelayer *Oglala* and the cruiser *Helena*. As Catherine watched, horrified, the *Helena* erupted in smoke and flame as a huge explosion rocked it. Next to it, the *Oglala* shuddered and began to heel over.

By this time, the other nurses in the lounge were at the window with Catherine, and one of them cried, "Oh, my God! What is it? What are they doing out there?"

"War," Catherine said.

Then one of the planes—Japanese planes, Catherine knew now—veered toward Hospital Point, and orange flame flickered under its nose as its pilot opened fire with his machine guns.

Spencer's room was in the old BOQ, on the northeast corner of Ford Island. He was sleeping soundly and dreaming of Billie Tabor. Dreams of the sweet, redheaded nurse were quite a change—and quite a relief—from the images of Joscelyn that had haunted his sleep over the past few months, ever since he had left Chicago. He hated Joscelyn for what she had done to him, but at the same time he knew he had played right into her hands. Some of the blame really and truly belonged to him. And deep down, although he was loath to admit it even to himself, a part of him still wanted her. His ability to reason went completely out the window when he thought too long about the things they had done together in bed.

That was why he was determined to take things slow and easy with Billie. *Sweet Billie*. So far he hadn't done anything except kiss her, even though she had made it relatively clear that she wouldn't mind if he went a little further. He was going to try holding back for a change, instead of giving in to every impulse. Maybe things would work out better this way.

He was smiling in his sleep when the bombing began.

The blasts were so loud and shook the building so hard that Spencer came up out of the sheets yelling. He twisted and rolled and fell hard on the floor next to his bunk. People were shouting in the halls. Spencer pushed himself to his feet and stumbled to the door, yanking it open as another explosion sounded somewhere nearby. A man running past in the corridor called out, "Air raid! Air raid! This is no drill! Air raid!"

Who the hell's bombing us? Even as the question formed in Spencer's mind, the answer came to him. It had to be the Japanese, of course. Everyone in the fleet knew that relations between the United States and Japan had grown worse over the past year. That was why the war alert had gone out from Washington. But no one seriously thought the Japs would hit Pearl Harbor. They were much more likely to strike at the Philippines or Borneo, according to everything Spencer had heard.

Somebody had made a *big* mistake, he thought as he ran toward the exit, dressed only in his skivvies.

He emerged from the BOQ just in time to see the battleship *Oklahoma*, moored just outside the *Maryland* only a couple of hundred yards away, take a hit amidships from a bomb or a torpedo, Spencer couldn't tell which. Japanese planes were coming in from the southeast on torpedo runs, launching their deadly missiles into the Southeast Loch so that they had a straight shot at the line of battleships. At the same time, Spencer saw as he looked up, high-level bombers were also dropping explosives, and Jap fighters flitted around the sky over Pearl Harbor as well, strafing anything that moved with deadly machine gun fire.

An officer trotted past and paused to call to Spencer and several other men, "Get to an AA gun!" He pointed toward the shore. Spencer and the others started running in that direction. Some of them were fully dressed in their uniforms, some wore pants and undershirts, others like Spencer were barefoot and clad only in their underwear. But Spencer supposed that being out of uniform didn't really matter all that much when you were under attack. He could help man an antiaircraft gun just as well in shorts and undershirt as he could in a full uniform.

And if they didn't start putting up a fight pretty soon, he thought, they might as well roll over and play dead for the Japs. It was almost that bad already.

He knew he should have been scared. In a way, he was. But he was more concerned with reaching the AA emplacement and doing whatever he could to help knock some of those planes out of the sky. A hot anger took the place of some of the fear he should have been experiencing.

Then a new fear went through him like a knife. *Catherine!* A second later, he remembered that she'd said she had the duty this morning. She would be at the hospital. Surely the Japs would spare the hospital.

But Billie and Alice were at the bungalow, and there was no telling what would happen there. At least Catherine ought to be relatively safe, he told himself.

"Get down!" Catherine screamed at the other nurses as she saw bullets chewing up the trees and the sidewalk and the lawn next to the hospital. The women threw themselves back away from the window. Catherine landed face down on the tile floor and covered her head with her arms, expecting to hear the window shatter under the onslaught of Japanese machine gun fire.

Instead, with a roar, the plane pulled up and zoomed past the hospital without firing into it. Catherine heard the sound of its engine diminish and dared to hope that they had been spared. She pushed herself onto her hands and knees as a doctor stuck his head in the lounge and yelled, "Get down to the ER! Now!"

They were going to be busy, all right, Catherine thought grimly. As she came to her feet, she cast one more glance over her shoulder through the window toward Ford Island and wondered if Spencer was all right. She couldn't even see the island anymore because of the thick black and white smoke rising from the battleships that were on fire.

Spencer didn't know anything about firing an antiaircraft gun, but he could pass shells as well as the next man. That was what he did, taking his place in the line of men that transferred ammunition up to the loaders and gunners. No one had been able to find the key to the ammunition locker, but one of the men had smashed the lock with a chunk of concrete he took from a fresh bomb crater. The sight of the smoking, gaping, ragged hole in the ground made Spencer feel cold inside when he looked at it, so he tried to ignore it.

The gun began to fire, slamming back heavily on its mount with each blast. The noise would have been deafening under normal circumstances, but there were so many explosions rocking Pearl Harbor that the sound of the gun was lost in them. Spencer glanced up and saw a few bursts of black smoke from the AA shells high in the sky. There were pitifully few such bursts. Only a little resistance was coming from the ships that were under attack, and on the ground everything was still too confused for an effective defense to be mounted. This AA gun where Spencer was located was one of the first to get into action.

He was covered in sweat, and it dripped into his eyes. He paused long enough to drag his arm across his forehead, then resumed passing ammunition. The next instant, a massive explosion staggered all the men and knocked some of them off their feet. Spencer caught his balance and looked toward the *Arizona*. The battleship was almost hidden by the black smoke that poured from it, but Spencer could see red flickers of flame within the smoke.

He became aware that someone was screaming, "Ammo! Ammo!" into his ear. He had a shell in his hands. He passed it on and then reached for another one. One of the men tapped him on the shoulder and pointed up. Spencer looked and saw a Japanese plane spiraling down toward the water, trailing smoke. The man next to Spencer mouthed gleefully, *We got him!*

Spencer nodded, then looked past the man. Another plane was barreling toward them, dropping lower and lower as it came straight at them. Spencer grabbed the man's shoulders and threw him aside. Red streaks came from underneath the plane's nose.

Spencer was knocked backward as something hit him heavily in the chest and side. Bullets whined and ricocheted around him as he fell. He didn't hurt, and his mind was clear, but a wet heat seemed to permeate his entire body. He saw men tumbling and bleeding around him, saw sparks shower through the air as machine gun fire from the strafing plane struck the antiaircraft gun and its mount. The sparks were almost pretty, he thought, and they became brighter and brighter to him, like a fireworks display, as the rest of the world grew dark.

The first casualties were in the emergency room by the time Catherine and the other nurses got there to help out.

Men were lying on the examining tables and on stretchers on the floor, and many of them seemed to be covered with blood. The doctors were working as fast as they could, trying to stop the bleeding and determine the extent of each man's injuries. Some of the wounded men died before anything could be done for them.

Catherine was at one of the tables, trying to cut away a blood-soaked shirt from a young man who looked barely old enough to shave, when his head jerked to the side and a horrible rattle came from his throat. Even in the chaos and confusion that filled the emergency room, Catherine heard the sound and knew she would never forget it. A doctor paused on the other side of the examining table, used two fingers to close the young man's staring eyes, and said to Catherine, "Go on to the next one, nurse."

Catherine had never seen anyone die before.

Her head spun, but she forced herself to try to calm down. She started to take a deep breath and found her nose and mouth filling with the coppery smell and taste of blood. She gagged a little and turned away from the examining table. Another man lay on a stretcher, practically at her feet. She knelt beside him. Both of his legs appeared to have been shattered by machine gun fire, but his torso was untouched. She cut away the ragged, sodden remains of his trousers and tried not to wince as she saw the jagged white pieces of bone that protruded from his flesh. The doctor who had spoken to Catherine a moment earlier leaned down and gave the wounded sailor an injection of morphine. "Get compresses on those legs," he said.

"Aye, aye, sir," Catherine heard herself saying.

After a while, all the blood and death and suffering began to blur together for her. She kept working, but she was numb inside. She didn't even pay attention to the explosions that rocked the hospital as bombs rained down on the *Pennsylvania,* the *Downes,* and the *Cassin* in the nearby drydock. Maybe a career in medicine hadn't been such a good idea after all.

A hand gripped her arm. "Hey, Catherine, you doing all right?"

She looked over and saw Missy Mitchell. Missy's hands and arms were stained with blood up to the elbow, and for a second Catherine thought she had been hurt. Then Catherine looked at her own hands and arms and saw that they were just as bloody. She nodded and said, "I'm okay. Have you seen Billie or Alice?"

Missy shook her head. "Haven't seen either of them."

Catherine prayed that her friends were all right. She hoped not even the Japs would be heartless enough to bomb the nurses' quarters.

Then she thought that from up there, the pilots wouldn't always know exactly where their bombs were going to fall. A lot of who lived and who died was up to nothing but Fate.

And today, on what should have been a tranquil Sunday morning, Catherine had learned just how arbitrary that was.

She went back to work with Missy beside her. The explosions and firing outside died away for a short time, then resumed with even more intensity. As she worked over the injured men, Catherine heard snatches of conversation: the Japanese were bombing all over the island of Oahu, at Hickam and Ewa and Schofield Barracks and Wheeler . . . the whole Japanese fleet was just offshore . . . an invasion force had landed in Honolulu and taken over the city . . . the mainland was under attack, too, with Los Angeles being shelled from the ocean and Japanese troops swarming ashore in San Francisco . . .

Catherine had no way of knowing what was true and what wasn't. All she could do was try to help save the lives of the men who were right in front of her. The rest of the world would just have to take care of itself for now.

Again the sounds of the attack faded. The big doors of the emergency room were wide open, and Catherine became aware that although she still heard some antiaircraft fire, the explosions and the strafing had stopped. The Japanese planes must have left. But they could come back at any time, she thought.

Still, there was a respite, and the rescue forces had to take advantage of it. Sirens wailed as ambulances raced around the naval base. Any vehicle that could still move was pressed into service as well to bring wounded men to the hospital. The Army hospital at Hickam Field was probably just as busy as the one here at Pearl Harbor, Catherine thought as she paused in her grisly tasks. Smoke still filled the air, but when she looked out through the doors toward Ford Island, she caught glimpses of small boats cutting through the water, looking for survivors.

A couple of corpsmen brought in a stretcher and set it in front of her. Catherine started to kneel beside the wounded man. She looked at the wounds where Japanese bullets had ripped through his chest and side, and she knew that he wouldn't make it. It was a miracle he had lived long enough to be brought to the hospital. She was about to move on when the man's hand suddenly came up and grasped hers with a terrible strength. She looked at his face. His mouth moved.

"Sis . . ."

"Spencer," Catherine whispered brokenly.

A grief the likes of which she had never even known could exist smashed through her, closing her throat and snapping a tight band of sorrow around her chest. She caught hold of his hand with her other hand and said again, "Spencer. Oh, God, no."

"L-love you . . . love you . . ."

Tears spilled from her eyes and she held on harder to his hand. "I love you, too."

"T-tell Mom . . ."

"I will," Catherine promised. "I'll tell her, Spencer." Her voice was so choked she could barely get the words out.

"Love you . . . tell Pop . . . Catherine . . . it hurts . . ."

She couldn't see anymore for the tears, but she felt his hand squeeze hers one more time, then go limp in her fingers. She fell forward across his body, and outside, the sirens wailed and men shouted and ran and the smoke climbed higher and higher into the blue Pacific sky.

FIFTY-TWO

By dusk on December 7, 1941, an almost eerie calm had descended on the island of Oahu. The Japanese were gone, but even though the rumors about an invasion of the island had proven to be false—at least for the time being—no one knew what was going to happen next. If war could come out of nowhere on a peaceful Sunday morning, anything could happen.

Catherine stepped out of the hospital onto the bullet-pocked front porch and gazed across the channel at Waipio Peninsula, where the battleship *Nevada* lay beached. The *Nevada*, the only vessel on Battleship Row that had had enough steam up to get moving at the time of the attack, had tried to make it out of the harbor and head for the open sea, even though it was badly damaged. It had made it only as far as Hospital Point before it went aground. From there, later in the day, it had been towed free and maneuvered across to the peninsula to keep it from sinking completely.

Smoke still hung thickly over the harbor. Fires were burning in a great many places, including on some of the ships. The *Arizona* had suffered the largest blaze of all before sinking so that only her topmost structures were still above the water. The *Oklahoma* had rolled over, trapping many of her sailors inside. Rescue parties now clambered over the upturned hull, trying to locate survivors and cut them free. Right now there was no way of knowing how many men had died here today, or how much damage the Japanese attack had done. The only thing anyone could be certain of was that the toll would be high.

Wearily, Catherine rubbed her eyes. She had cried them

dry over Spencer's body, and then Missy had lifted her and gently pulled her away. Catherine's place had been taken by Billie Tabor, who had knelt next to Spencer and sobbed wrackingly, mourning not only his death but what might have been.

Then, along with Alice Sutherland, who had also made it safely to the hospital, they all got back to work. That was the only thing they could do.

Now, Missy and Billie followed Catherine out of the hospital, and the three women in their blood-stained nurse's uniforms stood on the porch as twilight settled down over the island. Behind them, inside the building, wounded men still fought and gasped for every breath, and makeshift morgues filled every available space. There would have to be mass burials, perhaps as early as tonight but certainly by tomorrow. The area around the hospital showed some damage—trees toppled by bomb blasts or sawed off by strafing, craters in the lawn—but compared to most of the rest of Pearl Harbor the hospital had gotten off lightly.

Catherine slipped her hands into the pockets of her uniform. When she and her friends had been relieved for a short time, she had tried to scrub the blood off her hands, but most of it wouldn't come off. The stains would be there for a long time.

Missy came up beside her. "What are we going to do?"

"Catch our breath and then get back to work."

"I . . . I never dreamed . . ."

Catherine shook her head. "None of us did."

She lifted her eyes from the appalling destruction all around her and gazed to the west. Clouds had moved in during the late afternoon, and between them and the smoke, all the stars that would normally be starting to shine were blotted out.

If the Japanese had been daring enough to strike at Pearl Harbor, at the heart of the Pacific Fleet, there was no way of knowing where else they would attack. No place in the world was safe tonight.

As they turned back toward the door, Alice came out of the hospital. There were streaks of dried blood on her face where she had pushed her hair back out of her eyes during the long, terrible day. She was pale and exhausted like the rest of them, but there was concern in her eyes as she lifted a hand and reached out toward Catherine.

Catherine stopped short, dread washing over her. What else could possibly happen today?

Then she knew the answer without ever putting the question into words.

"Adam . . ." she breathed.

"I just heard some of the doctors talking," Alice said. "The Japanese have attacked Wake Island, too. A message came through from there about bombers and an invasion fleet, and then communications were cut off."

For a moment, Catherine thought she was going to faint from fear and horror. Her husband, the man she loved more than anyone or anything in the world, might already be dead, a victim of the same evil that had struck earlier today at Pearl Harbor. To keep herself from collapsing, she put a hand on one of the columns that held up the porch roof, and the other three young women stepped toward her worriedly.

Then Catherine stiffened. A few moments ago, before Alice had brought the news of the Japanese attack on Wake Island, she had made a brave statement about going inside and getting back to work. The memory of those words sounded hollow to her now, and yet she knew they were true. With the enormity of what they were facing, no one could afford to buckle, to give in to grief and fear and loss.

"I'm all right," she told her friends. "Let's go." Catherine took a deep breath and walked back into the hospital, and the others followed her.

EPILOGUE

The next day, December 8, 1941, Congress met in emergency session to hear an address by President Franklin Delano Roosevelt. Accompanied by his son, Marine Captain Jimmy Roosevelt, the president entered the House chamber at 12:29 P.M. Always a keen judge of the country's mood, Roosevelt knew that as the news of Japan's attack on Pearl Harbor spread across the nation, it washed away any lingering opposition to the involvement of the United States in the war. He had written an address to Congress in a black loose-leaf notebook, but the words he spoke today would really be meant for the entire country, not just the politicians who sat solemnly in the Capitol.

Gripping the rostrum tightly, giving no sign of the weakness in his legs, the president said, "Yesterday, December 7, 1941—a date which will live in infamy—" Roosevelt had originally written "history," then crossed it out and penciled in "infamy" above it "—the United States of America was suddenly and deliberately attacked by the Empire of Japan . . ."

He could have stopped right there and asked for a vote to declare war, and given the mood that was already in the chamber, the outcome probably would have been exactly the same. Instead he talked for a few more minutes before sitting down. When the vote did come, less than an hour later, the tally in the House of Representatives was 338 to 1 in favor of declaring war on Japan. The lone holdout was Representative Jeanette Rankin, a longtime Congresswoman who had also voted against the country's entry into World War I. The vote in the Senate was unanimous, 82 in favor, none opposed.

At long last, America was at war.

Here's a peek at the
next exciting novel in

★ **THE LAST GOOD WAR** ★

---

by
JAMES REASONER

BOOK 2

TRIAL BY FIRE

NINE

Gurnwall picked up his M1, rolled onto his belly, and snugged the butt of the rifle against his shoulder. He started firing at the twin-tailed Japanese dive bombers as they swooped down toward the air station. More bombs exploded around the runways.

Adam reached over and gripped Gurnwall's shoulder hard. "Stop it!" he said. "You're just wasting ammo!" It would be a million-to-one shot if any of Gurnwall's bullets hit one of the Jap planes and actually did any damage.

"Sonsabitches," Gurnwall was saying as he continued to pull the trigger. "Lousy stinkin' sonsabitches."

Adam grabbed the barrel of the M1 and wrenched it upwards. "Gurnwall! Cease fire, damn it!"

Gurnwall's grip on the rifle relaxed, and he blinked rapidly as if just waking up from a sound sleep. He looked up at Adam and said tentatively, "Corp? What do we do now?"

"This is an observation post. We observe."

The water tank shuddered under them again as several bombs detonated at once. Adam understood how Gurnwall was feeling. His every instinct told him to strike back at the attackers, too, but there was really nothing they could do that would accomplish anything. The 3-inch anti-aircraft guns and the .50-caliber machine guns were throwing a curtain of lead into the sky. That was the only real defense Wake Island had.

The Japanese planes were attacking in V-shaped waves. Adam was able to count the third such wave and saw that it had twelve planes in it. That seemed to be the final wave, at least for now, so that meant a total of thirty-six planes were bombing the atoll. As he watched, the first two waves continued across the lagoon toward Camp Two. Adam hoped all the civilians over there were hunting some cover by now. The third wave broke off from the formation and swung around to the west, making a broad circle.

Gurnwall was watching those planes, too. He said, "Holy shit, they're comin' at *us* now!"

It was true. The Japanese planes came out of their circle, zoomed over Kuku Point at the far end of Wilkes Island, and flew southeastward, straight toward Camp One. The .50-caliber batteries on Wilkes were pointed the wrong direction to bring their fire to bear on the planes, and the Japanese weren't even slowed down by the sparse anti-aircraft fire thrown up by the lone 3-inch gun on the island.

"Get down!" Adam shouted at Gurnwall as tracers flickered through the air around them and a line of machine gun bullets stitched across the edge of the water tank a few feet away from them.

Adam stretched out on his belly beside Gurnwall. Both men kept their heads down as the planes strafed the camp. As the low-flying aircraft passed over them, the roar of the engines was so loud that the pounding of the surf on the coral reef was finally drowned out. Rain continued to fall, soaking Adam's uniform. He rolled over, blinked water out of his eyes, and saw that the bombers were past the camp.

"Gurney, you all right? Gurnwall?"

Adam sat up sharply when there was no response from the private. He was afraid Gurnwall had been hit by the machine gun fire from the Jap planes.

Gurnwall still lay on his stomach, his arms crossed over his head. He was shaking violently, so he was still alive. Adam didn't see any blood. He reached over to touch Gurnwall's shoulder. "Gurney?"

Gurnwall jerked and pulled away. "Lemme 'lone!" he

shrieked, his face pressed against the water tank. "Lemme 'lone!"

He was too scared to function, Adam realized, but nothing could be done about it now. Adam turned instead toward the air station and picked up the binoculars. He wiped rain off the lenses as best he could and trained the glasses on the runway area. Despite the rain, clouds of black smoke billowed up. From the location, Adam knew that the big avgas tank that had been built by Lieutenant Conderman's men must have been hit by one of the bombs. The tank had been filled only a couple of days earlier with 25,000 gallons of fuel, and now it was all going up in smoke. Small spurts of flame were scattered around the blaze. Those were fifty-gallon drums of avgas exploding from the heat, Adam thought.

He tried to check on the Wildcats through the smoke. During the interval since the first news of the attack on Pearl Harbor had reached Wake, the eight American planes on the ground had been scattered as widely as possible given the limited area that was available for parking them. The idea was not to let one Japanese bomb take out more than one plane. Unfortunately, enough bombs had fallen so that a lot of damage had been done anyway. Adam was no aviation expert, but he could tell that some of the F4F-3s were now nothing but twisted wreckage.

The human toll must have been high, too. The tents and huts where the men of VMF-211 had been housed were either ablaze or totally destroyed. Adam had no idea how many men had been killed over there, but he knew there had to have been casualties.

The sound of engines made him look up. The Japanese bombers were forming into their triple V pattern again and flying south. They must have expended all their bombs and ammunition, Adam thought.

The attack was over. Adam looked at his watch. It was 1210. He wasn't sure when the Japanese planes had first come out of the clouds and dived toward the atoll, but he thought it had been a few minutes before noon. *A quarter of an hour, maybe less.* It seemed a lot longer than that, but at the same time it had been almost the blink of an eye.

"It's over, Gurney. The Japs are leaving."

Gurnwall paid no attention to him but continued trembling. Adam saw smoke rising from across the lagoon and swung the binoculars in that direction. Fires had broken out in Camp Two, and on Peale Island the Pan American Airways hotel was burning, too. The fact that those were civilian installations hadn't given the Japs a second's pause. They had bombed them anyway.

Adam thought again about the naval hospital at Pearl Harbor. He closed his eyes for a second and prayed that Catherine was all right.

Again, the sound of engines made Adam look up. His heart hammered wildly for a moment as he spotted more planes speeding toward Wake from the north. After a few seconds, however, he realized that there were only four planes, and shortly after that, he recognized them as Wildcats. The patrol that had left earlier was returning.

But they were coming back from the wrong direction. They had been scouting north of the atoll, while the attack had come from the south along with the rain squall. The Japanese had been lucky those clouds had concealed their approach. In fact, they'd had all the luck today. Adam didn't think a single one of the Japanese aircraft had gone down during the raid, or even been hit seriously. He couldn't recall seeing flames or smoke coming from any of them.

"Are . . . are they coming back?"

Adam looked around and saw that Gurnwall had finally lifted his head to stare around wild-eyed. "The Japanese are gone," he said. "Those are our Wildcats coming in. Are you hit, Gurney?"

Gurnwall lifted himself on his left hand and used his

right to feel along his torso. "I . . . I don't think so. I don't feel anything."

"They just strafed us with that one burst, and it missed." On hands and knees, Adam crawled over to the edge of the tank where the bullets had struck. The bullets had gone into the top of the tank and punched out through the side, leaving a row of holes out of which water was spurting. That loss would cut down on their supply of drinking water, Adam thought, but there were enough catchment basins and evaporators set up so that nobody was going to die of thirst. In fact, that would probably be one of their lesser worries.

"Can . . . can we get down offa here, Corp?"

"In a minute." Adam sat up and brought the binoculars to his eyes again. The air raid could have been just the first strike, something to soften them up for an invasion. He scanned the horizon, turning slowly through a complete circle, looking for Japanese ships. He didn't see anything but water. The Pacific was living up to its name. It was as peaceful as could be.

"We'll go down and see if we can help," Adam decided. "Maybe one of the other guys can climb up here and keep an eye out."

Gurnwall scuttled over to the ladder, clinging to the tank as if he were afraid that it might leap out from under him. He was still shaking so hard that he had trouble finding the rungs with his feet as he started down. Adam thought he might have to help him, but then Gurnwall's nerves seemed to settle slightly and he was able to begin the descent. Adam climbed down after him and had to admit to himself that he was glad when his feet were back on solid ground.

Gurnwall wiped the back of his hand across his mouth. "Sorry, Corp—" he began.

"Forget it." Adam knew Gurnwall was ashamed that someone had witnessed his fear, but there was no time for worrying about things like that now. He looked around, spotted Magruder, and called out to him to climb onto the water tank. Magruder nodded and took the binoculars that Adam offered him.

"Where are the other guys?" Adam asked as Magruder started up the ladder.

"At our battle station, Corporal," the lean, serious Magruder answered. "I got sent back up here for more ammo."

"I'll see that they get it," Adam said. "Come on, Gurnwall."

As they trotted through Camp One, Adam saw that many of the tents had been shredded by machine gun fire from the Japanese planes. Bomb craters were scattered around the camp. Adam didn't see any bodies, though. When the alarm had been sounded earlier, the Marines of the 1st Defense Battalion had scattered all over the three islands of the atoll, manning the guns they had set up over the past few weeks. The camp had been practically deserted when the attack began, which might have been, at last, a stroke of luck.

It was fortunate, as well, that no bombs had fallen on the ordnance depot. Adam and Gurnwall found it unattended. Each of them slung several belts of .50-caliber rounds over their shoulders and then started down the road toward the air station. The squad's regular defense post was about halfway along the southwestern shore of Wake Island, at one of the machine gun emplacements that was part of Battery E.

Rolofson, Stout, and Kennemer had all come through the attack unharmed, Adam was glad to see when he and Gurnwall reached the gun. They grinned at the newcomers and took the belts of ammunition. "Glad to see you again, Corporal," Rolofson said. "We were afraid you and Gurney were sitting ducks up there on that tank."

"They made one try for us but missed," Adam said. "How did you boys do?"

Stout, from the mountains of Kentucky, said, "We

burned a lot of powder but didn't hit anything, far as I could tell."

Adam nodded. "I'm afraid that was the case all over the island. I didn't see any of the Japs go down."

The machine gun was reloaded and its muzzle tilted toward the sky just in case the Japanese came back. The rain had stopped now, the squall moving on at the same speed with which it had come, and the clouds were breaking up overhead. If the Japs returned, they wouldn't be able to hide their approach quite so easily.

And they *would* be back, Adam thought as he looked at the black smoke rising from the air station and, beyond that, from the civilian installations on the other side of Wake Island and on Peale Island. The Americans had been hit hard today, damned hard, but their flag still flew over the atoll. He had a feeling that the Japanese wouldn't be satisfied until the Rising Sun had been lifted in its place.